TIMELESS MOMENTS

a novel

MICHELE ASHMAN BELL

Covenant Communications, Inc.

Covenant®

Cover image © Brand X Pictures/Getty Images, Inc.

Cover design copyrighted 2003 by Covenant Communications, Inc.

Published by Covenant Communications, Inc.
American Fork, Utah

Printed in the United States of America
First Printing: August 2003

10 09 08 07 06 05 04 03   10 9 8 7 6 5 4 3 2 1

ISBN 1-59156-255-4

*I would like to dedicate this
book to the many men and women
who have served and are now serving
to protect and defend
this great land in which we live.
Thank you.
God bless America!*

CHAPTER ONE

Vietnam
July 1972

The smell of fuel, jungle, and death surrounded the seven soldiers as they walked across the mist-covered tarmac and climbed aboard the Huey helicopter.

Their orders were exact, their mission top secret.

Low-hanging fog cloaked the landing zone as the helicopter lifted off, but a few moments later the craft broke into the clear. Vietnam, even in war, was scenic with its green jungle, thickly forested mountains, and slashes of silver rivers crisscrossing the terrain.

About four miles from X-ray, their assault landing zone, the pilot, Bryan Randall, gave the signal, and the helicopter dropped down to treetop level to fly nap-of-the-earth on the final approach. It wasn't even daylight and already, 105mm artillery pounded the area below them. Startled birds took flight as the Huey roared along at 110 miles per hour.

Dalton "Mac" McNamara's stomach tensed. The cornflakes he'd had for breakfast roiled and rumbled inside of him. He always felt this way before a mission, but today it was worse. Wondering if he would be fortunate enough to defy death yet one more day, he drew in several slow, calming breaths. Still, the question nagged at the back of his mind.

Mac sensed that the most critical part of the operation was coming—the drop. The timing had to be perfect. Not close. Not almost. Perfect. The choppers had to get in, get out, and get gone—otherwise they were an easy target. If everything didn't go precisely as planned, the enemy would be waiting when the Hueys came in. That wasn't the greeting any of them wanted. Not today. Not ever.

Still two minutes out. Below, smoke and dust flew from artillery fire where broad, low-rolling plains were dotted with trees thirty to fifty feet tall and interspersed with a few old Montagnard farm clearings and dry streambeds. There were no villages. No people. Just the enemy, shells, and hatred.

With the precision of months of training and the experience of battle, the operation continued, on time and on target. The small, tightly knit band of men was a reconnaissance group, part of the Fifth Special Forces Group out of Nha Trang, South Vietnam. At great risk, these men managed to bring in critical information that saved the lives of many American soldiers—yet often at the expense of their own. The area they were to enter was crawling with Viet Cong. The trick was to find them, close in, track their position, strengths, capabilities, and hopefully their intentions, then get out.

Mac and his men prepared themselves for the drop into battle. They had seconds, not minutes, to get out so the Huey could get back in the air. No one spoke, but the look in everyone's eyes told Lt. McNamara that they were brothers; they were a team. They would fight together, and if necessary, die together.

Randall gave the signal as they touched down, and in a split second, following Mac's lead, the men jumped out of the Huey and ran for cover. No one moved and no one breathed as the *whump whump whump* of the chopper roared away from them, then drifted further away. Tense, the men waited, a collective prayer in their hearts for Randall and his crew not to be shot down as they flew out.

Straining, they listened as an eerie stillness settled in. In the distance, several explosions shattered the silence. Smoke and gunpowder hung in the moist, tropical air.

Clinging to the last moments of peace, Mac glanced at each of his men before giving the signal. He knew it was impossible for them to land without notice, but hopefully the Viet Cong weren't aware of their exact location. The quicker they moved out and evaded the enemy, the safer they would be.

Staying low, hidden by elephant grass, the seven men crept toward an island of trees a hundred yards away. Mac paused a brief moment to listen, wishing for the sound of gunfire. The artillery would indicate the position of the enemy. But the silence remained.

Creeping stealthily, they arrived at the cluster of trees. Again, Mac and his men watched and waited, their movements unnoticed and nearly invisible.

After waiting for what seemed like an eternity, Mac nodded his head, and they walked toward the mountains. The early morning sun, hot and blazing, turned the moist jungle terrain into a steaming sauna. Sweat trickled down Mac's forehead and cheeks, trailing a path down his neck and between his shoulder blades. Brush and vines grew so thick that at several points, every step had to be carved out with a machete. Progress was slow and arduous, but progress just the same. They hoped to reach the appointed spot before nightfall.

Mac knew their route like the back of his hand. He'd studied the map, memorizing every hill, stream, and boulder. Yet knowing what they were headed for didn't bring him any comfort. The tree line ended up ahead, where they would cross several hundred yards of open field before they could disappear into the dense mountain foliage. If they made it across that field, the rest would be easy.

Sinking low in the brush, they inched their way to the edge of the clearing and looked out. The hair on the back of Mac's neck stood up. Something didn't feel right, and he motioned for them to stop.

Mac felt the other men watching him, waiting for his signal. Three of them would cross the field while the others covered for them. Once those three were safe on the other side, the other four would go.

Chambers, the recon platoon radio operator, nodded toward the clearing, but Mac shook his head. He couldn't explain it, but something told him to wait.

Just then, a rustle in the bushes across from them caught their attention. A young Vietnamese boy no more than sixteen years old stepped into the clearing wielding an AK-47.

Mac held his breath and watched, unsure if the boy was Viet Cong or not, since not all of them wore uniforms. Just as he suspected, several other soldiers no older than the first followed, heading straight at them. Mac now knew they were indeed VC.

Chambers eyed Mac, who remained motionless. If anyone moved, it would give away their position. If they fired, they would attract every Viet Cong soldier within a mile. No, it was better to wait.

Willing the enemy to turn and head west, Mac felt his heart pound in his chest. He didn't want to fire, but if the VCs got much closer, he'd have to.

Brady, the man to Mac's left, shifted his weight. A twig cracked, the noise magnified by the tension in the air. The VCs halted, drawing their weapons as they scanned the bush.

Mac's heart stopped.

Peering directly at their hiding spot as if they could see through the trees, the three young soldiers trained their gun barrels directly at Mac and his men, who remained frozen in their positions.

Mac knew if he and his men opened fire at such close range, the VC soldiers wouldn't know what hit them, but he resisted the signal until the last possible moment. Blowing their cover would defeat their mission and probably cost them their lives. He wasn't ready to make that call.

The men beside him flinched, their muscles taut and ready, their nerves sparking with the instinct to fire. Still they waited.

Just then, someone shouted from across the clearing where several other VC soldiers motioned for the three young men to join them. Mac expelled air from lungs that were ready to burst.

Two of the soldiers immediately retreated, but one narrowed his gaze and studied the bush. Suddenly, he exclaimed something in Vietnamese and raised his AK-47.

Mac's split-second decision to fire was one he'd regret for the rest of his life.

At the signal, Chambers quickly fired and shot the soldier. Just as Mac had feared, a dozen more VC emerged from the trees and pelted them with bullets. Two of Mac's men went down while the rest of them continued firing at the advancing troops.

A bullet whizzed passed Mac's head, but he continued firing. He heard a hollow thud as another one of his men went down.

"Jackson's hit!" Chambers yelled. Mac glanced down to see Jackson's helmet in front of him with a bullet hole in it. Mac kicked it out of the way, reeling from the gruesome sight.

Another man went down—Beckett, the youngest man on their team. From the very day Beckett had joined his team, Mac had felt protective of him, almost like he was a kid brother. Mac was close to all his men, but Beckett was young—too young to be killing people. The boy had already lost a brother in the war. No family deserved to lose two.

Mac grabbed the M-79 grenade launcher lying next to Beckett, whose arm and chest were both bleeding freely.

"Help," Beckett called to him, lifting his bloodied arm toward Mac.

Chambers grabbed the M-79 from Mac and launched a grenade. Mac tore off his shirt and wrapped it tightly around Beckett's arm. "You're going to be okay," he shouted over the din. Grabbing his M-79 again, Mac took aim and pulled the trigger, but nothing happened. He opened the feed cover, flipped the gun over, and hit it on the ground, jarring the shells loose. Debris had caught in the ammo belt. Mac flipped it right side up, slapped the ammo belt back in, slammed the feed cover, and began firing again.

Even though they were getting pummeled, the men in Mac's group who were still standing held off the NVA troops, and one by one, the enemy dropped.

The rat-tat-tat-tat of an enemy machine gun mowed down the foliage in front of them, taking Chambers, who screamed in pain as he writhed on the ground. Mac looked at Chambers, whose shoulder had been hit. Bullet fragments had also shredded the side of his face.

Raging anger filled Mac, and he fired, taking out two of the advancing troops, leaving only four or five standing. "Hang in there, Chambers, we've almost got 'em!" he yelled.

Mac heard a shot and glanced over to see Brody Thorpe fall backward without a whimper.

"I'm out of ammo," Sinclair hollered, throwing his M-60 on the ground and grabbing another one. He immediately began firing, taking out another soldier from the NVA—the North Vietnamese Army.

Then, out of nowhere, Mac felt a hot stinging in his head. A wave of nausea washed over him, and he knew he'd been hit. Still, he continued shooting, wondering why he wasn't feeling any pain. Another bullet whistled past, hitting the tree behind him.

"Lieutenant Mac," Sinclair yelled. "You okay? There's blood—"

"I'm fine," Mac yelled. But he spoke too soon. Right as the words left his mouth, a stick grenade passed through the trees and exploded at his feet. Mac reached down to his right leg and touched grenade fragments, suddenly feeling like he'd just touched a red-hot poker, sizzling his hand. He collapsed back as agonizing pain worse than anything he'd felt in his entire life consumed him.

A North Vietnamese soldier plowed through the trees and stumbled over some of the dead men on the ground. Mac gripped his gun, but it was Sinclair who fired, putting a full magazine through the enemy soldier before he went down.

Mac heard Vietnamese voices coming toward him. The three NVAs charged through the trees and began kicking at the American soldiers on the ground. Opening one eye just a slit, Mac saw the men removing guns, ammunition, watches, and other valuables from the American soldiers. Lying still, Mac prayed the North Vietnamese soldiers would just take what they wanted and leave them for dead.

Mac watched as they searched Beckett, then kicked him hard in the ribs. Beckett's body jackknifed with the blow, then stilled.

Certain the young boy was dead, Mac fought the urge to scream. Then he stopped. One of Beckett's eyelids fluttered, and the boy made eye contact with him.

A prayer of gratitude flashed through Mac's mind, as well as a plea for the rest of his men.

But the NVA soldiers had other plans. After they'd taken what they wanted, they made sure all of the Americans were dead by shooting a few extra rounds into their bodies. Mac's heart sank. All of his men were gone, and most likely he was next. If only he hadn't given the signal to fire, maybe that young Viet Cong soldier would have moved on. Maybe he wouldn't have discovered them hidden in the bushes.

His muscles tensed, waiting for the final bullet that would take his life. Mac's only thoughts were of his buddies. They'd fought together, and now, they would die together.

Yet the bullet didn't come. Mac waited, then saw the NVA soldiers leaving.

Confused, Mac wondered why they hadn't put a bullet through him. Was his injury so bad that they took him for dead?

He watched them leave, and just when he thought it was safe, one of the NVA soldiers unexpectedly turned. Mac closed his eyes, but not before they saw one another. Mac tensed. He was certain that it was over. His moment had come.

But he wasn't that lucky.

The soldier shouted an order to the other two men who were with him. They stopped, turned, and approached Mac with murder in their eyes. Fear claimed him.

Take me, God, he begged. *Death is better than prison.*

Just as the prayer escaped his lips, the men grabbed his arms and legs and jerked him off the ground, causing a horrific pain in his leg.

He panicked. This wasn't right. He wasn't supposed to get captured; his men weren't supposed to get killed. He was supposed to seek out the NVA and radio their location back to the base. Hundreds of American soldiers' lives depended on this information.

NO! Mac wanted to scream. He knew what happened in North Vietnamese prisoner of war camps, and he knew he'd rather die now than spend years rotting away in a camp, inhumanely tortured and stripped of all dignity.

Realizing he wasn't wearing his helmet, he squirmed to find it and received the butt of a rifle in his ribs, several of them cracking with the blow.

Mac cried out in pain, wondering how much more he could bear. Leaving his buddies and helmet behind, God's grace finally fell upon him as he passed out.

* * *

Mac woke up in excruciating pain. Where was he?

Disoriented, he took several shallow breaths to get a grip on the pain and a bearing on his surroundings. The last thing he remembered was being dragged by North Vietnamese soldiers away from his company, who all lay dead amidst the trees, but here he was, in the middle of a field somewhere with the sound of artillery flying all around him.

His mind processed the situation slowly. Maybe the NVA had been attacked or ambushed, and in their effort to combat the enemy, had left him for dead. Either way, he knew he was one lucky soldier. Maybe. He was in the middle of enemy territory. He was as good as dead. He didn't know how serious his other injuries were, but the chance of using his leg was slim. But he wasn't going to lie there to be used for target practice. If he was going to die, he was going to die trying to survive.

He reached to his side and discovered that he still had two or three frag grenades, a smoke grenade, and two or three hundred rounds of ammo, but his M-16 was gone. He felt around his waist and located his canteen and a small mirror.

As his mind cleared, he realized that the first thing he needed to do was get out of the open. His chances of survival were better in the trees.

Crawling army style, he dragged himself slowly, elbow by elbow, through the grass. Any movement could bring artillery and mortar his direction, so he held his breath and proceeded cautiously.

Eyeing a clump of bushes, he crawled over to it, planning to wait until he was concealed before he assessed his wounds and came up with a plan.

Several times he froze as the sound of enemy voices carried on the air. If he were spotted, there certainly wouldn't be any second chances. Yet each time, the voices rose and then faded. Still, he wouldn't breathe easy until he found cover.

With muscles tensed and trembling, he pulled himself the last few feet before snaking his way through a low opening in the branches and finding space to sit.

Sweat poured down his face, neck, and back. The unbearable heat and thick humidity made breathing difficult, yet in the shade, he was able to find some reprieve. He couldn't get a good view of his leg wound, but judging by the blood, pain, and gaping hole, he knew it wasn't good.

Ripping the sleeve off his shirt, he fashioned a bandage to help stop the bleeding and to lend some support to his knee. Hopefully, even if he had to limp the entire way, he would now be able to move on foot.

He waited several hours for the siege of battle to move away from his position, and then, using a dead branch for support, he slowly, painfully, got to his feet.

Wincing as he put weight on his injured leg, he moved a few steps and stopped. The base of the mountain was five to six hundred yards in the distance. He had to cross through a patch of tall elephant grass to get there.

Keeping his head down, he hobbled his way through the grass, noticing that each step actually seemed to become less painful.

After a hundred yards he stopped again. Artillery suddenly sounded from the treetops, and before he dared take another step, the grass in front of him started to move, suddenly parting to reveal a NVA soldier.

With razor-sharp reflexes, Mac threw a frag and a smoke grenade and cut sharp to the left, his heart pounding faster than the bullets flying overhead. He dragged himself as fast as he could, away from the explosion of the smoke grenade behind him.

Without looking back, he headed for the mountains and soon came to a stream. There he waded upstream for a hundred yards to conceal his route, stumbling on the slippery rocks, filling his canteen along the way, and gulping in all the water he could hold. He found a rocky bank where he could exit without leaving a trail, and he hobbled across a valley where he could have a clear view of his back trail. Once there, he took a break, concealed in the brush.

For now he was safe, as he noted that the sound of battle was receding to his rear. But he knew as night closed in that he needed to find a place to hide.

A constant prayer ran through his mind, a plea for guidance, help, wisdom, strength, and protection. Mac knew he couldn't get more isolated than he was right now. He was alone yet not alone, for he was surrounded on all sides by North Vietnamese soldiers who wouldn't think twice about killing him.

But he was on his own. There was no one to help him. No one but God.

He'd been in battle enough to know deep down just how much courage he had. He'd experienced feelings of sheer terror, and of bravery beyond belief. In any given situation, he knew that he would sacrifice his life for any of his men. He'd prepared himself to die, and he was at peace with death.

But that was not how it had happened. Each and every one of his men had been slaughtered right before his eyes. He'd heard their cries, seen them gasp for their last breath. And here he stood, living and breathing. It seemed cruel and unfair.

Not that he wanted to die. But he didn't know how he would ever live with the memory of those last moments with his friends . . . his buddies . . . his brothers.

An ache filled his heart, rending it in two, until the sound of artillery started closing in on the mountain. He scrambled between two large trees and crouched low, scanning the surrounding area for a place to hide.

Locating an area near another tree where thick grass grew, Mac hobbled over and settled in for the night. He shivered against the damp night air, trying as best as he could to keep ants and bugs out of his wounds. A throbbing in his head upset his stomach, and with each drink of water he threw up. In misery he lay there, looking at the stars, thinking of his men. They'd depended on him, and now they were all dead. All because of him. All because of one decision he'd made.

Mac couldn't help but second-guess those last few moments before he'd given the signal to open fire. Would the North Vietnamese soldier have seen them hiding in the bushes?

He would never know, and he was afraid the question would haunt him for the rest of his life. The images of his buddies, bleeding and dying, were indelibly etched into his memory.

The next morning, he woke up and lay there, listening. In the distance, helicopters landed and took off. United States choppers flew over him, and he tried to signal them with his small mirror but had no luck. He heard gunfire between him and the site where his men still lay.

Staying low and hidden as much as possible, he climbed to the top of a hill and found a large log, which he used for cover. Another battle soon ensued, and he found himself caught in the middle. The artillery and mortars continued until dark and on through the night. Mac covered himself with brush and leaves, trying to conceal himself. Between the ants, the cold, and the sound of artillery, he didn't get much sleep that night either, but he knew he was close to the American landing zone, which gave him the hope of rescue.

Daybreak greeted Mac with a shower of artillery that sprayed all around the slope where he hid. When it quieted down, he began moving toward the landing zone, crossing a wide, shallow creek and rocky terrain until he finally approached the perimeter of the landing zone where he knew he would be recognized as an American soldier.

When he broke into the clearing, the landing zone was empty. In shock, Mac realized that the Americans had pulled out and abandoned the site.

An empty despair replaced his earlier hope. He wondered by how many hours—or was it only minutes?—he had missed them. They'd been there throughout the night, and he'd been so sure that they would still be there this morning. But they were gone, and he was still on his own.

With shoulders slumped and a weariness born of a lack of food and sleep, Mac revisited his plan. He hadn't come up with a Plan B, so certain was he that Plan A would work. But it hadn't, and now he was back to the drawing board.

Closing his eyes, he balanced on his left foot to take weight off his injured leg. It had begun to stink, and he knew the wound was infected. He didn't allow himself to dwell on it—there was nothing he could do until he found help—but he feared the damage was severe. At least he could limp. He'd be dead by now had he been unable to walk.

A rustle in the brush behind him sent a bolt of fear through Mac's body. He froze, straining to hear any further sound, praying it was nothing. But the furious beating of his heart and the dread that filled him left no room for hope.

Slowly he turned his shoulder, then his head . . . and looked straight into the barrel of a Vietnamese patrol soldier's gun. Behind that soldier were five others with their sights set on Mac.

He'd almost made it. But the eyes staring back at him had no mercy, no compassion. Just hatred. And he knew that he was just about to discover what purgatory really was.

CHAPTER TWO

Salt Lake City
September 1973

"I'm in love," Paige Anthony said as she collapsed onto her bed and looked dreamily at the album cover of the new Donny Osmond record she'd just purchased.

"He's not as cute as Michael Jackson," her best friend, Louisa Nichols, countered. "He sure as heck can't dance as well either."

"I don't care if he can't dance," Paige proclaimed. "Besides, he's got the most incredible eyes. He doesn't need to dance with eyes like these." She gazed into the dark brown, thickly lashed eyes of the popular singer. "I could get lost in those eyes."

Lou groaned. "I swear you've had a crush on Donny Osmond since you were twelve." She opened Paige's closet and looked at the clothes hung neatly on hangers. "You're going to be sixteen tomorrow, and it's time you started looking at the boys around here instead of the ones on album covers." She pulled a chocolate-brown pantsuit from the closet and took it off the hanger. Trying it on, she continued, "Someone like Mark St. Claire."

"Mark St. Claire!" Paige exclaimed. "C'mon, Lou. He doesn't even know I'm alive."

Lou hooked the chain fastener on the vest and turned around to model it for Paige.

"Looks good, especially with that purple blouse you're wearing," Paige teased.

Lou pulled a face. "Don't be so sure Mark doesn't know you're alive." She struck a pose, then turned to her friend. "Today at lunch I overheard what he said to one of his friends when you walked into the lunchroom."

"Why didn't you tell me?" Paige asked excitedly.

"I am telling you," Lou answered. "He thinks you're really cute and that you have the prettiest hair in the sophomore class."

Paige's mouth dropped open. "You're lying."

"I swear." Lou held up her right hand. "Those were his exact words."

"Mark St. Claire," Paige said breathlessly. "You're sure it was him?"

"Of course I'm sure," Lou said.

"But he's like, like—"

"The most popular boy at school?" Lou finished her sentence.

"Yeah. I mean, why would he notice me?"

"Paige, don't you ever look in the mirror? You're beautiful. Besides, it's just like my mother always says, 'It doesn't matter how pretty you are outside if you aren't pretty inside.' You're pretty inside, Paige. You'd do anything for anybody. Mark would be lucky to have a girl like you."

Paige smiled warmly at her friend. "Thanks, Lou."

"Besides, it's not like Mark's all that perfect. Sure he's a hunk, but sometimes he can be so obnoxious. I thought Mr. Thomas was going to throw Mark out of science the other day because he kept talking back. I think Mark likes to have all the attention."

"But he gets it already because he's a star athlete—and because he's so cute."

"I know. I don't get it either. I guess that's why it's easy to forgive him for being obnoxious. If he wasn't cute, he'd just be annoying. Now tell me," Lou turned from side to side, "with my cream-colored blouse, what do you think?"

"Looks cute, but the pants will be floods on you."

With a sigh, Lou turned back to the full-length mirror in the corner of Paige's room. "I'm a giraffe," she said.

"You're not a giraffe. You've got gorgeous legs."

"But why do they have to be so dang long?" she complained. "No one's ever going to ask me out. There's only a handful of boys taller than me at school, and they're all basketball geeks or in the chess club."

"I thought you liked basketball players."

"I do, but not the ones from our school." Lou hung the pantsuit on the hanger and put it back into the closet. With her olive skin and thick, dark hair, Lou was the complete opposite of Paige, a petite blonde with green eyes.

"Let's face it," Lou complained, "I'm never going to meet a guy who's tall, good-looking, intelligent, and who has a sense of humor."

"You will," Paige assured her. "Maybe not at our school, but somewhere out there is the man of your dreams."

"Yeah, if my dad will ever let me date. He's so old-fashioned. He won't even let me get my ears pierced until I'm eighteen."

Paige shrugged. She'd heard her friend complain plenty about her father and his apparently overprotective ways. But Paige liked Lou's dad, and no matter what Lou said, Paige could tell he loved his children with all of his heart.

"Here," Paige said, going to her closet. "My mom got me this skirt, but it's kind of long on me, so I don't ever wear it. I bet it would fit you and look great with your orange sweater and matching kneesocks." She held out the skirt for her friend to try on.

To Lou's delight, the skirt did fit. It was even long enough to wear to school.

"Let's go show my mom," Paige said. "She'd love to see someone wear this skirt. Maybe she'll let you stay for dinner. She's making spaghetti."

They walked down the hall toward the kitchen and suddenly stopped. Voices carried from the living room—angry, shouting voices.

"How could you do this to me?!" a woman's voice screamed. It was Paige's mother. She was crying and yelling at the same time.

"It just happened," her father's answer bit back.

Paige felt as if she'd just taken a blow to the stomach. Did her father say what she thought she'd just heard him say? The implication of what he'd done was apparent, and it was confirmed as the yelling continued. Her legs went weak at the knees. Lou held on to her as they hid in the shadows.

"So that's it? After twenty years of marriage, you're leaving me?" her mother cried, her voice full of desperation.

"Barbara, I just don't love you anymore," he answered in an exasperated tone.

"What about the kids, Don?" she asked.

"Their needs will be taken care of," he replied, his voice sounding cold and devoid of feeling.

Paige's heart broke when she heard her mother's sobs.

"Don't leave me, Don." Barbara's voice quieted, but the pleading became more obvious. "We can work this out. I'll try harder. I'll lose weight and fix myself up more often so you'll want to be with me—"

"There's nothing to work out," Don interrupted. "It's over."

Paige knew her parents had been having problems. They argued nearly every day and were never affectionate with each other. She'd also heard her mother cry at night, many times when her dad was away on business. Still, the news came as a complete shock.

"I have to go," Don said. "I'll come back for my things."

"No, Don, please," Barbara begged, reaching for the man who had promised her his love in happier days. "I'll do anything. Don, I love you."

Paige cringed to see her mother grovel. Anger flared inside of her, and she ached to run to her mother, to pull her away from the source of misery and betrayal. Paige's father had always taken his wife and family for granted, and the stark reality of his disregard for them was cruel.

"I'm sorry. I just don't love you," he said.

"Don . . ." Barbara collapsed to the floor, sobbing loudly.

Don looked down at his wife, his face still unmoved. "Good-bye, Barbara." The words were punctuated by the slam of the front door echoing through the emptiness of the house.

With tears running down her face, Paige looked at Lou, who also had tears in her eyes. Silently, they cried together.

* * *

It turned out to be her worst birthday ever. Paige had looked forward to turning sixteen, getting her driver's license, and dating. Now none of it seemed important.

"Come on," Lou said. "Let me just take you out for pizza or something. Cissy and Janine said they'd meet us. We could go bowling after."

Paige sat on her bed, hugging her pillow, wishing she could just go to sleep and never wake up. Her life was miserable. She hated her father, who'd left without even saying good-bye. He'd called, but she refused to talk to him over the phone. Didn't he love her enough to even tell her in person that he was leaving? Paige's mother was another issue altogether. She was so distraught and depressed that Paige couldn't bear to be around her any longer.

"Please, Paige," Lou coaxed. "It'll make you feel better."

Paige sighed and wiped the tears from her cheeks. She knew there wasn't any food in the house. Whatever they ate was what Paige prepared. And she was sick and tired of macaroni and cheese. If she went with her friends, at least she'd have something decent to eat.

"Okay, I'll go," Paige said.

"Good!" Lou exclaimed, and hugged her friend. "We're gonna help you through this, Paige. We're all here for you."

* * *

The pizza place was packed when they arrived. Pyles Pizza was a favorite Friday night hangout for the local high school kids. Their arcade was the best in town, and their pizza was a local legend.

Paige, Lou, Cissy, and Janine arrived and were shown to a corner booth. Paige appreciated the distraction of the crowds, the loud music playing in the background, and the pinging and clanging of the games in the arcade room. They ordered a large deluxe pizza with a pitcher of root beer. Paige hoped there would be a few pieces left over to take home to her little brothers. They probably had eaten peanut butter and jelly sandwiches for dinner.

"Guess who's here," Cissy said with a teasing lilt to her voice.

Lou was all ears. "Who?"

"Mark St. Claire," she said.

With a shrug, Paige slid the strap of her purse off her shoulder and relaxed back into the seat. She no longer cared about Mark St. Claire—or any boy for that matter. Anyone from the opposite sex was taboo, as far as she was concerned. After what her dad had done to her family, she never wanted another man in her life. Even Mark St. Claire.

Lou stretched up tall to look across the room. "There he is," she announced. "And he's wearing his light blue shirt. You gotta see him, Paige."

"I don't care," Paige said.

"You wouldn't say that if you could see him," Lou cajoled.

Just then, their pizza arrived, saving Paige from further pressure to swoon over Mark like the rest of the girls at Pyles.

"Let's do gifts while we eat, then we can go next door and see what's going on at Super Bowl-a-Rama," Janine suggested. Cissy and Lou agreed.

"You go first, Janine," Lou said.

Janine brought out a small box with a silver ribbon tied around it and handed it to Paige. Paige untied the bow and lifted the lid. Inside was a black velvet choker with a cameo on it. Paige smiled shyly, a warmness making its way into the cold emptiness of her heart.

"Janine, it's beautiful. Thank you." Paige admired the jewelry.

Cissy was next and gave her a macramé pot hanger for her room. It was avocado green and had wooden beads on it.

"Is your room still yellow and green?" Cissy asked.

Paige nodded. "This will look really cute. Thanks."

"I made it in art class. Took me all quarter," Cissy announced proudly. Paige smiled again, touched at her friend's sacrifice.

Lou spoke up. "My turn." She handed Paige two gifts. "Open the big one first."

Inside the first box was a tie-dyed shirt with matching socks. "I was going to do a bra and underwear, but my mom didn't think that was a good idea," Lou said. Then she leaned in and whispered, "But I did some anyway. I'll give them to you later. Just don't show my mom."

Paige smiled and thanked her friend. "These are great," she told her. "What's this?" she asked, unwrapping the smaller gift.

"That's the best part," Lou said. "Open it already."

Paige opened the lid from the small box and pulled out a wide, flat, silver bracelet. On it was engraved *Lt. Dalton McNamara, 5th Special Forces Group, July 1972.*

"What's this?" Paige asked.

"That's an MIA/POW bracelet," Lou told her. "That's the name of a soldier in the Vietnam War and the date that he was lost. You're supposed to wear it until the day the Red Cross is allowed into Hanoi and can find out if he's missing or if he's been captured and is receiving humane treatment."

Paige read aloud the label attached to the bracelet. *"Distributed by VIVA (Voices in Vital America) a non-profit, non-political national student organization dedicated to the fact that progress and freedom can only be achieved and maintained by rational and responsible action."*

This was certainly the most unusual present she'd ever received, but then, it was from Lou. Lou had a style and a taste all her own. Paige loved that about her and wished she possessed the same inner confidence.

"You need to write to his family and tell them you're wearing their son's bracelet and that you'll pray for him," Lou told her. "See," she held up her wrist, "I have one too. We should all wear them."

"This guy is lost in the war?" Paige asked, reading the name again.

"Yeah, and who knows what's happened to him. Sometimes the newspaper publishes the names of soldiers who've been located. We can watch for his name to find out if he's alive and safe."

Paige wasn't sure about wearing the bracelet. She didn't even know the guy. Yet her heart went out to his family, not knowing whether their son was dead or alive.

"Okay," Paige said, bending the soft metal and sliding the bracelet onto her wrist.

"Good," Lou approved. "Now he's *your* POW or MIA soldier. And here's the address of his family so you can write," Lou instructed and handed her a paper. "I wrote to my soldier's family. They were really super. I cried when I read their letter."

Lou suddenly stopped talking. Her eyes grew wide and her mouth gaped open. Paige looked at her friend, wondering what was wrong with her. Not many things left Lou speechless.

"Hey, Paige," a male voice said from behind her.

A chill went up Paige's spine. She knew that voice. She'd memorized it and had learned to detect it in the hallways at school. Mark St. Claire!

She swallowed and slowly turned, tilting her head upward to see the six-foot-two form of "Mr. Incredible" standing behind her.

"Hi, Mark." She barely got the words out.

"Someone told me it's your birthday today," he said.

Paige nodded. She couldn't pull her wits about her enough to say anything.

"So," he said with a shrug and a lopsided grin, "do you think I could dance with the birthday girl?"

Paige's chin dropped. Cissy elbowed her, and Paige closed her mouth and nodded again.

Mark held out his hand, and Paige stood on shaking legs.

"Oh, just a minute," she exclaimed. "I need to, uh, put on my shoes." She hated wearing shoes and kicked them off whenever she could—in school, at church, at the movies. She'd lost more shoes than she cared to admit, but she couldn't help it.

Lou bent down beside her. "I thought you'd sworn off guys," she teased.

"Shhhhh!" Paige hissed, not wanting Mark to hear. "Okay, forget what I said. Did you see how great he looks in the light blue shirt?"

"Yeah, I noticed."

Paige sat up from tying her laces and smoothed her hair. And once again, Mark took her hand and guided her to the corner of the room where the jukebox played loudly. Paige glanced back at her friends, who waved and cheered at her.

Omigosh! Her stomach did back flips. *I'm dancing with Mark St. Claire.*

A slow song began to play, and Mark turned toward Paige and stepped closer, sliding his arms around her waist. She closed her eyes, wondering if she was going to die right then, right there.

"Mmm," he said. "Your hair smells good."

She felt his breath on her neck and knew for sure her heart was either going to stop or explode. For that one moment in time, nothing else existed. Everyone and everything in the room disappeared, and all that mattered was dancing with Mark.

Mark leaned back and looked into Paige's face. "Happy birthday," he said.

Paige smiled. "Thanks," she said. *It is now,* she almost added.

"I've been wanting to talk to you since school started," he said.

She couldn't believe she was hearing this. She wasn't in the popular group at school. Why would Mark even notice her?

"Why haven't you?" she asked, gazing into his smoky-gray eyes.

He shrugged, then laughed. "Afraid, I guess."

"Afraid? To talk to me?" She was incredulous, but tried to laugh lightly.

"Yeah, you're the prettiest girl at school."

Oh my heck, she thought. *How much neater can this guy get?*

"I guess you're sixteen then?" Mark asked.

"Sweet sixteen and . . ." she said without thinking.

"Never been kissed?" he finished for her.

She didn't want to admit that she'd never been kissed, but couldn't seem to find the right words to answer.

Mark bent his head and peered deeply into her eyes.

Paige reminded herself to breathe.

He leaned in closer, and Paige instinctively lifted her chin, their gazes locking.

And then, ever so gently, with soft, romantic music playing in the background, Mark kissed her.

Paige kept her eyes closed to prolong the moment, and when she opened them, Mark was looking at her.

And she knew in her heart that this was only the beginning.

CHAPTER THREE

Salt Lake City
Present day

Every man Paige St. Claire had ever loved had walked out on her. And now her son was doing the same thing.

Sure, UC Irvine was only an hour plane ride away from her home in Salt Lake City, but to her it didn't matter if Jared was moving across the country or across the street. Even though she was thrilled that he was going to realize his dream of playing college basketball, she regretted that she wouldn't be able to come to many of his games. She was going to miss out on some of the most important moments of his life. But worse, he wasn't going to be home with her—and that's what brought on the terrifying and engulfing feeling of loneliness that ate away at her insides.

She'd survived breast cancer and divorce. But this—the emptiness and loneliness that descended on her like a dark cloud—seemed as though it was the one thing that just might kill her.

Forcing herself to stay busy, Paige went to the storage room in the basement and searched for the large brown suitcase and an extra box for the rest of Jared's things. Paige knew it was silly to think that he was taking nearly everything with him—almost as though he were never coming home—but that's how it felt. And it didn't help that he would be living closer to his father than to her!

Thoughts of her ex-husband, Mark, only deepened her sense of loss. She didn't love Mark anymore, but that was only because she'd turned off her heart and had taught herself to bury those feelings deep down inside. He'd been her first kiss, her first love. But he'd been a terrible husband, and they had been miserable together. She was better off without him, she knew that without a doubt. And now he was going to be the one who watched Jared play basketball instead of her. The once-welcome distance that had kept them apart was the very thing that would now keep her from her son. Mark had attended as many of Jared's high school games as he could, but it was expensive to fly back and forth from California to Utah. Paige knew she couldn't afford the trip very often.

Flipping on the storage room light, Paige scanned the room, trying to remember where she had put the suitcase. She hadn't traveled in such a long time she didn't know where it could be. "Maybe Mark took it," she mumbled out loud. *Why not?* she thought. *He took everything else when he left.*

The divorce had left her bitter. Not only had she struggled with breast cancer and a mastectomy, but her husband told her in the midst of it all that he couldn't handle seeing her go through so much pain anymore. *Nothing like getting kicked when you're down,* she thought with cynicism born of the knowledge that he'd left her for an attractive, younger woman.

Moving a pair of old armchairs and a dusty world globe out of the way, she rummaged for the suitcase. Jared would be home soon to finish packing, and she needed to find it. Wondering why she didn't just haul all this stuff to Deseret Industries, Paige continued moving cans of paint, boxes of books and magazines, record albums and cassette tapes, and an old television.

"There you are!" she exclaimed when she discovered the suitcase underneath the pile of dust-covered storage items. Dragging it out, hoping she hadn't uncovered a nest of black widow spiders in the process, she wiped the dust off the suitcase and set it aside.

Just as she was about to restack all the items, a box caught her eye. *Jared's stuff* was written on the side in black Magic Marker. She smiled and pulled the box off the shelf. Lifting the flaps, she uncovered the contents and chuckled out loud. A deluge of memories flooded her mind, along with visions of Jared and his friends running around in superhero costumes or pretending to be Teenage Mutant Ninja Turtles. Jared had collected every conceivable superhero figure and accessory ever made. And when that phase had faded, he'd moved right into Ninja Turtles. The box was full of action figures.

A door slammed overhead followed by Jared bellowing, "Mom!" at the top of his lungs.

"Downstairs," Paige hollered back.

Sounding like an elephant tromping down the stairs, Jared appeared moments later in the doorway of the storage room. "Hey, Mom. What's for dinner? I'm starved."

"I thought we'd order pizza," she answered. "C'mere and take a look at this."

He joined her in the center of the room and kneeled down next to the box. Peering inside, he thrust in his hand and pulled out a Batman figure. "Cool! You found my stuff." He dug through the toys and found Robin. "Oh, man. I wondered where all these were."

"Are you glad I kept them?" she asked, pleased that he was so happy to see his childhood toys. She'd always known that someday he'd be glad she hadn't tossed them even though he'd lost interest when basketball, girls, and friends took over his life.

"Are you kidding? I love this stuff." He pulled out some more toys and examined them for missing parts. "I hope my Batmobile is in here. Oh, and Mom," he looked up at Paige, "can some of the guys come over and have pizza with us? You know, cuz it's my last night here and everything."

Paige had hoped that she and Jared could have the evening to themselves, but it *was* his last night, so if he wanted "the guys" there, she didn't want to disappoint him.

"Sure," she answered. "How many pizzas should we get?"

"Four or five," he said, digging deeper into the box.

"You know," Paige joked, "I'm probably going to save money having you in college."

"What do you mean?" The pile of toys next to his knee continued to grow as he rifled through the contents of the box.

"Without you and your friends here to feed, I'm going to save a fortune. I may be able to finally go on a cruise or buy a Ferrari or something."

Jared laughed. "A Ferrari? Right, Mom." He pulled more toys from the box. "I found it," he exclaimed suddenly, pulling out the sleek-winged Batmobile. He clicked a button, and the headlights flipped on. "Whoa! It still works. Wait till I show the guys."

Paige looked at her grown son holding the toys of his youth and felt a knot of emotion clog her throat. This was a turning point. Their lives would never be the same again. Jared would go to a year of school. Then next May, he'd leave on his mission. It would never be just them again. Not the way it used to be.

Tears filled her eyes, and she quickly looked away. She didn't want to bring down his good mood. She'd told herself she had to stay strong until he drove away. She could fall apart when he was gone.

Pulling herself together, she glanced at a box on the shelf with *Paige's stuff* written on the outside. Taking it from the shelf, she placed it on the floor next to where Jared was seated.

"What's that?" he asked, noticing her much smaller box.

"This is my box of junk."

"Really? What kind of junk?" He left his treasures for a moment to check out hers.

"I don't remember what all's in here." She pulled off the strip of packing tape and opened the flaps. "There's probably not much. I didn't keep a lot of my high school stuff."

"Let's see," he said anxiously.

"Okay," she said with a laugh. He seemed more excited than she did.

Along with her yearbooks were prom pictures and ribbons from cheerleading camps. She found her tassel from graduation, as well as her graduation announcements. Jared leafed through her senior yearbook and laughed at her picture, then, after looking awhile longer, said, "Actually, Mom, you weren't bad lookin' back then. In fact," he checked it out again, "you're kinda hot."

"Hot?" she asked, knowing that was the ultimate compliment to pay a girl.

"Yeah. Except for that flippy bang thing you've got going on with your hair, you're hot."

Paige sat up straight and smiled at her son. "Well, thanks, Jared. That's the nicest thing anyone's said to me all day."

"Gol, Mom," Jared said as he rummaged through Paige's box, "you're still nice lookin' . . . in a mom sort of way."

Paige laughed. "Thanks, hon." She reached out and patted him on the shoulder, resisting the urge to pull him into a hug and not let go. This was her son, the little boy who used to need her as much in his life as she needed him. But not anymore. He was excited to get out on his own, to experience the real world, to see what life had to offer.

But she still needed him, and his leaving tore her apart inside.

"Hey, what's this?" He held up a white, legal-sized envelope with a lump inside.

"Wow." Paige took the envelope from him. "I haven't thought about this in years."

"What is it?"

She tore open the envelope and pulled out a wide, silver metal bracelet. "It's an MIA/POW bracelet."

By the look on his face, it was obvious he didn't have a clue as to what she was talking about. "Lou gave this to me for my sixteenth birthday," she continued. Even though they lived in separate states now, Lou and Paige were still best friends. "It was during the Vietnam War, and these bracelets represented soldiers in the war who were either missing in action or prisoners of war."

Jared read the name and date on the bracelet. "So this guy is Dalton McNamara. Did they ever find him?"

She shrugged. "I don't know. I wrote to his family and told them I was wearing their son's bracelet, but I never heard if he came home."

"Did his family write back?"

"Yes." She held up the envelope. "The letter's right here."

"Read it to me." Paige could tell that her son was growing interested. Paige unfolded the letter and began to read.

December 14, 1973
Dear Paige,

> *Thank you for wearing Dalton's bracelet and for writing. I am his older brother, Brenden. Dalton is twenty-two, single, and grew up here in Chicago. I'm his only brother, and we have a younger sister. Dalton is an officer in the Green Berets, 5th Special Forces Group, Airborne Division. He went to Vietnam in July 1970*

*and was assigned to work with Montagnard tribesmen at
an outpost in the Central Highlands. There he was
awarded three Bronze Stars. In December 1970, the
outpost was turned over to the South Vietnamese Army.
Dalton volunteered for highly secret work out of Nha
Trang. He was leading a six-man reconnaissance team on
a secret mission when captured. He is still listed as a prisoner of war. Thanks again for wearing my brother's
bracelet. Please continue to pray for him and the other
1300 men still missing in action or prisoners of war.*
    Sincerely,
    Brenden McNamara.

Jared looked at her, his expression serious. "You need to write to
them again."

"Why?"

"You need to find out if he came home." Jared took the letter
from her hand and read it again.

Paige waited for him to finish. She didn't know what to say. She'd
always assumed the man had died since she had never heard from his
family again.

"Just think of it, Mom," Jared said handing the letter back to her.
"He wasn't much older than I am when he went to Vietnam. What if
I were going to war instead of to college?"

"Good grief," Paige laughed ruefully. "Grandma would be proud
of the way you lay on the guilt. Must be in the genes."

Jared shrugged. "I just think you should find out. I'd want to
know."

"Okay, okay," she said, ready to change subjects. "I'll think about
it. Now, we better get that pizza ordered before your friends show up."

They loaded the toys back into his box.

"Remember to bring the letter from his brother," Jared reminded
her. "So you can have the address."

"I know," Paige retorted. "I've got it."

Deciding to put everything away later, she followed her son out of
the storage room and turned off the light, pulling the door shut
behind her.

Memories. Funny how half the time she couldn't remember what she was supposed to get when she went to the grocery store, but she could remember vivid details of her son's childhood as well as her own youth. Not just in her mind, but in her heart. The emotions came back as strongly as the images. Where had time gone? How had her son grown up so quickly?

Sometimes the days during his teenage years had seemed to last forever. But looking back, Paige realized that the months and years had flown by. She'd tried to cherish the moments with her son, and she had been as involved in his life as possible. But looking back, it still didn't feel like she'd spent enough time with him—at least not enough for her to feel satisfied and ready for him to leave.

Whatever was she going to do when he was gone?

CHAPTER FOUR

"Hi, Mom," Jared said when Paige accepted his collect phone call. Paige's heart grew warm just hearing her son's voice. She'd just gotten home from work and was just about to jump in the shower. It had been a long, exhausting day.

"Sweetie, hi. How's school? Are you getting settled? How are your classes? Do you like the coach? How are you doing in practice?"

"Geez, Mom, slow down," Jared joked. "You act like we haven't talked in a year instead of four days ago."

"I know," Paige said. "It's just that you hadn't started school last time we talked. What's it like?"

"Awesome. I've got a great roommate. His name's Nate and he's from Atherton, California—somewhere around San Francisco. He's on the basketball team too, and he drives the greatest car ever. It's a black BMW Z4 and he said I could borrow it anytime I want. His parents are loaded."

"That's nice, Jared," Paige said, knowing that whether right or wrong, her son judged a person by the car they drove. "What about school?"

"It's okay. They sure like to pile on the homework, though."

"College is like that," Paige commiserated. "The teachers sometimes act like theirs is the only class you have."

"No kidding. I've got like five chapters to read in biology before my next class," he told her.

"How's basketball?"

"It's awesome! Lou's husband, Coach Curtis, is the coolest ever." Bryant worked as the assistant basketball coach at UC Irvine.

"Yeah," Paige agreed, "Bryant is pretty cool." Lou's parents had been determined to help their daughter find an upstanding, strong, LDS boy for a husband, so they'd sent her to BYU, where she met and fell in love with Bryant Curtis, a North Carolina boy who played basketball for the Y. Upon finding out that he wasn't LDS, Lou's parents had forbidden her to continue the relationship with Bryant. Yet Lou's patient persistence and strong testimony had interested Bryant enough that he began investigating the Church. A year before he and Lou married, Bryant was baptized. Paige knew he was a wonderful husband and father and that Lou had been right to be patient. As for Lou's parents, they had grown to love him like a son.

"I already like it here," he said, "and even if I don't get to play much this year, I'm glad I decided on UC Irvine instead of playing for a JC back home."

Paige felt herself flush. She had prayed fervently that her son would play for one of the local colleges that had wanted her son desperately. But he'd wanted to go "away" to school, especially after the opportunity to play for a division-one school opened up. It was an offer he couldn't refuse, and Paige had shed many private tears over his decision.

"That's good," Paige said, not admitting that she secretly wished he hated it in California and came back home to play.

"And I saw Dad on Sunday. They had me and Nate over for a barbecue."

Paige knew that "they" meant Jared's dad, Mark, and his girl-friend, Brindy.

"Dad's new house is amazing, and Brindy made the best dessert ever. I'll get the recipe for you."

Paige didn't tell her son that she'd rather have her hair set on fire than get a recipe from her ex-husband's girlfriend. In fact, just hearing her son talk about it all turned her stomach. One of her biggest fears having Jared move to southern California was that he'd become closer to his father than he was to her. Jared insisted that having his father nearby hadn't swayed his decision to go to college in Irvine, but Paige wondered if her son felt a need to strengthen his relationship with his father. Still, no matter what her feelings for Mark were, she wanted what was best for Jared.

Of course, she'd never shared any of her feelings about this with Jared. She doubted he'd understand just how difficult it was for her to hear him talk fondly about his father or his father's girlfriend. She was glad when he changed the subject.

"So what's going on there?" he asked.

"Not much," she told him. "Everyone asks about you—people at church, neighbors, the guys at work."

"Cool!" Jared exclaimed. "How is work anyway?"

Paige sighed. "It's fine. You know I get frustrated with Ross. He still won't let me try out some of my ideas, so I get stuck doing the same old thing, day after day." Her job as a graphic designer for a local design company had her working on brochures and marketing materials for various companies. She'd had several ideas over the years to pull in more business by branching out into other design opportunities, but her boss, Ross Langerfeld, gave all the unique and challenging jobs to two other designers—both men—who weren't nearly as good as her. Apparently, though, she was the only one who seemed to think so.

"I thought he liked your idea to do sports programs for high schools," Jared said.

"He did," Paige answered. "But he said he had to run the idea by the other partners before I could move on it. That was six months ago." During Jared's senior year in high school, Paige had helped the basketball coach put together a program for the team, complete with pictures and information about each of the players. They'd sold the program at ball games and had made enough of a profit to buy new uniforms for the team. She'd been approached by several other high schools requesting her help on their programs, but she didn't have enough spare time to do it outside of work.

"Don't give up, Mom," Jared said. "Ross will come around."

"I hope so," Paige answered. She didn't tell her son that she scoured the paper every Sunday for a new job, one that would allow her creativity to grow and would provide a sense of fulfillment, something she would look forward to each day with anticipation, not dread.

"So, Mom," Jared once again changed the subject, "I have an idea."

Paige liked the excitement in his voice. She'd missed the energy his presence brought into her home and her life. Without him, it was as if all the 100-watt lightbulbs in the house had been changed to 40 watt. Life just wasn't as bright and glowing with Jared gone.

"Why don't you come to California over Labor Day? It's a three-day weekend. Maybe you could stay with Lou since she doesn't live very far away. There are tons of places we could visit."

Every day Paige thought of going to visit her son, but to actually have him ask her to come to California filled her with sudden anticipation and made her willing to move heaven and earth to find a way. It would be exciting to have something to look forward to—seeing Jared, visiting Lou, getting away from her empty house . . .

"That sounds like a great idea," she told him. "I'd love to."

"You'll come?"

"Sure," she said. "I'll call Lou and make sure she's going to be in town."

"Cool!" he exclaimed. "Okay, I guess I'd better go hit the books. It's going to take hours to read all that biology stuff."

They said their good-byes, but this time when Paige hung up the phone, she didn't feel quite so down and lonely. The prospect of seeing her son had lightened her heart.

* * *

The letter haunted her. Twice she had put it in her top drawer, and twice she had gotten it back out again. She didn't know why it was so hard to sit down and write to the family of the soldier missing in action, but it was. What would she say? Would it remind them of their great loss? Would it only bring them pain? Had he been one of the lucky few who had been found and survived the prisoner of war camps? She'd heard of the atrocities of the Hanoi prisons—the severe torture, the extreme conditions reducing the men to skin and bones, robbing them of their dignity and their identities. Had this man suffered such a fate . . . this Dalton McNamara?

She read the letter again and thought about Jared. How did a mother ever send her son off to war? Paige would have a hard enough time sending him on his mission. In a way, having Jared away at school was probably good because it prepared her for the two years he would be in the mission field.

After deliberating about the letter while she ate a microwave dinner, she finally took a paper and pen and started a reply. Seven attempts later, she held up the short note and read what she'd written.

Dear Mr. and Mrs. McNamara,

My name is Paige St. Claire. Back in 1973, I wore your son Dalton's MIA/POW bracelet. I wrote you a letter to tell you that, and I received a reply from your son Brenden, telling me about Dalton. I recently found the letter and the bracelet and thought about your son and wondered if he'd returned home. I hope I'm not out of line writing to you after all these years.

The letter was stupid. She was tempted to wad it up and toss it in the garbage, yet she truly had begun to wonder what had happened to her soldier, and her curiosity was getting the best of her. She'd recently watched a PBS special on the American prisoners of war from Vietnam. Had her soldier's face been among those she'd seen on the screen?

Signing and folding the letter, she placed it in an envelope and addressed it to the return address from the soldier's family. Their letter to her was nearly thirty years old, and she knew the chance of them still being where they lived then was slim. She placed a stamp in the corner.

Her thoughts drifted back to thirty years ago. The events of that time had altered her life and reshaped it forever. She'd been forced to assume great responsibility at age sixteen, when her parents divorced. Her father walked away from their family, rarely returning to see them. He'd always fulfilled his financial obligations, but her mother always found something negative to say about him and had convinced her children that he was a worthless, heartless monster incapable of love. Their mother never did remarry, but grew more bitter and angry with each passing year. Their father avoided his ex-wife at the cost of not seeing his children, so Paige and her siblings were forced to deal with his absence, and it had taken its toll on them. Paige's two younger brothers both turned to drinking and drugs in their teens, causing their mother even more heartache. Her youngest brother, Nick, had actually managed to get his life together and had built a successful computer business, but he'd been in and out of three marriages and couldn't seem to have a healthy relationship with a woman. Her other brother, John, didn't even bother with marriage. Even at forty, he refused to settle down and get married, though he'd had several children out of wedlock.

Then there was Paige with her own failed marriage. For years she had blamed herself for its demise, figuring it had been caused by her own psychological problems spilling over into their relationship. But she soon realized that this thinking had only been encouraged by Mark to distract her from his own selfish desires for someone young and beautiful . . . and whole.

Unbidden tears filled her eyes. It didn't seem to matter how many years passed by. The pain of her experience with breast cancer was always there if she dug deeply enough. She just had to quit digging. She had to quit allowing herself to dwell on the past, especially when there was nothing she could do about it. She'd done the best she could do with what she'd been given. That was all she could do. She couldn't change things now.

Both of her parents were gone. Her father had passed away from colon cancer at age sixty-nine, and her mother from congenital heart failure just last year. Paige had been able to make peace with her father. After he was diagnosed with cancer, he came to her a changed man. Paige noted bitterly that cancer had a way of doing that to a person. He was full of remorse at leaving his family, but Paige had grown to realize that the divorce was not wholly his fault. She had been able to forgive him and finally have the relationship with him that she'd always wanted in her life. She'd learned that he was a good man, and she cherished the few years they'd had together before he died. Her brothers hadn't been so lucky. Neither of them had been able to forgive him for what he'd done. They were a lot like their mother.

Paige's mother never did forgive her ex-husband for leaving her and her children. Paige's father tried to make peace, but she had clung to her anger like a barnacle to a ship's hull. It was her constant companion, her identity. It had turned her into a bitter old woman whose last years on earth were sad and lonely.

Paige swore she'd never be that way, yet she wondered if it truly was by sheer coincidence that her own marriage had followed the same course as her mother's. And was she handling the aftermath of her failed marriage any better than her mother had?

Maybe on the outside. She always tried to be pleasant to Mark. She encouraged her son's relationship with his father and allowed Mark and Brindy to come and visit whenever they wanted. But on the inside, she still felt anger and betrayal. His selfishness still got to her, and that bothered her—or was it the fact that he was wealthy, lived in a beautiful home, and appeared to be in a happy relationship that irked her so much? Maybe she worried that his lifestyle would become appealing to her son and that he would see the material, worldly pursuits of his father as a formula for happiness. She hadn't been able to offer that kind of life to Jared. They'd always had what they'd needed—food, clothes, a roof over their heads—but not the lavish lifestyle his father offered. But Paige knew she had also provided Jared with something his father never would . . . the gospel. Even though Mark hadn't served a mission, they'd gotten married in the temple. But Mark had gone inactive within the first five years of their marriage. As for having a family, Mark had wanted them to wait until they were both out of college, settled in a house, and established in their careers. But Paige had never wanted a career outside the home. She'd always envisioned herself as the mother of a big family that took care of one another and worshiped together.

Paige recalled that helping Jared see the joy in living the gospel hadn't always been easy. There had been times he hadn't wanted to get up for church or go to his midweek activities or bless the sacrament, but he was a good kid, and she knew he had a testimony. And he was determined to share that testimony on a mission.

Rinsing her utensils off in the sink, Paige tossed the remains of her microwave dinner into the garbage and turned out the kitchen light. The house was eerily silent. She turned on the television and all the lights in the family room. She didn't care what program was on, she just needed some noise, some company. She flipped through the

channels but found nothing good to watch, so she went to her
bedroom and changed into her pajamas. She used to complain about
how late Jared and his friends kept her up at night. What she'd give
right now to have them in the kitchen making smoothies and
popping popcorn.

She pulled the top of her pajamas over her head and tugged them
into place, glimpsing her reflection in the mirror. Smoothing the shirt
on her chest, she turned from side to side, noting the glaring flatness
of her left side. She didn't know which was worse—the physical scars
left by her surgery or the emotional scars left by her husband. The
wounds had healed, but the scars remained, serving as blatant
reminders of her battles with cancer, with her marriage, with life.

She sat on the bed and squeezed her eyes shut, not wanting to cry
but unable to stop the tears. She'd resigned herself to the fact that she
would probably never marry again. She probably wouldn't date again
either. It would be too awkward and uncomfortable now. Besides,
how would she bring up the subject anyway?

An even bigger reason she would never marry again was the fact
that she wasn't stupid enough to trust a man again. She'd been burned
and still remembered how painful it was. Relationships were just too
much work and too risky to be worth the effort. She was lonely, but
there were worse situations she could be in.

She rested her face in her hands and sighed, thinking about her
cancer. She'd already gone through all the stages of disbelief, denial,
and anger, and now she was just grateful to be a breast cancer
survivor. She'd stopped asking why a long time ago because she knew
how fortunate she was to be alive. She'd made it through some incredibly rough times, and she hadn't done it alone. Heavenly Father had
helped her every step of the way. But wasn't she due for something
good to happen? Wasn't it her turn to get off the roller coaster ride
from—

The ringing of the telephone broke her thoughts. She wiped her
cheeks with a corner of her shirtsleeve, and, clearing her throat, she
answered the phone.

"Hi, Mom," Jared said.

"Jared, what is it?" she exclaimed. "Is something wrong?"

"No, no, nothing's wrong. I just wondered if you'd written that letter yet."

Paige shook her head. How about that? With all Jared had going on, he wasn't going to let her forget about her promise to write a letter to her soldier's family. She was grateful she'd sat down and done it.

"You'll be happy to know I wrote the letter tonight. I'll mail it first thing in the morning."

"I'm surprised," Jared confessed. "I thought it would take more than that to get you to write that letter."

Paige laughed. She knew she had a tendency to avoid tasks she didn't enjoy. For some reason, Jared seemed to think it was his obligation to push her to follow through with these tasks. At times she wondered who was the parent and who was the child.

"I knew you'd be calling to bug me about it, so I just got it over with," she explained.

Jared chuckled. "You'll let me know when you hear back from them?"

"Honey, don't get your hopes up. It's been thirty years since I corresponded with them. Who says they're still in that house? Or even alive?"

"You don't have anything to lose by trying though, right?" he reminded her.

"Right," she answered.

"Okay then. Now, I really have to start reading. Good night, Mom. I love you," he said.

"I love you, too," she replied.

"Thanks for being the best mom in the world," he added.

"Thanks for being the best son in the world," she answered.

That night after reading her scriptures, Paige knelt down to say her prayers. She didn't know what she'd do without the knowledge that Heavenly Father loved her and was aware of her, that she wasn't really alone. She thanked God for all He had done for her and for her son, and she prayed for Jared and his success in school and in basketball. And finally, she thanked Him for helping her through yet another day.

CHAPTER FIVE

Early the next morning, Paige was awakened by the telephone. She glanced at the clock, which read five minutes to seven. With her voice still sleepy, she said, "Hello," while trying to force open her eyes.

"Paige, did I wake you? I'm sorry, I just couldn't wait. I had to call," the frantic voice came over the phone.

"Lou?" Paige yawned and propped herself up on one elbow. "I was going to call you today. What's up? Is something wrong? You sound funny."

"Oh, Paige," Lou said, her voice full of emotion, "I had to talk to you. You're the only one who can help me."

Paige's thoughts raced. What had happened? Had Bryant done something to upset Lou? Had something happened to one of her children? Then fear struck her heart . . .

"You know how I was going in for my annual mammogram?" Lou said.

Paige didn't need to hear any more. The grief in Lou's voice rang familiar in Paige's memory and caused an ache in Paige's heart, an ache she never wanted to associate with again. "Lou, no," she whispered.

"I got the results from the biopsy, and . . ." she wept for a moment, "oh, Paige, it's cancer."

Tears filled Paige's eyes as she collapsed back into her pillow, covered the phone, and sobbed. Though neither of them spoke, together they cried.

* * *

Paige learned that Lou's surgery date was scheduled on Wednesday, two weeks from tomorrow. As soon as Paige got to work she went to see her boss. Lou needed her, and she was willing to move heaven and earth to be there for her friend.

She presented the situation to Ross, trying not to get emotional. But talking about it brought her feelings to the surface.

Ross sat behind his desk, rolling his gold Cross pen between his fingers as he listened. Nodding his head thoughtfully, he said, "How long will you need to be gone?"

"I'm not sure," Paige answered. "Most likely a week, but I just won't know until I get down there and Lou has her surgery."

Ross looked down at his planner. "I've got the number where you can be reached?"

Paige nodded.

"How's the layout for the Meads Medical Plaza brochure?"

"Almost done," Paige told him. "I won't have any trouble finishing it before I leave." She wondered if he'd forgotten who he was talking to. She was the one who finished her projects either on time or ahead of schedule and constantly asked for more work—particularly for more challenging projects.

As much as she liked Ross, he had a very chauvinistic way of handling his employees. Whether he meant to or not, he obviously valued his male employees more than his few female employees, even though the women in the office were more productive and met their deadlines more often than their male counterparts. It was frustrating for Paige, but in spite of it all, she still felt loyal to Ross. He'd hired her five years ago even though she didn't have as much experience as some of the other applicants for the job. He'd recognized her drive and her desire, and he'd told her many times since she'd been hired that he was glad to have her on the team.

On the way back to her office, she pondered the reasons the women in the firm seemed to be more productive and take their jobs more seriously. She decided that it was because they competed in a man's world and had to try harder. Additionally, all three women in her office were sole breadwinners of their families, single parents trying to keep a roof over their children's heads.

Whatever the reason, it still wasn't fair that the men produced less, didn't work as hard, and still got paid more. It irked Paige to no end, but there was nothing she could do about it. What made matters even worse was that even though Ross loved her idea of providing a service to junior high schools, high schools, and colleges to help them put together the programs for their sports events, he had taken such a long time getting it approved that she'd lost her desire to pursue it. What had started out as an exciting career was quickly becoming simply a boring job.

* * *

A week later, Paige left work early and headed home to pack and get ready for her trip. Her plane left at eight the next morning, and she needed to do some laundry and shopping before she left. She wanted to go to California a few days before Lou's surgery so she could help Lou around the house and spend some time with Jared.

Jared had been excited to learn she was coming to visit so soon, but was saddened by the news about Lou's breast cancer. Lou and Bryant were like family to him. His "Aunt Lou" had never missed sending him a little something for his birthday or Christmas. In fact, her gifts were the ones he looked forward to the most.

Feeling anxious and fidgety, Paige paced the house. She'd done all the cleaning and packing she could do, but she still had nervous energy to spare. She was worried about Lou and knew all too well the horrors her dearest friend was about to face.

Convinced that she'd never fall asleep that night, Paige decided to soak in the tub and read a magazine, hoping it would help her relax and distract her mind for a while.

Her plan worked as far as the relaxing bubble bath went, but fell apart when she opened the woman's magazine to find it full of stories about cancer survivors. Even though Paige herself was a cancer survivor, reading other women's stories proved to be too harsh and painful of a reminder of her own battle—something she didn't need when she had one every day when she looked in the mirror at her lopsided chest.

She looked at the pictures of the smiling women in the magazine. Some had gone on to make huge contributions to society—organizing cancer runs, fund-raisers, and free cancer-screening clinics in their communities. Others had become motivational speakers, CEOs of large corporations and even political figures.

Paige tossed the magazine onto the floor and let her body sink slowly into the steaming water. Apparently now it wasn't enough just to survive the horror of having cancer, of knowing that your body had turned against you. It wasn't enough to stare death in the face, to lose your hair, your energy, your appetite, and at times feel like you'd lost your very soul. No, you not only had to survive, you had to come out better than before, even to the point of changing the world. Paige could barely change a furnace filter, let alone start a new business and become a millionaire in less than a year.

She glanced down at her chest and groaned. She'd thought about having reconstructive surgery at the time of her mastectomy, but her doctor had recommended she wait a year or two after her initial surgery. Now she wished she would have had it done at the time of the surgery. Maybe if she had, it would have been easier to put her cancer behind her. Maybe if she looked more "normal," life would become more "normal." Maybe she would have been able to get on with her life and not feel like a perpetual victim of breast cancer.

Sometimes she also wondered if she'd had the operation done initially that things with her and Mark would have been different. Her illness had been a tremendous strain on their marriage. At times Mark had seemed frightened of what she was going through, like he didn't know how to treat her or take care of her. Then at times he seemed so frustrated and angry that she felt guilty for having cancer—as if she'd had any choice. It didn't help that he no longer wanted anything to do with the Church. Except for Jared, they'd had nothing in common.

The marital problems they'd had before her cancer seemed to be intensified after it. Instead of growing closer together, gaining a greater appreciation for life and each other, they grew apart. Paige knew she hadn't handled her cancer and its treatment with as much strength and dignity as she could have, but she also realized that she'd been scared and worried. She knew she'd feel miserable after radiation, chemotherapy, and tamoxifen, but she ended up feeling worse than she'd expected. She'd become so withdrawn and overwhelmed trying to cope with her own plight and discomfort that she'd neglected her husband and her son. It was painful to be so honest with herself, but lying to herself and trying to place all the blame on Mark hadn't helped handle the breakup of her marriage.

Maybe being in the "breast cancer survivors club" was an elite and prestigious membership, but the dues to get in had been much too high, and the sacrifices weren't worth it. Sure, she was grateful each day to be alive and to have a wonderful son, but she'd also experienced trials she knew she could never face again.

Toweling off, she wrapped herself in her thick, fleecy robe and went to the kitchen. She was hungry, but she wasn't in the mood to cook. She scanned the shelves and cupboards for something tantalizing but found nothing . . . until she looked in the freezer.

Paige didn't have a lot of vices, but she did have a serious addiction to ice cream—especially mint chocolate chip with caramel fudge sauce. Unable to resist, Paige pulled the carton from the freezer, popped the topping into the microwave, and proceeded to create a delectable sundae worth every calorie.

Noticing the stack of mail on her counter, she sifted through bills and junk mail as she enjoyed each smooth, creamy bite of ice cream. She pushed a handful of bills aside and picked up an envelope addressed in unfamiliar handwriting and studied it. The letters were formed carefully, the tiny writing uneven and shaky, as if written by an unsteady hand. The words were hard to make out, but Paige finally deciphered the name of the sender: *Naomi McNamara.*

Paige blinked. She couldn't believe her eyes. This letter had to be a response to the one she sent last week to her soldier's family.

"That was fast," Paige said out loud, taking a sip of water to moisten her suddenly dry mouth. Opening the flap, she pulled out the single sheet of rose-colored paper and unfolded it.

Dear Paige,

> *How wonderful to receive your letter. Even though it's been many years, it was still nice to know you thought of us and of our son. It's amazing that you kept our letter all this time. Isn't it funny how our past can catch up to us?*
> *To answer your first question, yes, my son Dalton did return from the war. He was missing in action, and for many months we didn't know if he was dead or alive. After six months of wondering and heartache, we found*

out that he had been captured by the North Vietnamese and was being held prisoner in Hanoi. He was one of the lucky ones, and by some miracle he was only there a year, but the scars and effects of the war were devastating to him, and he returned home a different man than the son I sent. He's faced many challenges and has had a very hard life. But Dalton also has an amazing attitude and never gives up. He has gone on to make something out of himself that he can be proud of and that we are very proud of.

Still, as a mother, I would love to see him free from the pain and horror he experienced so he could once again have peace and joy in his life. He doesn't talk about the war much. Many things he won't tell us, but you can see it in his eyes—unspeakable, horrible things he saw and experienced. My heart still aches for him and what he went through during the war.

He lives in Newport Beach, California, now. We don't see him much, but he visits as often as he can. I couldn't be prouder of my son. He's truly a hero, even though many don't see him that way.

You are welcome to contact him if you'd like. He would enjoy talking to you, especially if he knew that you wore his bracelet and that with the help of your faith and prayers, his life was spared and he returned from the war.

Naomi McNamara then closed the letter with her son's address and phone number and one last encouraging word to contact him.

Paige stared at the letter for several moments. She hadn't ever entertained the idea of meeting her soldier. She'd mainly been interested in finding out if he'd returned alive. Now that she knew, she didn't feel a need to pursue the matter further. But there was something about Naomi's suggestion for Paige to contact him.

Folding the letter back into the envelope, Paige tucked it into her purse. She wasn't about to make it a point to look up the man while she was in California, but Jared would ask if she'd heard from the soldier's family. As far as she was concerned, her goal had been achieved and there was no need to pursue the issue.

Still, her heart grew warm with the information that he was alive. He'd actually survived a prisoner of war camp and returned home—the stranger whose bracelet she'd worn, the man for whom she'd prayed month after month. It was a miracle. Certainly God's hand had spared his life and brought him home to his family. She could only imagine what a profound experience it would have been if it had been her own son.

Paige went to her bathroom to moisturize her face before bed. She looked at the lines around her eyes and across her forehead, lines etched by the passing of years and the experiences of life. She'd earned those lines, yet she didn't want them. Inside she felt nothing like the forty-six years her physical body reflected.

Smoothing on the silky cream, she was startled when the telephone rang. She wiped her hands on a towel, then answered the phone.

"Are you packed?" Lou's anxious voice asked.

"I'm packed and ready," Paige told her. "How're you doing?"

"I guess I've already moved onto the next stage of acceptance," Lou replied, her voice sounding strong and solid.

"Which stage is that?"

"I'm past denial and pity and way into the anger phase," Lou explained. "I'm so into the anger phase that I'm into the foot-stomping, not-going-to-let-this-beat-me phase."

Paige chuckled. Lou was a fighter, thank goodness. If anyone could beat cancer by sheer will and determination alone, it was Lou. "That's good," Paige told her. "This is the best phase to be in."

"I feel like I'm going into battle," Lou explained, "yet I don't feel weak or vulnerable. I feel strong and empowered. Bryant has been so awesome. He gives me even more strength."

Lou's words stirred Paige's soul, but reminded her of her own experience, one that sadly wasn't the same. "I wish I would've been as brave as you. It would have made things much easier." Paige had wanted to be strong, but she'd felt so alone. Mark had withdrawn from her, and she'd had no one to lean on. No one but the Lord. Consequently, her relationship with Mark had eventually dissolved into nothing, but thankfully her relationship with the Lord had become stronger and much more personal.

"You're wrong, Paige," Lou told her. "Your example has given me the strength to face this with courage. You are my hero."

Paige laughed out loud. "That's going a little far."

"It's true," Lou said. "You've always been a rock for me."

"And you've been one for me," Paige told her. She would never be able to repay her friend for all the support, love, and encouragement she'd given her through the years.

"I'm glad we have each other," Lou observed.

"Me too," Paige agreed. "It's funny you called. I was thinking about you—actually, about us—when we were sixteen."

"Oooo," Lou exclaimed, "don't remind me. I was such a geek back then. I've tried to block out that phase of my life."

"You weren't a geek," Paige assured her. "You were a cheerleader and in the homecoming royalty. Most of the girls in our class would have given anything to be in your shoes."

"Well, unless they were a size ten they would have had a hard time wearing them. And besides, the only reason I made the cheerleading squad was because they needed someone big and tall to use as a base for the pyramids. I was the one all the other girls climbed on, remember?"

"That doesn't matter," Paige scoffed. "You were still the prettiest cheerleader on our squad."

"You're just saying that because you're my best friend. Besides, it doesn't matter anymore, right?"

"Right," Paige agreed.

"So I'll be there to pick you up in the morning?" Lou reminded her.

"I'm excited to see you and Bryant and the kids."

"And Jared."

"And Jared," Paige echoed. She couldn't wait to see her son.

"We're set then. I better go. It sounds like the kids are trying to kill each other again," Lou said.

"Thanks for calling," Paige told her.

"Thanks for answering," Lou said. "I just needed to hear your voice."

Paige had needed to hear Lou's voice just as much. The television provided noise to her empty home, but not conversation or companionship.

That night when Paige went to bed, she thought about everything that she and Lou had gone through together—marriages, divorces, births, deaths, good times, bad times, health . . . and sickness. They'd been through it all. Sisters couldn't have been any closer than they were.

With gratitude in her heart for her friend and a fervent prayer for God to spare Lou's life, Paige drifted off to sleep.

CHAPTER SIX

Lou and Paige talked nonstop from the John Wayne Airport to Lou's home in Irvine. Riding with the top down in Lou's sporty new Infiniti convertible was exhilarating and fun. Lou had a Beach Boys CD playing, and suddenly Paige felt young and free again. For a moment their cares were gone, their worries behind them.

The warm glow of the sun, the blue sky, and the palm trees transported Paige from her desert home in Utah to what she saw as a lush, tropical paradise. Even the traffic on the road seemed more tolerable because of the view.

"Jared is such a doll," Lou bragged about Paige's son. "He's so fun with the kids. Little Maddie has such a crush on him. I mean," Lou brushed a strand of hair from her mouth, "the boy will sit and play Barbies with her!"

Paige smiled proudly, picturing her six-foot-five son down on the floor with Lou's six year old, playing Barbies. "He's always loved action figures and toys like that. I'm glad your kids like him."

"Are you kidding? Carter is in heaven every time Jared takes him outside to shoot basketball. They would love it if Jared just moved in with us." Carter was Lou's nine year old. Both of the children were beautiful with their creamy olive skin and dark hair.

"The way you cook, he'd probably take you up on it. But he's kind of a slob, so I wouldn't be too quick to invite him if I were you," Paige warned.

"He and Bryant would get along great," Lou said. "Bryant's not exactly the King of Clean. I mean, how many men drop dirty socks *one foot away* from the hamper?"

Paige shrugged. "I don't know. All of them?" she guessed.

Lou laughed out loud. "Probably."

Soon they wound their way up the palm-lined street to Lou's sprawling home, a lovely stucco structure decorated in rich Tuscan style with doses of Mediterranean flavor. The home was surrounded by beautifully manicured lawns with leafy shade trees and patches of colorful flowers tucked here and there amidst ferns and bushes. Lou owned a furniture and design business, and even had stores in San Diego and the Bay area. Her own home reflected her success as well as her decorating style.

The house was quiet when they arrived, the children still at school. Paige got settled in the guest room while Lou made them some light lunch.

"This looks fabulous," Paige exclaimed when she joined Lou on the terrace overlooking the backyard, where the aqua-blue pool, sprawling lawn, lush gardens, tennis court, and even a guest house were located. Lou had offered the guest house to Paige, but Paige had wanted to stay in the main house where she could be with Lou and her family.

Tempting chicken caesar salad–filled pitas and glasses of cold lemonade enticed Paige to the table. "You didn't need to fuss," she told her friend.

"Are you kidding? Bryant made these last night for dinner— you're having leftovers," Lou told her.

"Well, leftovers at your house beat microwave dinners at my house anytime."

"It's hard being alone, isn't it?" Lou said.

Paige nodded and swallowed. "The house doesn't get as dirty though," she remarked.

Lou studied her face for a moment. "Are you okay?"

Paige was taken aback. "I'm fine. My life isn't terribly exciting, but things are good." She looked at Lou's doubtful expression. "Really. I can't complain. Now," she poked a piece of chicken back into the pita pocket, "let me ask you that same question. How are you, really?"

Lou licked her lips, then dabbed them with a napkin. "I'm okay," she said. "But I wonder, is it okay for me to be okay? I mean, shouldn't I be freaking out or something? Not that I didn't already freak out. You should have seen me when the doctor told me the news. I was a mess."

Paige recalled her own experience of learning she had cancer—the numbness, the disbelief, the fear that came with the doctor's shocking announcement.

"You seem to be handling it well now," Paige complimented.

"There were times when I thought I would fall apart. I even had a panic attack one day in the grocery store. They called 911 and everything . . ." Lou laughed cynically at the memory. "They thought I was having a heart attack."

Paige cringed. "That must have been awful."

"It was. I still can't go shopping there now. But Bryant was so amazing. He's so strong physically, but nothing compared to how strong he is spiritually. He gave me a blessing in the emergency room, and . . ." Lou flashed an embarrassed smile at Paige, then blinked as tears filmed her eyes. "Sorry. It's still hard to talk about without getting emotional."

Paige reached out and gave her friend's hand a squeeze.

"Since then, I've felt greater peace and faith," Lou said. "I still get myself worked up at times, but I'm doing so much better."

"I'm glad," Paige said. "I think I walked around in a daze for a long time. I guess I was in shock and denial." She didn't say that she'd struggled desperately to face the challenge alone. Mark hadn't been worthy to give her a priesthood blessing. She'd had to ask her home teachers to do so.

"Anyway, I'm learning that I'm a fighter. I don't let many things get in my way," Lou continued. "And I'm not going to start caving in to challenges now."

Paige looked at her friend with amazement. Lou really was an incredible woman. "So what kind of surgery and treatment are you going to have?"

"I've decided to have reconstructive surgery done at the same time as my mastectomy. My doctor tried to tell me to wait a year or two, but I did some checking around and decided that I didn't want to wait. Even though my insurance company won't pay for the reconstruction, Bryant and I discussed it and decided it was worth it. So, I go in Wednesday morning for the surgery to remove my left breast, and while I'm there my plastic surgeon will place a spacer inside my chest, just under the muscle. I guess over the next two months, I go in and he'll inject it with a saline solution that's supposed to expand and reshape the muscle."

Paige wished that she'd done the same. She'd decided that the scar from her cancer was no badge of honor, just a constant reminder of what she'd endured.

"As for my treatment, they have to delay the radiation until the reconstruction is done because radiation destroys skin elasticity. The skin simply won't stretch. I'll undergo chemotherapy and most likely tamoxifen. I'm not looking forward to all the side effects, but I plan on living to see my grandchildren and great-grandchildren. Even if I am bald."

Paige smiled at Lou.

"This sure would all be easier if you lived closer though," Lou told her.

"I'll come and visit often," Paige assured her. "I promise."

* * *

Paige watched out the front window of Lou's house as the sports car drove up the driveway. Her scalp tingled with excitement.

Watching the car door open, she held her breath as Jared stepped out and stood, his tall, solid frame bronzed by the California sun.

Was it possible he could change after only a few weeks? He looked more mature, his shoulders broader, his face chiseled and handsome. Certainly he had his father's dark complexion, strong nose, and high cheekbones, but he had Paige's broad smile and her same sandy blonde hair color, bleached lighter by the sun. He was a good combination of both parents.

Running for the door, she opened it before he made it up the stairs.

"Jared," she cried, running to her son.

He pulled her into a giant hug, lifting her off the ground. "Hey, Mom," he said, setting her back on the ground. "You look great," he complimented.

"I was thinking the same about you," Paige said. "Bigger, tanner," she ruffled his hair, "blonder. You getting any homework done or are you spending too much time at the beach?"

"I've only been to the beach twice," he defended himself. "But we do have a pool at the apartments, remember?"

"I remember," Paige said, hooking her arm through his and walking with him into Lou's house, where the fragrance of salsa and Mexican food spiced the air.

"Jared," Lou called from the kitchen, "is that you?"

Jared gave Lou a hug when he saw her. "Hungry?" she asked.

"Always," he replied.

She laughed. "I've got some pitas left over from lunch. Would that hold you over until dinner?"

"It might," Jared replied, opening the fridge and gathering an armful of food and drinks as if he were a member of the family.

"Jared," Paige scolded as he carried the load to the counter, where he sat down on a bar stool.

"What?" he exclaimed, apparently unsure of what he'd done wrong. He picked up a bunch of red grapes and popped one into his mouth.

"You cleaned out the fridge," she complained.

Lou looked at Paige and said, "He's fine. I've told him that this is his home away from home. I want him to feel like he can plop down on the couch and watch television, get whatever he wants to eat. He can even bring friends over to swim or play tennis whenever he wants."

"Well, don't wear out your welcome," Paige advised her son.

"I won't, Mom," Jared said, his mouth full of pita sandwich.

The kitchen door leading to the garage suddenly burst open and in barged Maddie and Carter with Bryant directly behind them. Paige jumped from her seat to hug the two children, then him.

Bryant was a linebacker-sized man with a gleaming white smile and a generous dose of good humor. He had a contagious laugh and was one of Paige's favorite people.

"Well, look at you!" Bryant exclaimed to Paige. "You look ravishing. Doesn't she, Lou?"

"Paige's always looked good in red. It's her best color," Lou told him. Paige had on a simple geranium-red linen blouse with light tan linen pants.

"Gee, thanks," Paige told both of them. "I need to come and visit more often."

"You sure do," Bryant said, leaving her side to give his wife a hug and a brief kiss. "I've been waiting all day for that," he said.

Paige blushed at their romantic display, not out of embarrassment but with jealousy. Even when they were their happiest, Mark had never treated her with such admiration and love. She'd never known a sweet relationship like Lou and Bryant's. She was glad when Jared asked her some questions about friends back home and about her job.

"I ran into David's mom at the store. She says he's anxious about getting his mission call. It should come this week. He'll call you when it does. As for Brenton and Cam, they're both having fun at the community college, trying to date as many girls as they can before their missions."

Jared laughed. "Wish I had time to date."

Bryant pointed a finger at Jared and said, "No girls! They mess up your game. You keep your head on basketball."

Paige raised her eyebrows, impressed at his fatherly tone. She certainly didn't need to add anything to that.

"I know, I know," Jared complained. "But Coach . . ."

"Don't 'But Coach' me, nothin'," Bryant said. "You remember our talk before school started. And your blessing . . ."

"What blessing?" Paige asked. This was the first she'd heard about a blessing.

"I asked Bryant to give me a blessing. You know, a first-day-of-school thing," Jared said, obviously exasperated to have to explain.

Paige knew her son well. Talking about personal or spiritual things wasn't easy for him.

"Thank you, Bryant," she said, her throat constricting. Jared had received blessings from many great men in his life, none of them his father.

"It was an honor to do it," Bryant said. "Jared's kind of like a son to me."

A squabble upstairs broke out between Maddie and Carter. "Excuse me," Bryant said. "I'd better go break it up before Carter gets what he probably deserves. Maddie's got quite a punch, and Carter loves to tease her. You'd think he'd learn after three bloody noses."

Lou shook her head. "Those two are constantly fighting. I don't know what I'm going to do with them. And Maddie . . ." She shook her head. "The child's four years younger than her brother!" Lou pulled a pan from the stove and set it on a hot pad.

Paige gave her friend a knowing smile.

"What?" Lou insisted.

"Nothing, it's just that I remember what a spunky kid you were, that's all," Paige said with a shrug.

"Spunky!" Lou exclaimed, taking off her apron and hanging it on a hook near the fridge. "I wasn't spunky."

"You were the spunkmeister," Paige told her. "The Queen of Spunk. The—"

"Okay," Lou stopped her, grinning, "enough already. I get your point."

"Like mother like daughter," Paige added, remembering how long Lou and Bryant had wanted to have children.

"Poor kid." Lou checked a pot on the stove and turned down the heat. "Dinner's ready. I'm just going to dash upstairs and change into something a little more comfy. I'll be right back, and then we can eat."

Paige and Jared smiled at each other. Just being involved in an active, happy home like this was pure joy. Paige always wished she'd been able to have more children. But every time she'd approached Mark about it, he had plenty of reasons for them to wait. She knew he didn't want anything else tying him down, and maybe in a way, that in itself was a blessing given her and Mark's stormy relationship.

"So, what's new?" Jared asked, finishing the last grape on the stem.

"Nothing really," Paige said. They'd already talked about his friends, her work, the ward. That pretty much covered her life. Then she remembered something she wanted to show him.

"Except for maybe this." She handed him the letter from her purse.

"What is it?" he asked, reading the return address on the front. He looked at her, his expression puzzled. Then the realization hit him. "Is this what I think it is?"

Paige nodded.

"You already heard from that soldier's family?"

"It came yesterday."

"This is so great!" he exclaimed. Then he stopped. "Did he make it home?"

"Read the letter," she told him.

He unfolded the note, and as he read, a smile broke out on his face. "He made it home. Cool!" Then he continued reading. "Whoa! The guy lives in Newport Beach. That's so close. We have to go see him!"

Paige looked at her son as if he'd suddenly become an alien. "No, we don't."

"His mom wants you to, and I want to meet this guy, Mom. I've never known anyone who fought in a war, especially someone who was a POW. Why don't you want to meet him?"

"Well . . ." Paige scraped words together in her mind, "I, ah . . . well . . ." She glared at her son. "You just don't go looking up strangers like that. What would I say? He'd think I'm a nut."

"Mom, you wore his bracelet. He was a war hero. It's your patriotic duty."

Paige burst out laughing.

Lou walked into the room just then. "What's so funny?"

"Nothing." Paige shook her head, snatching the letter away from Jared and shoving it into her purse. Jared reached in and grabbed it, then threw it to Lou before his mom could grab it away again.

"What is this?" Lou glanced down at the letter and read the first line. Her mouth opened and she gasped, pointing at Paige, speechless.

Paige rolled her eyes.

"Your soldier. Paige, you heard from his mother? This is incredible."

Paige quickly explained about finding the bracelet in storage, writing to the family at Jared's insistence, and receiving the reply.

"You have to go see him," Lou insisted. Jared smiled triumphantly.

Paige glared at both of them. "I am not going to see him. I don't know him from Adam, and he doesn't know me from . . . Eve!" she burst out. "You guys are crazy if you think I'm going to see him."

Jared and Lou looked at each other. "She has to go," Jared said.

"Absolutely," Lou agreed. "No question."

To Paige's relief, the telephone rang.

While Lou spoke, Paige placed the hot dishes of food on the table. Bryant and the kids came down the stairs, and everyone took their place at the table. Lou hung up just as Maddie was about to say the prayer. She quickly took her seat and bowed her head.

Maddie began, "Dear Heavenly Father, thank You for this food and for all we have. Thank You for our family and for Jared and Paige. Thank You for my turtle, Sneaky, and that my birthday is in two weeks and for the new bike that I'm going to get."

Paige lifted her eyes and glanced at Lou, who was trying hard not to laugh.

"Please bless our food so we can be healthy and strong. Please especially bless my mommy. Help her so the cancer will go away and she will get to live with us until she's an old, old lady."

Even though part of Paige wanted to laugh, the other part of her wanted to cry. *Please,* Paige's own prayer echoed, *let Lou be with us until she's an old, old lady.*

CHAPTER SEVEN

"So, who was on the phone?" Bryant asked while everyone enjoyed Lou's delicious meal.

Lou sighed. "Linda. She can't—"

"Don't tell me she can't come in again," Bryant interrupted.

Lou shook her head. "I've tried to be patient with her, I really have, but with my surgery and treatment . . ." Lou's voice grew shaky. "I need someone I can depend on at the store. More now than ever."

Bryant filled Paige and Jared in on the situation. "Linda is Lou's general manager. She went through a divorce recently, and now she's got a new boyfriend who keeps her distracted most of the time."

"Don't get me wrong, I'm happy for her," Lou said. "But she calls in sick, sometimes twice a week, so she can be with him. I know she's not really sick because Bryant saw her downtown last week with her boyfriend, and I passed them together on the freeway the other day. I can't depend on her anymore."

"You're not looking for a new job, are you, Paige?" Bryant asked.

Paige chuckled, but Lou's face showed more than amusement. "Paige," Lou said, her tone serious, her expression intense, "that's a great idea. I would love to have you manage my store. You would do a spectacular job. Have you ever thought about moving here? You could be closer to Jared and to us. You don't have any family in Utah. Your only tie there is your job."

Jared's expression matched Lou's. "She's right, Mom. And you don't even like your job."

Lou's eyes opened wide. "Paige," she exclaimed, "is that true?"

Paige flashed a "thanks a lot" look at her son and said, "I'm just a little frustrated right now."

"What's going on?" Lou wanted to know. Paige didn't want to get into it, but Lou wouldn't give up.

"Ross is a really great guy," Paige began. "He's been wonderful about everything I've been through, giving me time off when I've needed it, very understanding."

Lou nodded.

"It's just that he tends to give all the good projects and assignments to the men in our company. And I'm not the only one who feels this way," she qualified her complaint. "There are other women in our department who feel the same way I do."

"Mom had a really great idea to go around to high schools and colleges and help them put together their programs for football and basketball. She helped with ours at school last year and did a great job," Jared interjected.

"We're working on ours right now," Bryant said. "Coach Hale was just complaining about it to me today. The person who's supposed to lay out the program backed out on us. The guy's done it for three or four years, but he got a new job or something. Anyway, Coach Hale is not happy about it."

"Mom," Jared piped up, "you could do it. You've got all the software at home."

Paige shook her head. "It would be difficult with me in Utah, Jared. Besides, there are probably hundreds of people here who would be better qualified."

"Are you sure you wouldn't consider doing it?" Bryant asked. "We're ahead of schedule, so we'd have time to send you all the pictures and information. I mean, if you're at all interested. We'd pay you for your time and expenses."

Paige didn't doubt she could do the basketball program. She enjoyed designing and laying out sports programs. She'd been the yearbook editor in high school and in college, and she had a knack for placing pictures and text on a page and having it turn out appealing and professional.

"Mom, it would be so awesome," Jared said with excitement. "The only thing that would be better is if you moved here."

Lou agreed, and so did Bryant. Even Maddie and Carter piped up and said she should.

"She could live in our guest house," Maddie suggested without hesitation.

Lou looked at her child, wide-eyed, as if she'd suddenly spoken in tongues. "That's brilliant," she exclaimed. "Our guest house is just sitting there."

Paige's brows narrowed. Lou was serious. So was Jared. They wanted her to move to California.

"Mom, it would be so great," Jared continued. "You could even come to my games." He knew that the worst fear his mother had about him going so far away to school was that she'd never get to see him play.

But to give up her job . . .

"If you wanted to pick up more jobs doing sports programs, I could recommend you to the coaches in some of the other colleges. I know they deal with this kind of stuff every year too," Bryant encouraged, somehow knowing her worries.

"And I would love to give you that management position at the store," Lou said. "You're perfect for the job with your design background and great taste in decorating." Paige had studied interior design in college while gaining her degree.

Stunned and speechless, Paige placed a hand on her chest and looked at the eager, excited faces in front of her. "You guys are serious, aren't you?"

"What's holding you in Utah, Mom?" Jared asked.

"I have roots there. It's been my home my entire life," she said.

"But your home is where your loved ones and family are," Lou tried to persuade her. "Jared's here, and we're about as close to family as you can get."

It was true. Paige enjoyed her ward, her neighbors, and the people at work, but she had no close friends, no relationships she treasured as much as those with the people sitting in front of her.

"I don't know," she finally said. "This would be such a drastic change. I'd need to think about it."

Jared's face lit up. Lou clapped her hands and smiled with joy. Bryant high-fived Carter and Maddie.

"Wait!" she exclaimed. "I didn't say yes. I just said I'd think about it."

Lou and Jared quickly erased any trace of excitement from their faces, but they continually glanced at each other and grinned throughout the remainder of the meal.

Could she do it? Could she really move from the place she'd called home for over forty years and start over in California? It would be difficult, but the best part would be being near Jared, Lou, and Lou's family.

"If you lived in the guest house, could I come visit you?" Maddie asked Paige.

"Of course you could," Paige told her.

"Could we make cookies?"

Paige smiled. The deal seemed even sweeter knowing she'd have youngsters around. If she moved in, she could help with Lou's kids, loving them and spoiling them.

"I know this is selfish, but having you around while I'm losing my hair from chemo would honestly be about the only way I could get through it," Lou joked while tears filled her eyes. "Who else would go wig shopping with me?"

Paige reached for Lou's hand and gave it a squeeze and nodded. She understood exactly how Lou felt. She would have given anything to have had Lou by her side when she herself watched handfuls of hair go down the shower drain or spent so much time over the toilet turning her stomach inside out.

"I'll think about it," she told them once more with an encouraging smile.

* * *

Saturday morning, Lou and Paige went to Lou's store, appropriately named *Louisa's*. The showroom was breathtaking, her furniture selection ranging from casual country French to elegant Mediterranean and a little of everything in between. Paige particularly admired some of the rich leather couches and gorgeous wood pieces.

From the moment the doors opened for business, the place had a steady stream of customers. Some just wanted to browse and furniture shop, others needed to meet with Lou or one of her designers. At noon, Lou's assistant manager, Candace, came in out of breath but ready to work.

"Candy," Lou called, "I'd like you to meet Paige, my dearest friend in the world."

Paige smiled and shook Candy's outstretched hand.

"Lou talks about you all the time," Candy said. "I feel like I know you already."

Paige flashed Lou a sidelong glance.

"Don't worry, Paige, it's all been good," Lou said.

"I'm glad I finally get to meet you," Candy added. "Especially since I'm transferring to the San Francisco store next month."

Lou's expression fell at the reminder. "I'm promoting Candy to manager. She's taking over the Bay Area store for me. We're going to miss her around here. She always brings doughnuts and cookies to work to share." She slipped an arm around Candy's shoulders and gave her a squeeze. "Of course, she's going to whip the Bay Area store into shape for me, and I'm excited about that."

Candy smiled at the compliment. "So, are you two going to lunch or out shopping?"

"Lunch and shopping, then we're going back to my house to lounge by the pool," Lou told her.

"Sounds wonderful," Candy said. "Have fun, and don't worry about a thing here. You just enjoy yourself. By the way, Lou, I've got a couple of applicants coming in this afternoon to interview for my position. They seem pretty sharp, so keep your fingers crossed."

"I will," Lou replied. "And my toes and my eyes." She crossed her eyes and made a face.

Candy and Paige laughed. Paige admired her friend for keeping her wit and sense of humor no matter what was going on in her life. Lou was a fighter and a survivor.

* * *

"This is living," Paige said as she paddled her hand in the water to turn her floaty around. "If I had a pool, I'd quit my day job."

"Sometimes I wish I could. I get so busy in the summer I've gone months without even putting my big toe in the water. Maybe," Lou lifted her head from the inflatable mat, "that's one of the things I'm supposed to learn through this cancer thing."

"To stop and swim in your pool?" Paige teased.

"Something like that, you know? Smell the roses, spend more time with my husband and children . . ." Lou lay back down and shut her eyes. "Right now, every day seems like a gift to me, one I can't take for granted or waste. I know I have to go to work, but I'd rather be with loved ones or out in nature appreciating the world, experiencing life because I don't know when it's going to . . ." her voiced drifted to a whisper.

"Hey," Paige said, "you're going to beat this, Lou. You have so many things going for you—early detection, and you take good care of yourself. You're doing everything right. It's not going to be easy, but you are going to win. I know you are."

Lou rolled her head to the side and shielded her eyes as she looked at Paige. "That's why you're here," she said. "You're my cheerleader. I need you to keep telling me this stuff."

"It's true. Every word."

They floated lazily while the California sun sprinkled them with bronze kisses.

"So when do you plan on going to see your soldier?" Lou asked without hedging.

"I am *not* going to see him. I really don't know what I would even say to him. Maybe if it had been only a year or two after the war, but thirty? The last thing he probably needs is a reminder of Vietnam," Paige argued.

"Well, tonight would be a good night since Bry and I have to run to that wedding reception. I mean, you're welcome to come with us, but I'm sure it will be boring since you don't know any of the people who will be there."

"Don't you need me to help with the children? I planned on tending them."

"Are you kidding? I've got a neighbor girl across the street who tends for me. The kids love her. She always brings treats and games for them. They have a party while we're gone. I hate to tell you this, but they'd be brokenhearted if Lindsay didn't tend them."

Paige frowned. She didn't want to intrude on the family's plans, but she also didn't want to go see her soldier.

"Then Jared and I will probably go to a movie or something," Paige said. "He wants me to come and check out the campus and his apartment now that he's moved in. Tonight would be a good chance to do so."

"You can do that tomorrow," Lou said.

"I need more time to think about going to see him."

"Well, you're not going to be here that long. I hope you think fast."

* * *

That evening, just for fun, Paige and Jared went to Downtown Disney to eat dinner. They hadn't been to Disneyland since Jared was ten years old, and now there was a whole new California Adventure park built right next to the main theme park. Between the two parks was an area called Downtown Disney with places to shop and eat. The atmosphere was festive and fun, and just being around Disneyland brought out the kid in Paige. She yearned to go in and hit some rides, but it was near closing time and wouldn't be worth the entry fee. They decided that the next time she came to California, they were definitely coming back.

"How about driving to the beach?" Jared suggested after dinner. "There's still time before it gets dark."

"I'd like that," Paige said, marveling at how well her son maneuvered his friend's BMW around the busy streets of the city. She was nervous having him borrow such an expensive car, but he assured her that his roommate wasn't worried about it. In fact, Nate sounded like he was generous to a fault. Jared had also borrowed his Ferrari sports shoes, his Polo jeans, and his cologne.

"Is Nate LDS?" she asked as Jared changed lanes. She'd talked to Nate on the phone but hadn't had a chance to meet him yet.

"No, I think his mom's Catholic and his dad's Jewish, or the other way around. I can't remember for sure."

They traveled farther down the congested road.

"Is he a good kid? You know," she tried to play down her interrogation, "he doesn't party and bring girls home or anything like that, does he?"

"I think he drinks a little, but he's pretty focused. He wants to be a doctor like his dad, so he doesn't mess around much."

Paige wondered what exactly "much" meant. She was still concerned for her son even though he wasn't at home anymore. He'd done well so far in making right choices, choosing good friends, and not having a steady girlfriend. She just didn't want anything to happen to change his course.

Suddenly, the air smelled fresh with the tang of salt, and a silver stretch of ocean sparkled in the distance. Just being this close to the sea made her want to walk barefoot in the sand and watch the sunset over the water. It had been ages since she'd been to the beach. The last time had been one Christmas long ago when Mark had surprised her and Jared with a trip to Disneyland. They'd gone to all the fun places, all the hot tourist spots, and had spent some time at the beach. They'd been happy then, and the vacation had been the perfect getaway. That was just before everything went bad.

"There's a parking spot." Paige pointed toward a perfect parallel space along a quiet road.

"I think I'll go down here a little farther," Jared said, finally slipping into a spot near a McDonald's on a busy, crowded street. Paige couldn't see why this spot was more appealing than the other one, but she figured he was the one who knew the area.

They crossed a busy street and followed an alleyway between rows of colorful beach houses to the sand and ocean ahead. Most of the homes were cozy little bungalows, brightly painted and framed with thriving plants and vivid flowers. But some of the homes facing the ocean were large and spacious, elegant and elaborate.

"Let's walk over to the pier," Paige suggested. But Jared was staring at something off in the distance. "Jared?"

Startled, he replied with a quick, "What did you just say?"

"I wondered if you wanted to walk over to the pier."

"Sure," he answered. "We can check out that cool sunglasses store over there."

The temperature was comfortable, and the fragrance of flowers and patio barbecues filled the evening with wonderful scents of the end of summer. A gentle breeze brushed against Paige's cheek. They walked along the beach dotted with joggers, frisbee throwers, and strolling couples. The steady rhythm of the pounding surf brought Paige serenity, a relaxing, welcome peace. Sharing these beautiful surroundings and private time with Jared filled her with gratitude. Moments like these wouldn't come very often, and she cherished every minute they had together.

She glanced at her tall, handsome son and smiled. He'd been so easy to raise and such a joy in her life. Sure, he'd had his moments of bad attitude and rebellion. She'd felt him occasionally tugging against the restraints of rules and expectations, but not so hard that she couldn't enforce them. He had an obedient spirit and a sweet disposition. He was the best thing that came out of her marriage with Mark.

They walked along the oceanfront boardwalk to the end of the Newport Pier and looked out over the ocean. Three sailboats cut through the choppy water, their sails floating like billowing clouds against the clear blue sky.

"Out that way is Catalina Island." He pointed west.

Paige nodded, imagining just how lovely Catalina was.

"South of here there are tons of shops and restaurants and a place called the Fun Zone."

"The Fun Zone?" she asked.

"You know, where the Ferris wheel and carousel are. There are all kinds of arcades and souvenir shops," he told her. "I came down here with Nate the first weekend I got here."

They watched the sailboats awhile longer, then decided to get ice cream at one of the shops along the boardwalk. With waffle cones in hand—Paige's with pralines and caramel swirl, Jared's with Oreo cookie—they found a bench and sat down. They talked about Jared's classes and teachers while they watched the people along the beach and ate the smooth ice cream. There were people on bikes and on roller blades and an abundance of tourists milling about. There were even three teenagers in full-body wet suits bobbing on the surface of the water, waiting for the perfect wave.

In the midst of the stream of people, Paige noticed a handsome man, probably in his forties, roller blading with a young Asian girl. At a distance she wondered if maybe they were a couple, but as they came closer Paige saw that there was a substantial difference in their ages and that their actions were playful and casual, more those of a father and daughter.

The girl, maybe fifteen or sixteen years old, said something to the man, then bolted away, skating ahead with quick strides. The man, surprised at first, picked up his pace and tried to catch up to her.

The girl turned and saw him in pursuit. She laughed out loud as she pushed ahead even farther, her long, glossy black ponytail swaying from side to side beneath her helmet.

By now Jared was also watching the pair approaching as they sped along the boardwalk. Suddenly, the girl pitched forward, landing on her side, then rolling to her shoulder and tumbling over several times before she came to a stop in the sand.

Jared and Paige sprang from the bench and ran to her, arriving just after the older man. "Skyler, are you okay?" he cried, kneeling down beside the girl. "Sky?"

The girl groaned and lifted her head. "My shoulder." The man helped her roll onto her back, in the process exposing a scraped, bleeding wound on her shoulder.

"Is there anything we can do to help?" Paige said, her stomach turning at the sight of the blood.

The man looked at her, his friendly, suntanned face and aqua-colored eyes expressing thanks. "Yes, please. My daughter could use some ice."

"I'll get it," Jared announced.

"Here," Paige untied the sweatshirt she had around her waist, "put this under her head."

The man folded the sweatshirt and helped his daughter get more comfortable.

"What happened?" he asked Skyler, whose face grimaced with pain.

"I hit a rock and my wheel jammed," she explained. "It happened so fast I couldn't do anything."

Jared returned with ice and a clean dishcloth from the refreshment stand. "The guy wondered if you wanted him to call 911," Jared said to the man.

"I'm fine, Dad," the girl said, trying to sit up.

"Take it easy, Sky, I'm not calling the paramedics," he assured his daughter. "But we probably should take you to the doctor."

"I'm fine, Dad," she said again, wincing when the bag of ice was placed on her wound. After a moment, she admitted it felt much better.

The man turned to Paige and said, "Thank you for your help."

Paige smiled. "You're welcome. I'm just glad she's okay." Paige looked at the girl with raised eyebrows. "You *are* okay, aren't you?"

Skyler's eyes were closed, but she nodded her head.

"Good thing we wore our pads and helmets." The man examined Skyler's knee and elbow pads, which were scraped and worn from the rough cement surface.

"Guess I need to start wearing shoulder pads now, too," Skyler joked.

Paige noticed the darkening sky as she stood.

"Can we go home now, Dad?" Skyler asked.

"Sure, hon. Let's see if you can stand, though."

Skyler circled her arm around her father's shoulder and let him pull her slowly to her feet. Just as she stood, her left leg buckled.

"Whoa!" Jared exclaimed as he helped catch her. "I think I better help you get her home," he offered her father.

"That would be nice," the man answered. "We don't live far."

Sky rolled along the pavement on her right leg as her father and Jared supported her on either side. Paige walked beside her son.

"You folks just visiting?" the man asked.

"Kind of," Jared answered. "I just moved here to go to college, and my mom came to visit."

"Which college do you go to?" Skyler asked.

"UC Irvine," Jared answered. "I play basketball there."

"You do?" the man exclaimed. "We're big fans of UC Irvine's basketball team. I get season tickets every year."

He asked Jared about the team and his position. Paige was pleased to see how well Jared conversed with the man—not as a boy, but as a man, a grown-up.

Yet in a way, she knew it was a sign of Jared's truly becoming independent. Her son had always given her life such purpose, such importance. In a way he was her identity. She was "Jared's mom." Of course, that hadn't changed, but she realized that the apron strings had truly been severed. While she knew Jared would always love her, he also needed to move on and build a life of his own.

"Here we are," the man said, stopping at one of the lovely homes facing the ocean. It was a light gray stucco with a terrace on top overlooking the ocean. Paige immediately loved the contemporary architecture and abundance of large windows. It was very classy and welcoming.

Skyler eased herself onto a bench outside the front door while her father and Jared helped remove her skates, testing her shoulder and elbow.

"Is it pretty sore?" her father asked.

"Not too bad," Skyler answered. "I think I'll soak in the tub for a while."

"Good idea, hon," her father said, giving her a kiss on the forehead.

"Thanks for your help," she said to Jared and Paige.

"Glad we could do it," Paige replied, noticing that Jared was too busy appraising the man's house to answer.

With a wave of her hand, Skyler limped into the house.

"Could I offer you something to eat or drink?" the man asked.

"Thank you, but we need to get going," Paige answered.

"Of course. Well," he extended his hand toward Jared, "I'll look forward to watching you play this season. They sure can use a good outside shooter."

"Thanks, Mr.—"

"I'm sorry," the man chuckled self-consciously. "I guess we never introduced ourselves. My name is Dalton. Dalton McNamara."

Paige froze. Had she heard him correctly? Had the man actually said his name was Dalton McNamara?

CHAPTER EIGHT

"I'm sorry, what was that?" Paige said, certain she'd heard the name wrong.

"Dalton McNamara," he said again, enunciating his name for her.

Paige looked at Jared, whose expression of feigned innocence alerted her suspicions. Something was up.

"Is there something wrong?" Dalton asked.

"Ah . . . no." Paige swallowed. "It's just that . . ." How did she even begin to explain to him why she was in sudden shock?

And, she wanted to know, what were the chances of them running into him on this particular beach? One in a million? One in a billion? Just a coincidence? Somehow, she didn't think so.

Her suspicions grew into a hunch, her motherly instincts fine-tuned by years of living with a teenage son. "Jared?" she accused, giving him a stern look in the eye. "Did you know . . ."

"Know what?" Jared replied before she finished. But his wide-eyed "who, me?" expression was marred by mischievous glints of guilt. He turned his head away, but it was too late. Paige always knew when Jared wasn't telling the truth, and now was one of those times. He couldn't look her straight in the eye. Paige realized that he'd brought her here on purpose, knowing precisely whose house it was.

"Is something wrong?" Dalton asked, looking a bit unsure of the two standing in front of him.

This wasn't how she'd wanted to meet this man. In fact, she hadn't ever wanted to meet him at all. But it was too late now.

"I'm sorry," she apologized. "I guess I should explain."

Dalton's gaze narrowed.

Paige flashed a scathing glare at her son, wondering if she could ground him while he was away at college.

"I think we better sit down," she suggested.

"All right then." Dalton loosened the latches on his skates. "Why don't we go inside?" He removed the roller blades and opened the door for them.

His entryway and living room were stunningly decorated in elegant pieces of black-lacquered wood with black leather couches placed against taupe-colored walls and carpet. Here and there were splashes of deep red, burnt umber, and sage green. A baby grand piano anchored the corner of the room against giant picture windows revealing scenes from the ocean in the distance. Paige thought she recognized some pieces from Lou's store, but decided not to ask about them now. There was something more important to tend to.

"Please, have a seat. Are you sure I can't get you anything to eat or drink?" Dalton asked one more time.

"We're fine," Paige answered for both of them, knowing that if Jared and his appetite spoke up, Dalton would be fixing a double-decker peanut butter and jelly sandwich or a half dozen scrambled eggs.

"So," Dalton said, looking at her and then at Jared, "you wanted to tell me something?"

"Well," she started, "you see . . ." She searched carefully for the right words to say since she was unsure of how he would react to her news.

"Just tell him, Mom," Jared whispered.

Paige gave her son an annoyed look. "You see, Mr. McNamara—"

"Please, call me Dalton."

She nodded, still trying to figure out what to say. "I guess I should first ask you if you served in the Vietnam War."

"Yes," he replied. "I did."

"Were you a prisoner of war over there?"

His forehead wrinkled with confusion. "Yes."

"Well," she dug at the cuticle of her left thumb, "while you were being held prisoner of war, I was wearing an MIA-POW bracelet with your name on it."

Dalton's eyebrows lifted with surprised. "Mine? You wore my bracelet?"

"I did," Paige said, then went on to explain. "When we were getting Jared packed to move here to college, we found the bracelet in storage. I had written to your family when I received the bracelet, and your brother replied with a touching letter telling me a little about what you'd done in the war."

Dalton nodded but said nothing.

"Anyway . . ." she cleared her throat, trying to get a sense of Dalton's discomfort. Detecting none, she went on. "When we found the letter, Jared suggested—actually he insisted—that I write your family again. He, I mean, we, wondered if you'd returned from the war."

Dalton exhaled slowly. "That was many years ago."

"It was, and I was hesitant to bother you," she stumbled with her apology. "I didn't know if it would be painful . . ." She panicked, not wanting to suggest it was painful for him. "I mean . . . difficult for you . . ." *Criminy,* she scolded herself, *get a grip.* "I'm sorry," she weakly added, wishing she could disappear and take her son with him so she could throttle him for putting her in this position.

Dalton raised his head and, with kindness in his blue eyes, looked at Paige, then at Jared. He nodded slowly, as if processing the information.

"Please," he said, "you don't need to apologize. I'm touched that you would go to so much trouble." He smiled. "And that you wore my bracelet. No one ever told me about it."

"We still have it if you want to see it," Jared told him.

"Yes," Dalton said, his grin widening, "I would."

"It's back in Salt Lake," Paige said. "But I could send it to you."

"Salt Lake?" Dalton clarified.

"Yes," Paige answered. "That's where we're from."

"Both of my grandparents lived there," Dalton said. "Salt Lake City was like a second home to me. Our family spent entire summers there when we were kids. I loved those mountains. We went hunting, camping, and fishing." His expression grew distant. "I haven't been fishing in years."

"Is that where your parents are from?" Paige asked.

"They grew up in Salt Lake, but met at Brigham Young University," he told them. "I went to BYU for a year before I went into the service," Dalton told them. "I'm planning a trip to Utah next month."

"Do your grandparents still live there?" Paige asked, hoping she wasn't getting too personal.

"Both of my father's parents have passed away, as well as my mother's father. But my grandmother lives in Chicago with my parents. My sister just went through a divorce and lives with them, too. My brother, Brenden, who wrote to you, has passed away."

"I'm sorry," Paige said, wishing she could think of something more meaningful to say.

Dalton nodded. "I guess my mother wrote back and told you how to get in touch with me?" he asked.

Paige nodded. "She gave me your phone number and address."

"I keep trying to get my parents to move out here so we can be closer, but I haven't been able to talk them into it. Luckily my job takes me to the Chicago area three or four times a year, so I'm able to see them often."

"What do you do?" Jared asked, looking around at the nice furnishings.

"I'm a health benefits consultant. I've been in the health care industry for years, and now I consult with large companies about their health plans, helping them save money while meeting the needs of their employees," Dalton explained. "Because of my experiences in Nam, I also do a lot of motivational speaking at business conventions and graduations. As horrible as the war was and as awful as the prisons were, I learned a great deal and am blessed to have the opportunity to share that with others." He looked directly at them when he spoke, his voice strong and powerful.

In the short time they'd been with him, Paige had sensed what a solid, grounded individual Dalton was. He was sure of himself, focused, and full of purpose. She felt his strength.

"I'd enjoy hearing you speak sometime," Paige found herself saying.

"Me too," Jared added, his face reflecting admiration for the man in front of them.

"I'll be in Salt Lake next month for general conference," he said. "I'm giving a presentation to a group of health care professionals the following week," he added. "You're welcome to come."

Paige knew then that he was LDS, and she felt even more intrigued by this amazing man in front of her. She hadn't meant to be so forward, inviting herself to hear him speak, but she couldn't help herself. She felt drawn to something inside of him. Perhaps it was his self-assured, inner strength that she only hoped one day to possess herself.

"Thank you," she said.

"Dad?" Skyler's voice broke in.

Dalton looked up and saw his daughter limp into the room. "Honey, hi, how are you feeling? Come and sit down with us."

Skyler didn't join them. "I'm feeling lots better now. I wanted to go over to Abigail's for a little while. She just got a new CD."

It was difficult, but Paige tried not to gape at the girl's outfit, a midriff-baring T-shirt, low-rise, tattered jeans, and the glint of a silver ring piercing her belly button. Was this even the same fresh, sweet girl who'd been skating with her father an hour ago?

"It's late, Sky," Dalton said.

"It's not even ten, and it's not a school night," Sky pleaded.

"What CD is it that's so important?" her father asked.

Sky rolled her eyes, her impatience growing with her obvious frustration at her father's questions.

"You don't even know the group, Dad," she said.

"I'm just asking," Dalton replied.

"Okay, okay," she said, "they're called Psyche Ward."

"Psyche Ward?" Dalton looked at Paige with raised eyebrows in what she knew was a parental gesture of "Is she serious?"

Paige shrugged helplessly. She recalled the days when some of Jared's choices in music had actually made her toes curl. The lyrics she still remembered made her cringe even now. She was grateful he'd moved past that phase.

Dalton sighed. "I guess you can go, but call when you get there and be home before midnight. Okay?"

Sky immediately brightened, the annoyance in her voice changing to a sweeter tone. "Thanks, Dad. I won't be late. Promise."

"Be careful driving," he warned before she slipped out the back door.

"I will," she called behind her before the door swung shut with a bang.

Dalton shook his head as the house grew silent again. "It's like these kids don't even get started until ten o'clock at night." He pinched the bridge of his nose for a brief moment, then exclaimed, "Psyche Ward! What kind of group is that?"

Paige glanced at Jared's expression of distaste. "Jared," she said, "have you heard of this group?"

He shrunk back in his seat.

Dalton sat up with concern.

"Jared," Paige prompted, knowing her son wouldn't want to say anything to cause trouble.

"I just . . ." he started. "They're kind of a . . ." He rubbed his palms on the knees of his jeans.

"Kind of a what?" Dalton asked.

Paige gave her son a level look, indicating that they weren't leaving until he told Dalton what he knew about the music group.

"They play pretty rough stuff. You know, angry, heavy-metal kind of stuff. Some people think they're . . ." He hesitated.

Paige and Dalton waited.

"Some people think their stuff is evil. Dark. You know what I mean."

Dalton nodded as if attempting to make sense out of what he was hearing.

Jared continued, "I knew a kid who was killed at one of their concerts in a mosh pit. He was trampled to death."

His face washing pale, Dalton swallowed. "You're kidding."

Jared shook his head. "Lots of concerts have mosh pits though, not just this group."

"Why would Sky want to listen to that garbage?" he asked no one in particular. "She knows better than that. She's taken eight years of classical piano lessons. She knows what good music sounds like."

Paige looked at him with compassion, understanding what he was feeling. A parent's love and concern for their child created an all-encompassing umbrella of protection. It was natural to want to guard a child from bad influences, but since that wasn't possible all the time, the most difficult part of being a parent was watching a child make mistakes and pay the consequences for their choices. She knew Dalton was worried that his daughter had gone looking for trouble when trouble had no problem finding many sixteen year olds anymore.

"She'll probably get tired of it soon," Jared offered. "She'll be okay."

Dalton sighed and closed his eyes for a moment, seeming suddenly weary, a look Paige understood as a parent. She appreciated her son offering some words of encouragement for this distressed father. Then she wondered about Skyler's mother. Where was she? Dalton wore no wedding band, and there was no indication of a woman around the house. Was she Vietnamese? Had Dalton been like many of the soldiers who had met someone while in Vietnam and brought her back to the States?

Dalton sat in silence for a moment. Paige's heart went out to him.

"We should get going." She stood and motioned for Jared to get up, assuming Dalton would probably rather be alone. Besides, it was getting late.

But instead of getting up, Jared reached for a framed picture on the end table. "Is this a picture of you in Vietnam?"

Paige was anxious to leave, not because she didn't enjoy Dalton's company, but because she didn't want to wear out their welcome or bother the man any more than they already had.

But Jared's question seemed just the thing to pull Dalton from his worries. "Yes," he answered. "Before I was captured." He leaned over and pointed at the lush green mountains in the background. "Such a beautiful place. The war destroyed so much of it."

"It looks like Hawaii," Jared said.

Dalton chuckled. "Some parts of it are just as beautiful," he replied. "Here." He reached underneath the glass-topped coffee table and pulled out a picture album. "Would you like to see some more pictures?"

Jared didn't even glance Paige's way. "Sure, if you don't mind."

Dalton joined Jared on the couch and opened the album. "Paige, do you have a few more minutes, or do you need to go?"

She didn't want to tell him that she was more concerned about being in his way than anything. Lou and Bryant wouldn't be home until late anyway.

"I'm fine to stay," she said, making her way around to sit on the other side of Dalton.

When they all got situated, Dalton opened the book to the first page, then stopped. "Tell you what," he closed the book again, "why don't we take this to the counter in the kitchen? I'm dying of thirst, and we could look at the pictures over chips and salsa. What do you say?"

Jared was in the kitchen before Dalton or Paige had reached the door, more than willing to oblige when food was involved.

The three settled in at the bar with cold glasses of raspberry lemonade, chips and salsa, and a plate of chocolate chip cookies Skyler had made earlier that day. Dalton pulled out the picture album again.

"What's that?" Jared pointed to a picture that showed merely a hole in the jungle floor, difficult to see unless looked at closely.

"That's an entrance to an underground tunnel," Dalton said, wiping his mouth with a napkin. "You see, the Viet Cong are small people, and they dug these tunnels that went all over underground. This is where they hid and lived. They stored weapons and food and could survive underground for long periods of time."

Paige shuddered. "I couldn't do it. I'm too claustrophobic."

Dalton nodded. "I tried to climb down through one of the entrances and couldn't even get through."

Paige nodded, noting that Dalton was probably six-foot-three and close to two hundred pounds.

"When were you over there?" Jared asked.

Paige wasn't surprised at Jared's interest and unending questions. He'd loved history all through school—so much, in fact, that she wouldn't be surprised if he majored in history in college.

"The end of 1969," Dalton said.

Jared thought for a moment. "Same year as Woodstock, and Neil Armstrong walking on the moon."

Dalton's eyebrows arched, his eyes wide with surprise at the boy's knowledge of historical facts.

"I like history," Jared told him.

"I can tell," Dalton said, flashing Paige an impressed look.

"What was it like being in the war?" Jared probed.

Paige hoped her son wasn't getting too personal, but Dalton didn't seem to mind.

"Oh, it was first-class accommodations all the way," Dalton joked. "Pup tents, C-rations, we even had showers . . . when it rained."

Jared laughed. "Sounds like scout camp."

"Every day we had to choke down a yellow-colored malaria pill about the size of dime. And to protect us even further, we had to sleep inside a mosquito net no matter how hot it got. And some days it was hotter than Hades. Even with all the precautions, though, fifty-six troopers from my battalion alone were evacuated to hospitals because they were suffering from serious cases of malaria."

Paige shivered, not wanting to imagine enduring sickness under such conditions.

"What's that?" Jared pointed to a picture of a man holding a weapon in his hand. "I've never seen a gun like that."

"That's a flamethrower," Dalton explained. "It delivered napalm, a gasoline-type substance that was jelled by soap."

"What did they use that for?" Jared asked with fascination.

"It clung to any surface it touched and would continue burning," he said. Dalton shut his eyes for a moment. "It was very effective stuff," he went on. "It burned trees, buildings, barriers . . . and sometimes, people," he said softly.

Paige noticed a look of pain in Dalton's eyes. She wondered about the horrors he must have seen in the war.

"Your brother said in your letter that you were a Green Beret," Jared said.

Dalton nodded. "Actually, we prefer to say 'wore' a Green Beret."

"Oh." Jared processed the information. "What kind of training did you have?"

"Special Operations," Dalton told him. "I was one of the first soldiers to make a night jump into enemy-controlled territory inside Cambodia."

"Cool!" Jared exclaimed. "Is it hard to get a Green Beret?"

Dalton nodded. "The training was tough and dangerous. One of our soldiers died on our fourth parachute jump when his chute didn't open," Dalton said. "But I think the hardest part was the survival phase."

"What was that like?" Paige asked, finding herself mesmerized by the fact that this handsome, well-groomed man sitting in front of her had been a real-life Rambo.

"Let's just say I got to the point of being so weak and hungry that I ate raw goat, water moccasins, and berries to stay alive. I survived on one and a half hours of sleep a night."

Paige held her stomach. "Water moccasins?" Just the thought of eating raw snake gave her the creeps and sent a shiver up her spine.

"Only twenty-eight men out of our class of seventy-two completed training."

"What makes the Green Beret different from the other branches of the service?" Paige asked, looking at a picture of a much younger, very handsome Dalton McNamara with several of his buddies, flexing their biceps and smiling broadly for the camera.

"Green Beret don't recognize the Geneva Convention," he said.

"They don't?" Jared asked with surprise.

Dalton went on to explain. "Even though there are rules of war, the Special Forces don't abide by them. Besides our survival training, we were trained in unconventional warfare, psychological warfare, demolition, interrogation, intelligence, logistics . . . We had to get FBI clearance because some of our training was classified and secret. We were even under armed guards during a few classes."

"Whoa," Jared said in complete awe of this man sitting in front of him.

They looked through more pictures showing beautiful beaches, thick, green jungles, many of Dalton's buddies and . . . unbelievable destruction.

Paige swallowed hard as she looked at this vivid, firsthand account of the ravages of war, at the horror and hatred between humans. "There had to have been a better way," she said, remembering the United States' involvement in the war. "Too many innocent people died, too many young men gave their lives."

Dalton nodded slowly. "Over a ten-year period, a million American soldiers rode to battle in Huey helicopters. The Vietnam War cost the lives of fifty-eight thousand men and divided the nation."

Paige recalled that at such a young age, she had never fully understood what the fighting was all about. The main thing she remembered was watching Bob Hope specials at Christmas, news reports about the fighting, and all the demonstrations and riots against the war. It had been a scary, confusing time to grow up.

"Was it hard to come back home and resume normal life after everything you went through?" she asked.

Dalton nodded thoughtfully. "Normal life isn't possible again. The war changed me and everything about me—the depth of my faith, my priorities, my outlook on life. Thankfully, I've been able to move on, and I've been so blessed. I've worked through a lot of the nightmares. But there are still things that haunt me. I don't know if I'll ever get some of the memories, some of the images, out of my mind." He breathed a weary sigh. "I don't sleep more than three or four hours a night."

"That's awful," Paige said. "How do you get through the day?"

"I'm used to it after all these years, but I've dozed during meetings or while talking on the phone. I've even fallen asleep at stoplights before."

Paige looked at him, her heart full of compassion. He'd truly given everything to serve his country and fulfill his patriotic duty. He'd risked his life for freedom. The least he deserved was a good night's sleep!

The three of them remained quiet for a moment, and then Jared turned a page and studied one of the pictures. "Tell me about all your medals," he requested, looking at another picture of Dalton in dress uniform, his chest covered with various pieces of brass.

"Well, I was awarded Vietnamese Jumpwings." Dalton pointed at a specific medal decoration on his uniform. "Combat Infantryman's Badge, two Bronze Stars, and Vietnamese Crosses of Gallantry with Silver Star and with Palm," he said. "Maybe someday I'll show them to you."

Jared smiled. "I'd like that."

Just then the telephone rang.

While Dalton took the call, Paige began cleaning up their snack. She'd noticed the lateness of the hour and thought they should get back to Lou's.

"I can get that," Dalton said when he hung up the phone.

Paige put a clip on the bag of chips and stacked their plates. "I hate to leave you with a mess. We didn't mean to take your whole evening."

"Don't worry, it's not like you're keeping me up." He smiled warmly at her. "It's been my pleasure. I hope I didn't bore you with my stories and pictures."

"No way," Jared exclaimed. "It was amazing. You're a hero."

Patting Jared on the shoulder, Dalton said, "No, son, I just did what I was asked to do and prayed that God would protect me."

"Thank you for your time," Paige told him. "I'm really glad we came to meet you."

"I am too," Dalton said, reaching out to shake her hand.

Their gazes met, and for a moment, they stood, locked by eye contact. It felt as if an unspoken understanding passed between them. Paige wasn't sure what she felt or how she felt it, but she knew that Dalton was a good man, kind and caring. Suddenly she realized she was staring, and she blinked to return from her thoughts. "Good night, then."

"I'll walk you out to your car," Dalton said, opening the front door for them.

They stepped into the warm, star-filled night, the sound of waves rolling on the shore like night music.

"So, have you been doing a lot of fun things while you've been here? Have you got a lot planned?" Dalton asked.

"We haven't got much planned," she answered. "We went to Downtown Disney for dinner tonight, but didn't have time to go into the park. I'm actually here to be with my friend while she has surgery on Wednesday. But until then, we're just hanging out and having fun." She looked at her son, making sure he thought it was fun having his mom around.

Dalton's forehead wrinkled for a moment as if he were thinking, and then a smile grew on his face. "I just had a great idea," he told her.

Paige couldn't help smiling back at him. "You did?"

"Speaking of Disneyland, Skyler doesn't have school on Monday, and we were going to go to Disneyland. We haven't been to the California Adventure yet."

Paige noticed Jared's interest level soar to new heights.

"Any chance you two could come?" Dalton invited.

"Yes!" Jared exclaimed, pumping his fist in the air.

Not wanting to jump into anything, Paige weighed his invitation with caution. Why would he ask them to join him and Skyler? They were practically strangers. Yet Paige felt comfortable with this man. And she couldn't deny the fact that she was fascinated by him. Obviously Jared felt the same.

"C'mon, Mom," Jared coaxed. "I have an early math class on Monday, then weight lifting. Bryant won't care if I miss it once."

"Are you sure?" Paige asked Dalton, unsure of what would prompt him to invite them.

"It would be fun to have you join us. I'd, I mean, we'd enjoy the company," Dalton said, looking exclusively at Paige, who couldn't help blushing under his eye. She was grateful for the darkness around them.

"It does sound fun," Paige said.

"We were just saying how we wanted to go to Disneyland and the new theme park," Jared reminded her.

Paige looked at both eager faces in front of her. "I need to check with Lou first," she told her son. "Just to make sure she doesn't need me for anything."

Dalton smiled broadly. "Why don't you call me as soon as you decide? We're planning on being at the park about eleven."

After one look into his amazing blue eyes, Paige knew she couldn't turn him down. "We'll let you know tomorrow." She turned toward the car.

"Here, let me give you my cell phone number just in case I'm not home when you call." He dashed into the house and brought out a piece of paper with both numbers written on it. "I hope you can make it," he said in parting.

They thanked Dalton for their evening, then waved good-bye. Paige had been prepared to blast her son with a lecture on pulling tricks on her like he had that night, but in all honesty, she had to admit that she was glad he had tricked her into meeting Dalton McNamara. Very glad.

CHAPTER NINE

The next day, Paige and Jared went to Bryant and Lou's ward together. Paige was glad to have Jared with her. She'd missed sitting with him in sacrament meeting. Even though she knew all the members of her home ward, it was still difficult to go to her meetings alone. There were a few other single women who sat with her occasionally, but one was a nurse who worked every other Sunday and the other one traveled a lot with her job.

From the moment they walked into Lou's ward, Paige was impressed with the members. Lou's upcoming surgery was no secret, and she was showered with love, concern, and hugs from many of the members. A special ward fast had been arranged for the day of Lou's surgery, and the Relief Society had arranged for meals and care of the children for two weeks following. Paige wondered exactly why Lou had felt she needed her there when her ward had amply filled all of the family's needs. But Lou assured her that she needed her best friend there for moral support more than anything.

The meetings were enjoyable, the teachers knowledgeable and entertaining, especially the Relief Society instructor. The woman was a visual-aids nut who had pictures, props, and all sorts of extras to make her lesson unforgettable. Overall, Paige hadn't enjoyed going to church meetings that much in a long time.

After church, Paige and Jared walked out into the bright, warm southern California sunshine with Lou and her family. The day took Paige's breath away. All the palm trees, flowers, and bushes in bloom gave her a new appreciation for nature. There was something therapeutic about the sun and the surrounding beauty that felt like a healing balm, lifting Paige's spirits, making her feel happy and care-free for the first time in many months. She was laughing at something Carter said when she looked up and stopped in her tracks.

Walking toward them were Dalton and his daughter.

"Hey," Jared exclaimed before Paige said anything. "Look who's here, Mom."

Paige couldn't help smiling when she saw Dalton, and to her pleasure, he smiled when he noticed her too.

She was immediately glad that she'd worn the slim-fitting black skirt and teal-green silk sweater set she'd purchased before she came to California. Teal green had always looked good with her blonde hair and emerald-colored eyes.

"Who is that?" Lou whispered, but Paige couldn't answer since Dalton approached them quickly, obviously happy to see them.

"What a surprise," he said, shaking Jared's hand. He reached for Paige's, but instead of shaking it, he held hers with both of his hands for a lingering moment. "It's wonderful to see you again."

Lou cleared her throat behind them, breaking Paige's spellbound gaze into Dalton's eyes. He looked sharp in light tan slacks, a deep navy double-breasted jacket, and a starched white shirt.

"Dalton," Paige said, "I'd like you to meet my dear friend, Louisa Curtis, and her husband, Bryant Curtis."

Dalton shook their hands and smiled when Paige introduced the children. He shook their hands also, and Maddie giggled when Dalton told her what a pretty girl she was.

"This is Dalton McNamara and his daughter, Skyler," Paige said. "I didn't have a chance to tell you, Lou, but we met Dalton and Skyler last night."

Lou's eyebrows arched with sudden "tell me more" interest.

"You remember that letter I showed you from Dalton's mother?" Paige reminded her.

"The letter . . ." Lou thought for a moment, then gasped with the realization of who Dalton was. "You're . . ." she pointed at Dalton, "the bracelet . . . Paige wore . . ."

Dalton nodded. "She wore my bracelet when I was a POW in the Vietnam War."

"You found your soldier!" Lou exclaimed to Paige. "This is so neat."

Skyler appeared to be completely uninterested and unimpressed. The look of sheer annoyance on her face wasn't lost on Paige. She'd worked with the young women in her ward enough to know how easily girls this age got annoyed. It was apparent that Skyler wasn't excited about being at church, nor about meeting some boring people. Thank goodness Jared stepped up.

"Hey, Skyler," he said. "What's up?"

She shrugged. "Not much." She still didn't straighten her slouched posture, but a hint of smile turned the corner of her lips. She wasn't stupid. Jared was handsome and had a charming personality that even Skyler couldn't resist.

Engaging her in a conversation about her friends and school, Jared kept the girl talking so the others could enjoy their conversation.

"It was so late when we got home last night that I didn't have a chance to tell you about meeting Dalton," Paige explained to Lou and Bryant.

"It was my fault they got home so late," Dalton jumped in. "I was boring them with war stories."

Paige shook her head. "That's not true. It was fascinating. We enjoyed every minute of it, especially Jared. It was like having one of his history books come alive."

As Bryant listened, he studied Dalton's face intently, then said, "You look familiar. Have we met?"

Dalton thought for a moment, then shook his head. "I don't think so."

"I know I've seen you somewhere," Bryant insisted.

"You're one of the coaches at UC Irvine?" Dalton asked.

Bryant nodded.

"I spoke at graduation a few years ago."

"That's it!" Bryant exclaimed. "You told about your capture and being in the Hanoi prison. I've never forgotten your talk. It was incredible."

"I remember, too," Lou said. "Bryant couldn't quit talking about it for weeks after."

"Thank you," Dalton said. "I'm glad you enjoyed it."

"Maybe we could have you and your daughter over for dinner while Paige's here," Lou invited.

"That would be nice," Dalton accepted. "Thank you." The organ music from inside the chapel played the opening hymn for the next ward's meeting. "I guess we better get to sacrament meeting. You ready, Sky?"

Skyler and Jared were laughing at Lou's daughter, Maddie, who had her shoes and socks off and was wading in a puddle of muddy water she'd found by a drain pipe.

"Madison Curtis!" Lou scolded. "Get out of that mud. Look at your dress!" She bid Dalton good-bye, promising to call soon about dinner, then rushed over to help Maddie out of the mud.

Jared and Bryant rounded up Carter, who was trying to fry a bug by holding the lens of his glasses just right so the sun's rays could hit the bug.

Skyler walked inside the building, leaving Dalton and Paige alone together for a moment.

"They're a great family," he commented.

"They sure are. Lou and I have been friends since high school. We've been through a lot together. They're like family to me," she said.

"Do you have family back in Salt Lake City?" he asked, looking down at the empty ring finger on her left hand.

"I'm divorced, and both of my parents have passed away. I have two brothers, but I don't see them very often," she told him. "What about you?" She felt it only fair to ask the same question. Besides, she was dying to know about his wife.

"My wife, Soon Lee, died when Skyler was ten," he said, not offering much more information than that.

Judging by the brevity of his answer, Paige sensed there was much more to the story than he was telling, yet she respected his privacy.

"I'm sorry," she replied.

"Sky could really use having her mom around right now. She's having such a difficult time. I don't seem to relate very well to her."

"You seemed to be doing a pretty good job last night," Paige said. "I don't know many dads who roller blade with their daughters."

Dalton chuckled. "I try."

Lou waved to Paige, letting her know they were going to the car. "I've made you late for church," Paige told him.

"No problem," he said.

They looked at each other for a moment longer until the door opened and Skyler poked her head out. "Are we going in or not, Dad?"

"You better go," Paige said. "I'll call you later."

Dalton smiled. "I hope you can come tomorrow."

She didn't reply as he rushed into the church, but a sweet, wonderful warmth washed over her. What was it about his smile that caused such a reaction inside of her?

* * *

After church, over shrimp and chicken grilled to perfection on the barbecue, the Curtis family, along with Paige and Jared, ate outside in the shade. They relaxed on the deck overlooking the pool and back-yard. Paige loved Lou and Bryant's backyard, a veritable Garden of Eden, lush and flowering, with a waterfall in one corner and the English cottage–style bungalow in the other. They'd built the bungalow when Bryant's widowed mother came to live with them. She'd only lived there six months when she suffered a stroke and died after several weeks in the hospital.

While the kids jumped on the trampoline, the adults ate slices of lemon meringue pie and enjoyed the relaxing Sunday afternoon.

"Before I forget," Bryant exclaimed, "Coach Hale wants to talk to you, Paige."

"Me?" Paige nearly choked on her bite of pie. She shot a look at Jared. "What did you do?"

Jared's mouth dropped open. "I didn't do anything."

Bryant laughed. "It's nothing like that. He's very interested in having you design our basketball program. We'll take care of getting the pictures and advertising. We just need someone to create the look, something really spectacular."

"He wants me to do it?" Paige asked, flattered at the offer. "He hasn't even seen any of my work."

"Maybe you could send us a sample of some of the things you've done," Bryant suggested.

"That'd be cool, Mom," Jared said. "You could sneak in some highlight pictures of your son doing one of his amazing dunks."

"Oh, I could, could I?" Paige asked with amusement.

"No, wait, I have a better idea," Jared said. "How about a center-fold poster, you know, something girls, I mean kids, could hang on their wall."

Her son didn't lack confidence, Paige decided with a chuckle.

"I'll think about it," she said, knowing full well that he wouldn't get any preferential treatment if she did, in fact, end up doing the layout of the program.

Lou put her plate of half-eaten pie on the table and covered a yawn. "If I don't get up and move around I'm going to fall asleep. Why don't we walk through the bungalow?" she asked Paige. "It's completely empty now. You could picture it with your stuff in it," she tempted.

Paige gave her an unappreciative look, then laughed. "Okay, enough joking around. I would drive you guys nuts if I moved here."

Lou's expression fell. "Paige," she looked her straight in the eye, "there's no way you'd drive us nuts. I can't think of anything better than having you next door. You're practically family."

Realizing that she'd hurt Lou's feelings, Paige apologized. "You really are serious, aren't you?"

"Yes," Lou said earnestly. "There's nothing in Salt Lake for you anymore. You should be here with us. And between doing freelance design work and managing my store, you'd probably make twice as much as you do in Utah."

"I'd insist on paying my share of the rent," Paige replied.

"It's paid for," Bryant piped up. "The place is sitting there empty. All you'd need to cover are the utilities, which aren't that much. You'd be doing us a favor."

Paige struggled to prevent tears from filling her eyes. These two were the most giving, loving people she could have in her life. Their offer tempted her just because she couldn't imagine anything better than living so close to the people she loved the most—Lou and Bryant, and of course, Jared.

She got to her feet. "All right, let's go look at the cottage. I don't think Jared's even seen it yet, have you?"

"Not inside," he said.

The cottage reminded Paige of something from a storybook. It was cozy, charming, and inviting, decorated in a French country style with cobbled walks, vines of ivy clinging to eaves, and rosebushes in various colors. Paige could hardly imagine herself living there because it would be like living in a fairy tale.

When they opened the front door, a spacious living room greeted them, where plenty of large, paned windows let in ribbons of golden sunlight. The loft overhead had shelves for books and a corner for a computer. There was a small but cozy kitchen, a dining area, and a small main bathroom. The spacious bedroom had a tall, vaulted ceiling with beautiful wooden beams, French doors leading out to a private patio, and an equally spacious bathroom with a jetted tub.

Jared looked at his mother. "How can you turn this down?" Then he turned to Lou. "If she doesn't live here, I will. I love this place."

Paige did too. It was charming and beautiful. But still, she wasn't the type of person who made big decisions easily or acted spontaneously. Her life was organized, predictable, and routine. That's how she liked it. Could she really pull up her Utah roots and transplant them in California? Could she really leave her job and home and the security of Salt Lake and move here to this lovely cottage, surrounded by her son and dearest friends?

She was thinking about it.

CHAPTER TEN

"We're coming," Paige told Dalton over the phone. Her stomach had been in knots as she dialed his number and waited for him to answer, but once she heard his voice, she relaxed.

"That's great!" he exclaimed. "I'm so happy, and Skyler will be, too. She wasn't very excited about just the two of us going together."

"If you're sure she won't mind," Paige said, knowing how moody and unpredictable teenage girls' emotions were.

"She doesn't say much, and you probably can't tell, but she does like you and Jared. Of course, it doesn't hurt that Jared's 'hot'," Dalton said with a laugh. "But she thinks you're really nice." This was welcome news to Paige. "We can pick you up if you'd like," he continued. "Or you can meet us there, whichever is easiest."

"Why don't we meet you?" Paige suggested.

"Okay, then we'll see you right out in front of the ticket booth at eleven in the morning. Bring a hat and sunscreen. It's going to be a sunny day."

"Will do," Paige answered, feeling excitement course through her veins. She wasn't sure if it was from the fact that they were going to Disneyland or that she was seeing Dalton again, but then, it didn't really matter. It felt great just to be excited about anything again.

* * *

Before going to bed that night, Paige and Lou laid out a plan for the next week. Paige wanted to help Lou get everything ready before her surgery so she could relax and recover quickly without feeling stressed about her family, home, or work.

"I've got everything at work covered for the next two weeks, but I need to get a display finished for the front window."

"We've got time in the morning to work on it," Paige said. "Why don't we go in early before the store opens?"

"That would be great," Lou said with obvious relief in her voice. "You sure you don't mind helping?"

"Mind!" Paige exclaimed. "It sounds fun. Besides, that's why I'm here."

"It will be fun," Lou said. Then she grabbed her friend and gave her an enormous hug. "It's so great having you here."

Paige laughed but didn't respond. She didn't want to start up the discussion again about her moving. Her stomach knotted up when she thought about the huge change everyone wanted her to make in her life. She needed time to process, ponder, and weigh the decision.

She looked over at Lou's to-do list. "Is there anything else? I don't want to abandon you tomorrow if you need me."

"We've got everything covered. Besides," Lou had mischief in her eyes, "I wouldn't dream of spoiling your chance to go to Disneyland. You know," she smiled, "it's the place where dreams come true."

Paige looked at Lou like she was crazy. "What are you talking about?"

"Going to Disneyland with Dalton," Lou reminded her.

This was another topic Paige wanted to avoid. Quickly she said, "How is it that you haven't seen Dalton before? I mean, he goes to the same church building as you."

"I might have seen him before, but obviously I didn't know who he was," Lou said. "He looked kind of familiar, like maybe I'd seen him at stake conference or something, but it's not like I go to church and check out guys."

"I know," Paige said, figuring there were many men in her own stake back in Salt Lake she didn't know. "I was just wondering if you knew him or anything about him."

Lou shrugged. "Sorry. I wish I did. I am surprised, though."

"At what?"

"At the fact that a man as handsome as he is hasn't got a dozen women after him. We've got quite a few available women in our stake. I'm sure he's at the top of everyone's list."

"I guess," Paige said with reserve.

"If I were you, he'd certainly be at the top of my list." Lou eyed her friend for a reaction.

Paige cast a level glance at Lou.

"Come on, Paige." Lou acted surprised at Paige's expression. "The man is very good-looking and so classy. And he seemed quite interested in you as well."

"Ha!" Paige scoffed.

"Couldn't you see it?"

"See what?" Paige exclaimed. "Lou, there's nothing to see. The man is just being nice to invite us along to Disneyland. I think he wants Skyler to spend some time with Jared to get her away from her friends. That's all."

Lou snickered. "Yeah, that's it."

"It's true," Paige insisted.

Lou rolled her eyes. "Sorry, but I saw what was going on between you two yesterday at church."

Paige's mouth dropped open. "There's nothing going on between us."

"Will you calm down?" Lou grinned. "You're acting like it's a bad thing. Paige," Lou took one of Paige's hands in hers, "whether you could tell or are willing to admit it or not, there's a spark between you and Dalton. Call it chemistry, call it infatuation, call it love at first sight, I don't care. But I saw the way you two looked at each other."

"The sun must've been in your eyes."

"We were in the shade," Lou said.

Paige didn't dignify this with an answer.

"Paige, look at me," Lou insisted.

Paige looked at her with pure annoyance.

"Tell me straight to my face that you didn't feel anything when you were talking to Dalton, and I'll believe you and I won't say any more about it."

"There's nothing—"

"Look me in the eye," Lou said.

Paige stared straight into Lou's chocolate-brown eyes. "I didn't feel any . . . there's nothing going . . ." She couldn't finish the sentence.

A smile broke onto Lou's face.

"Okay," Paige finally admitted. "I might have felt a little something. It's been so long since I've been around a man I probably wouldn't recognize what it felt like to be attracted to one."

"Trust me," Lou said. "By the look in your eye and on your face, whatever you felt was real. And . . ." she paused teasingly, "he had the same look on his face."

Paige tried but couldn't hide her smile. "He did? How do you know? How can you tell?"

"Even Bryant said something about it when we got home."

"What did Bryant say?"

"He wondered if something was going on between you and Dalton."

Paige sighed with exasperation. "What do you mean 'going on' between us?"

"Sometimes it takes longer for your head to catch up with what your heart already knows. But, dear friend, I think there's something more to this meeting with Dalton than you realize."

"Like what?"

"I think this has all been by design," Lou said. "You wearing Dalton's bracelet, then finding the letter from his brother, then writing to his mother, and then . . . finally meeting him in person. It's so wonderfully romantic, and it's so obvious."

"It is?" Paige was lost.

"Something like this would never happen on its own. You're a recipient of heavenly intervention, Paige. Somebody much more powerful and much wiser has brought you two together."

"I've only seen the guy twice. You're making much more of this than there really is. I appreciate what you're saying, but you've got to admit, Lou, the idea is far-fetched and absolutely crazy."

"Sure it is, but that's what makes it so exciting! Besides," Lou's voice became serious, "what are the chances of you meeting a man in Salt Lake unless you happen to broadside him in an intersection? I mean, there's no one at work and there's no one at church. The only other place you go is the grocery store, and all the baggers there are too young."

"You've always had a vivid imagination," Paige said.

"Are you saying that you don't mind being alone the rest of your life? Do you really have no intention of getting married again?"

Paige couldn't look Lou in the eye, but the answers screamed inside her head. No, she hated being alone and lonely. Lou was right. Her chances of meeting someone else were slim to none. But up until now, she'd had no desire to meet someone else. Her marriage with Mark had been much too difficult to risk making that mistake again. Sure, she'd love to have a companion, but unless the man came with a stamp of approval and guarantee from heaven itself, she wasn't ready to take the risk. Being alone was easier than being married in misery.

"Paige?" Lou asked quietly.

"It's hard," she said. "I'm not opposed to marriage at all, I'm just opposed to unhappiness, and for me that seems to come with being married." She cleared her throat. "When we were teenagers, I used to think about my husband and what he'd be like. I always wanted someone who would make me laugh, you know? Someone who was my best friend."

Lou smiled and nodded.

"And I always wanted to be married to a guy who was a protector, someone, I guess, who was strong and brave and would take care of me and my children." Paige took a deep breath and sighed. "Maybe it's because my father walked out on our family and because Mark didn't have a nurturing bone in his body, but I've come to realize that most men are selfish and cruel."

"Not every guy is going to be Mark or your father," Lou counseled.

"Who would've thought that Mark would turn out like he did, though?" Paige reminded her.

"I know, I know," Lou admitted, "I was as charmed by Mark as anyone. Looking back, I realize that we should've seen what he was like. You know, always wanting to be the center of attention, obnoxious, outspoken, selfish . . ."

"He grew up to be the adult version of the same thing. I was willing to overlook those flaws because I was so infatuated by his looks and personality. He just didn't have what was important inside."

"Like I said, we all were charmed by Mark. He had us all fooled. But Paige, I think this time is different. If heaven is going to so much trouble to bring you two together, there must be something pretty special in store for both of you."

Tears stung Paige's eyes. She swallowed a knot of emotion in her throat. "I don't think so."

"I do," Lou assured her. "I know you're gun-shy and afraid, but a wonderful, fulfilling relationship full of love and companionship is worth the risk. And I can't think of anyone who deserves a wonderful husband more than you."

Paige's heart swelled with gratitude for her friend. Even though Lou was a hopeless romantic and certainly overexaggerating this simple meeting with Dalton, Paige knew her friend's heart was in the right place.

* * *

"I just don't know what to do with all of this." Lou gestured toward rolls of fabric and several pieces of furniture she'd been saving for the window display.

"These colors are beautiful," Paige said as she felt the textures of the rich cloths in vivid earth tones that reminded her of leaves changing in the fall. Paige's eyes opened wide. "That's it!" she exclaimed.

"You have an idea?" Lou asked.

"What's fall like around here?" Paige asked.

"Pretty much like the rest of the year," Lou said. "A little windier maybe, cooler in the evening, rainier, that's about it."

"I don't know if you remember how gorgeous the fall leaves are in Utah, but that's exactly what these colors remind me of. Why don't we make a fall scene with large leaves cut out of these different fabrics, hanging by fishing line from the ceiling?" Paige suggested.

"We could get a wheelbarrow and a rake," Lou said, "and dress the mannequins in cable-knit sweaters and jeans." Her eyes widened with excitement. "I love it."

"How about pumpkins? We could use pumpkins."

"Big pumpkins and apples—bushels of apples." Lou clapped her hands together. "It's so simple and so perfect! We've got a lot to do, but as soon as some of the other help gets here, we'll put them to work." Lou gave Paige a huge smile. "You're brilliant!"

Paige rolled her eyes. "Hardly."

"Come on, let's get started."

They cut out fabric leaves and glued the material onto stiff card-board. Several employees showed up and were put to work finishing the project while Lou and Paige ran to a nearby home and garden store to find props for the display.

* * *

"I'm glad we're getting this done today. It's the last big item on my 'to do' list," Lou told Paige as she drove along the busy streets of Newport Beach.

"Are you sure you don't mind me going to Disneyland? I feel terrible leaving when you've got so much to do," Paige said. Then she confided, "And to be honest, I'm not sure this is such a good idea. I don't even know this guy. Why would I want to spend an afternoon with him and his daughter?"

"Are you kidding? I wouldn't dream of having you miss your date with Dalton," Lou said.

Paige opened her mouth to assure Lou that it wasn't a date. Then she saw the teasing look in her friend's eye. Classic Louisa. The woman loved to tease people just to get a reaction out of them. Paige didn't give her the satisfaction.

"But I can go to Disneyland another time," Paige offered. "I came here to be with you, remember?"

"And you are with me. Until my surgery, I plan on staying as busy as possible. That way I won't sit and worry about it, and it will make the time go faster. I'm full of nervous energy. I need to capitalize on it while I've got it. Besides," Lou signaled to turn into the parking lot, "I've got five full-time employees that can help with this window. I was just having trouble coming up with an idea for the display. But thanks to you, that's something I can finally cross off my list." Lou pulled into a parking space. "I'll be able to relax and rest easy once I get this window done."

"You're sure there's nothing else I can do? Cleaning, errands, yard work?" Paige asked.

"I'm sure I'll need you to throw in a load of laundry or vacuum a rug or two," Lou assured her. "But for now, I just need to know you're here."

"I'm glad I could be here with you. It would drive me crazy being back home while you were going through your surgery." They remained in the car for a moment. Paige noticed a faraway look in Lou's eyes. She reached over and patted her friend's leg. "You okay?"

Lou licked her lips, then swallowed. She opened her mouth to speak, but her bottom lip trembled. Paige had prepared herself for this. Stalwart and brave, Lou kept up a good front, but Paige wondered just how calm her friend really was inside.

"I am, really." Lou's voice shook as she spoke. "I'm not afraid of the surgery or the recovery or treatment. I'm not looking forward to it," she said with a forced laugh, "but I know it will all go well. I'm just worried that . . ." She stared straight ahead, clutching the steering wheel with a viselike grip. Clearing her throat, she fought for control, then went on. "I just don't want this to be the beginning of the end."

Paige's own eyes filled with tears. She nodded her head with understanding.

"I know I should be brave and not be afraid to die," Lou said as emotion reduced her voice to a forced whisper. "I'm just not ready to leave my family. I mean, my kids are so little . . . and even though Bryant is such a good dad, it would be . . . hard for him . . ." She couldn't go on.

Right in front of Paige's eyes, Lou crumbled.

Circling her arms around her sobbing friend, Paige held Lou while together they cried. "I know, Lou. I know."

Paige recognized all of Lou's feelings. In fact, watching her friend deal with the reality of cancer brought back memories of her own experience in facing the possibility of dying. Paige knew she could offer strength and advice, words of hope and encouragement, because she knew, deep in her heart, that Lou truly would be okay. But the time for those things would come later. Right now was the time for tears, to work through the fears and the emotions. Lou would feel better and be stronger once she dealt with this part of the process.

Paige expressed a silent prayer of gratitude that she could be there for Lou. In some strange way, she also knew that there was more to being there with Lou than just supporting a friend. Perhaps going through this experience would also help Paige finally heal and move on. For once she had to be the strong one, the rock, Lou's source of encouragement. She added another prayer, asking for wisdom and strength and comfort to be with them all. They were certainly going to need it over the next few weeks.

* * *

With the window display underway, Paige didn't feel quite so guilty leaving for Disneyland with Jared. Still, she kept hoping Dalton would call and cancel their plans. She just wasn't up to making small talk with a stranger. What had she been thinking when she accepted his invitation?

Jared picked Paige up at Lou's store, roaring up to the curb in his roommate's sleek X4. Paige didn't say anything, but she worried about Nate's influence on Jared. Nate was a nice guy, but he was very materialistic, and if Jared had a weak spot, it was his love for nice cars, nice things, and lots of money.

"You're sure you don't mind hanging out with Dalton and his daughter?" Paige asked her son, hoping he'd say he had too much homework or that he had other plans.

To Paige's disappointment, he just said, "Sure, it'll be fun."

Inside, Paige argued with herself. Surely Dalton knew that her time in California was short, and if she claimed something had come up, he would understand. Her reasons for wanting to turn around and go home were simple. Sure, she admired Dalton and was attracted to him, but she hadn't expected their meeting to turn into anything more than just a brief introduction and a simple good-bye. It was silly to turn it into anything more than that, even if a connection between them had been made. After all, she wasn't naive. She knew connections could be made with total strangers virtually anywhere. She and Dalton shared a common bond, but that didn't mean they were destined to spend eternity together.

Criminy, Lou! she scolded her friend mentally. Paige should have prepared herself for Lou's reaction and her need to make more of the situation than actually existed.

All right, fine, Paige thought. *I'll go and have fun and enjoy a day at Disneyland. Then we'll shake hands and say good-bye.* Satisfied that the situation was under control, that when the day was done she could return to Lou and tell her that there was nothing between them, Paige finally relaxed.

Besides, she thought, *I'll probably spend most of the day with Jared anyway.*

She nearly laughed with relief. She'd let Lou psyche her out about spending the day with Dalton. It wasn't a date—it wasn't even anything close to one. The four of them would hit a few rides together, maybe even grab a burger for lunch, then they'd go their separate ways.

"Are we almost there?" she asked her son, finally able to get excited about the fun afternoon ahead.

"It's just down the street," he told her.

CHAPTER ELEVEN

A light cloud cover masked the burning rays of the sun, keeping the temperature cool and comfortable, just right for standing in lines at a theme park.

Jared nearly skipped to the ticket booth he was so excited to be there. Every summer after their first trip to Disneyland, he'd asked if they could go back, and every year the answer had been, "Not this summer, maybe next year." But it never happened. Mark had never made the time or the effort to take them again.

In some ways, going there would be like coming full circle, even more so, since Mark wasn't there. Paige felt a small victory in doing something for Jared that he'd wanted for so long, something she hadn't been able to give him before now. Each task she succeeded at, each house payment she made by herself, each month her savings grew, she felt more and more independent and strong, able to stand on her own two feet without leaning or depending on anyone. And she was proud that she was making it on her own.

They walked past rows of buses and approached the ticket area, but there was no Dalton or Skyler to be found. Checking her watch, Paige noticed that it was just a few minutes after the hour, and she figured they were probably just caught in traffic or something.

Taking a seat on a bench, they watched as families with excited children made their way through the turnstile to the "happiest place on earth."

Behind them, directly across from Disneyland, was the new California Adventure park. In the distance, the roar of the roller coaster was punctuated by wild screaming. Paige looked at her son with apprehension. He laughed and said, "You're going on all the rides!"

Paige had always loved thrill rides, but it had been awhile since she'd been on any, and just seeing pictures of some of the new roller coasters made her stomach curdle. However, she was determined to be brave even if it killed her! Just then, the clouds broke and the sun shone through, pouring down warmth upon them. "Let's move into the shade," Jared said. Paige looked toward the parking lot hoping to see Dalton and Skyler, but they weren't there. She decided that even if Dalton and Skyler didn't show up, she and Jared would buy a ticket and enjoy the park by themselves. Still, even after wishing Dalton would cancel, Paige realized she'd be disappointed if they didn't make it.

"I wonder where they are?" Jared asked.

"Traffic maybe," Paige said. "Or something might have come up."

"It's almost eleven-thirty," Jared said. "How much longer should we wait?"

Paige stretched her neck to look toward the parking lot again. Nothing. A half an hour was plenty to wait. "Let's go ahead and go in," she said. "Maybe we'll see them inside if they show up."

The entrance to the park had gotten more crowded. They took their place at the end of the ticket line and waited their turn. One of the Disney characters, Pluto, came out from the park to greet the children and welcome them to Disneyland. Jared and Paige got a kick out of watching the overgrown dog interact with the children, signing autographs and posing for pictures.

"Sorry we're late." Paige jumped when she heard the voice beside her. She turned and saw a haggard-looking Dalton and a sullen-faced Skyler.

"Hi," Paige said with hesitation, wondering if either of them had slept the night before. "I'm glad you made it. Is everything okay?"

Skyler rolled her eyes. "One of Dad's friends called and needed him to come and jump-start her car." Paige noticed the distaste with which Skyler said the word *friends*.

"Mary Anne couldn't help it if her battery went dead," Dalton said.

"I'm sure she could have called a dozen other people," Skyler shot back.

"Well," Dalton said calmly, "it doesn't matter. We're here now. I'm just sorry we kept you waiting."

"It's times like this that I wish I had a cell phone," Paige said, trying to ease the awkwardness.

"I've been telling you to get one for months, Mom," Jared piped up.

"I don't really need one," Paige confessed. "I'm either at work or I'm home. I have phones at both places."

Jared just shook his head and stepped forward as the line moved ahead.

"I've already got our passes," Dalton said, fishing them out of his wallet. "Here," he stepped out of line, "we can go right inside."

"I'm starving, Dad," Skyler complained.

Paige noticed that Dalton ignored his daughter's request. The girl seemed to be high maintenance, demanding, and maybe even a bit spoiled. But Paige felt sympathetic for her knowing that she didn't have a mother and that she was in the throes of being a teenager with hormones, peer pressures, and mood swings worse than any thrill ride at this park. In fact, now that Skyler mentioned it, Paige couldn't remember eating breakfast that morning and felt a little hungry herself.

They got through the gates and stood inside the park. A brass band in the corner played a jazzy Dixie tune, which attracted a crowd of excited guests.

"Where to first?" Dalton asked. "I guess you're familiar with the park, aren't you?"

"It's changed a lot since we were here last," Paige told him.

"How about the Indiana Jones ride?" Jared suggested. "I hear it's awesome."

"That's my favorite ride," Dalton said. "Let's go."

"Dad . . ." Skyler started to say, but Jared and Dalton were already ten steps ahead of them.

Paige turned to Skyler. "You know what? I'm starving too. Let's go get in line with them and while they wait, we'll go get something to eat."

Skyler's eyes lit up. "Okay."

They followed the men through the crowded main street of the park and then took a sharp left to Adventure land.

"Something smells wonderful," Paige said as delicious aromas surrounded them.

"There's a place around here that sells turkey legs," Skyler told her.

"Mmmm," Paige answered. "That sounds delicious. But I have to have a churro too."

"I love churros," Skyler said.

Dalton turned and waved at them to hurry up. Skyler and Paige looked at each other and laughed for no reason. Maybe it was because they were in cahoots together or just feeling the effects of being in the "happiest place on earth," but they stepped up their pace and closed in on Jared and Dalton.

"There it is," Jared said as the sign for the ride came into view. "The line's not that long either."

Jared and Dalton darted into the maze of ropes leading to the ride.

"What about our food?" Paige asked Skyler.

"This is a pretty cool ride," the girl said. "And I've never seen the line so short."

"I can wait if you can," Paige said.

Skyler nodded, and they ran to catch up with the others.

The ride was indeed fun and exciting, so much so that as soon as they got off, they took advantage of the short line and got right back on.

Laughing until her sides hurt, Paige was surprised at how much she loved the Indiana Jones ride with its twists, turns, and thrills.

"Pirates of the Caribbean," Jared said as the four exited the ride. "We have to go there next! Then Splash Mountain."

"Jared," Paige quietly reminded him, "Dalton and Skyler may have other places they want to go first."

Dalton overheard her and said, "Doesn't matter to us, does it, Skyler?"

Skyler shook her head. "I like those rides."

Jared smiled. "Okay. Let's go."

Racing down the path that wound through Adventure land, Skyler and Paige kept their eyes open for the stand selling turkey legs.

"Are you two coming?" Dalton hollered back as he kept pace with Jared.

"You guys get in line, and we'll catch up," Paige suggested, happy to see that Dalton looked like he'd perked up a bit.

Dalton waved, and he and Jared took off for the Pirates of the Carribean ride, giving Skyler and Paige a chance to grab some food.

"Is your dad okay?" Paige asked, hoping she wasn't being nosy.

"He had another one of his nightmares last night. He has a hard time getting back to sleep after he has one."

"Nightmares?"

Skyler shrugged as she took her place at the end of the line for food. "I think it's Vietnam stuff or something. He won't talk about it with me. My mom used to rub his back and help him fall back to sleep when it happened. With her gone, he just paces around the house or goes out for a walk on the beach. That's why he looks like a zombie today."

Paige shook her head slowly, her heart aching for the man and what he was going through. "Is there anything he can do?"

"My mom said there's something that happened during the war that he can't let go of. I guess it upset him so much that he can't forget about it. I wish he would, though. It freaks me out when he wakes up screaming in the middle of the night."

Paige looked at the girl and swallowed. "He wakes up screaming?"

Skyler pulled a face and nodded. "He's drenched with sweat and looks like he's seen a ghost. Then he paces."

"That is so sad."

"It's kind of gotten worse since my mom died."

It was their turn to order, so they couldn't continue the conversation, but Paige pondered it. What was it that haunted Dalton? She'd heard about Post-Traumatic Stress Disorder. After some of the things Dalton had told them about the war and what she'd heard about the horrors of Vietnam, she wouldn't be surprised if the man's dreams had turned into nightmares. She just wished that after thirty years, he could find peace.

* * *

Even though Jared and Dalton hadn't asked for anything to eat, Paige got them some food and drinks anyway. Knowing Jared, he was probably hungry but just too excited to think about eating.

"This is so good," Skyler said with her mouth full.

Paige took a bite of the turkey leg and agreed. "It's so tender and sweet," she said.

It took a minute for them to make their way through the crowded walkways to the ride, where a long line of people waited for their turn. They found Jared and Dalton about halfway to the front. Dalton was busily talking on his cell phone.

"Thanks, Mom," Jared said when Paige handed him the turkey leg, churro, and apple juice.

Dalton finished his phone conversation rather abruptly and accepted the food. It was obvious that he was uncomfortable continuing his conversation "You didn't need to do this," he said.

"I know," Paige replied. "But we were starving, and we didn't want to share our own."

Skyler grinned and cleaned the last bite of meat off the turkey bone. "Yeah, Dad," she said with her mouth full. "You ask for one bite and take half of whatever I'm eating."

"I don't do that," Dalton said defensively, but he was grinning. Paige could sense that the earlier friction that existed between him and Skyler had vanished.

Skyler cast a sidelong glance at Paige, who winked.

"This is great," Jared said, licking his lips. "I might need another one." Paige rolled her eyes, knowing her son could eat an entire turkey by himself.

The guys ate while the line moved forward. Paige watched Dalton closely as he interacted with Skyler and Jared and was impressed again at his tenderness and sincerity. He was a good man, but, she was learning, he was also a complicated man. But then, who wasn't complicated? Most people had issues, things to deal with, emotions and experiences that took years to work through. She, herself, had plenty of issues to work through—or at least to keep buried away until she was ready to work through them. Right or wrong, everyone dealt with life the best they could. She was grateful for the strength that came from her faith in God and her beliefs in the gospel. How did people without the gospel deal with life's constant challenges?

Finally, it was their turn to climb into the boats that transported them back to the time of pirates in the Caribbean. Paige had forgotten just how much fun Disneyland was. It brought out a side of her that she'd forgotten she had.

Next they hit Splash Mountain, which gave them a thorough drenching, making Paige grateful for the warm sunshine to dry out their clothes. They seemed to be going the opposite direction from the rest of the throng of people and managed to find short lines on many of the rides. When they did, they made sure to ride twice. Paige had never known anyone to be as big of a fan of theme parks as her son was, but Dalton seemed to be a close second. By early afternoon they'd ridden all the rides they wanted to and were ready to go across to the California Adventure.

Jared and Skyler walked ahead of Dalton and Paige, planning which rides to go on first. Paige smiled as she watched her son listen eagerly to Skyler explain some of the exciting rides in the new park. "There really isn't a ride that takes you up high in the air and drops you, is there?" Paige asked Dalton after overhearing a bit of their conversation.

Giving her a wry smile, he didn't offer much comfort. "I'm afraid so, and I hear it's as scary as it sounds."

She knew Jared would never let her miss a ride. For some reason, he felt it his obligation to not let his mother miss out on any fun, whatever the cost.

As they waited in line to go through the turnstile, Paige noticed Dalton resting against the gate, rubbing his right thigh. They'd been whipped around on Space Mountain, and she wondered if maybe he'd gotten hurt.

"Are you okay, Dalton?"

He nodded and followed the kids into the park.

"My leg gets stiff on me when I'm on it for long periods of time. I'll be okay."

"I wouldn't mind taking a rest for a little while," Paige offered, wishing she'd worn a more comfortable pair of shoes. Jared tried to talk her into wearing her cross-trainers, but she'd wanted to wear the cute sandals that matched her capris and striped shirt.

Dalton lifted an eyebrow. "Are you sure?"

"My feet would really appreciate it."

They arranged a meeting spot with Jared and Skyler who, to Paige's chagrin, acted like they were glad to unload the parents and took off for more fun.

"They seem to be getting along well," Paige observed.

"Jared's a sharp kid," Dalton complimented. "I appreciate him being so nice to Skyler. She could use an influence like him in her life."

They sat on a bench in the shade, out of the way of the crowds but close enough to watch all the people walking by.

"This is a hard age for girls. I worked with a lot of young women in our ward, and it seemed like this was the age we worried about the most with the girls." Paige slid her feet out of her sandals and stretched her toes. "Their self-esteem is very fragile right now. It doesn't take much to shatter their confidence—a mean comment from one of their peers, not fitting in, getting hurt by a friend, getting dumped by a boy. It seemed to me like the girls who had a strong set of goals or who were involved in a sport or pursuing a talent were the ones who got through these years the best."

Dalton listened intently, nodding. "Skyler used to play the piano. I never had to tell her to practice. She did it on her own. She's naturally gifted with music and can play anything by ear. I've missed hearing her play. She also used to take dance—jazz and ballet. She danced en pointe for four years. She couldn't get enough of it."

Impressed by Skyler's accomplishments, Paige asked why she quit.

"She tried out for the dance company at school. When she didn't make it, it nearly killed her. She didn't come out of her room for days. Swore she'd never go back to school."

"Why didn't she get in?"

"Bad luck mostly," Dalton said. "She'd been going to dance six times a week, rehearsing for the school play, going to the dance company workshops, and it got to be too much. She caught a cold and ended up getting pneumonia because she was so worn down."

"How awful." Paige felt for the girl. All that hard work, then to get sick.

"She could barely get through the tryouts she was so weak and sick. But she was determined not to give up, and I'm proud of her for that. She coughed so hard she nearly passed out, but the judges didn't seem to care that her sickness affected her performance. She could dance circles around most of the girls who made it."

"What happened?"

"She ended up quitting dance. She stayed with the piano for a while longer, but she started spending time with a group of girls who seemed to have no ambition or restrictions. They'd rather spend time at the mall, or 'hanging out,' as Skyler calls it. Piano lessons and practicing didn't fit into her schedule anymore. Ever since then, it's been a source of contention between us."

"That's such a shame. Especially when she's invested so much time in it and is so accomplished." Paige had seen it happen many times, usually without a happy ending.

"I can see why she couldn't continue to pursue both," he said, "but I wish she'd stayed with one of her talents. There's a big dance competition coming up at the end of October that I wish she'd try out for. She tried out last year and took second place. The girl who won beat her by just a few points. I know Sky could win this year if she'd get back into dance and work hard. Her teacher has called me many times begging me to talk Skyler into coming back, but I think Sky's too afraid of losing again."

"But she'll never know if she doesn't try," Paige replied.

"I agree. It would be such a good experience for her. The winner receives a scholarship to the New York City Ballet for a month in the summer and a cash award, plus an opportunity to compete in a national competition."

"There's no way you can convince her to try?" Paige asked with disbelief.

"I've tried everything from punishing her to paying her to do it, but she won't even consider it."

"I had something happen my junior year in high school that taught me a lesson I'll never forget," Paige told him.

"Do you mind telling me?"

It was painful for Paige to recall the incident, but she concluded that if it helped Dalton with his daughter, then it was worth it. Paige told him how she'd wanted to try out for the school play. They were doing *The Sound of Music,* and she'd always loved the part of Maria. She'd had small parts in a couple of the school plays before then, but she thought this would finally be her chance to play a character she loved so well.

She practiced the songs and rehearsed the part for hours. Her voice wasn't as strong as some of the other girls, and that worried her, but still, she wanted to try. And then, the day of tryouts, as she sat in the back of the auditorium waiting for her turn and watching the other girls try for the lead in the play, her confidence faded. Before her name was called, she left, convinced that she didn't have a chance.

It wasn't until her ten-year high school reunion, when she ran into her old classmate Julia Martin, who'd won the part of Maria, that

Paige learned the other side of the story. Julia had told her that she'd almost not tried out for the play because she knew Paige would be chosen for the lead. Julia had overheard the drama teacher telling another teacher how impressed she'd been with Paige's abilities during rehearsal. Julia felt that Paige already had the part and she had almost changed her mind about trying out. They'd all been surprised when Paige backed out.

Paige knew her drama teacher was disappointed when she didn't try out, but assumed she was just being nice. Julia had assured her, "You would have been Maria in the play."

Even now, talking about it, Paige felt the same regret and disappointment in her heart that she'd felt that day after talking to Julia. If she'd only tried.

"I hate living with regret," Paige confided in Dalton. "I've made so many mistakes in my life and have lived to regret most of them. I hate to see Skyler pass by this opportunity. I think one day she'll look back and wish she'd done things differently."

Dalton nodded. "I wish I could go back and do some things over too." He sighed as though he still bore heavy burdens from his past. "I'd give anything if Skyler could hear your story. Maybe it would make her think about what she's giving up."

"You think she'd listen?" Paige asked.

"Yes," he answered. "I think she would."

"I'll see if I can work it into a conversation sometime," she promised.

"Thank you," Dalton said, smiling warmly at Paige. His blue eyes connected with hers, holding her gaze for a moment. As if in a trance, Paige felt like she was floating on air.

"Hey," Dalton said, sniffing the air, "do you like cotton candy?"

"I can't remember the last time I had any," she said.

"Let's go get some before the kids come back." He stood and reached for her hand. She slipped on her sandals and accepted his outstretched hand.

CHAPTER TWELVE

It took all three of them to talk Paige into going on the "Maliboomer," one of the more terrifying rides at the California Adventure theme park. She promised them that if she had a heart attack on the ride, she would come back to haunt them all. Against her better judgment, Paige found herself sitting in a seat, facing outward with her feet dangling in the air and a clear shield in front of her from head to waist. She wondered if it was for the purpose of containing the contents of someone's stomach were they to throw up as they were catapulted hundreds of feet into the air.

While standing in line, she'd watched other people go on the ride, heard their screams and watched their pale, startled faces as the ride literally shot them straight up into the air, then let them free-fall toward the ground.

Shutting her eyes she waited for the blast off, feeling as though she was going to need that shield in front of her any minute. Checking to make sure the strap was securely fastened around her waist, Paige waited, wanting the thing to just hurry up so they could get it over with.

A loud *whoosh* sounded and up they shot, streaking toward the sky, the gravitational force pulling them hard into their seats. The ride paused on top just long enough for them to see practically to the Mexican border. Paige held her breath as she lifted out of her seat.

A loud holler to her left her caused her to glance sideways. It was Dalton.

He looked over at her, wild-eyed, and yelled, "Hang on!" as they plummeted earthward.

Feeling as though her stomach remained above her somewhere in the air, Paige clutched the armrests tightly as they bottomed out and . . . shot back up again! With the shock of the first launch out of the way, the second ride to the top was actually kind of fun, and Paige found herself laughing.

Jared whooped and hollered, "This is awesome!" and Skyler "woo-hooed" right along with him.

Again the ride peaked, and just as they started downward, Paige yelled to Dalton, "Here we go again!"

By the time the ride ended, Paige decided that she liked how thrilling and fun it was. In fact, she wanted to do it again. Dalton thought she was crazy, but the line had died down, and it was now or never. This time it took some convincing to get Dalton to go, but, being the good sport that he was, he didn't ditch out when he had the chance. And afterward, he even admitted that the second time was more fun than the first.

They stopped for an early dinner and enjoyed grilled hamburgers and thick-cut fries. Jared was famished and finished off his mother's burger as well as the rest of her and Skyler's fries. When they finished, Dalton gathered up the remains of the meal and took them to the trash while Jared ran to the men's room.

Paige was sharing a milk shake with Skyler when a tall, blonde woman with more curves than a roller coaster strolled toward Dalton. Judging by Dalton's reaction, Paige assumed he must have known the woman. He seemed happy to see her, and rightly so. The woman was stunningly beautiful, probably in her late thirties, but with the body of a twenty year old. She wore slim-fitting white capris and a vivid turquoise T-shirt that accentuated her shape and looked gorgeous with her golden suntan.

"Oh, great!" Skyler exclaimed when she noticed who her father was talking to.

"Is something wrong?" Paige asked.

"It's Darlene, one of Dad's girlfriends," Skyler said. "*Old* girl-friends I should say."

"*One* of his girlfriends?" Paige felt like she'd just been doused with cold water. Of course he had girlfriends. He was incredibly hand-some, extremely charming, and completely available. If he ever came to Salt Lake, he'd get eaten alive.

"They were pretty serious for a while. They almost got married."

"They were engaged?" Paige managed to keep her voice calm.

"For a while. But they broke it off. I don't really know why, but I don't really care. I'm sure glad they did. She would have been the ultimate wicked stepmother." Skyler studied the woman, who was standing comfortably close to Dalton. "She hasn't been around much lately. I was hoping she'd moved or gotten married or something." She tossed her empty cup into the garbage.

"She's very pretty," Paige remarked, not sure what to say. If that was the type of woman Dalton went for, then Lou was going to be disappointed. Paige couldn't compete with someone like that.

"I guess," Skyler scoffed. "I think she's like some QVC makeup lady—she has her own line or something. She used to be a movie star. She was even in a James Bond movie."

"Wow. So how come you don't like her?"

"She's like Barbie—outside *and* inside. Some of the other women Dad's dated have been like that. You know, the kind who've had so much plastic surgery they'd melt if they stood to close to a fire. Then there are the ones who are career women who have no time or patience for kids. I'm just a thorn in their side. There have been some cool ones, too, though—you know, nice and fun. But nothing ever seems to work out. Darlene's the closest he's come to a serious relationship."

"Sounds like your dad dates a lot."

"It seems like everyone we know is trying to fix him up. I get tired of all of his dates. I know he does too."

"You and your dad seem to get along pretty well."

Skyler shrugged and dug a container of lip gloss from the pocket of her denim shorts. "Not as well as we used to."

Paige listened while Skyler kept talking.

"Instead of trying to understand what I'm saying and just listening to me when I talk to him, he jumps in and begins to lecture and tell me what to do and how to do it. Sometimes I wish he'd just let me talk—even if he doesn't like what I'm saying—and try and see things from my perspective. It's like he can't remember what it was like to be young."

"I think your father feels protective of you. He's just trying to prevent you from making mistakes or wrong choices and having to pay the consequences for them." Paige would have given anything to have had a father who cared as much for her as Dalton did for Skyler. "My father and mother divorced when I was your age, and my dad was never around. I really missed having him in my life."

Skyler sighed. "I know he's just trying to be a good dad, but sometimes I wish he'd just try and be my friend instead of my parent. It's so hard to talk to him. Like now." Skyler folded one knee up underneath her. "I could never talk to him like I'm talking to you right now."

"Don't give up on him," Paige said. "He loves you so much. Someday you'll see how hard it is to be a parent and watch your kids make mistakes."

"Did Jared ever make any mistakes? He seems like the perfect kid." Skyler quickly added, "But he's so cool, too."

"Thanks. He is pretty cool."

"He would've been a great big brother," Skyler told her. "You're cool, too," Skyler complimented her shyly.

"Me?" Paige sat up taller. "Gee, thanks. I never thought of myself as 'cool' before."

"Are you kidding? A woman like Darlene over there would never ride the Maliboomer once, let alone twice!"

"And I might ride it again if we have time before the park closes," Paige declared.

Skyler laughed. "I'll ride it with you."

A pause in the conversation seemed to signal the perfect chance for Paige to change the subject. She felt like the lines of communication were open enough for her to bring up Skyler's dancing. With a prayer for help, she proceeded with caution.

"Your father tells me that you used to be a dancer and a piano player."

"When did he tell you that?"

"Earlier today. I was asking him what kind of things you were involved in. You know, what you liked to do."

"What did he say?" Skyler tried to act uninterested, but Paige could tell she really wanted to know what her father had to say.

Paige recounted the most positive and glowing comments Dalton had said about his daughter.

"I'm not as good as he says I am," Skyler told her.

"You must be better than you think," Paige replied. "I bet there aren't too many girls who have a dance teacher calling to beg for them to come back and dance at their studio."

"Miss Mandy was a great teacher." Skyler traced the hem of her shorts with her finger.

"Your dad said something about a dance competition in October. I guess Miss Mandy thinks you have a good chance of winning this year."

"Yeah, right!" Skyler scoffed.

"You don't believe her? Would she have a reason to lie to you about it?" Paige wanted to get her thinking.

It worked. Paige watched as Skyler pondered the question for a moment before answering.

"No, I just think she's being nice. I couldn't do it. Even if I wanted to compete, I haven't danced for months."

"She still thinks you could win," Paige encouraged.

"She does?"

Paige noticed a flash of hopefulness in the young girl's eyes that was quickly replaced by fear.

"Would you mind if I told you a story about me when I was your age?"

"No," Skyler said, glancing over at her father, who was still talking to Darlene. "We can't do anything until Darlene lets my dad out of her clutches."

Paige chuckled, then began her story, explaining about her own struggles and self-doubt as a youth.

"So you see," Paige looked directly into Skyler's eyes, "I didn't even give myself a chance to find out if I would have been given the part of Maria in the play because I didn't even try. Who knows? Maybe being in that play would have made a difference in my life. And had I tried out for the part, maybe I wouldn't be sitting here nearly thirty years later, regretting that I didn't try and wondering what would have happened if I had tried out. Regrets are killers."

Skyler nodded, and then her eyes widened as she saw her dad finally walking toward them.

"You ready to do the Maliboomer again?" Dalton asked when he joined them.

"Are you?" Paige replied, surprised that he even considered going again.

"Yeah, right, Dad," Skyler said, her voice thick with sarcasm. "You screamed like a girl when you went on it."

"That wasn't me screaming," Dalton corrected.

Skyler flashed a "yeah, right" gaze to Paige, who did her best to keep a straight face. She'd heard him scream. He'd sat right next to her.

Dalton looked at Paige with an imploring gaze, leaving her no choice but to lie or change the subject.

"Oh look," she said, "there's Jared. I'd wondered where he wandered off to."

Jared stepped out of a sunglasses shack wearing a sleek pair of mirror-lensed sunglasses. He sauntered over to the table.

"Not bad," Paige said. "But we can't look directly at you when you're facing the sun or we'll go blind from the reflection."

Skyler nodded her approval of his choice of glasses.

"Hey, Mom," Jared said, "how much longer are we going to stay? I have a team meeting tonight."

It was just like Jared not to mention it until now.

Paige looked at Dalton. They'd had a long, full day, but she hated to see it come to an end.

"Sky does have school in the morning," Dalton answered, glancing at his watch.

"But we were going on the roller coaster. And Paige and I want to hit the Maliboomer one more time," Skyler reminded him.

"Do we have time?" Paige asked Jared.

He checked his own watch and shook his head. "By the time I take you to Lou's, then get to the gym, I'll be late."

"I can take your mom home," Dalton offered. "It's not that far out of the way for me."

"Are you sure?" Paige asked, not wanting to be a bother.

"It's no problem at all," he assured her.

"All right!" Jared exclaimed. "Then let's hit the roller coaster."

He and Skyler were off and running. It took Dalton and Paige a little longer to get going. By the time they caught up with the two kids, they were in line and ready to get on the next car that pulled in.

"Hurry," Skyler urged. "We saved you a space."

Dalton and Paige took their place in line just as the car pulled up. Sharing a look of fear with each other, they climbed into the seat behind their children, buckled up, and held on tight. They didn't even have time to scream as the ride suddenly blasted off.

* * *

Still breathless from their last ride on the Maliboomer, the two parents and their children walked together to the parking lot, laughing and recounting the fun of the day.

They arrived at Jared's car and said their good-byes, and Jared was on his way. Paige was pleased that Skyler and Jared had hit it off so well. At first she'd thought maybe Skyler had a crush on her son, but the more she saw them together, the more it seemed as though she looked at him as a friend or a big brother.

They walked to Dalton's sleek, silver Audi, and he opened the door for Skyler and Paige. Paige was impressed by this since the entire time she was married to Mark, he'd never opened a door for her.

"Dad, can you drop me off at the house first?" Skyler requested. "I have to finish a report tonight."

Paige felt terrible for making Dalton drive her all the way to Lou's house, but he was her only ride home.

"Sure, hon, you need to straighten—"

"My room, I know, I know," Skyler finished for him.

Heading west down Harbor Boulevard, they arrived at Dalton's house in fifteen minutes. "I won't be long," Dalton told his daughter as she got out of the car.

"Bye, Skyler," Paige said to the young girl. "It was fun today."

Skyler smiled. "It was the best!" she exclaimed. "Thanks for, you know, for talking with me."

Paige returned her smile. "You're welcome. Good luck with everything. You'll let me know what happens?"

Skyler grinned. "I will."

After waiting until she was safely inside the house, Paige and Dalton were soon back on the road.

"I'm glad you had a good time today," Dalton said as he pulled onto the busy street.

"I did," she answered. "How about you?"

"One of the funnest days I've had in a long time. I'm glad Skyler and Jared hit it off so well."

"I noticed that too."

"She's so different when she's not around her friends."

Paige noticed that Skyler hadn't put on as much makeup today and her clothes were comfortable and modest. She was a beautiful girl, and Paige wondered if she looked a lot like her mother.

"Somehow I need to think of a way to get her away from her friends," he confided.

"I had a chance to talk to her while you were talking to your . . . er . . . friend," Paige said, not sure what to call Darlene. "I know Skyler's thinking about the competition. She misses dance, I can tell. Knowing that her teacher believes in her is just what she needed to hear."

"Paige, that's great!" Dalton exclaimed, throwing a quick glance of appreciation. "How can I ever thank you?"

"She's a wonderful girl," Paige said. "I just hope I said something that helped."

Dalton slowed the car as traffic became more congested, his gaze focused straight ahead. For a moment, he looked as though he'd slipped into a world of his own. A honk of a horn from the car behind them snapped him out of his trance.

Paige didn't want to pry, but she felt comfortable enough with him to ask, "Is something wrong?"

Dalton didn't answer for a moment, then he licked his lips and drew in a deep breath, which he expelled slowly, as if pondering his reply. Finally he spoke. "I try to be both father and mother to her, but obviously I'm not doing a very good job of it. I worry that not having a mother is going to make being a teenager harder for Sky than it already is."

Paige remembered well how difficult some of Jared's high school years had been. She'd waited up many nights until well past his curfew, wanting to beat him and bawl her head off at the same time when he finally returned. She knew that not having a father actively involved in his life was difficult for Jared, but she was convinced that having no father was almost better than having a bad one. Mark wasn't nurturing, nor did he live his life according to the gospel. His influence on Jared was more negative than anything.

"I know it's none of my business, but what happened to Skyler's mother?"

Dalton looked at her, his clear, blue eyes etched with pain. Instead of taking the freeway on-ramp, he pulled over to the side of the road next to a park filled with kids on the playground and a group of young men playing football.

"Do you have a few minutes?" he asked.

Paige looked into his pain-filled expression and nodded.

CHAPTER THIRTEEN

"She had the most beautiful face of anyone I'd ever seen, like an angel's, with eyes so full of sadness it broke my heart."

He rolled down the windows so the evening breeze could flow through the car.

"I met her during the war. Some of my buddies and I were in Da Nang." He swallowed. "I'll just say that even though they were my friends, I didn't always approve of some of the things they did, like going to bars and finding women. Nothing was different on this particular night. We left the restaurant after dinner and some of the guys were on their way to the bar. The rest of us were on our way to see a movie. Anyway, I saw this young girl—sixteen, almost seventeen—as sweet and fragile as an orchid.

"She, along with dozens of other young Vietnamese girls, stood near the bars, hoping for the American soldiers to pick them up, buy them dinner, and maybe even give them some money. I knew most of these girls were forced to beg because they were starving and desperate and willing to do anything to earn money to keep themselves and the rest of their families alive. They were forced to be this way because of their circumstances, not by choice."

Paige's heart constricted in her chest.

"One of my buddies noticed this same girl right off and started to talk to her and make crude comments. I didn't appreciate them, and I told him so. Before I knew it, he and I were having a fistfight on the street because he wouldn't leave her alone.

"Of course, the other guys broke it up quickly before any authorities got involved and we got into trouble. For some reason, I just couldn't leave this girl there to be preyed upon, so I invited her to a restaurant to get her something to eat. I figure that was the least I could do. Her English was good enough that we could have a conversation, and I found out that she was actually a few years older than I had thought—eighteen—and she was trying to save money so she could get out of Vietnam.

"I asked her why she wanted to leave her family, but she told me that she had no family. She explained that she had been married and had a child, and she had lived with her parents and brothers. One day, the American soldiers came to their village and took all the men out into a field and executed them right before the women's and children's eyes. Soon Lee lost her father, her husband, and her two brothers that day."

"No," Paige said, covering her mouth with her hand, imagining the horror.

"Later, more soldiers came to their village. The women were frightened of what the soldiers would do to them, and they knew that the only way to be safe was to play dead, so the women hid themselves and the children underneath a pile of garbage. Soon Lee had her three-month-old baby with her. He was sleeping until one of the soldiers fired his gun. The baby started to cry, and Soon Lee knew if she didn't get the baby quiet, they would all be dead."

A sense of dread filled Paige. "What did she do?"

Dalton swallowed, his eyes closing, then slowing opening. "She put her hand over his mouth to quiet him, but after a minute, she noticed he wasn't breathing. He had died."

Paige wiped at the sudden tears that formed in her eyes and threatened to fall.

"The saddest part is that they were still captured and put in prison and tortured. The prison was bombed soon after that and those who lived were able to escape. Soon Lee never could find her mother or friends from her village. She didn't know if they were dead or alive, so she struck out on her own. She finally made it to the city, where she was forced to do anything she could to survive."

"How horrible," Paige whispered. "That poor woman, to suffer so much at such a young age."

"She never got over it," Dalton told her. "After dinner that night, I told her I would help her get out of Vietnam. I made arrangements for her to get the money she needed to go to my parents' home. My family was willing to help her and give her a job and a place to live."

"And that's how she got out?" Paige asked.

Dalton nodded. "That was before I was captured and held in prison in Hanoi. But when I returned home, she was there at my parents' home. A year later we got married. It was as if we were kindred spirits even though we were from opposite sides of the war and the world. She suffered tragedy at the hands of the Americans, and I endured unspeakable torture in that prison at the hands of her people. Still, we could relate to each other and had a deeper, stronger bond because of what we'd suffered. I loved Soon Lee with all of my heart," he said.

There was a distinct look of pain in his eyes.

"We were married almost fourteen years when she finally had Skyler." His expression softened as he spoke of his daughter. "Soon Lee didn't think she could have any more children. She was convinced God was punishing her for killing her first child." His voice grew quiet. "It was a miracle when she became pregnant. I thought for sure having Skyler would change things and bring Soon Lee the closure and peace she needed, but she just couldn't escape the nightmares and the pain from the past. She was on many different medications to help her with depression and sleeplessness, but one day she decided she just couldn't deal with it anymore."

Paige's mouth dropped open with horror. "No."

Dalton nodded. "It was the only way she felt she could finally have peace. She took a whole bottle of sleeping pills and never woke up."

"That's so sad," Paige said.

"She'd tried for years to contact her relatives to see if her mother was still alive as well as any of her extended family, but she never had any luck. Almost a year after she died, I got a letter from one of her relatives saying that her mother was, in fact, still alive, along with many of her cousins. But the rest of their relatives and family had all died in the war, the war they called 'The American War.'"

With a heavy heart, Paige imagined the horror of watching loved ones getting shot to death, of sacrificing her own child for her safety and the safety of others, of enduring the horrible torture and unspeakable acts inflicted upon her in an enemy prison. The memories would be enough to drive a person to drastic measures. Her soul ached for Soon Lee's tragic life.

"I always felt that if she could have gone back, looked for her relatives, revisited her home, and seen her people, she would have found some sort of peace or closure. Before she died, she had even begun to consider it. I thought we were finally making some progress . . ."

Paige could barely speak. "I'm so sorry," she managed.

Dalton shut his eyes for a moment, then he looked at her. "I can't believe I just burdened you with all of that. We don't even know each other that well, and here I am telling you all of this. You must think I'm a . . . I don't know what you think I am."

"I think you're a wonderful father and person, and I'll bet you were a wonderful husband."

Dalton was silent.

Paige didn't know what else to say. Words seemed intrusive to the silence between them. They'd both suffered heartache and pain, had both stared death in the face, and had overcome physical challenges that took every ounce of strength and courage to conquer—both in different ways, but survivors still the same.

He started up the car and drove to Lou and Bryant's house. Before he helped her out of the car, he turned and said, "I haven't told many people those things about Soon Lee. Thanks for listening. It feels good to talk about it."

"I'm glad you feel comfortable talking to me," Paige told him, her admiration for him growing with each meeting and each conversation.

"Paige?" He looked down at his hands for a moment before speaking. "I'd like . . . to see you again," he said.

Paige wanted to see him too, but she knew that for the next few days she needed to be with Lou.

"Maybe if you have time after your friend's surgery," he went on, "before you go back to Salt Lake City."

Paige smiled. "I'd like that." She didn't allow herself to stop and analyze the wisdom of seeing him again, for once listening to her heart.

"Maybe when I come to Utah for general conference next month, we could . . ." he paused as if weighing his words carefully, "that is, if you'd like, we could get together then, too."

Paige was glad the darkness partially hid the broad smile on her face. The feeling was momentary but wonderful. This man wanted to see her again! This wonderful, charming, spiritual giant of a man who had the choice of all the Barbies in southern California wanted to see her—*her*—again.

"That would be nice," Paige said, reining in her enthusiasm so she didn't risk scaring him off or freaking herself out. She would process all of this once she got inside Lou's house.

She noticed him release a long breath, almost as if he was relieved she'd said yes.

The porch light of Lou's house flicked on just before Bryant stepped out and retrieved the evening paper off the doorstep. He looked out at the driveway and saw Dalton's car. He waved, smiled, and went inside.

"Suddenly I feel sixteen again," Paige said, remembering how her mother used to flip the porch light on and off if she sat in a boy's car too long after a date.

Dalton laughed. "Your parents did the light signal too?"

"Every time. And as much as it annoyed me, I've done it a time or two with Jared in the past."

"Not me," Dalton said. "I'm not going to bother with the light. If Skyler ever spends more than five minutes in a parked car in our driveway with a boy, I'll be out of the house and in his face in a second."

Now it was Paige's turn to laugh. "Skyler will really appreciate that."

"Yeah, I know." He was thoughtful for a moment. "This teenager stuff is hard as a single parent, isn't it?"

"It's not easy when there are two parents, but I think it is harder with only one. I spent most of Jared's high school years on my knees, praying him through those tough times."

"He's a great kid. You did a wonderful job."

Dalton's compliment made Paige feel warm inside. She appreciated the comment but knew she couldn't really take much of the credit. "I was blessed with a great kid. He's always had an obedient spirit, but he does have weaknesses. I think as long as he keeps up his guard, he'll be fine. I'll be glad when he's on his mission, though."

"It's wonderful he's so committed to going on a mission. I would have given anything to have served a mission. I keep hoping that someday I'll be able to somehow serve."

"But you are a missionary. I'm sure you touch many people's lives every time you give one of your speeches. And in the service, I'll bet your example made an impression on all the soldiers."

Dalton didn't reply.

She wondered if she'd said something wrong, something to upset him. So she checked her watch in the patch of light from the porch and said, "It's getting late. I guess I'd better go inside."

"And I better get home and help Skyler finish her project." He opened his car door and stepped out. Paige had to stop herself from opening the door before he got around to her side.

Together they walked to the front door.

"I had a wonderful time today," she said once more, looking up into his face, admiring for the hundredth time his chiseled good looks and warm smile.

"Me too. Especially the Maliboomer," he joked.

They both laughed at the fun and terror of the ride.

"Give Lou my best," he said. "I'll keep her in my prayers."

"I'll tell her," she promised.

She didn't know if it was her imagination or not, but he seemed to have inched closer and was leaning in toward her. Her heart sped up as she found herself drawn toward him. Once again, that young, naive schoolgirl feeling she'd had earlier returned. Crickets chirped in the warm night air, a light breeze tickled the leaves on the trees, and a full moon cast shadows around them.

Their eyes made contact. She was nervous, but not frightened like she'd thought she'd be if this moment ever happened again in her life.

Just as he reached for her, the front door flew open. It was Carter.

"Paige, you're wanted on the phone," he yelled, then pushed the door shut. Then it opened again. "Oh, yeah, it's Jared." The door closed once again, and the spell was broken.

With a weak smile, Paige faced Dalton. They couldn't recapture the moment, but it wouldn't be forgotten, and hopefully, someday . . .

"I'll call you," Dalton said, reaching out and giving her hand a squeeze.

"Okay," Paige replied, the touch of his hand sending waves of electricity up her arm. "Good night."

CHAPTER FOURTEEN

The day of Lou's surgery arrived, and Paige found herself more nervous for Lou than she'd been for herself. Perhaps it was because she knew what Lou was getting into—the pain, the adjustment, the change in her physical appearance, the treatments. She herself had gone into her operation not caring what the doctor did nor what she had to go through; she just wanted the cancer out of her body.

With the kids at school, Paige and Bryant paced the floor of the waiting room, wondering, worrying, and putting on a front of strength and optimism. She felt she had to be strong and positive for Bryant.

But when the doctor came out of surgery and told them everything went well and that Lou was resting comfortably in the recovery room, they both broke down, hugged each other, and cried tears of relief.

It was over, but it was also just beginning.

* * *

"I hate having you feed me like a six month old," Lou complained as Paige spooned cream of chicken soup into her mouth.

"You're welcome to try to feed yourself," Paige said, but she knew it would be too painful for her friend to move her right arm.

"Okay, okay, but when can I have something else besides soup? I'm dying for Chinese takeout."

"Maybe tonight for dinner," Paige said. "No, wait, I think the Relief Society is bringing dinner in again."

"Not another casserole." Lou rolled her eyes. "I can't stomach any more casseroles or Jell-O," she stated.

"Maybe they'll surprise us," Paige said, doubting her own words.

Lou finished her soup, and, while Paige read articles to her from a women's magazine, drifted off to sleep. She was still on a prescription painkiller, and the pills knocked her out within twenty minutes of taking them. But sleep was just what she needed.

After rinsing the lunch dishes in the sink and placing them in the dishwasher, Paige looked around at the immaculate house and wondered how she was going to fill her afternoon. She'd done all the light housework that need to be done—dusting, vacuuming, sweeping. The laundry was even done.

Plopping down on the sofa in the family room, Paige flipped on the television and clicked through channel after channel of emotionally charged talk shows, annoying game shows, boring shopping shows, and an overabundance of sports shows. Nothing caught her interest except a cooking show featuring dishes from somewhere in Europe.

Wondering how many calories were in the dessert the chef made with straight cream and butter, Paige jumped when the telephone rang.

"Paige?" the voice asked, a voice she immediately recognized as Dalton's.

She couldn't help smiling. He'd called every day since Lou's surgery.

"How's Lou doing today?"

"Better. She's got her spunk back. In fact, I'm afraid it's time to call off the Relief Society dinners. She's fed up with casseroles and Jell-O."

Dalton laughed. "Tell them they can bring the dinners to my house. I'd love not having to cook dinner one night."

He was certainly no ordinary man, Paige thought. That was one of the things she liked about Dalton. His experience as a single parent seemed to make him more sensitive to the opposite sex. Being forced to play both parents gave him a keener understanding of a woman's role in the family.

"I'll see what I can do," Paige said. "Lou's craving Chinese food, but I don't feel comfortable leaving her to go get some."

"I'm free," he volunteered.

"No, that's okay. I'll see if I can reach Bryant. He might be able to swing by and get her some."

"I insist," Dalton proclaimed. "Skyler's staying at a friend's house tonight, and I'm stuck home with a TV dinner. This would give me an excuse to get some real food and see some real people."

Paige didn't want to discourage him too much. She'd thought about him a lot during the last few days, and the fact that she was leaving soon made her want to see him at least one more time.

"I know she'd appreciate it," Paige said. "But don't feel like you have to."

"I'll be over around five o'clock," he said. "If the Relief Society brings a casserole, just hide it from Lou. She doesn't need to know any different."

Paige hung up, anticipation coursing through her veins, trying to tell herself not to let her emotions run away with her imagination. She was leaving in two days, and then things would go back to normal. He'd stay here in California with his beauty pageant girl-friends, and she'd return to Salt Lake City to . . . what? Her meaning-less job, her quiet house, and her empty life.

She shook her head to clear the unwanted thoughts and got to her feet to go check on Lou. After thinking long and hard these last few days about Dalton, she'd convinced herself not to build up an expec-tation about their "relationship." That way, she wouldn't get disap-pointed when nothing worked out between them. Realistically, nothing ever could work out between them. She'd enjoy their time together and have fond memories of her visit in California. Hopefully they would be friends who stayed in touch occasionally, maybe exchanged Christmas cards once a year.

Yet deep in her heart, Paige knew she wanted more than that.

* * *

As soon as Maddie and Carter stepped through the door from school, they headed straight upstairs to see their mom. Lou had show-ered and cleaned up after her nap and was now feeling refreshed and rejuvenated, which made it difficult to keep her down.

With one eye on the clock, Paige waited with nervous excitement for Dalton to pull into the driveway. A few minutes before five, she heard a car engine, and her heart beat triple time. Glancing out the window, she saw Jared step out of his roommate's BMW.

However happy she was to see her son, she couldn't help the nagging thought in the back of her mind that Jared seemed to drive Nate's car more than Nate did. And now that she thought about it, she never saw him when he wasn't wearing something of Nate's, too— an expensive, name-brand shirt, shorts, or even Nate's favorite shoes.

"Hi, hon," Paige greeted him as he walked in. "How was school?"

"Hey, Mom. School is school." He kissed her on the cheek like he did every time they saw each other, a habit she hoped he never got out of. "How's Lou?"

"Good," Paige told him, updating him quickly on Lou's progress. "I thought you had practice today."

"Not until later," he said. "I wondered what you were doing for dinner."

Paige explained that the Relief Society was bringing in dinner and so was Dalton.

"I like casserole," Jared said. "I'll eat it."

"You just might have to. Lou swears she'll never eat another one as long as she lives."

They'd only had three meals brought in so far, but all three of them had been a different version of the same thing: meat, vegetables, and some kind of potato or pasta covered with sauce and melted cheese. They had so many leftovers Paige couldn't fit another thing into the refrigerator, yet she felt guilty just dumping out the food.

The doorbell rang, and Paige hurried to answer it.

There, holding a cardboard box full of Chinese takeout containers, was Dalton, all smiles.

"Hi," Paige said, her gaze locking with his for a moment. She knew there was no denying that there was something going on between them, some kind of bond that she couldn't explain. She knew Dalton was aware of it too.

She invited him inside, and again, before they walked to the kitchen, their eyes met.

"It's good to see you," Dalton said.

"You too," Paige replied.

There wasn't a chance to say more because just then, Maddie and Carter charged down the stairs. "Is it Daddy?" Maddie hollered, flying into the entryway.

She skidded to a halt with her brother at her heels and stared at Dalton.

"You're not my daddy," she scowled.

"Is that pizza?" Carter questioned.

Dalton lifted the box and said, "Sorry, Chinese."

"We want pizza," Maddie complained.

"Yeah, Dad said we could have pizza tonight."

"The Relief Society is bringing in some more food," Paige reasoned with the children. "Maybe you'll like what they're bringing."

"Where do you want this?" Dalton asked.

"In the kitchen," she answered. "Come on, you guys," she said to the kids, "you can help with dinner." Even though they were disappointed about the no-show pizza, they were excited when they learned Jared was there.

No sooner did they reach the kitchen than the doorbell rang. "Hide the Chinese food," Paige exclaimed. "It's the Relief Society." Sure enough, there at the front door were two women from the ward, their arms loaded with food. The sisters introduced themselves and walked straight into the kitchen, where one woman turned on the stove, put a nine-by-thirteen baking pan into the oven, and said, "Let it heat for fifteen minutes or so until the cheese melts over the tater tots and hamburger." The woman didn't notice Paige, Dalton, and Jared exchange knowing looks.

There were rolls, vegetables, salad, cookies, and of course, Jell-O, to go along with the meal. Paige couldn't stifle a laugh, but she faked a cough to cover her amusement.

"We'll just pop up and tell Louisa hello, then be on our way," one of the sisters said before venturing upstairs.

One look at the Relief Society dinner and Maddie and Carter both pulled faces. "Mommy's not going to like that," Maddie said. "She hates casserole."

"I hate it too," Carter said. "I'll have a peanut butter and jelly sandwich."

"Can I have a peanut butter and jelly sandwich, too?" Maddie asked.

Paige looked at the children, then at Dalton. She shrugged, knowing it wasn't her place to discipline the children or insist they have what was being served for dinner. "Sure, why not?" With the kitchen rapidly becoming a food court, Paige got out plates and utensils and spread out the buffet.

The children heard the garage door open and close and ran to greet their father, who was home just in time for dinner. To everyone's surprise, he walked in with two boxes of pizza.

"I didn't think Lou could take another—"

"Shhh," Paige stopped him before he could finish his sentence. "The Relief Society just brought a nice *casserole* for dinner." Bryant quickly caught her message and put the boxes discreetly out of sight until the Relief Society sisters left. The children were ecstatic that he'd remembered their pizza, and after he opened the boxes, they didn't waste any time digging into the first one.

Lou soon joined everyone in the kitchen. "Good heavens!" she exclaimed. "Where did all this food come from?" Jared was working on a pile of casserole and vegetables, the kids were on their second slices of pepperoni pizza, and Dalton was helping Paige open cartons of Chinese food. They all got a good laugh out of Paige's recounting of how the three meals arrived.

"I can't thank you enough," Lou said, managing to eat her egg roll with her left hand. "I've been craving this for two days. And thank you, honey," she said to Bryant. "The pizza was perfect for the kids. We've had our fill of casseroles, haven't we, kids?"

"This stuff is pretty good," Jared said, squirting a stream of ketchup on top of his food. "Why didn't you ever make this at home, Mom?"

"Because your mother loved you more than that," Lou told him. "My mom was the Relief Society president in our ward for five years when I was growing up. I ate so many casseroles as a kid I seriously thought they were their own food group. I'd rather have a peanut butter and jelly sandwich for dinner."

Everyone laughed, and Maddie explained to her mother that they'd just requested the same thing before the pizza showed up.

"You better take it easy," Bryant told Jared. "You eat too much of that casserole and you won't get off the ground at practice tonight."

Jared groaned and shoved his plate away from him. "Too late, I've already had three helpings."

"Take the rest with you," Lou offered.

Jared pulled a face. "As much as I liked it, I don't want to ever see any of that stuff again."

After Lou finished her meal, Bryant helped her to the family room couch, where he propped pillows around her to make her comfortable. She was sick of her bedroom and felt well enough to join the family.

"I better get Nate's car home and get changed for practice," Jared said. "Hey, Mom, too bad you're leaving Sunday. Nate invited us to go on his dad's yacht with their family."

Paige immediately wondered if Jared was planning on going to church first, but she didn't bring it up, deciding she'd ask him privately. Jared continued to tell her about the million-dollar yacht Nate's family had and the condos they owned in Hawaii and Cozumel.

As he spoke, Paige felt a twinge of worry cross her mind. Jared's father was already a negative influence in his life, representing a lack of values and a complete focus on material things. Jared didn't need Nate working on him as well.

"Thanks for dinner," Jared said to Lou as he got ready to leave.

"No, thank you," Lou said. "You did us a huge favor by eating it."

Jared kissed Paige on the cheek before he left. "I'll see you tomorrow, Mom. We still gonna hang out?"

"You bet," she answered. "Have a good practice."

"Speaking of practice," Bryant said to Paige, "Coach said he'd give me the files and disks for the program tonight so I could send them home with you."

Home. Paige wasn't ready to go back home to the drudgery of her life. Mustering a smile, she tried to give him an enthusiastic reply, but her heart just wasn't in it.

The kids occupied Lou's time by doing their homework in the family room where she could help Carter with his spelling and Maddie with her reading. Bryant also had to change his clothes for practice, so Paige cleaned up the kitchen. Dalton volunteered to help, and they soon had previous leftovers in the garbage and new leftovers in the refrigerator.

"I better head home," he said.

"I'll walk you to your car. I haven't been outside yet today," Paige said.

The evening was calm and cool, and Paige and Dalton walked slowly to his car, as if to prolong their time together as long as they could.

"Lou and Bryant have a beautiful yard," he said.

"They've done most of it themselves. Before he got this coaching job, Bryant spent his summers landscaping. You should see the back-yard—it's really amazing. Picture the Garden of Eden."

"That nice?" he asked.

Paige nodded.

"Do you think they'd mind if you showed it to me?"

"I'm sure they wouldn't," she replied. Paige took him around the side of the house to the backyard, where the pool lay like a shim-mering gem in the evening shadows. The flowering trees and shrubs perfumed the air with exotic fragrances, creating a sense of escape, as if they were in their own private paradise.

"Incredible," Dalton said. "If I had this yard, I'd never leave." He pointed to the cottage. "What's that?"

Paige explained the story of the cottage to him. "Lou and Bryant have offered it to me," she said. "They want me to move here and live in the cottage."

Dalton's face lit up. "Are you going to?"

His enthusiastic response made it hard not to say yes.

"I haven't really had time to think about it. I'll go back to Salt Lake and see how it feels. It's a big decision for me, but a fresh, new start surrounded by the people I love sounds appealing."

"I toy with the idea of moving, starting over somewhere else, but I think that would be very difficult for Sky right now. And I really love my home. It would be hard to leave," Dalton said.

"My home in Salt Lake isn't anything special to me," Paige confided. "A few happy memories, but nothing I couldn't leave behind."

"Too bad we don't have the key for the cottage. I'd like to see inside." He tried to peek inside through a small frosted window on the front door, but couldn't see anything.

"I just happen to know where they keep the spare." Paige retrieved the hidden key and let them inside. Dalton was immediately impressed by the charming structure, the attention to detail, and the architectural beauty.

"The loft is up here," Paige said, climbing the stairs to the cozy library overhead.

"This is great." He looked around at the vaulted ceiling and built-in shelves. "I think this is already my favorite room in the house."

"Mine too," Paige said, looking up into his face.

Dalton returned her gaze, and once again, her heart pounded in her chest.

Inching her way closer, Paige tilted her chin to keep eye contact with him. Dalton dipped his chin, closing the space between them.

"I think you should seriously consider their offer," he said softly.

Paige swallowed. "You do?"

He nodded as he reached out for her.

She stepped into his arms, and slowly their lips met.

The brief but tender kiss spoke volumes to her heart and soul. Dalton didn't demand or expect anything from her. For one short moment, their feelings for one another were mutually understood, and their hearts beat in sync. And even when the kiss was over, the sensation still lingered.

"I will," she replied to his suggestion. "I definitely will."

CHAPTER FIFTEEN

"I hate having you leave so soon," Lou said, wiping at the corners of her eyes. "Are you sure you can't stay another week? Or at least a few more days?"

"I wish I could," Paige answered, knowing Lou had no idea just how badly she wanted to stay, not only so she could help Lou and be with Jared, but, she realized as she packed her suitcase, to be with Dalton.

Her heart ached when she looked into Lou's tear-filled eyes and glimpsed a fear that she'd never seen in them before but one she had recognized in herself. It was the uncertainty of what to expect, a sense that the treatments would be difficult, and a fear of what the future held.

"Lou." Paige placed a stack of folded clothes into her suitcase, then walked over to her friend and took her by her hands, giving them a warm, assuring squeeze. "Everything is going to be okay. You're going to get through this, and I'm just a short phone call away."

Lou nodded as tears slipped down her cheeks. "I know. I just feel so much better having you here."

Paige encircled her arms around her friend and hugged her tightly. "I know. I know."

When they faced each other again, Lou reminded her of her promise. "You're going to think about moving, right?"

Paige didn't want to get anyone's hopes up until she had a chance to get home and really think seriously about making such a huge change in her life. But she couldn't find it in herself to tell Lou no.

She just couldn't. "Of course I am," she said. "We'll talk after I get back to Salt Lake."

Lou gave her a tremulous smile.

"You've gotten through this surgery amazingly well," Paige encouraged her. "I've never seen anyone recover from major surgery as quickly as you have."

"Really?" Lou questioned. "I do feel pretty good."

"See, you'll be fine. And I'll be back real soon. I won't be able to stay away when basketball starts." Paige gave her a reassuring smile.

The door to the guest room opened, and little Maddie stepped inside holding the cordless phone. "It's for you, Paige," she said, handing it to her. Jared was supposed to take her to the airport, and she hoped he wasn't calling to tell her he had been held up in traffic.

"Hello?"

"I'm so glad I caught you before you left."

Paige's heart soared. "Dalton, hi."

Lou's face brightened at the mention of Dalton's name, and she winked at Paige.

"I wanted to come over and tell you good-bye in person, but I ended up having to go to Skyler's school," he continued.

"Is everything okay?" Paige asked.

"She was caught sluffing with her friend and some boys. This is actually the third time she's been caught sluffing. She managed to keep me from finding out about the other two times."

"Oh, Dalton, I'm so sorry."

Lou motioned to her that she'd step out of the room and give her some privacy.

"She's been put on detention and has a lot of school work to make up. She's not very happy with me since I basically grounded her until she graduates from high school."

Paige chuckled, knowing how he felt. There had been times she'd wanted to lock Jared in his room for a few months to help him wake up and see what kind of friends he was hanging out with and what kind of trouble they were getting into. She was so glad those days were behind her.

"Is there any chance she'll get a reduced sentence for good behavior?" she joked.

"Not today. But maybe when I have a chance to calm down, I'll think about it." He gave a weary sigh. "Anyway, this wasn't how I planned on spending my morning. I wanted to tell you good-bye in person."

The mere fact that he wanted to see her touched her. "I understand," she said. "I would have loved to have seen you too."

"I also wanted to ask you what you were doing the first weekend in October."

She didn't have anything planned any weekend in the entire month of October. "Nothing," she said. "Why?"

"I'm definitely coming to Utah for general conference and will be there until the following Wednesday to give a presentation. I'd like to see you when I get to town."

Paige hugged the phone to her ear even though her head scolded her for being such a pushover. She didn't consider herself a spontaneous, jump-in-with-both-feet kind of girl, but deep down she really wanted to see him again.

"Paige?" he said.

She shook her head as if to clear the noise inside. "Yes," she answered.

"Would you like to get together, maybe go to dinner, while I'm in town?"

Paige paused for just a moment so she didn't appear too anxious or nervous. Unsure of pursuing a relationship but enjoying Dalton's friendship too much to not see him again, she finally said, "I think that would be wonderful."

Suddenly the singsong sound of dialing played in their ears. Paige wondered if someone was trying to use the phone.

"Hello?" Dalton said. "Sky? I'm on the phone."

"Sorry, Dad," Skyler said.

"You're not supposed to be using the phone anyway," he reminded his daughter.

"I know," she said, the anger in her voice apparent.

"Wait," Paige said quickly. "Skyler?"

"Yes?"

"Hi, it's me, Paige."

"Hi, Paige. What are you doing?"

"I'm getting ready to go back to Salt Lake City."

"You're leaving?" The girl sincerely sounded sad at the news.

"Yeah, stinks, huh?"

"Sure does. Not as bad as my life, though."

"Yeah, I heard," Paige commiserated. "Hey," she said, "listen, Sky. We all make mistakes. Just don't take your eye off your goal, okay? I'm expecting big things out of you. I know you can do well at this dance competition, but you have to focus on it. You have to work hard and make it happen. It will be worth it, I promise."

"I know," Skyler said. "Sometimes I let my friends talk me into doing stupid things, you know?"

"Yeah, I did my share of stupid things when I was young, and Jared did his share of dumb things too. But he's turned out okay. I know you will too."

"I wish you could be here for the competition," Skyler said.

"Me too," Paige answered. "But you never know. Maybe something will work out."

"I'm glad I got to talk to you before you left."

"So am I. You hang in there. And if you want, you can call me anytime, okay?" Paige offered.

"Okay," Skyler agreed.

After Skyler left the line, Dalton immediately exclaimed, "That was amazing!"

"What?" Paige asked.

"She didn't say two words to me on the way home from school, but in one minute she told you more information than I'd get from her in a week of prying."

"That's because you're her father. I may be an adult, but I'm nonthreatening. I don't have the power to ground or discipline her. I can just be her friend."

Dalton didn't say anything.

"Dalton?" Paige wondered if she'd said something to upset him.

"I'm here, I was just thinking about all of this—the bracelet, meeting you and Jared, and now hearing you have conversations with my daughter that I could only dream of having. I can't help but think . . ."

Paige waited for him to continue, but he remained quiet.

"Yes?" she prompted.

"I don't mean to sound corny, but I have to wonder if all of this has happened for a reason."

Paige had wondered the same thing more than once. "All I know," she said, "is that I've enjoyed getting to know you and Skyler. And I'm glad we're going to stay in touch, otherwise . . ." Now it was her turn to be silent. She didn't want to give away too much of her feelings, but there was so much in her heart.

"Otherwise what?" he asked.

She debated whether to continue her comment.

"Paige?"

Letting down her defenses, she confessed, "It would be hard to say good-bye."

"For me too," he said.

This time they were both quiet.

Finally Paige broke the silence. "You'll let me know how Skyler's doing and when her competition is?"

"I sure will. And I'll keep an eye on Jared. We'll have him over for a barbecue or something."

"He'd like that," she said, appreciating his gesture.

With hesitation, they both said good-bye and hung up the phone. Even though Paige felt a sense of sadness, she also felt joy. She would see him again. She knew it.

* * *

"Sister St. Claire, come in," the bishop said when Paige appeared in his doorway. She'd been requested to meet with him immediately following their Sunday church meetings.

Her palms felt clammy, and she rubbed them against her cotton knit skirt to dry them. Meeting with the bishop always made her nervous because it meant some sort of change, usually an unwelcome one.

Paige took a seat across from the desk and waited while he shut the door and took his seat. With a smile, he told her how nice it was to see her and asked about Jared. Paige gave him a brief overview of her son, tempted to finish her sentence with, "Can we just cut to the chase?" She restrained herself.

After the small talk was out of the way, the bishop finally approached the reason he'd called her in there. "You know, Paige, I've seen you in various callings in our ward and have always been impressed at your dedication and strength. Even with all you've been through, your testimony has been a tremendous example to the rest of ward."

Paige smiled at his kind words. "Gee, thanks," she said.

"That is why I've called you in here today. I feel you have a lot to offer. You are a great leader and teacher."

Paige listened as anxiety squeezed her heart and stomach. *Please let it be a Sunday School teacher,* she prayed, *or Primary instructor. I love being in Primary.*

"After weeks of fasting and prayer, we'd like to call you to be our ward choir director."

Paige burst out laughing, but the bishop wasn't joking.

"Me?" Paige asked, wondering if they realized that her choir skills were pretty much reduced to singing, and that was only if she sat next to someone who sang her part.

"I know you don't have a huge music background," the bishop said.

I don't have any music background—at least not leading it!

"But don't forget, many times the Lord gives us callings for the growth they can provide us, not so much for the abilities we have to fulfill those callings."

Paige nodded, wondering why, after all the years that she'd had relatively low-key, background callings, the Lord would see fit to give her such an out-in-front calling like this?

"Would you like some time to think about it?" the bishop asked, obviously sensing her shocked reaction.

She nodded, unable to voice her inadequacies and lack of musical ability.

"I'll give you a call in a day or two and see how you're feeling about it," he said.

Again, she nodded and stood, accepting his outstretched hand.

Giving her a reassuring smile and words of encouragement, the bishop showed her to the door. Still stunned, Paige walked out. Choir director. Either the bishop was desperate to fill the calling or the Lord knew something about her she didn't. Whichever it was, she still didn't have a clue as to how to direct a choir.

* * *

After her meeting with the bishop, Paige went back to her empty house and pulled a Marie Callender's frozen pot pie from the freezer. She liked pot pies because they were microwavable and disposable. She could eat without even having to dirty a dish.

While she waited for the pie to cook, Paige changed out of her church clothes and into a comfy denim jumper and T-shirt.

Choir director!

She chuckled at the thought. She'd participated in the choir for several years only because the previous director, Amber Nelson, who was also one of her close ward acquaintances, had cornered her in the hallway one day at church and begged for her to join the choir. They'd worked together in the Relief Society presidency several years previously, and Amber had stood by Paige when she went through her divorce. Paige felt obligated to join.

Now here she was, asked to be in charge of the choir.

Grabbing her ward list from the drawer by the telephone, Paige dialed Amber's number, hoping that a talk with Amber would expel some of the panic and anxiety welling up inside of her.

* * *

After work each evening, Paige worked on the program for the UC Irvine basketball team. She referred to the layout of previous programs from the university to get a general idea of the contents and the feel of the school. Grateful to have something to keep her busy in the evenings, Paige worked hard to create a stunning presentation of the men's and women's basketball teams at the college.

But the project didn't prove to be enough of a distraction, and she found herself taking frequent breaks from her computer to wander into the kitchen and find something to nibble on or to turn on the television and flip through channels.

Her concentration was shot. No matter how hard she tried to focus on her work or her calling, her mind wandered . . . all the way to southern California and Lou, Jared, and Dalton.

* * *

"Good morning, Paige," Ross Langerfeld said as he stepped into her office.

"Ross," Paige replied, massaging her neck. She'd gone in early to work to finish a brochure so she could meet a deadline, and her shoulders and neck were stiff from working in front of her computer for three hours without a break.

"How's the Brecken Ridge condominiums brochure coming?" He leaned against the doorjamb.

"Just about finished. I'll have it ready when they come in at three."

"Good, good." He nodded. "They liked your other work and are on a tight schedule. I knew I could count on you."

Paige slid her pen behind her ear and her feet into her shoes. She worked better without her shoes on, especially when she was stuck at her desk for long periods of time.

"Do you have a minute?" he asked.

Paige looked at her boss, trying to determine whether she needed to prepare herself for bad news or not.

She swallowed and said, "Sure, what's up?"

Ross closed the door behind him and took a seat.

"You've been a good worker, Paige. You're talented, disciplined, and very dependable."

"Thank you," Paige replied, worry tightening her chest.

"That's why . . ." he hesitated for a moment, making Paige hold her breath with anxiety, "I'm giving you a promotion. And a raise."

Paige's mouth dropped open. For a moment she'd let her insecurities get the best of her and worried that he was going to let her go.

"A promotion?" she said for clarification.

"And a raise," he repeated. "This is long overdue. I'm sorry it's taken me so long to get around to it."

"That's okay." Paige chuckled. A promotion and a raise. This was a cause for celebration—except she had no one to celebrate with.

"I've also given your suggestion a lot of thought and, well, with all the high schools back in session and basketball season just around the corner, I'd like to assign you an assistant and have you draw up a proposal to launch our new sports programs service. Of course, you'd still have other assignments and projects, but I'm looking to have you head up this new area."

Stunned was about the only word Paige could come up with to describe how she felt.

"Well?" Ross asked.

"I . . . don't know what . . . to say."

"Say you'll do it," he replied. "I've contacted several high schools in the valley to see how they provide this service for their schools, and each coach I talked to said what an enormous headache it was for them every year. Putting these programs together took a great deal of effort and time that they didn't have. They were more than thrilled at the prospect of paying a little extra to have an expert put it together." He nodded his approval. "I should have listened to you earlier. You were absolutely right. So, what do you say?"

It was all Paige could do not to pinch herself to see if she was dreaming. She'd been waiting for a break like this for years. And now, out of the blue, he was delivering her dream job on a silver platter.

Stunned but pleased, Paige said, "I'll do it."

* * *

"I'm telling you, Jared," Paige restated for her son, "it came as a total surprise. Ross didn't ever hint about this promotion or raise. But he's pretty tight-lipped about stuff like this. He won't say anything until it's carved in stone."

"I wish I could be there so we could celebrate," Jared said.

Paige appreciated his comment because she'd had the same thought more than once that day.

"Next time you come down we will," Jared said.

"I'd like that," she said, wondering when the next time would be that she went to California. "How's basketball going?"

"I've never worked so hard in my life. We spend hours in the weight room and on the court, but I've really stepped up my game. It's weird going from being the biggest on the team—like I was in high school—to being one of the smallest on the team like I am here. But my shot's never been better, and I'm playing out of my head."

Paige assumed that meant he was doing well.

"I won't start, but Coach thinks I'm going to get some serious playing time. Dad's been coming to my practices to watch."

Paige sat up with a start. "He has?"

"Not every day, but two or three times a week. It's cool. He missed most of my high school games because he was living in California, but now that we live so close, he'll be able to see all of my games here."

An explosion of jealousy filled Paige's chest. It wasn't fair! Mark did nothing to deserve to sit in those stands like the proud father and show support. Yet he was there and she wasn't. The thought of him taking her place as the parent supporter, their son's anchor, irritated her.

"Mom?"

"Sorry," Paige said, keeping her voice from betraying her emotions. "I'm glad, honey."

"Oh, and guess what? This weekend I'm going home with Nate. His dad's receiving some award in San Francisco, so we get to go and stay in this fancy hotel and attend this important ceremony and stuff. His parents are flying us up there."

"They are? What do you mean, flying you there? How much is the plane ticket?"

"It's free, Mom. They have their own jet. They're sending it down to pick us up."

Why Paige wanted to encourage him not to go she didn't know. It seemed as though all Jared could talk about was Nate and how much money his family had. She appreciated them being so generous to her son, but she worried about the influence and message they were sending him.

"Just remember that not everything that glitters is gold," she told her son.

"Huh?"

"It means that even though something seems appealing and attractive, it doesn't mean it's the real thing and will bring you joy. You know, the concept that money can't buy happiness and all that."

"Mom," Jared complained, "what are you saying? Why are you telling me this?"

"I don't know, I just . . ." Sometimes she wished there was a way to take back words once they came out of her mouth. "Never mind," she said. But Jared persisted.

"What is it, Mom? Don't you want me to go this weekend?" She appreciated him respecting her enough to ask her opinion, but she knew how he'd feel if she told him no.

"I just don't want you to think that all of the money Nate's family has and all their possessions are what's important in life."

"I know, Mom," he answered, sounding completely annoyed.

"I don't mean to ruin your fun. It sounds like a great time."

Jared didn't answer, and Paige knew she'd upset him.

"I gotta go," Jared said. "I'm going to be late for practice."

Paige's heart ached. She hated to say good-bye when he was upset with her, but she still felt a need to steer him in the right direction. Just because he was gone from her home didn't mean he was gone from her heart. She was still his mother, and he still needed guidance and counsel, even though he didn't want it.

CHAPTER SIXTEEN

"I'm telling you, Lou, I can't help but worry about the effect this Nate is having on Jared. Mark has always shown him such a worldly view of life, and it's been all I could do to keep Jared focused on what really matters. I think I'd feel better if I could actually meet Nate."

"I've met Nate," Lou reminded her. "He's a good kid. You can tell he was born with a silver spoon in his mouth, but I think he's pretty harmless. If anything, I think Jared's good for Nate."

"You do?" Paige said with relief.

"I do. Nate has a lot of respect for Jared. I can tell."

"I'm so glad you and Bryant are there near him. I sometimes feel like my son is being preyed upon."

"But you've taught him well. Jared is strong and valiant. He's a stripling warrior. He'll be fine. You have to have faith in him."

"I know," Paige replied. "It's hard to be so far away from him and not be able to interact with him. We used to stay up late at night talking about everything—girls, friends, school, his goals. I miss that closeness. We don't have it anymore."

"You could," Lou said. "It wouldn't be that hard."

Paige knew what Lou was implying, and she felt torn across three states. Her heart was in California, but everything else was in Utah.

"I know. I still think about it."

"I'm glad," Lou said. "I can't think of anything better than to have you here with us. Even though I'm feeling better, I still miss you."

"I miss you guys, too."

"What about—"

"Don't say it!" Paige tried to stop her.

"What?"

"You know what."

"You mean, don't say, 'What about Dalton?'"

Paige groaned. "Please, Lou. I've already told you, I haven't talked to him. He hasn't called, and I'm not about to call him."

"But you two hit it off so well. I can't understand why he hasn't called."

"It's no big deal," Paige lied. "He's busy with all his Barbie-doll girlfriends anyway."

Lou laughed. "Not all of them are Barbie dolls."

"What do you mean?"

"I've been doing some asking around," Lou said. "I know a lady in his ward, so I thought up a reason to call her. I casually asked about 'Brother McNamara.'"

"Lou, you didn't!"

"Of course I did. Are you kidding? You know me better than that. I had to find out everything I could about our friend Dalton."

Paige didn't want to encourage her friend, but, truth be told, she was dying to know what Lou found out. But Lou was having too much fun teasing her and remained silent until finally Paige couldn't stand it any longer.

"Okay," Paige blurted out, "what did you find out?"

"Ha! I thought you'd want to know," Lou snickered.

"I'm just curious, that's all," Paige padded her eagerness.

"Well," Lou paused, then said, "I guess Dalton is *the* most sought after guy not just in my stake, but in all of southern California. We're talking fan club popularity here."

Paige laughed. The poor man.

"I hear, though," Lou continued, "that the one thing that keeps a lot of women from getting serious with him is his daughter."

"Skyler!" Paige exclaimed. "Why?"

"I guess that girl can get mean and vicious. She's been known to sabotage dates and mess up messages between him and some of these women."

"I don't believe it," Paige defended the girl. "Skyler's confused and she's struggling just like every other teenage girl her age, but she's not vicious."

"She's probably just very protective of her father," Lou offered. "But I'm sure she'd do better if she had a mom around the house."

Paige didn't have Skyler figured out yet, but she knew the girl still struggled with the loss of her mother. She probably also struggled with wanting to know why her mother had done what she had. "All I know is that Skyler is a very complicated girl. She may be confused, but she's not vicious."

"Hey, you don't have to convince me. That's just what other women have said."

Paige's heart dropped. How cruel for these women to judge Skyler without really knowing her. Maybe if they stopped pursuing Dalton long enough to give Skyler a chance, to take time to get to know her, understand her . . .

"Anyway, I'll keep you posted on what I hear. One thing I do know is that he got very close to a woman a year ago—I mean, engaged-to-be-married close—a woman named Darla. No, Doreen."

"You mean Darlene?"

"That's it. But the woman called it off. And once again, I heard it was because of Skyler. I guess it was pretty hard on Dalton. He really loved this lady."

Paige knew Skyler wasn't fond of Darlene, and she also knew how much Dalton loved his daughter. If Skyler didn't want him to marry Darlene, she was positive Dalton wouldn't marry her.

Personally, she couldn't imagine trying to cope with dating along with trying to form a second family. It was too risky, and there were no guarantees that the stepparent and stepchildren would ever develop a nurturing relationship.

Wanting to change the subject, Paige asked, "So, how are you doing? How's work?"

"I'm doing better. I'm still really sore, though. I wish I could do more, but I just have to take it easy. My doctor says I'm doing better than most of his patients, though, because I exercise and eat right and I don't smoke and drink. He's not even LDS, but he knew a lot about our church and said that the health care industry would save millions of dollars if all people would follow the Word of Wisdom."

"That's pretty amazing," Paige said.

"Yeah, I thought so, too. And as for work, my new manager isn't working out so well. Because of his strong business background, I thought he'd take charge and whip the store into shape for me. Well, he's great with the business end of the job, but he has horrible people skills. He's the kind of guy who should just stay in an office and not work with the public. I need to get rid of him, but I can't until I find a replacement."

"Sorry it hasn't worked out," Paige told her. "You don't really need this right now, do you?"

"No, but I'll get through it. In fact, I probably ought to say good-bye because I need to get some work done tonight. When are you coming back to visit?"

"Soon, I hope. Right now, though, I have to concentrate on getting this new department going. Ross went out on a limb for me, and I want to prove to him that I can do this. I want to make this a success."

"Good for you," Lou encouraged. "It seems like men follow a career path that's already been laid out for them, but women have to carve the path out for themselves every step of the way."

"That's how it's been for me. That's why I don't want to mess this up. This is my first real break. I feel like this is my chance to prove myself."

"Well, you go girl," Lou quipped. "You're a fighter. That's why I admire you so much. I'm behind you all the way."

"Thanks, Lou."

* * *

Paige's days grew increasingly hectic, starting early and ending late, but she liked having something she could throw her heart into, something that challenged her mind even though it exhausted her physically. Fortunately, Ross assigned her two assistants, both fresh out of college and eager to learn. They were like sponges, and she enjoyed the energy they brought to work with them each day.

The first step in making the department a success was contacting schools and building a clientele. That was Paige's job. She set up appointments with the coaching staffs of each school and then visited them in person. Paige enjoyed visiting with the coaches and office staff at the schools. She was always well received, and in fact, most of the coaches were grateful and relieved after her visit. None of them had time to do the sports programs themselves. Her company was equipped not only to do the layout and design of the schools' various sports programs, but they could also act as a liaison between printing companies and the schools, taking the projects all the way to the end. Between the long hours at work and time in the evenings working on the program for Jared's team, Paige rarely had a free moment anymore.

One morning during a planning meeting with her assistants, Paige was interrupted by the receptionist.

"There's a delivery for you, Ms. St. Claire."

"Thanks, Kelli, we'll be through here in a minute and I'll come and get it."

Paige had each assistant report on the progress of each high school account they were responsible for, and together they made decisions regarding projected deadlines and follow-up. The programs required coordinating photo shoots and lining up business advertisements.

After her assistants left, Paige leaned back in her chair and ran her hand through her hair, overwhelmed at the job ahead of her. She'd just found out that a disk containing all the ad layouts for one of the high schools had been wiped clean. A week's work had been deleted with the push of a button.

"Got a minute?" Lance from the office next door said as he tapped on the door to her office before stepping inside.

Paige untangled her fingers from her hair and looked up. "No, but come in anyway. I need a diversion."

"Ross mentioned you were getting a little overwhelmed with your new project and thought you could use some help. I've got some free time. Is there anything I can do?"

"You're offering to help?" She saw the first glimmer of light at the end of the tunnel.

"Yeah, I just completed some big jobs and haven't got much lined up right now. What've you got?"

Lance sat down, and Paige proceeded to go through a list of concerns she had, grateful that Lance had done some similar work and was already trained in the computer program they used.

They worked until lunchtime, when Paige had one of the assistants run out for food so they could keep working. By the time they finished their meal and their meeting, Paige noticed that Lance's list of "to do's" was longer than hers, but when she pointed it out to him, he insisted on keeping it. He assured her he was happy to have something to work on, and even offered to take on more if needed.

Feeling as though she'd conquered Everest, Paige finally got up from her desk and stretched her legs. It had been a long morning. Then she remembered that something had been delivered for her.

The receptionist was away when Paige went to inquire about the delivery, so she looked around the desk and checked the in-box for manila envelopes addressed to her. Many of the high schools sent their team pictures and their ads on disk. But she couldn't find anything with her name on it.

Paige admired a flower arrangement sitting on the credenza behind the receptionist's chair. It was especially pretty because right in the center of a dozen long-stemmed red roses was one pristine, white rose.

"I see you found the flowers," Kelli said when she returned to her desk.

"They're beautiful. I didn't know you had a boyfriend," Paige said to the young girl. Kelli was just out of high school and worked part-time for them.

"Oh, they aren't for me," Kelli told her. "Those were delivered for you."

Paige's mouth dropped open. "Me?"

"There's a card in them somewhere," Kelli told her, reaching for the vase of flowers.

Paige found the card tucked into the flower stems. "I'll just take it back to my office. Thanks."

Her cheeks flushed the same color as the roses. Who in the world would send her flowers?

Closing the door, Paige put the flowers on her desk, then found the card and opened it.

To Paige, a woman who stands out in a crowd.
I've been out of town, but I'll call you soon.

Thinking of you,
Dalton

Paige smiled and reread the card. He thought she stood out in a crowd. Her? He was the man who was surrounded by gorgeous women like the host of a beauty pageant.

She stood out? Ha!

She chuckled at the thought, but gazed for a moment at the roses and felt her insides grow warm. Even though she didn't think she stood out, it was nice of him to say so.

* * *

Soaking in the tub that night, Paige thumbed through a *Good Housekeeping* magazine, her mouth watering at some of the delicious dishes and recipes it showed. She'd enjoyed cooking in the past, but never really had a reason to do it anymore. It wasn't worth cooking a fancy meal for one person. She usually just stopped by one of her favorite take-out places for dinner or cooked something in the microwave.

She jumped when the telephone rang.

Fumbling to get the phone to her ear, she lost hold of the magazine and dropped it into the water.

"Hello?"

"Is Paige there?"

She immediately recognized Dalton's voice.

"Hi," she said, fishing the soggy magazine out of the water and tossing it onto the floor.

"How are you?" he asked.

She scooted up in the water so her voice wouldn't echo off the sides of the tub. "I'm great," she said. "How are you?"

"Pretty good." She shut her eyes, relishing the fact that he was on the other end of the line. "Oh," she remembered, "I got the lovely roses you sent. Thank you. You didn't need to do that."

"I wanted to. I didn't want you to think I'd forgotten about you."

She slid down into the warm water a few inches. He was thinking about her. "They're lovely. And the card was too."

"I'm glad you liked them. How have you been?"

She told him about work and the new calling she'd just accepted, and he told her about his recent trip to New Orleans to meet with a group of medical professionals.

"How's Skyler?"

"That's the best part," he said. "She's doing so much better."

Paige couldn't have been happier with the news. "What's happened?"

"About a week ago she finally said she was ready to go back to dance. She changed her mind three times on the way to class, but I talked her into giving it one shot just to see how she felt. I told her I'd stay and watch, and if she changed her mind, we'd leave. I didn't want to put any pressure on her, but I knew if she just got back to the studio, everything would be okay."

Paige admired his intuitiveness with the teenager. She knew from her own experience with Jared that sometimes all it took was a push in the right direction and things took care of themselves. She'd done plenty of pushing while Jared was a teenager.

"And it was?"

"Paige, it was incredible. Her teacher and the girls in her class literally surrounded her to each give her a hug. Skyler was so happy."

"That's wonderful," Paige replied, knowing how difficult it would be to go back after quitting.

"She's had so much fun being back in dance that she's been taking extra classes just to get back in shape. And the best news is she's definitely trying out for the dance competition. Her teacher was thrilled and promised to do everything she could to help her get ready."

Paige's cheeks hurt from smiling so much, but she couldn't help it. The news was truly wonderful. "Skyler's lucky to have such a caring teacher."

"She is. Her teacher told me that Skyler reminded her a lot of herself when she was Sky's age. She was fortunate to have someone step into her life and help her down the right path. I think she feels like she can be that person for Skyler, and I think she's right."

"When is the competition?"

"The twenty-fifth of October, so she doesn't have much time, but she's really working hard. It's been . . ." He trailed off and cleared his throat. "I feel like she's getting back to her old self again."

"I'm glad, Dalton," Paige said. "Skyler's such a sweet girl. She just needed a little redirecting."

"Well, you were the one to do it. You reached her when no one else could."

"I just got lucky that we hit it off," Paige replied. "It wasn't anything I did."

"I happen to disagree, but the most important thing is that those talks you had with her made a difference, and for that I'm very grateful."

"I'm glad I could help."

"How's everything in Salt Lake?"

As Paige talked to him, she marveled at how nice it was to talk to someone who actually listened to what she had to say and cared about how she was feeling. Mark had never taken time to listen.

"Sounds like you're pretty busy," he commented.

"Swamped," she replied.

"Too busy to get together when I come up for conference?" he asked.

Her heart jumped. He still wanted to see her when he came to town.

"I think I can squeeze you into my schedule. Is Sky coming?"

"She needs to stay here. She's got rehearsal that weekend, and she'd have to miss school."

"That's too bad. I'd love to see her again."

"I'll tell her you said so. She really wishes you could come to her competition."

"I'll see what's going on then. I'd love to come if I can get away."

They continued talking and laughing, sharing day-to-day experiences and finding out about each other's lives, pasts, and families. It was past eleven when they finally said good-bye. They'd talked for nearly two hours, but it had seemed like fifteen minutes. Paige was amazed that they could have so much to talk about and that they hadn't had to search for topics. In fact, they'd run out of time before they ran out of conversation.

That night when Paige went to bed, she spent longer than usual on her knees, her prayer filled with gratitude. She hadn't been sure how she would fill her days once Jared left home, and now she barely had time to read the newspaper. It felt good to be busy.

Yet being busy still didn't make her any less lonely or confused. She couldn't deny that she enjoyed Dalton's company, but she didn't trust her ability to make decisions when it came to men. She'd loved Mark with all her heart when they'd gotten married, and when he walked out on her, it had shattered her heart and world into a million pieces, causing an ache that had pierced her soul. She couldn't go through that again. Loneliness was bad, but being miserable in an unhappy marriage was by far worse.

CHAPTER SEVENTEEN

"So we're waiting on the final approval for Valley View's basketball program, and then it's ready to send to the printer?" Paige asked Lance.

"I'm expecting it any day now," Lance replied.

Paige nodded and checked the item on her list. Lance had been a lifesaver. He'd worked many long, hard hours laying out the programs for many of their accounts. He had a natural knack for seeing exactly how each page would work best, and his talent was paying off in a major way.

"I guess that's all then." Paige closed her planner and looked at the two assistants and Lance. "I know it's been hectic lately, and I appreciate you being willing to work overtime to meet some of these deadlines. You guys have been great."

"Valley View's our last program. We ought to celebrate," Lance suggested.

"I agree," Paige said, "We should go to that new Brazilian restaurant that opened. I hear it's great."

"I've been there," Lance said. "It is good."

"What do you say?" Paige asked her assistants.

"Sorry," Cheryl said. "I have other plans for tonight."

"Me too," Karl said. "My three year old's birthday is today."

"Oh, okay," Paige said with disappointment. "Maybe we can do it another time—hopefully before baseball season starts. I'm afraid we're going to live by feast or famine in this department."

Cheryl stood and bid her farewell. It was obvious she was anxious to leave, and Paige didn't blame the girl. They had all stayed late four out of the last five nights.

"I'll see you Monday," Karl said.

Paige and Lance slumped back in their chairs, not possessing enough energy to stand. It had been a long week.

"I'm still free tonight," Lance said. Paige looked at him and could tell by his expression that he was serious. "What do you say?" he added.

Taking a deep breath and releasing it slowly gave Paige a moment to think. It wouldn't be like a date or anything—just friends and coworkers going out to dinner. Besides, it wasn't like she had anything else going on. Her evening was free, and she'd spent way too much time lately with her microwave.

She looked at Lance. He was two years younger than her, divorced, and boyishly handsome. She didn't flatter herself into thinking that there was more to his offer of going out to dinner. Still, he was fun to be around, and Brazilian food sounded much better than a Lean Cuisine and a half-pint of Ben & Jerry's ice cream.

"Sure," she said. "Why not?"

* * *

"He tried to kiss me," Paige said with disgust when she called Lou after dinner that night.

"Did you let him?"

"Of course not!" Paige exclaimed.

"Why not?" Lou asked.

"Lou, it wasn't even a date. We work together, for heaven's sake, and . . . a . . ." Paige stumbled. "I don't know. I just didn't think it was appropriate. I'm his boss . . . kind of."

"It was just a harmless kiss," Lou said.

"It just didn't feel right." Paige still shivered when she thought about how Lance had walked her to her car in the dark corner of the parking lot, slipped his arms around her, and pulled her close. They'd had such an enjoyable time at dinner too. Why did he have to go and ruin it like that?

"Good grief, Paige, you're not a nun. You're an attractive, grown woman. A man is bound to want to kiss you."

"Still, it gave me the creeps. I don't know how I'm going to face him Monday morning."

"Paige, don't make such a big deal out of this. I'm sure he's not going to dwell on it."

"I hope not," Paige said. "I like working with Lance. He's been really awesome to help out so much. I wouldn't have made it this far without him. I mean, the guy knows more about all of this than I do."

"Then you've just let him know by your reaction that all you want is a professional, business relationship. He'll be fine."

Paige thought about Lou's words and realized she was probably right. Certainly Lance had more important things to worry about than Paige's cold response to his advances.

"You always know just what to say to help me feel better."

"That's what friends are for," Lou said. Paige didn't know what she'd do without Lou. The woman was an amazing strength to her. "By the way, Jared and Nate came over tonight," Lou told her. "They're going to San Diego for the weekend."

"They are?"

"Yeah. Jared wanted to borrow some snorkeling equipment. Nate, of course, has his own."

"Why were they going to San Diego?" Paige asked.

Lou's voice reflected hesitancy. "They were going to visit Nate's girlfriend and her roommates."

"What?" Paige said, mortified. "Where are they staying?"

"I don't know," Lou answered. "I'm sure they have a hotel or something."

Paige forced herself to calm down. Jared was levelheaded and had good judgment. She had no reason not to trust him. It was Nate she wasn't sure about.

"Paige, you don't need to worry. Jared's a good kid. And Nate is too."

"I know," Paige answered, hoping for some assurance of this in her heart. Yet she wasn't naive enough to believe that just because Jared had his sights set on a mission that he was out of reach of the adversary. If anything, his goals probably made him even more of a target for temptation. "I wish I weren't so far away. At least I'd feel like I was still involved in Jared's life."

Lou didn't comment.

"Lou, are you still there?"

"I'm here," Lou replied. "You already know what I have to say about the matter."

"I know, I know. You think I should just pick up and move to California. But it's just not that easy. I mean, now that I have this new position at work, Ross is really relying on me to make it successful. Plus I have this new calling, and except for singing, I haven't got a musical bone in my body. I don't actually know how to *lead* music!"

"You still haven't given me any valid reasons that you can't leave."

Paige sighed. "I know. It's just that this has been my home forever. It's kind of scary to just pick up and move."

"But you have a place to live here, a job to come to, plus your son and your best friend. And we don't have snow. What else do you need?"

"I don't know," Paige said. "It just doesn't feel right yet."

"Well, keep praying, girl, because it feels right to me. I need you desperately at my store, and I can guarantee that you would not only be perfect for the job, you'd love it."

"But—"

"And," Lou continued, "Bryant told me today that the entire coaching staff went nuts over the program you sent. They loved the cover, the artwork inside, the whole thing. It was better than they expected. I think the baseball coach wants to talk to you about doing his program for spring, and they would be happy to refer you to other coaches looking for help."

Paige appreciated the vote of confidence. She thought the program had turned out nicely, and was happy to get the final approval.

"I have a question for you," Lou said. "Have you fasted and prayed and gone to the temple to find out if you should do this or not?"

Paige didn't want to answer, but she knew she had no choice. "No."

"No wonder you don't feel right yet," Lou scolded. "You know how I feel about—"

"About people who complain but aren't willing to do anything to change their situation," Paige finished for her. "I know, I know." Lou's pet peeve was people who griped about their problems but weren't willing to do whatever it took to fix them. Generally Paige agreed. But this time the philosophy applied to *her*, and she didn't like it.

"I'm thinking that now that you have your big projects out of the way, you need to spend some time this weekend deciding your future."

Paige would love it if it were that easy, but she knew it wasn't. Answers to prayers didn't come so simply to her. She struggled and stewed and analyzed every situation before finally making a decision. But she knew she needed to give the matter some serious thought. She couldn't help wondering why all of a sudden her life changed from dull and boring to being swamped at work and church. And then having men trying to kiss her in parking lots!

With some degree of reservation, she told Lou she would put some effort into finding out what the Lord would have her do, but she didn't expect much to happen.

* * *

Paige woke up in a cold sweat. Try as she might, she couldn't shake the image of Jared's mangled and dead body inside Nate's smashed and twisted BMW. It was only a dream, but it had seemed so real.

The picture in her mind continued to haunt her as she got up and went to the kitchen for a drink. She ached to talk to her son, to call him and just hear his voice to know that he was okay. But it was three in the morning, and he was somewhere in San Diego.

She filled a glass with water, then remembered she was fasting.

She dumped the water and left the glass by the sink, then sat down at the kitchen table. Resting her head in her hands, she thought about Jared and the road ahead. After this school year was over, he would head out on his mission. Then, after two years on his mission, he would most likely go back to Irvine to play basketball again and continue his education. There was a good chance he would never return again to Salt Lake for any length of time. He would visit, maybe spend a week here or there, but he would never live at home again.

Paige shut her eyes as tears threatened.

Her mother used to always say, "Home is where the heart is." Paige's home was here, but her heart wasn't.

With that thought and a nagging urge to call her son to make sure he was okay, she made herself go back to bed, but sleep was a long time in coming.

* * *

Sunday morning, the first thing Paige did was call her son's apartment. She doubted he'd be home, but she was frantic to get ahold of him, unable to stop thinking about the dream she'd had the night before.

When no one answered, she slammed down the receiver in frustration. Nate had a cell phone, but she didn't have the number. She wondered when they'd be home. They had school the next morning, so hopefully it would be sometime Sunday afternoon.

Shoving her feet into her shoes, she grabbed her set of scriptures and her purse and headed for church. It was a beautiful fall day, and the Rocky Mountains to the east were glorious with color, but she couldn't appreciate the sight nor relish the crisp freshness of the morning air. Worries about Jared consumed her.

Saying a prayer in the car on her way to church, Paige swallowed the knot of emotion that kept forming in her throat. *He's fine*, she told herself, but the words didn't convince her.

Paige carried a constant prayer in her heart through the block of church meetings and immediately checked the answering machine when she returned home. Nothing. She resolved that when she finally did get ahold of Jared, she was going to let him know that even though they lived far apart, she still needed him to let her know if he went somewhere. She was his mother, and just because he'd moved didn't mean she didn't worry about him anymore.

She said a prayer before breaking her fast, pleading with Heavenly Father to help her with her decision, to enlighten her mind. After eating a tuna fish sandwich for lunch, she sat down to read the Sunday paper, but her eyes soon grew heavy. Within minutes, she fell asleep.

* * *

"What!" she exclaimed with a start when the phone rang. She shook her head, disoriented. The phone rang again. This time she got up and answered it.

"Paige," Lou's voice came, the frantic tone unmistakable.

"Lou, what's going on?"

"Has Jared called you yet?"

"Jared? No, I've been trying to reach him, but he's not home—"

"I just talked to him," Lou said.

"He called you?" Paige didn't need to hear more. Something was wrong. Something had happened.

"He's going to be fine. Bryant's with him now, but he and Nate got in a little accident coming home from San Diego."

"An accident? What happened? Is he okay?"

"He's fine, Paige. He just got a bump on the head that needed a few stitches. They were both wearing seat belts, thank goodness."

"What about Nate?" Paige asked.

"He wasn't so lucky. He has a broken collarbone and a concussion. He'll be fine, but he's going to have to stay in the hospital a few days."

"How did it happen?" Paige asked, remembering her dream. Had she had the dream to help her prepare for the news of the accident?

"Jared's not sure—he was asleep—but he thinks Nate might have dozed off. Nate was going to drive for the first hour while Jared rested, and then Jared would take over so Nate could nap. I guess Nate just got too tired."

"Because they'd had such a wild weekend?" Paige asked, feeling anger and concern well up inside of her.

"Now, Paige," Lou spoke in a motherly tone, "they're kids. I'm sure they stayed up late, but that doesn't mean they were doing anything wrong."

"I know," Paige replied as a tear slipped onto her cheek. "I'm just worried and frustrated. I feel helpless being so far away."

"Bryant's going to bring Jared home with him. We want him to stay the night, you know, to make sure he's okay. I'll have him call you when he gets here."

"I would appreciate that." She wouldn't feel better until she talked to her son. "Thanks for being there for him."

"Hey, you know he's like a son to me. I promise we'll take good care of him."

Paige didn't doubt for a second that Lou would take care of Jared, but *she* wanted to take care of her son. *She* should be there with him. He needed her.

I should be there.

She sat in stunned silence as the words sank in.

I should be there, she thought again, consciously this time.

"Father," she whispered heavenward, "should I be there?"

After attending the temple yesterday, as well as fasting and praying fervently, striving for some indication as to what she should do with her life, she'd felt as though she'd come up short in the answer department. She'd tried to do everything in her power to receive divine guidance, but nothing had come into her heart or her mind. They had been blank. Until now. All she could think about was being there, near Jared.

And her heart grew warm as her eyes grew moist. It made so much sense.

* * *

"So you're fine. You don't need me to come out?" Paige asked her son for the second time.

"You can come if you want, but I'm fine, Mom. Nate's in pain, but he's doing better. You should see his car, though."

Paige squeezed her eyes shut, trying to block out the image of the crashed car. The vision had haunted her since she'd heard of the accident.

"Guess what?" he said excitedly. "Since Nate's car is totaled, his dad is buying him a new one. Can you believe it?"

Paige didn't dare tell him what she thought of Nate's father. Maybe they had a lot of money, but giving out cars for free didn't seem like sound parenting skills. To Jared it seemed like the perfect situation, but Paige knew that learning to work and save and earn would teach her son more life skills and pride in his accomplishments.

"Hey, I gotta go, Mom," Jared said. "I'll talk to you later."

"Wait!" she exclaimed. "I have to tell you something."

"What, Mom?"

"I had a dream that something had happened to you and Nate. A car accident."

"You did? Wow, Mom, that's freaky."

"Jared, I know you think I worry too much, but I can't help it. I just don't want anything to happen to you. And I wonder about you spending so much time with . . ."

Jared gave her a moment to finish, then said, "With who?"

She knew he'd get mad if she said anything, but she did worry about him spending so much time with Nate.

"Mom?"

"I just don't know much about what kind of boy Nate is."

"What do you mean by that?"

Paige closed her eyes, praying for guidance. "I don't know anything about him, that's all. And you seem to spend so much time together."

Jared didn't speak.

Paige knew the conversation was over.

"I gotta go, Mom."

"Okay. Be careful, Jared," Paige tried to squeeze in before he hung up the phone, cutting her off midsentence.

* * *

"Paige," Ross said. His voice came through her thoughts like a voice in the fog. She was distracted, uninterested, and disheartened.

"Sorry." Paige blinked and forced herself to focus on Ross's face across the desk from her. "Guess I let my thoughts drift."

"You haven't been yourself these last few days. Is everything okay? How's Jared and his roommate?"

"Jared's fine," Paige replied. "They both are. It's just that I feel so guilty not being there for him. He's never had stitches before."

"He's a big boy now, Paige."

Typical male answer, Paige thought.

"Why don't you take the afternoon off? Go shopping or go to a movie. Relax and get your mind off things. There's nothing going on here that Lance and your assistants can't handle."

Paige looked at him with amusement. Shopping? A movie? How much fun were either of those things by yourself? She would never set foot in a movie theater by herself.

"Take a drive up the canyon," he continued. "The last of the fall leaves are out. A break from the office might be just what you need."

Appreciating his effort at sympathizing with her concerns, Paige smiled. Even if she just went home and immersed herself in a good book and overindulged with Chinese takeout, the break would be nice. It wouldn't make her concerns disappear, but she wasn't dumb enough to pass up an opportunity like this.

"I'll find something to do. Thanks, Ross." Paige got up from her chair and shook his hand. As far as he was concerned, the problem was as good as solved and Paige would return to work tomorrow her old self, ready to work and tackle her job.

Wishing it were that easy, Paige shut the door to her office after Ross left, then sat in her black leather chair. Closing her eyes, she willed the throbbing between her temples to go away. She'd had a headache for the past three days. Stress did that to her. Some mornings she woke up and her jaw hurt from clenching her teeth so tightly in her sleep.

Moving was sounding better all the time. Starting fresh, starting over, making a new life for herself—maybe that was just what she needed. She would be near the only people she truly loved, people she needed in her life more than just over the phone or on an occasional weekend.

The buzzing of her phone broke her thoughts. It was worth leaving the office just to get away from that annoying buzz.

"Hello," she said begrudgingly, kicking herself for not just grabbing her purse and walking out. She wasn't in the mood for a crisis.

"Hello, Paige."

"Oh, great," she muttered under her breath, then said, "Hello, Mark."

CHAPTER EIGHTEEN

"Bet you don't remember what day it is?" he asked.

Paige didn't answer for a moment. She knew what day it was. It was the first of October. "It's Tuesday. At least that's what my calendar says," she finally said.

He spoke with annoying enthusiasm. "It's our anniversary today. Or *was,* I guess I should say." He chuckled, which annoyed Paige even more. He always thought he was so charming. She'd fallen for it once, but now whenever he tried to be charming with her she just wanted to throw up.

"It is?" Paige answered, not sure what he expected her to say or do.

He laughed. "Come on," he said. "This day is still special to me."

She shook her head. "Mark, why do you do this every year? You didn't even remember our anniversary when we were married. Why do you remember it now?"

"Paige, we may not still be married, but that doesn't mean I don't still care about you. You're the mother of my son. We spent some really great years together."

And some really crummy ones, too, she wanted to add.

"And . . ." she said, wondering what the point was.

"So I just wanted to let you know I was thinking about you today."

"I'm glad, Mark," she said. "By the way, how's Brindy?" Paige wanted to highlight the fact that he shouldn't be calling her when he had someone else in his life.

"She's great. That's another reason I'm calling."

"Yes?" she asked, shoving her feet into her shoes. Somehow she had to tell him good-bye and get out of there. He was apparently under the impression that their divorce had been amicable, but it was just that she'd never really told him what she thought. For Jared's sake, she didn't want him to suffer just because his parents had divorced. But amicable?

"We have some exciting news."

He really was asking a lot. Not only did he think they were on friendly terms, but he was dense enough to think she would ever be excited for anything good that happened to him.

Bitter? Yes, she was.

"What's that?"

"Brindy and I are getting married in Vegas this weekend."

"That's nice," she said, her voice hollow and empty.

"But that's not all."

Paige really didn't want to hear the rest, but she had no choice.

"Brindy's expecting."

"Expecting what?" Paige said with sarcasm, aghast at the thought of him being a father again.

"A baby," he said with a laugh. "She's due next May."

"Congratulations," Paige said, reaching the end of her cordiality rope. "You know what, Mark? You caught me on my way out of the office."

"That's okay, I've got to run too. I've still got to call my travel agent and book some flights to Hawaii for our honeymoon."

"Good-bye, Mark," she said, and hung up.

She shut her eyes and blew out a long breath. A baby?

* * *

Friday after work, Paige literally collapsed on the couch when she got home.

Lance had not only been distant since their dinner date, he'd also become less cooperative and willing to take on assignments from Paige. She felt his resistance and knew it was because of the kiss she'd refused him. Male ego. Wounded pride. Lance was letting her know what he thought of her by his actions, and Paige had finally had enough.

She'd called him into her office just before closing to confront him about it, telling him that she enjoyed working with him and had great respect for his creative ability and work ethic. She said that she hated to see their working relationship damaged by something that had happened outside of the office—something he'd assumed and attempted of his own volition, not by her invitation.

She'd only succeeded in fueling his frustration and fanning his anger. He wasn't about to admit that she'd damaged his pride. He acted as if he didn't know what she was talking about, and then laughed sardonically that she even thought such a thing. She'd tried to explain that she was just reading his actions as a signal that he wasn't comfortable around her, and she hoped that they could put what happened behind them.

He'd only shrugged and said, "Whatever." Paige didn't deal well with discord and knew that unless he got over whatever was bothering him, they couldn't continue working together.

With her arm covering her eyes, she lay lifeless on the couch. Why did there have to be an obstacle around every corner? Sometimes she felt like she was in a maze filled with dead ends and pitfalls.

The phone rang, and Paige groaned. She wasn't in the mood to answer it just in case it was a treat comparable to the phone call earlier that day. So she let it ring.

But try as she might, she couldn't ignore it. Curiosity got the best of her, and she strained to listen as the machine clicked on.

After the recorded message played, a man's voice came on.

"Hi, Paige, sorry I missed you . . ."

It was Dalton!

"I took an earlier flight and just got in town and wondered if you had plans for dinner."

Paige flew off of the couch and succeeded in ramming her shin into the corner of the coffee table as she charged for the phone. Fighting the urge to cry out in pain, she reached for the phone and said, "Hello?"

"Oh, you're home," he said.

Wincing, Paige rubbed the growing bump on her shin bone and said, "I just got in. Where are you?"

"I'm at the Marriott in downtown Salt Lake. I was just thinking about getting some dinner and wondered if you'd join me."

The pain vanished. Paige could only think about being with Dalton again. He would definitely be a bright spot in her dreary day.

"I need time to freshen up and change," she said. *And putty my leg,* she thought as she ran her fingers up and down her shin.

"No hurry," he replied. "I'm just getting unpacked myself."

"Do you want me to meet you downtown?"

"No, no, why don't you let me pick you up? I'm sure there's somewhere good to eat out by you, isn't there?"

"Do you like Italian?"

"My favorite," he said.

"There's a wonderful place called Bellini's. I've never tasted better Italian food than theirs."

"Sounds perfect."

Paige gave Dalton directions, and they decided to meet in an hour. Before jumping into the shower, Paige phoned the restaurant and made reservations, knowing that Friday nights got busy. She also asked for seats on the outdoor terrace with a view of the west side that included downtown Salt Lake City and the silver reflection of the Great Salt Lake. It was by far the most romantic spot in the area as well as Paige's favorite place to eat. After hanging up the phone, Paige held both hands over her stomach as her nerves bunched and twisted her insides, nerves that teetered on the edge of fear.

Truth be told, she enjoyed Dalton's companionship immensely. She loved his sense of humor and how comfortable she felt around him. Feeling that way around a man surprised her more than anything. She never thought she would ever venture far enough into a relationship for it to be considered even "friends," let alone "dating," but here she was, getting ready to go out to dinner with Dalton.

"Stop thinking about it," she told herself out loud as she turned on the water in the shower. But she couldn't stop herself. Where was this relationship heading? Most women, most "normal" women, would just enjoy the journey and let the relationship follow its natural course, but she wasn't like that. She wondered what Dalton was thinking. Did he like her? He must, or he wouldn't call. But he had so many other girlfriends—so many gorgeous girlfriends.

Her very own husband had rejected her. Why would a man she was merely dating want to further a relationship with her? And for that matter, what was she doing spending more time with Dalton anyway? All it was doing was complicating things. She wasn't up to getting involved with anyone, not after all she'd been through with Mark. Her heart couldn't take it.

There was just one problem. When she was with Dalton, she felt happier than she felt in years.

Steam from the hot water coated the mirror, blurring her reflection, matching the haze of emotions inside of her. There was only one thing she knew to do, one place she could turn to for help.

Sinking to her knees there on the bathroom floor, she bowed her head and uttered an earnest prayer for help from above. She'd learned long ago that the only way she could face her fears and get through her challenges was to turn to her Father in Heaven. He was always there for her. His comfort and love strengthened her.

* * *

Paige doubted she'd be able to get through a meal with her stomach in knots, but once she was with Dalton, her nervousness disappeared. They laughed together over memories of Disneyland and Relief Society casseroles. They shared concerns about their children, but most of all, they found enjoyment in each other's company.

After their meal, they shared a scrumptious piece of cheesecake with fresh raspberries. The dessert wasn't Italian, but it was a favorite of both of theirs.

"I can't eat another bite," Paige said, setting down her fork. She'd eaten way too much, but the meal had been so delicious and Dalton's company so relaxing.

"Look at that sunset," Dalton said as the brilliant rays of the sun ignited the clouds in a display of crimson and fiery orange.

It was indeed glorious, made only better by Dalton reaching across the table and taking Paige's hand in hers as they watched.

"There should be a law for people to stop whatever they're doing and watch a sunset like that," Dalton said.

Paige smiled. "I'm glad we could see it."

"How could a person see such a sight and not wonder about the Creator? Something that perfect and magnificent isn't by accident," he said. "And those mountains," he said, scanning the entire valley. "We take so much for granted . . ." His voice faded to a whisper.

Paige knew that was true and that she was as guilty as anyone for not stopping to smell the roses, to watch the sunset, to appreciate the changing leaves. Sometimes she was so wrapped up in her own challenges that she failed to recognize the blessings around her.

"Like freedom?" she asked him.

A look of pain crossed his eyes. With a slow nod, he said, "We probably take that for granted the most. Americans don't know what it's like to live in a country without freedom, without choice. If they did, they would hate it. They would do anything in their power to stop it, change it, or get away from it. Anything."

"I used to watch kids at Jared's ball games during the national anthem," Paige told him. "They wouldn't even put their hands over their hearts or stop talking and goofing around long enough to look at the flag."

Dalton nodded. "We're so much like the people in the Book of Mormon. When times are good and things are plentiful, we forget about what's really important. We even forget about God. Too often, it takes some kind of catastrophe or disaster or war to make people wake up. After something like that, you never take things for granted."

"Do you look at things differently since the war?" she asked.

He didn't answer for a moment, then took a breath, released it slowly, and said, "There was a time when I was in prison that I finally accepted the fact that I would probably die in there. I realized I possibly would never see outside of those prison walls again. I'd never see . . ." he looked to the west, where the last rays of sun were disappearing below the horizon, ". . . another sunset, or hug my mother, or taste ice cream, or take a warm shower."

Paige gave his hand a squeeze.

"It wasn't an act of defeat," he qualified his comment. "It was an act of acceptance. Until that day, the hope of being released nearly drove me crazy. I lived in denial. I didn't want to believe what was happening to me, where I was. The day I finally accepted my circumstances was the day I finally got peace back in my life without taking away hope. And once that happened, I was able to make the best of the situation instead of beat my head against the wall about it."

"That would take a great deal of inner strength," she remarked.

"The only way I did it was with God's help. His companionship and blessings have been the difference between a productive life and a destructive life. No one can see and experience the horrors of war that we did and not be changed and scarred for life. I still have challenges—I don't think I've had a full night's sleep since my return—and my dreams are haunted by my memories, but at least I can function and contribute to society."

Paige swallowed a knot that had formed in her throat as she listened to him talk. She remembered Skyler telling her about the nightmares and the nightly pacing.

"I have so much, and I am so grateful for all I have and every day I'm alive. I think about all of my buddies who died . . ." His voice cracked and he cleared his throat before continuing. "And I wonder, why not me? Why did I survive? I may never know the reason, but what matters is what I do with the blessing of life God gave me and what I learned from everything I went through."

Paige looked at him with wonder and respect. He *was* a special man. His life and his testimony touched and influenced the lives of many people. She knew this because he had touched hers.

* * *

"Would you like to come in?" she asked Dalton when he pulled up to the house after dinner. "There's something I'd like to show you."

After parking the car, he got out, walked around to her side, and opened the door for her, a gesture Paige had decided she liked a lot.

Dalton complimented her on her yard. Even though it was tiny, she kept it well manicured and the flower beds weeded. Her home wasn't extravagant, but it was cozy and clean and inviting.

Once inside, she showed him to the living room. "Have a seat," she offered. "I'll be right back."

She scurried to her bedroom and found the item she wanted to show him, then returned to find Dalton looking at pictures on the wall. Most of them were of Jared—some alone, some with friends, some with her. There was one, though, with Jared and his father.

"Who's that?"

"Oh," she grimaced, "that's Jared's father."

Dalton nodded. "I take it you're not fond of him."

"You could say that," Paige replied, holding a white envelope out to him. The last thing she wanted to do was get into a discussion about Mark. "Here, why don't we sit down?"

"What's this?"

"Look inside."

Dalton lifted the flap of the envelope and gasped. "My bracelet. I mean, your bracelet with my name on it." He read his name again, then saw the letters inside the envelope.

"This one's from your brother," she said, showing him the first letter. "And this one is the recent one from your mother."

Dalton took a moment and read the first letter. His expression seemed pinched with pain. She wondered if unwanted memories were surfacing.

He then read the second letter and chuckled. "That's my mom, all right."

He folded the letters and put them back inside the envelope.

"Are you okay?" she asked.

"Yes." He nodded slowly. "This is all so amazing, isn't it?"

"What do you mean?"

"You wearing my bracelet and wanting to find out if I'd made it out alive. And now, here we are, like old friends."

"I feel the same," she said. "I have to be honest, though. Jared was the one who pushed me to find out. I thought it might be too weird to show up on your doorstep. I wasn't sure what to expect."

"You know what?" he said, looking directly into her eyes. "I'm really glad that you did."

Paige smiled, feeling shy. "Me too."

He handed the bracelet back to her. "It's amazing how detailed the memories come back when something triggers them. Almost too detailed, like smells and sounds."

"Like what?"

He settled back into the cushion of the couch. "I don't know, like sometimes when I'm outside working in the yard and it's unusually hot and muggy, the smell of earth, sweat, and even some of the plants in my yard bring back sudden memories. Or the Fourth of July."

"Really?"

"I have a hard time with fireworks. I sit through them for Skyler's sake, but the noise is difficult for me. There were times in Nam when you'd have rifles and machine guns and mortars and grenades rattling, banging, and booming all around you. I remember being in a foxhole with two batteries of 105mm howitzers. Twelve big guns located on a landing zone five miles away were firing nonstop, their shells exploding and shaking the ground beneath us. It was deafening . . ." He looked at her. "And terrifying. Even though the recon missions were intense and dangerous, I preferred them over battle."

"What were they like?"

"I spent some time deep in the mountains with the Montagnard villagers. Walking through the jungle to get to these villages was like walking through Hades itself. The heat was unbearable. We fought our way through brush and vines so thick and thorny that every step was an effort. It would take four hours to cover three hundred yards. Then, we'd either get wet from crossing a mountain stream or from an afternoon thundershower and we'd be wet and freezing all night."

"How did you sleep? How did you eat?"

"Sleep was difficult, and so was eating. At night, ants crawled all over us—inside our clothes and ears and eyes. If we didn't move much, they were okay, but if we moved they bit us. Eating was another story. We used C-4 plastic explosive from our emergency supply packs to boil up a canteen of water."

"Plastic explosives?"

"Yeah. If you were careful, it could heat the water in thirty seconds, for soup, coffee, or oatmeal. If you were careless, it could blow off your arm."

Paige winced.

Dalton's expression grew alarmed. "I'm sorry. I'm sure you don't appreciate hearing about this."

"No," she assured him. "I do. It's fascinating, but so horrible." She couldn't help reaching out a hand to him. "Please, don't stop. Tell me—how were you captured?"

He shut his eyes, and the muscles in his face tensed, as if the question drove a piercing ache through his heart.

"I'm sorry," she said. "I didn't mean to pry."

"No." He released a weary sigh. "It's good for me to talk about it. Besides, there aren't too many people who will sit and listen. I'm grateful to you for being interested."

"I am interested," she told him, and she did want to find out more about this man who had experienced more pain and destruction than any ten people in an entire lifetime.

He recounted his experience to her, every tactile detail still fresh in his mind. But with each word, his emotions grew deeper, his story more difficult to relate.

"It happened so fast it was almost over before we knew it. All six men who were with me that day died. I was the last one to see them alive." He closed his eyes and pulled in a ragged breath. "Not a day goes by that I don't think of those men. Brave, good men—heroes in every sense of the word. I still see their faces, their eyes, looking at me for the signal, willing to give everything they had for their country."

Paige nodded as tears stung her eyes.

"And every day, I battle the guilt I feel that my life was spared and theirs were taken. I think of everything that happened—the shooting, the prison, the bloodshed—but the one thing I can't get past is their faces. It was all because of me that they died."

Paige reached out toward him. He opened his arms and accepted her hug as he struggled to choke down the emotion building up inside of him.

Paige had read about survivor's guilt. She understood Dalton's feelings, but wished she could help him understand that he couldn't take responsibility for what happened to his men.

"I know I can't change what happened," he struggled to say, "but I vowed that I would never let their deaths be in vain. I promised that I would do everything in my power to keep their memories alive."

He pulled away from her, clearing his throat and wiping the moisture at the corners of his eyes.

"I wrote a long letter to each man's parents. I wanted them to know that it had been a privilege to serve with their sons, and that those men had died with honor."

Keeping hold of one of his hands, Paige gave it a gentle squeeze. She yearned to comfort him, but she knew her words were feeble attempts at comfort, unable to explain her feelings or change his.

He shook his head and gave her a weak smile. "It's been such a long time. You'd think I would have been able to get past all of this and forget about it by now."

"I don't see how you could ever forget about something like that," she told him. "In fact, I think it would be wrong if you did. What you're doing now with your life, like talking to others, touching people's lives with your story, telling them what you've learned through all of it, is the greatest tribute you can pay to yourself and those men."

His smile broadened. "I hope so."

"It's true," she said. "God spared you for a reason—you've said that yourself. I guess that doesn't make it easier to accept what happened, but it certainly helps make sense out of it."

"I think God did something else for me too," Dalton said.

"What's that?"

"He brought somebody wonderful into my life."

Paige nodded, thinking he was talking about his wife. "Soon Lee sounds like an amazing woman."

"She was," Dalton agreed. "But I wasn't talking about her."

CHAPTER NINETEEN

Paige dipped her chin, feeling her cheeks flush with color.

Dalton lifted her chin with his finger so he could look her in the eyes. "It's true. I've always believed that our lives are in God's hands, that He guides our paths. We just have to have the faith and the strength to endure the journey. Paige," he gave her a wink and a smile, "He's brought us together for a reason. It wasn't by chance that you found that bracelet when you did and that your son went to school near the place I live."

"I know," Paige said softly. "I believe that too."

"It's been a long time since I've felt so comfortable with another person, especially a woman."

Paige couldn't help the way her eyebrows arched with doubt. With all the women he'd dated, he didn't feel comfortable with *any* of them? It was hard to believe.

"What?" Dalton responded to her questioning look.

"Nothing," she replied. "It's just that Skyler mentioned to me about all of your girlfriends."

"All of my girlfriends?"

"That's the impression I got."

Dalton looked irritated.

"Don't be too hard on her," Paige continued. "She confided in me because she doesn't see me as a threat like she sees those other women. I think she just considers me a friend, and I like that."

Dalton smiled. "I like that too. She needs a friend like you—someone wiser, an adult she'll take advice from and listen to."

"I'm glad. She's such a great girl."

Shaking his head, Dalton looked at Paige and smiled. "But she's exaggerating, you know. I don't have a lot of girlfriends. In fact, I don't have any girlfriends."

Paige's expression must have revealed her doubt because he quickly added, "I mean, someone I date regularly."

She smiled, thinking how cute he was when he was embarrassed.

"It is nice to hear that you like my daughter. Skyler has been called everything from a brat to evil."

Paige shook her head. "She's a great kid. The people who are saying those things about her haven't taken the time to get to know her. If they had, they wouldn't feel that way."

Dalton's smile broadened. "You really are something, you know that?"

Paige returned his smile, but sudden tears stung her eyes.

"What?" He grew alarmed. "Paige, I didn't mean to say anything to upset you."

"You didn't," she answered, feeling foolish as she wiped at her eyes. "It's just that I think that's why I can relate so well to Skyler. Except for Lou and her family, I've never had anyone take time to get to know me—you know, care about what I had to say or what I was feeling. My ex-husband didn't even bother when we were married. My boss really hasn't until recently." She looked at Dalton, noting the kindness in his blue eyes. "Until I met you, I didn't think I had anything worth saying, but you always make me feel as though what I say matters."

Dalton stroked her cheek. "Paige, you're a very intelligent, kind, and caring woman. You're strong and independent. And you're very beautiful, inside and out."

"Thank you," Paige said, once again feeling color rise to her cheeks. She knew she wasn't beautiful, but when he said it, it made her feel that way.

For a moment they remained locked in each other's gaze, in a connection so strong it went straight to Paige's heart, making it beat faster. Her palms grew clammy, her breath weak.

She felt a sudden need to change their conversation. "I have some lemonade in the fridge. Would you like something to drink?"

Dalton accepted and followed her to the kitchen, where she filled tall glasses with crystal-fresh lemonade.

After a few sips, Dalton said, "You don't happen to have anything salty, do you?"

"Salty, like chips or something?"

"Chips would be great. It's like when I have a milk shake . . ."

"And you want french fries to go with it?"

"Exactly."

She went to the pantry, where she found a bag of pretzels and a bag of chips. "The chips are barbecue flavored," she said, handing them to him.

"Even better," he said. He accepted the bag and dug in, relishing one of the heavily spiced chips. "Mmm, delicious."

Paige also had one and followed it with a sip from her lemonade. "I shouldn't have done that."

"Why?"

"Because I can't stop after one chip."

"Me neither—especially barbecued ones."

They munched and chatted, sipped and laughed, the minutes slipping by unnoticed. Paige found herself lost in the joy of conversation with someone who was both interesting and interested in what she had to say.

"So," Dalton said, licking his fingers, then pushing the bag of chips away, "you've pretty much heard my life story. What about you? All I know about you is that you have an outstanding son, you had a difficult marriage, which ended in divorce, and you have an amazing creative talent." He tilted his head and looked at her, studying her face. "Even though I feel I know you so well, I don't really know all that much about you."

Paige met his imploring expression and marveled that he would even care about her life. But his sincere desire to know her better unlocked the closed doors in her heart, releasing feelings and memories she'd kept hidden deep inside.

She began by telling him about her family, her parents' divorce, and her brothers. It wasn't as difficult as she'd thought it would be to tell him about Mark. And in all truth, as she reflected on it, their courtship and marriage had been remarkably romantic and sweet. Mark had taken her to the temple. Even though he hadn't served a mission and had to make big changes in his life to be worthy to marry her there, he'd made sincere efforts to prepare himself so they could be sealed together forever.

But the change hadn't even lasted a year. At first his excuses to miss church on Sundays were occasional, but with each passing month he missed more and more often until he finally quit going altogether. Even when Jared was born, he didn't make any better effort to go with them as a family. When Jared was eight, it was their home teacher, not Mark, who baptized Jared.

"I knew things weren't good between us," she told Dalton. "And I'd talked with Mark about going to a counselor together, but then I got diagnosed with breast cancer."

"Paige," he said, looking at her with sincere concern.

"I'm fine now. I'm doing really well," she assured him.

Dalton sighed in relief, then glanced at her. "I have to admit, I thought it was amazing how you could relate to Lou and what she was going through. I wondered if you'd worked as a nurse or something."

"Nope," she replied, "just been through it myself."

"Was it hard on your marriage?"

"It was pretty much the final straw. Instead of bringing us closer together, it drove us completely apart."

"That must have been so hard, especially since that was when you needed your husband the most."

Paige couldn't really even think about it without remembering the pain and loneliness of those months during chemo. She'd felt so crummy, so down and distraught, so hopeless.

"Lou helped me a lot," Paige told him. "She was always just a phone call away. Jared, too. He took care of me, helped me to the bathroom to throw up, drove me to my doctor's appointments. Through it all, I rarely missed any of his basketball games."

"That's amazing," Dalton said.

"It really is when I think back about it. I'm not sure how I even did it."

"The human spirit is a powerful thing," he said.

Looking at him, a survivor of the Hanoi Hilton and the Vietnam War, she knew he spoke from experience.

"Is it hard to talk about, or can you tell me what the treatments were like?" Dalton looked at her with care and concern in his eyes.

Again, even though this wasn't a subject she was fond of discussing, she found herself opening up to him, sharing her deepest feelings, feelings she'd kept buried deep inside, feelings that now surfaced. Talking about them seemed to make them lighter and even disappear altogether.

"With radiation, the worst problems were the sore throat and this horrible sensation of burning skin. With chemo, it was everything— nausea, depression, weakness, hair loss . . . I didn't make a very attractive bald woman, I'll tell you that."

A pained expression crossed Dalton's face.

"Then there were the months of tamoxifen, which kept me feeling lousy most of the time." She knew her experiences were gruesome, but she felt compelled to be honest about her health. "I'm not considered 'healed,' but I've improved my odds of not getting cancer again." She looked at him, studied his expression, waiting to see the interest leave his eyes and to hear his excuses for why he suddenly needed to leave. But none came. There was no change in his expression.

"How did you deal with it?"

"The same as you," she said, looking at him directly, sensing understanding and kindness. "For a while I felt like having cancer defined who I was. I was the sister in the ward who had cancer, or the woman at work battling cancer, or the bald lady at the store who had cancer. I finally got sick of being sick and faced the reality that even though my illness finished off my marriage, I still had a son who depended on me."

"What made you change?"

"Most of it came about when Jared started having trouble at school and coming in late at night. He was either agitated or exhausted when he was home, and even though I was sick, I wasn't stupid. I knew he was struggling with my illness in his own way."

"Was Mark still around to help?"

"His belongings were still at the house, but he didn't spend any more time with us than he had to. Finally, one day while I was lying there fighting off the nausea," she stopped and took a breath to steady her emotions, "I took inventory of my life. Here I was, basically on death's doorstep, my husband had deserted me, and my son was becoming a juvenile delinquent. I hated my life."

"What did you do?"

"Up to that point the only thing I was able to do while lying in bed was listen to music. It's funny because I wasn't a super spiritual person before my diagnosis, but after it, all I wanted to listen to were instrumental hymns and Mormon Tabernacle Choir music. I also listened to scriptures on tape. This probably doesn't make sense, but those were the things that seemed to soothe my stomach and calm my body. I came to love many of the hymns not only for their sweet melodies, but also for their words of comfort and hope. And the scriptures . . ." Paige choked up and had to stop and clear her throat so she could go on. "You have to understand, I read regularly before, but it was nothing like during my treatments when I listened to the scriptures for hours. I went through all the standard works while I was ill—the Book of Mormon twice."

"Wow," Dalton said. "It takes me a year to get through the Book of Mormon once."

"There were many times that the words jumped out and grabbed me. I wasn't just hearing them with my ears, I was understanding them in my heart. There was one that helped me finally stop and make that 180-degree turn."

"Which one was that?"

"In section 58 of the Doctrine and Covenants," she said. "When I heard these two verses, it honestly was the most spiritual . . ." She had to stop again and blink several times to stop tears from forming. "I'm sorry."

Dalton stroked her arm with his hand while she gathered her strength to go on.

"I had been praying for help, for perspective. Because I had lost the will to try any longer, I didn't have any fight left in me. Sometimes I actually felt like there wasn't anything worth living for." She felt ashamed for admitting her weakness, but she didn't feel as though Dalton would judge her. Somehow she knew he understood. "It was then, at my lowest point, that I heard the words to these verses, words I'd heard before but that finally made sense to me."

"What were they?"

"I listened to them so many times I memorized them so that when I couldn't listen to the CDs, I could at least say the words in my mind. The verses are three and four of that section. They say, 'Ye *cannot behold with your natural eyes, for the present time, the design of your God concerning those things which shall come hereafter, and the glory which shall follow after much tribulation. For after much tribulation come the blessings. Wherefore the day cometh that ye shall be crowned with much glory; the hour is not yet, but is nigh at hand.'* That was all I needed to hear," she told him. "I suddenly realized that although I couldn't see the purpose of what I was going through, I didn't need to. I just needed to be reminded that my life was in God's hands and to have faith that things would work out. That didn't mean it would be easy, though," she said with a chuckle.

Dalton's gentle laughter joined hers. He nodded with complete understanding.

"I just needed a glimmer of hope, no matter how small—a light at the end of the tunnel. And that's what this scripture gave me."

"Then what happened?"

"It was like a seed was planted inside of me that grew stronger and stronger each day. I finally took charge of my life again and began to care, to want to get better. I wanted to live. I got more involved in my treatment, and I made myself go back to work for as many hours a day as I could. I was showered and dressed when Jared came home from school, and I had dinner ready each night. Basically, I made myself start living again. I realized that regardless of whether I lived or died, I wanted my days on earth to be as good as they could be. I wanted to leave my son with good memories. But, still, sometimes I can't help but wonder if . . ." She suddenly realized she was probably giving Dalton much more information than he really needed or wanted to know.

"Yes?" he asked.

"Oh, it's nothing really," she replied. "More chips?"

"Paige, what was it you were going to tell me?"

He evidently wasn't going to let her stop there, so she finished her thoughts. "I just sometimes wonder if I would have been stronger sooner, handled my surgery and the treatments better, maybe my marriage would have stayed together. I mean, I pretty much thought about myself and my needs most of the time."

Dalton gave her a skeptical eye. "Paige, are you saying that you still should have been a model wife and mother while you were fighting for your very life?"

Paige looked down, knowing it sounded irrational but nonetheless believing it in the corners of her mind.

He reached for her hand. "What did your husband do while you were lying in bed as sick as you were?"

"He was having an affair," she said bluntly.

Dalton raised his eyebrows. "How thoughtful of him."

"Like I said, we just didn't have the kind of relationship that could handle a trial like this. Every problem we had in our marriage before the cancer seemed even worse after."

Dalton nodded and let her continue. "How do you feel about everything now?"

"Well," she said with a thoughtful sigh, "I know that even though life still has its challenges, I'm very glad to be alive. I'm glad I got to become the woman I am now, because really," she smiled proudly, "I like myself better for who I am."

Dalton gave her an encouraging smile.

"I also feel blessed to have been given another chance at life. I believe that I will have to account for the extra time I've been given."

Dalton gave a nod of agreement.

"I feel like I need to do much more with my life than I'm doing now—you know, handle some of the things I'm struggling with better than I'm handling them," she said, not mentioning her scarred chest, "but I'm growing and coming to terms with certain things, and I know I'm going to be okay."

After she stopped talking, they remained in silence, looking at each other, appreciating the moment of understanding, each knowing full well of suffering and pain, of loss and discouragement, but also of finding faith and strength again.

And soon, as natural as the changing of the leaves or the waves of the sea, the physical gap between them grew smaller and smaller until for a brief but wonderful moment, their lips touched and their hearts spoke.

* * *

Saturday morning dawned beautiful and clear. Paige was up early even though it had been after one in the morning before she'd gone to bed the night before. Pulling her robe tightly around her, she walked outside to get the morning paper and stopped to watch the sun rise above the majestic Rocky Mountains to the east.

The nip of fall was in the air, but its refreshing crispness filled her lungs, energizing her soul.

Dalton. He was the last thing she'd thought of the night before and the first thing she'd thought of that morning when she woke up.

How wonderful, how refreshing, to have someone to talk to, someone whose focus and attention was right there, not wandering or distracted or divided among a dozen other demands. Just there.

She hugged the paper to her chest.

And he'd kissed her.

She blushed. If Lou knew about the kiss, she'd be having an absolute conniption.

Paige had almost forgotten how thrilling a kiss could be, especially one so sweet and tender as Dalton's had been. Just thinking about it now made her heart race.

The phone rang inside the house, and she hurried in to answer it.

"Hello?" she answered breathlessly, almost positive who it was going to be.

"Good morning," Dalton said. "Were you out jogging?"

Paige burst out laughing. If he only knew how much she hated jogging. "I just went out to get the paper."

"How far did you have to go to get it?"

She laughed again. "The end of the front walk. I just ran in to answer the phone because I didn't want to miss your call."

"How did you know it was me?"

"I didn't," she said, "but I was hoping."

"I was afraid I'd wake you."

"I couldn't sleep."

"Me neither. What are you doing?"

"I was going to get something to eat and read the newspaper."

"Oh," he said.

"Why?" she asked, noting his disappointment.

"I was hoping I could talk you into going out to breakfast with me."

"And give up my bowl of Raisin Bran? That's a lot to ask," she teased. "I'd love to go to breakfast."

"And we're still on for conference this afternoon?"

"I'm looking forward to it." She'd been excited when he'd invited her to attend the afternoon session of general conference with him. She hadn't yet been to the new Conference Center.

"Are you sure you won't mind if I monopolize most of your day?"

"Well, I will have to reschedule my massage and pedicure at the spa and cancel my plans for the theater, but . . ."

"I'm sorry, I didn't realize—"

"Dalton," she said, "I'm kidding. I was going to plant some bulbs and rake leaves. Believe me, that will wait until next week."

"You're sure?"

"I'm absolutely sure."

They made plans for breakfast, and Paige hurried to the shower, a swarm of butterflies filling her stomach. She felt so happy inside she couldn't stop smiling.

She told herself to calm down and take things slowly, but it felt so good to be excited and alive she just wanted to enjoy it, at least for today. Instead of overanalyzing what was going on between her and Dalton, she just wanted to enjoy it. She could think about it later.

There was one thing she did think about though—moving to California. A lot of good things were happening in Salt Lake, but her heart just wasn't there anymore.

CHAPTER TWENTY

So far the day had been as wonderful as Paige had wanted it to be. Breakfast was enjoyable, and Paige was still amazed at how much she and Dalton had to talk about. Skyler and Jared were always big topics of discussion, and the best part was that Dalton thought as much of Jared as she thought of Skyler.

Between breakfast and the two o'clock conference session, they wandered the mall in downtown Salt Lake, window shopping and grabbing a bite for lunch. While they lingered over Caesar salads and tropical smoothies, Dalton's cell phone rang. It was Skyler. Paige tried to act interested in her salad, but couldn't help overhearing the conversation and the concern in Dalton's voice.

"You know how I feel about those kids, Sky," he told his daughter.

Paige stabbed at a crouton with her fork and put it in her mouth. "What did Abigail's mother say?"

Paige chewed and swallowed, counting her blessings that Jared was past his teen years. Then she thought of Nate and rolled her eyes. Maybe she was kidding herself.

"All right. You can go, but you have to be in before midnight." He was obviously not happy about whatever it was he was giving permission for. "Anything else?"

He listened for a minute, his face taking on a curious look. "She did? What did she want?"

Paige tuned in to every word he was saying as she attempted to drain the last drops of her smoothie from the cup to appear uninterested in the conversation.

"I'll get in touch with her when I get home," he answered, then listened for another moment. "Actually, she's right here, do you want to say hi?"

He offered the phone to Paige. "Skyler wants to say hi."

Paige brightened, and she took the phone. "Hey, Sky, how are you?"

"Hi, Paige. Are you and my dad having fun?"

"We've had a really fun day. We're going to conference in a few minutes. How about you?"

"I'm having a blast with Abigail. Dad's letting me go with some friends tonight to Remix. It's a dance club. I'm so excited."

"A club?"

"It's for high school–age kids. There's no drinking allowed. They have security and all that, so it's cool."

"Still, you be careful. Sometimes you don't have to go looking for trouble in order for it to find you."

"I know. I will," Skyler said.

"How's dance coming?"

"It's awesome," Skyler declared with enthusiasm. "I'm glad you talked me into trying it again. Miss Mandy is working so hard with me. You have to come to the competition. It's on the twenty-fifth."

"I'll try, okay?"

"Okay, good," Skyler said. "'Cause maybe if Darlene knows you're coming, she won't come."

"Oh?" Paige said, not wanting to tip off Dalton about what Skyler was telling her.

"Yeah, she's been calling to talk to Dad and stuff, and every time I answer the phone, she sits and talks to me and asks me all these questions and pretends she's really interested in what I'm doing."

"And you don't buy it?"

"Not for a second. It's just a show to impress Dad. I think she wants him back."

Paige didn't know what to say. She certainly wasn't in a position to find out more information about the situation, even though she wanted to.

"I just hope Dad's not stupid enough to fall for her again," Skyler said. "She burned him big-time when she broke off their engagement."

"Oh, I see," Paige said, stunned and at a loss for words.

"I felt bad for him because he really loved her, and I know she hurt him. But I was glad it ended."

Paige chuckled. "That bad, huh?"

"Darlene wanted my dad, but she didn't want me. I knew that, and I'll be honest, I probably got into more trouble than I should have because I wanted to do everything I could to drive her away."

"Skyler, is that true?"

"Hey, it's been hard enough with my mom gone. We don't need Darlene to make things worse."

Paige wondered if Dalton knew his daughter had been so manipulative with his relationship.

"I feel kind of guilty about it, though," Skyler continued. "I mean, what if he would have been really happy with her? I want my dad to be happy . . . just not with her. I don't know if I'll ever be ready for someone to take my mother's place. I can't stand the thought of my dad with another woman."

Paige didn't respond.

"Well, I gotta go. I'll see you on the twenty-fifth?"

"I'll try," Paige said, unable to promise more than that. If Darlene were back in the picture, she didn't want to put herself in an awkward situation no matter how badly she wanted to support Skyler.

Again, she remembered her vow not to get hurt again.

But how could she walk away from someone as wonderful as Dalton?

* * *

The conversation with Skyler put a damper on Paige's mood, but she managed to cheer up when they took their seats in the immense Conference Center, where they sat close enough to the front that they could clearly see the prophet and other leaders of the Church. As usual, the messages and spirit of the meeting lifted the concerns and worries from Paige's heart and mind and fed her soul. She felt inspired and strengthened by words of hope and comfort.

On their way out of the session, Dalton and Paige heard someone calling his name.

"Lieutenant Mac?" a voice called out over the crowd of people. "Lieutenant?"

Dalton's head snapped up and turned toward the voice.

"Did you hear that?" he asked Paige when he didn't locate who it was.

"I heard someone calling for Lieutenant Mac," she said.

He nodded. "That was my nickname during the war. I haven't heard that name in years."

"Lieutenant!" the voice called again.

This time, both Paige and Dalton scanned the swarm of people and saw a man standing on a cement wall waving his arms.

Dalton squinted to get a better look.

"Do you know him?" Paige asked.

"He kind of looks familiar, but I can't place the face. Guess I should go see who it is. Do you mind?"

"Not at all," Paige said.

Dalton took her hand and led her through the masses until they got close to the man on the wall.

"Lieutenant!" the guy exclaimed as he jumped down from the wall. "I knew that was you."

He approached Dalton with outstretched arms and bear hugged Dalton, lifting him off the ground.

"This is amazing, just amazing," the astounded man said. Paige guessed that at one time he was probably a linebacker because he was tall and wide shouldered, with a flattop buzz cut and a scar on his chin and eyebrow.

"I'm sorry," Dalton said when the man released him. "I can't seem to—"

"Brewster," the man said in a booming voice. "Hobart Brewster."

"Brewster," Dalton repeated, obviously trying to place the name.

"Maybe you remember my nickname. The guys called me Brewsky."

Dalton's eyes grew wide. "Brewsky! Of course I remember you." He turned to Paige. "This guy saved my life."

Paige's eyebrows lifted in surprise.

"Not at all, sir," Hobart said. "I was just doing my duty."

Dalton shook his head. "I literally fell into this guy's arms when we were released from the Hanoi prison. All I remembered was coming off the truck with the other prisoners and seeing this big brute waiting there to take us to the hospital."

"It took him four days to wake up," Hobart said. "We weren't sure he was going to make it, but he did, and here you are."

"I can't believe you recognized me, especially in such a big crowd. What are you—"

"Doing here?" Hobart finished his sentence.

Dalton nodded.

"I just went to conference. I'm a Mormon."

Dalton looked shocked, glancing from Hobart to Paige, then back again.

Hobart laughed, a deep, hearty belly laugh. Paige guessed her expression must have reflected her confusion because the man went on to explain the cause of his laughter and Dalton's surprise.

"You see . . ."

"Oh, by the way, this is my friend Paige," Dalton introduced her quickly.

"Nice to meet you, Paige. The reason Lieutenant Mac here is so dumbfounded about my news is because, well . . . because I was known to do a bit of drinking over in Nam."

"A bit!" Dalton interjected.

Hobart chuckled. "Okay, all right, I was drunk every chance I got," he told her. "I'm not proud of it, but hey, it helped me survive that crazy war, and I'm living proof that people can change. I've been sober for over twenty years. Got a wife and three kids," he said. "My wife's mother is sick, so they went to visit her in Idaho this weekend. I'd love it if you could meet them."

"I'd love to meet them," Dalton said.

"You know," Hobart said to Paige, "it's all because of this guy that I even looked into the Church."

"Me?" Dalton asked.

"Maybe you don't remember the talks we had while you were in the hospital, but I do. And those things we talked about, the things you told me about the premortal existence and the whole plan of salvation, made me think a lot about my life and where it was going. When I got home, I decided to look up the missionaries. But it took a bad marriage and several times through AA before I was able to make the changes I needed to so I could get baptized. It was your example, Lieutenant, that made me want to find out more about the Church. I knew you had something special, and I wanted to have it too. And now I do," he announced proudly.

Paige looked at Dalton with admiration. Of course he denied doing anything out of the ordinary that deserved credit for Hobart's conversion, but Hobart assured him that he wouldn't have even been interested in the Church had it not been for Dalton.

"You know, Lieutenant, I have something of yours that I've kept all these years. Any chance of getting together so I could give it to you?"

Dalton told him his schedule until after his presentation on Wednesday when he returned to California.

"Why don't you come by the house tomorrow night? That way you can meet my family. And . . . someone else."

Dalton's forehead wrinkled, but he didn't press Hobart for details. "Paige," he asked, "is tomorrow night good for you?"

Paige smiled at his subtle way of inviting her to go along with him. "I don't have any plans," she said.

Hobart jotted down his address and a few directions on finding his house, and before leaving said, "I hoped that one day I would be able to see you again and thank you for the part you played in helping me change my life. Thank you, sir." He saluted Dalton, who returned the gesture.

Paige could hardly wait until Sunday evening to see what Brother Hobart Brewster had in store for Dalton.

CHAPTER TWENTY-ONE

Sunday morning as Paige was getting dressed for the morning session of general conference, the phone rang. It was Dalton, and by the tone of his voice, something was terribly wrong.

"I have to fly home today," he told her.

"Dalton, what happened?"

"It's Skyler. You remember how she went to that club with her friends last night?"

Paige's stomach turned.

"I guess some of the kids she was with had some problems with kids from another school."

"Oh no."

"They met up with them out in the parking lot."

Paige's heart skipped a beat.

"Skyler's fine, but one of the boys who was with her group pulled a knife on a kid from the other school. They fought, and the boy from the other school stabbed him."

"You're kidding." Paige still didn't have her breath. "Is the boy okay?"

"He's in critical condition. I hate to think what's going to happen if he dies."

She forced herself to pull in a lungful of air. "How involved was Skyler?"

"She wasn't involved at all, she says. But all the kids were taken in for questioning. She's pretty upset. I need to go home." Dalton paused for a moment. "Why didn't I follow my gut on this? I didn't have a good feeling about it when she asked."

"Thank goodness she didn't get hurt," Paige said.

"That may change when I get home," Dalton said sarcastically. "I'm telling you, Paige, I'm really worried about her."

"I know," Paige said. "I hate this age."

"I wish I had time to tell you good-bye in person, but I have to be at the airport in an hour."

"What about seeing your friend tonight? And what about your presentation?"

"I have to cancel both right now. I'll just have to see what's going on when I get home. I'll let you know."

"Good luck," Paige said, her heart aching for Dalton. She knew the heaviness in his heart, the concern weighing him down.

"Thanks. I'll need it."

* * *

Paige couldn't relax until she heard from Dalton. She paced and worried and ate double-fudge ice cream, her proven method for dealing with stress. While it didn't make the stress go away, it did make it more bearable. She wasn't sure there was enough double-fudge ice cream on the planet for her worries.

Skyler. Jared. Moving.

She walked outside with her scriptures and sat on a bench beneath the black walnut tree at the edge of the lawn. But her mind wandered.

Skyler. Jared. Moving.

She went back in the house and turned on some Tabernacle Choir music. Shutting her eyes, she relaxed into the softness of her recliner and tried to let the words and melodies soothe her.

Skyler. Jared. Moving.

"Ahhhhh!" she cried with frustration, jumping out of the chair and turning off the music. It wasn't working. Nothing worked. Her mind spun with confusion and worry. Skyler needed direction. Jared needed reminding. And she needed guidance.

She walked into her bedroom to put something away and plopped down on the edge of the bed. Then she fell back and lay on it, staring at the ceiling for several minutes as frustrated tears formed and fell from the corners of her eyes, rolling into her ears.

Overwhelmed? She'd felt that way before. Confused? That too. And frustrated. But all at once? It was just a little too much.

Then a thought came to her, an idea that was so simple and obvious it made her wonder why she hadn't thought of it before.

Pray.

She needed to pray.

She'd been praying, but for some reason she felt like maybe now she was ready to listen.

Rolling off the bed onto her knees, she rested her head in her hands for a moment, trying to gather her thoughts.

What did she do? All of it was pressing. All of it was equally important.

The impression came again, *Just pray.*

First she expressed her gratitude for the abundant blessings in her life and, most importantly, for her health and for the strength and comfort that came from knowing that Heavenly Father was there, that He loved her, and that she wasn't alone. She had learned to lean upon the Lord, knowing that without Him, she would have never made it this far.

Then she prayed for Dalton and Skyler. They were headed for some rough times, and she knew that they both needed heavenly blessings more now than ever.

Next, she prayed for Jared. He was a good son, but Paige worried about his vulnerability for material wealth—for sleek, fast cars, large, elaborate homes, and expensive clothes. His father's example hadn't helped any. Mark had sacrificed the gospel and his family for worldly possessions. It was a shallow existence, but Paige was unsure of how to communicate that to Jared. And while Jared had made the decision to serve a mission, she was concerned that his level of commitment was weakening.

Finally she asked for blessings for herself. Her thoughts and her heart were in one place, and her body was in another. Clearly it was time to make a decision. Reasoning her situation out in her mind while she prayed, she listed the pros and cons of moving. The pros sounded like reasons, the cons more like rationalizations.

She wondered who would miss her if she moved. Of course, there were many wonderful people in her ward, but their lives wouldn't be altered dramatically if she left. She thought about her coworkers. Many of them were good, caring people, but she realized that except for the time she spent with them at work, everyone was involved in their own busy lives. She made a contribution—she knew that—but would her departure bring anything to a screeching halt? Hardly.

"Father," she said out loud, "deep down in my heart, what I want to do is move. But my mind just doesn't seem to agree. Still, there is nothing keeping me here anymore. Everyone that matters to me lives in California."

Then she thought of Dalton.

"I can't even consider him in this decision," she said. "I am attracted and interested in him," she admitted, "but I'm not dumb enough to move to a new state for any man. Who knows where this relationship is going anyway?"

She shook her head, confirming the wisdom of being cautious. "I can deal with that issue later. Right now I need to decide what I'm doing. Because I'm leaning toward . . ." she could barely say the word because once it was out of her mouth, everything changed. She shut her eyes, took a deep breath, and said, ". . . moving. I think the right thing to do is move."

She kept her eyes shut and listened with her heart, waiting, yearning for the flooding warmth of an answer, of some indication that this, too, was the Lord's will.

And as she waited, she finally relaxed and rested her head on the cushioned softness of her bed. Visualizing herself in Lou's guest house, working at the design shop, attending Jared's games, she saw herself stepping easily into a new life. She already had a built-in comfort zone waiting for her. In her mind, she had already moved and was living there. And it seemed right. With that thought, she slowly drifted to sleep.

* * *

The next morning, Paige sat straight up in bed and looked around her room. She'd always hated her bedroom. The window was small and faced the north, never getting any direct sunlight. There was only one place to put the bed, the closet was small, and the carpet was a sickening shade of green.

Then there was the bathroom. It needed to be repainted, and she'd always wanted to put tile down in it and in the entry.

Then there was the family room. The wallpaper in there was out-of-date and so was her furniture. But she'd never had extra money to redecorate.

Throwing off the covers, she jumped out of bed as a surge of energy coursed through her veins. Quickly she said her morning prayer, changed her clothes, made her bed, then went to the kitchen to get her purse.

She had two choices: go to the home and garden store and buy paint and supplies to give her home an entire face-lift or buy a For Sale sign.

* * *

"You what?" Lou asked again, her voice still full of surprise and disbelief.

"I called in sick to work and stayed home and put my house up for sale today."

Lou laughed. "This is great news. I take it you got an answer?"

"Well, I would have liked a personal messenger from heaven to come and tell me exactly what I was supposed to do, but since that didn't happen, I'll just have to go on the really calm, sure feeling I have inside." That's exactly how she felt—calm and sure. She thought that after she put out the sign she'd have second thoughts, but they didn't come. In fact, seeing the sign in front of her house only deepened her resolve. Her decision had been made. She was moving.

"What did Jared say?"

"He went nuts," Paige told her. "He's so excited I'm going to live there. Of course, he says it's going to be weird not to have a place to call home when we go back to Salt Lake to visit, but he didn't care about having to stay in a hotel or with friends. He's fine with it."

"That's great, Paige. When are you going to tell Ross?"

"Tomorrow as soon as I get to work."

"And you're okay with all of this?"

"I am so okay with this," Paige assured her. "It's like now that I've made the decision, I can't make things happen fast enough. I'm just on my way out to find boxes. I'm ready to start packing up today."

"I want to ask you something else, and I don't want you to freak out, okay?"

"Okay," Paige agreed with some hesitancy.

"Has this got anything to do with Dalton?"

Paige smiled and sighed. "I knew you'd ask me that, and the answer is no. It really doesn't. I mean, do I like the guy? Yes," she said with a nervous chuckle. "He's awesome. But he's got some issues, and I certainly have issues and, well, you know how I feel about marriage. Unless the word *guaranteed* is stamped on his forehead, I'm not getting serious with any man. I can't move for anyone but myself and Jared. Believe me, I've learned that there's only one person responsible for my happiness, and that's me. I'm moving because there is nothing here for me anymore. I'm finally ready to make a new start."

Lou didn't answer for a moment, then finally said, "I've been praying so hard for you. Not that you would come here—even though that's what I wanted to happen—but that you'd know what to do, because as much as I wanted you near me, I wanted your happiness more, and whatever brought you the most happiness was the most important thing. I still can't believe you're coming! I can't wait to tell Bryant. We'll start cleaning the cottage and getting it ready for you."

"Don't you dare!" Paige exclaimed. "I can do all that when I get there. Right now I need to focus on this house and getting it sold so I can move."

"Why do you have to wait until your house sells? It's not like you have a payment here. Just move. You can let a realtor do all the work for you."

"I still need to give Ross at least two weeks' notice," she said.

"Then call him right now and get your two weeks started," Lou urged.

Paige laughed at her friend's enthusiasm. "Okay, okay," she said, "Gee, Lou, I'm glad you're so happy I'm coming."

"Are you kidding? You and I have always, always wanted to live close together, and we've never been able to, and now . . ." Lou suddenly went silent. Paige heard her clear her throat a few times. When she spoke again, it was in a whisper, "Now, you're going to be right in my backyard. This is a blessing from God," she finished resolutely. "There's no doubt in my mind He's giving me a special bonus blessing for going through this whole cancer thing."

"Is something wrong?" Paige asked with alarm.

"No, everything's fine. I'm good—really. Of course, all that will change when I start chemo, but for now everything's fine. Still, I won't lie to you. There are days when I have my own private pity parties. But not now. I feel like I can conquer anything with you close by."

"So do I," Paige said, feeling excited about the future. "So do I."

CHAPTER TWENTY-TWO

With close to a thousand dollars of cash in her hand, Paige was convinced that the garage sale really had been worth it. She'd wondered that a dozen times while getting ready for the crazy thing. It had taken tons of organizing and time, but it had been a huge success.

And now, as she looked around the bare rooms of her house, she felt a small twinge of sadness. She'd sold nearly everything—couches, dining table, bookshelves, clothes, small appliances, and even her lawn mower. All that remained was her bedroom set, a few favorite pieces of furniture, and personal items.

Lou had told her she would help furnish the cottage, and there was no use for yard equipment, so Paige had gotten rid of nearly everything she owned. And it felt great. Getting rid of that old stuff felt as though she were shedding her old skin and emerging with new, fresh skin and a positive outlook on life. It was cathartic and completely soul cleansing.

The phone rang, and she caught it on the second ring.

"How did the garage sale go?" Dalton asked.

"It was wonderful. I didn't think anyone would buy my old junk, but you know what they say—'One man's trash is another man's treasure.' I just got back from taking a huge load to Deseret Industries. My house is almost empty."

"Are you still coming on Friday?"

"It looks that way."

"Is it still uncomfortable at work?"

After she'd given Ross her two-week notice, he'd become anxious and eager to do anything he could to keep her there. He promised her more money and better job opportunities. In fact, after the success of her other project, he said he felt confident that she could handle even bigger, higher-profile work. He told her she'd become a valuable employee and he hated to lose her, but she didn't falter. She'd already emotionally said good-bye to her life in Salt Lake. She was just going through the motions before she could physically say good-bye.

"Uncomfortable enough that Ross was fine with giving me some vacation days so I could leave early. Besides, Lance has already been given my department, so I don't really have anything I can do except pack up the stuff in my desk."

"Have you had any regrets?"

"Not even one," she said. "I could never picture me ever leaving this place, and now it's like I can't get out of here fast enough."

Dalton chuckled. "Think you can make it three more days?"

"I've got so much left to do I'll be lucky if I'm ready in three days. I still have to finish packing, and then I need to clean the carpets and scrub everything really good."

"You sure you don't need some help? I hate the thought of you driving here all by yourself."

Paige smiled, liking the protective sound of his voice. "I'm staying overnight in St. George with a friend, and I finally got a cell phone just in case anything happens."

Dalton didn't answer right away. Paige heard Skyler's voice in the background.

"Paige," Dalton said, "Skyler wants to talk to you. Is that okay?"

"Sure!" Paige exclaimed. "Put her on." She waited while Skyler came to the phone.

"Hey, Paige. Are you really going to be here this weekend?"

"Friday afternoon sometime."

"Awesome! I'm glad you're moving here. Now for sure you'll be here for my competition."

"Are you feeling ready for it?"

"I broke one of my pointe shoes, so I have to get another pair broken in before the competition, but other than that, it's been going great. Miss Mandy has helped me so much."

"And you're staying out of trouble?" Paige asked with a teasing lilt to her voice, even though she was serious.

"I'm trying," Sky answered. "I never realized how much trouble you could get into hanging out with the wrong crowd—even if you weren't doing anything wrong."

"That's called being guilty by association. It's not fair, but that's how it goes."

"Well, I've learned my lesson—the hard way as usual."

Paige laughed. "You're in good company then. That's how I seem to learn most of the time."

"I don't believe it."

"It's true," Paige assured her.

"You know what, Paige?"

"What?"

"I'm really glad you're moving here."

"Me too, Sky." Then Paige couldn't help asking. "Is your dad right there?"

"No, he stepped out to grab the newspaper. Why?"

"I just wondered how Darlene's doing. Has she been hanging around much?"

"Yeah," Sky said with disgust.

Paige's heart sank.

"She tries to be all buddy-buddy with me, and I just want to throw up. She thinks we're all tight and best friends. She wants to come to my competition and all that. I didn't even invite her."

"You can't blame her for trying," Paige said.

"Yeah, but it's all fake. She doesn't care about me. She's just being nice to me to get to my dad."

"Is it working?"

"I can't tell yet." Just then, Skyler said, "Oh, here's Dad again. I'll see you when you get here."

"Okay, take care, Sky," Paige said with a heavy heart.

Dalton asked what they talked about, and Paige told him some of their conversation. The rest she kept to herself. But she couldn't help wondering about Dalton and Darlene, a woman he'd apparently been madly in love with and engaged to. What kind of situation was she walking into?

* * *

Paige pulled into Lou and Bryant's driveway around eight o'clock on Friday evening. She'd driven all day and was exhausted. Even though the U-haul trailer behind her Camry was small, it still slowed her down, making the trip even longer than she had anticipated. But she was here, and that was all that mattered.

With a weary sigh, she put the car in park and turned off the engine. She was home. Her thoughts drifted back to yesterday, when she'd closed the door on her house in Salt Lake City one last time. She'd had a moment of nostalgia and sadness recollecting Christmases, barbecues, after-game get-togethers, and Jared's birthday parties all spent in that house, a house that no longer felt like home. Even though her heart was touched by memories of the past, it was filled with anticipation for the future. A chapter in her life was closing, but another one was starting, one she prayed would be full of joy and fulfillment.

Ever since she'd made the decision to move, she hadn't turned back. She had no regrets in leaving, no second thoughts. Still, it had been difficult to tell her bishop she was leaving, especially since he'd just given her a new calling. But he'd been extremely supportive and encouraging, which was something she'd needed more than ever. Even Ross at work had softened and told Paige that if things didn't work out for her in California, she could always have her old job back. In fact, he'd tried one last time to entice her to stay, telling her that one of the partners was considering branching off and starting a sister business that would specialize in making professional video and DVD productions for companies. He confided that Paige's performance had been so impressive that there was talk among the members of the board to offer Paige a chance at becoming a partner. She'd proven herself to be a hard-working business woman, and they liked the perspective a woman could bring to their decision making.

Paige had been flattered and surprised at this announcement, but it hadn't changed her plans. This was something she was ready to do, something she needed to do. Besides, there was no guarantee a partnership would ever be offered. She wasn't about to hang around for something that "might" happen.

Just then, the front door of Lou's house flew open, and the first one outside was Maddie. "Mom, Dad," she yelled. "Paige is here."

Behind Maddie came Lou and Bryant and Carter, followed by two tall young men with bleached white hair and bronzed skin. Paige wondered who they were when her mouth suddenly dropped open.

It was Jared and his roommate Nate.

Lou practically had to pull Paige from the car because she was in shock at the sight of her handsome, clean-cut son with white hair gelled and spiked on top. She glanced quickly at his ears to make sure there weren't any other surprises, like earrings.

"I'm so glad you made it safely," Lou exclaimed as she hugged Paige.

"What happened to my son's hair?" she whispered in Lou's ear.

"I didn't know until they showed up tonight," Lou said. "He's expecting you to freak."

"Then he won't be disappointed."

"Try and be cool."

Paige turned to her son.

"Hey, Mom," he said. "Look what Nate and I did today." He turned his head side to side.

"You didn't get a tattoo to go with it, did you?"

"Yeah, Mom. Like I'm that dumb."

Paige held her tongue, resisting the urge to embarrass him.

"Hi, Mrs. St. Claire," Nate said, flashing a goofy smile. He wasn't the most handsome guy Paige had ever met, and the hair color did nothing to improve his looks, but because he had money, people—especially girls—tended to overlook his long, narrow face, domineering nose, and oversized ears. His cool car, expensive clothes, and cocky attitude seemed to make him more appealing than he really was.

"Hi, Nate. It's nice to finally meet you," she said, trying to appear friendly even though she was liking the kid less and less. Sure, she knew that Jared was old enough to make his own decisions, and neither Nate nor anybody else could make him do anything he didn't want to do, but it seemed like ever since he had met Nate, his good sense had flown south for the winter.

"You must be exhausted," Bryant said, giving her a hug with a few reassuring pats on the back. "Don't worry," he whispered to her. "The day the season starts, Coach will make those two either shave their heads or get their hair dyed back."

Paige was grateful for Bryant's place in her son's life. She knew she couldn't be both father and mother to him and was glad that a man Jared admired so much could help influence her son. And as for her influence, it looked as though she had gotten there just in the nick of time.

* * *

With Bryant and Jared's help, Saturday morning was spent moving Paige's few belongings into the cottage. Lou helped her put things away, and by noon she was settled.

She'd called Dalton the night before to let him know she'd arrived and to give him her new phone number, but there had been no answer. She left a message on his machine. Her mind jumped to conclusions about where he was and who he was with, but she tried hard not entertain them. Still, visions of Dalton and Darlene together seemed to materialize in her imagination without any effort.

Once she got her clothes put away, Paige got cleaned up and went with Lou to look at furniture for her new little home. She didn't need much—a couch, a chair and a lamp for the living room, a small dining set, and maybe a reading chair for the library in the loft, but Lou had different ideas.

"Listen," Lou said. "The manager of my store needs to live in comfort and beauty. I want you to have the best. Call it a moving bonus or whatever you want, but I want your place to feel like your dream home."

"I'm not sure I can even manage your store," Paige told her friend, worrying that Lou was giving her too much credit for business sense she wasn't sure she had. "Don't put too much confidence in me yet."

"Oh, pooh! How hard can it be? I'm going to teach you every-thing you need to know, so don't worry. Now," Lou pointed to a far corner of the store, "let's look over there at the leather sectionals. There's an oxblood leather that would be gorgeous in the cottage."

Several hours later, arrangements were made for Paige's furniture delivery. A couple of pieces needed to be transferred from their Bay Area store, so it wouldn't be until Wednesday of the following week until she got them, but Paige was in no hurry. She didn't need a big-screen television and entertainment center at all. She rarely watched TV, but Lou insisted.

"I'm planning a big welcome party for you next Friday," Lou said. "I would have had it tonight, but I wanted to wait until we got your place furnished so you can show it off."

"Lou, you are literally spoiling me. I'm never going to be able to repay you for all of this. And you don't need to give me a party."

"I don't expect you to pay me back, and yes, I do need to give you a party," Lou said. "I want to invite a bunch of our neighbors and ward members so they can meet you." Lou threw an arm around Paige's shoulders and gave her a squeeze. "You are going to fit in so well. I know you're going to love it here."

Lou's enthusiasm was contagious. Paige couldn't help feeling the same.

* * *

Sunday was a busy day, full of new faces and warm welcomes. Lou and Bryant's ward members went out of their way to make her feel welcome. She appreciated all the efforts they made to shake her hand and introduce themselves. The problem was, she knew she wouldn't remember any of their names the next time she saw them.

After church, Jared had joined them for Sunday dinner and then gone back to his apartment to study. Paige couldn't help noticing that even now that she was finally in California, he still wanted to spend time at his apartment. She wasn't sure what she'd expected when she moved, but she'd hoped he would hang out with her at the cottage. In fact, she wouldn't have cared if he wanted to set up a foldaway bed in the loft and use it for a bedroom.

She was exhausted when evening hit and was getting ready for bed when the telephone rang.

"Hi there, how's everything going?" Dalton asked.

Paige had hoped it was Dalton, but she had to wonder what had taken him so long to return her call.

"I'm all moved in, and I start work at Lou's store tomorrow," Paige said, trying to hide her disappointment that he hadn't tried harder to contact her or see her until now.

"Sorry I wasn't around to help," he said, not offering an explanation of where he'd been.

"That's okay," she told him. "I didn't bring much with me and I had plenty of help." She paused, waiting for him to continue the conversation, but he didn't say anything. "So," Paige said, trying to fill the awkward gap, "how are you guys doing? How's Skyler?"

She heard Dalton sigh, his frustration apparent. "I don't know what I'm going to do with her, Paige. Just when I think she's finally getting things figured out, she does something that leaves me wondering if she even thinks about what she's doing."

"What happened?" Paige wished she could help him understand his daughter better, but she didn't know what was going on inside Skyler's head and heart either.

"I went out Friday night, and when I got home around midnight I went in to check on Skyler. She was sound asleep. Well, you know how I've told you I don't sleep well at night? I got up to get a drink around two in the morning, and for some reason, I thought to check on her again. She was gone."

"What do you mean, gone?"

"She snuck out of the house. She went with some friends to a party."

"In the middle of the night? What happened? What time did she come home?"

"It was about four when she tried to sneak back into the house."

"What did she have to say?"

"She said that she was sorry."

"Sorry that she snuck out of the house?" Paige asked. "Or sorry that she got caught?"

"I'm sure she was sorry I caught her," he said, "especially since I grounded her for a month."

"What kind of party was it?"

"She was very up-front about the fact that there were kids who were drinking, but she promised me she didn't drink anything."

"Do you believe her?"

"I smelled her breath and couldn't smell any alcohol. I want to believe her, but honestly, Paige, I don't understand why she's doing this."

"Did you ask her?"

"Ask her what?"

"Why she's doing these things?"

"Not in those exact words, but I've tried to find out where her head's at. She just won't talk to me."

Paige remembered when Jared would clam up when he was upset about something, but invariably he would end up talking about it a day or two later. Sometimes it took longer than that, but Paige tried to make herself available for him so when he felt ready to talk, she was there to listen.

"You need to wait and ask her when you're not upset with her and when there's nothing else going on. Maybe you could go out to dinner or for ice cream or something. Make the mood relaxing and casual, and then talk to her. Ask her what's bothering her. Maybe she doesn't even realize herself that something inside is causing her to make poor choices."

"You sure you're not a child psychologist?"

"I'm quite sure," Paige said with a laugh. "Why?"

"You sound like you know your stuff."

"That's just years of working with the young women. A lot of kids struggle. Actually, all of them struggle to some degree. Skyler's normal. You just have to dig a little and find out what her concerns and feelings are. Then you'll know better how to help and support her."

"If I can just get her to open up to me."

"She will. You just have to be persistent and show her that you love her too much to give up." She still wished she knew where he'd been on Friday night, but figured it wasn't her place to ask. Besides, the most important thing was Skyler.

* * *

The week whizzed by. Paige barely had time to miss Salt Lake or worry about Dalton. Her job at Louisa's was demanding, but she was enjoying every minute. The people at the store were friendly, fun, and amazingly talented. Paige loved the environment, which was full of energy and enthusiasm. Everyone worked as a team, men and women alike. It was nothing like her job back in Salt Lake. There was a broad clientele built on repeat business and satisfied customers. In fact, Lou's business was made up mostly of referrals.

Even though Paige felt overwhelmed at times, Lou was patient and understanding, staying right by Paige's side, helping her step-by-step. Paige was grateful for all the business experience she'd had. A lot was unfamiliar to her, but she caught on quickly and the more she learned, the more excited she got about her job.

Before she knew it, Friday had arrived. Lou and Paige took off work early so they could go home and get ready for the party. Lou had invited close to fifty people and had gone all out on the food and decorations.

The backyard had been transformed into a tropical paradise. Tiki lamps, Hawaiian music, and the fragrance of marinated chicken and teriyaki beef grilling on the barbecue filled the air. Bryant, who loved to entertain and acted as resident chef, grabbed the two women when they entered the backyard after they'd changed their clothes. He placed flower leis around their shoulders and made them hula with him while he sang along with a Don Ho CD. Paige loved his fun-loving, easygoing nature. He loved to laugh, and a person couldn't be around him without catching his contagious good mood.

Jared and Nate came over and helped set up chairs. They each wore Hawaiian-print shirts and puka shell necklaces. Their hair was still white but seemed to have toned down enough to look more sun-bleached and natural.

Around seven o'clock, other guests started to arrive. The bishop of the ward, the Relief Society president, and other auxiliary leaders showed up in appropriate luau attire. Paige was grateful for the name tags Lou had the foresight to make ahead of time on her behalf. Putting the name with the face made it that much easier to remember the people from the ward and the neighborhood.

To her utter delight and relief, Dalton showed up with a stone-faced Skyler at his side. The girl looked like an island beauty with her creamy brown skin and long black hair, but Paige couldn't help noticing how hard the girl looked with her low-cut, belly-baring tank top and heavy eye makeup. She knew without asking that Dalton was mortified by his daughter's appearance.

Paige ran to greet them and give them a lei. She hesitated giving Dalton a kiss on the cheek, but he made it easy, kissing her before she had a chance to decide. She managed to keep her wits about her and gave Skyler a kiss on each cheek.

"Hey, Sky, thanks for coming."

Skyler gave her smirky smile. "You're welcome."

"Whoa," Paige teased, "try and control your excitement."

Skyler rolled her eyes.

"Had a better offer for tonight, huh?"

The girl shrugged.

"You know what?" Paige pulled her close. "You're going to have to work pretty hard to not have fun tonight. The food is great, and Jared and Nate have been waiting for you to play volleyball with them."

Skyler's expression brightened.

"And there's a couple of boys that live in the neighborhood who came with their parents. I think you'd categorize them as 'hot,'" Paige baited her.

Skyler looked over Paige's shoulder.

"Across the pool, by the deejay."

"There's a deejay here?" Skyler asked with obvious surprise.

"You thought this was going to be some old-fogy party, didn't you?"

One side of Skyler's face scrunched up as though she didn't want to admit Paige was right.

"You haven't partied until you've hung out with Lou and Bryant. Just wait—Bryant has some awesome karaoke numbers ready. He does a pretty mean Stevie Wonder impression, and wait until you see him moonwalk like Michael Jackson."

"Really?" Skyler asked with disbelief.

Paige nodded. "Look, there's Jared and Nate waving for you to come and play."

Skyler flashed Paige a grateful smile. "Save me some food. I'm starving."

Dalton and Paige watched the girl run over to the volleyball net.

"You're amazing," Dalton said. "She doesn't even intimidate you."

"Why would she intimidate me?" Paige asked.

"I don't know. It's like you know the perfect thing to say. I would have made her mad no matter what I said."

"That's because you're her father. You're doomed."

Dalton chuckled. "I'm just glad someone can get through to her."

Paige introduced Dalton to some of the ward members. A couple of them knew Dalton from work they'd done together in the stake. Lou and Bryant made a special fuss over him and helped him fill up a plate of some delicious food. Paige got some for herself, and together they sat down and ate while they watched their kids play volleyball. Just as Paige had predicted, Skyler was quickly joined by the two neighborhood boys on one side of the net against Jared and Nate.

"I'd say she's a lucky girl." Paige nodded toward Sky. "Not many girls get to be surrounded by such cute guys."

"I knew getting her here would be the hard part. I just wish . . ." He didn't continue, but Paige had an idea of what he was going to say. "I had a hard enough time getting her to come with me without battling her about her outfit. She knows how I feel about shirts like that."

Paige patted his hand. "If girls only understood what kind of messages they sent out by the way they dressed. Even Jared's admitted that he doesn't like girls who dress too skimpily. He says it makes him uncomfortable."

"Wouldn't it be nice if boys would let girls know they felt that way?"

"The problem is, most boys probably don't feel that way."

Dalton nodded.

"I'm still glad she came. I've missed her," Paige said, looking at Dalton. She'd missed him too but didn't say as much.

The volleyball game continued long enough for Dalton and Paige to finish their meal and for Dalton to go back for seconds on the teriyaki beef. Before too long, though, the group of kids took a break from their game so they could eat. Paige hoped there would be some food left for the rest of the people after Nate and Jared went through the line.

"Hey, Mom," Jared said as he and Nate joined her and Dalton at their table. Just as she expected, their plates were piled high with food. Jared continued, "I hope you don't mind, but I invited someone to the party tonight. Lou said it was okay if I invited some people."

Paige licked the sticky, sweet marinade from her fingers and said, "Who'd you invite?" She expected to hear that a couple of cute college coeds would be joining them.

"Dad and Brindy," he said, digging into a mound of potato salad.

CHAPTER TWENTY-THREE

Paige nearly choked on the piece of chicken she was chewing. She coughed several times to clear her airway.

"Paige, are you okay?" Dalton asked, patting her on the back.

She nodded and gasped.

"You what?" she asked her son.

"I invited Dad and Brindy," he said with some hesitancy. "I kind of had to because they called and invited me and Nate over to their place, and I felt stupid telling them we were having a barbecue with Lou and Bryant and not inviting them. I mean, Dad is their friend too."

Paige wanted to tell her son that Lou and Bryant were friendly to Mark because they were too nice not to be friendly.

"I hope it's okay," Jared added.

She didn't know what to say. She had managed to put on a good front for her son regarding Mark and Brindy because she wanted Jared to be spared any of the negative feelings she and Mark felt for each other. But this was her party. The last person she wanted there was Mark and his new wife, but she held her response and gathered her composure. There was nothing she could do about it except pray they didn't come. If they did, she'd just have to make the best of it.

Jared pressed her further for her approval, obviously picking up on the fact that she wasn't thrilled about the invitation.

"Mom?" he persisted.

Faking her most pleasant voice, she said, "It's fine."

Satisfied, Jared went to get some more food. He'd inhaled his first plate within minutes of sitting down.

Skyler finished her food quickly, then went to sit with the two new neighbor boys, Trevor and Landon. Paige was happy to see the girl having so much fun. Skyler was at a vulnerable age and had been through a lot in her young life. She needed to surround herself with good friends who would help her become strong and stay focused on her goals.

The food was so good that everyone ate to the point of bursting. While Dalton, Jared, and Nate talked about Nate's new car, Paige gathered up paper plates and cups and walked them over to the trash, where she bumped into the Relief Society president, Sister Gibbs.

"Lou tells me you're a wonderful teacher," Sister Gibbs said to her.

Paige smiled. That sounded like something Lou would say.

"We're looking for someone to teach a Relief Society lesson on October 27 and wondered if you'd be interested. It would be a great way for the other sisters to get to know you better."

Without even looking at her calendar, Paige knew she didn't have anything else going on. But the prospect of getting up in front of other people, especially a room full of women she didn't know, was terrifying. On the other hand, it really would give other sisters a chance to get to know her. And this was now her new home ward.

"I'd love to," Paige answered with a smile.

"We'll get a lesson manual over to you then. We're certainly thrilled to have you in the ward."

Sister Gibbs left Paige smiling, but the smile didn't last long. She turned to go back to her seat just as Mark and Brindy walked through the side gate into the backyard.

Paige closed her eyes, praying for strength. When she opened them again, she was disappointed to see the couple still there. It was one thing for Jared to invite them. It was another for them to show up.

Brindy was dressed so scantily that even in the warm evening temperatures, Paige wondered if the girl would catch a cold. Her white halter top and tropical-print capri pants were both so skintight that Paige found herself holding her own stomach in just looking at her. With long, platinum-bleached blonde hair and a deep, golden tan, Brindy's entrance stopped everyone in their tracks. The reaction didn't go unnoticed by Mark, who puffed his chest out like a proud peacock.

Jared jumped to his feet to greet his father and Brindy. And, gracious as always, Lou and Bryant also walked over and welcomed them to the party.

Paige hadn't seen Mark since Jared's high school graduation, and it had been horribly uncomfortable for her. Now, watching Jared interact so lovingly with his father made anger flare inside of Paige.

Jared and Mark stood chatting jovially with Lou, Bryant, and Brindy. Paige knew it was stupid and petty and juvenile, but she felt envious and excluded from the little gathering. That was her son and those were her friends. How dare Mark and Brindy walk in, acting like the royal couple!

Hot tears filled Paige's eyes, and she knew she needed to get out of there fast or she'd embarrass herself. Quietly, she slipped into the shadows and ran down the lit path toward her cottage. Once she was safely inside, she collapsed onto her couch and buried her face in her hands while her tears fell freely. Paige allowed her self-pitying thoughts to consume her for a time.

Mark had left her and Jared to fend for themselves and they'd made it all on their own. Now it seemed as though Mark wanted to reclaim what had once been his. And darn it, she wasn't about to let him. He had no right to meddle with their lives again. Hadn't he done enough damage?

A soft creak from the front door brought Paige's head up with a snap. Dalton softly called out her name. She wiped at her face with her shirttail and tried to dry her tears. Taking a quick, cleansing breath, she called out, "I'm here."

Dalton pushed the door open wider and stepped inside. "Hey," he turned on the lamp, "what are you doing sitting here in the—"

He stopped. She knew he could tell she'd been crying.

"Paige, what's the matter?" He sat next to her on the couch and rested one hand on her shoulder.

"I'm fine," Paige replied, wishing he hadn't caught her.

"One minute you were there talking to Sister Gibbs, and the next minute you were gone. I went looking for you, and someone said they saw you head toward the cottage." He was thoughtful for a moment. "Does this have anything to do with your ex-husband showing up?"

Paige closed her eyes, not wanting to answer that question. "Yes, I guess it does."

Dalton patted her shoulder. "Are you okay?"

"Yes." Paige nodded, wishing she had a tissue to blow her nose. She looked around the room, hoping she might have set a box of tissues somewhere, but she couldn't see any.

Dalton produced a paper napkin from his pocket. "Would this help?"

Appreciating his thoughtfulness, she accepted the napkin and wiped her eyes and nose. "Thank you." With the release of tears came a release of emotion. She felt much better and grateful to get rid of her frustration and anger.

"Can I ask you something, Paige?"

"Sure," Paige answered, wondering just how puffy and red her eyes were.

"Do you still love him?"

Paige looked at Dalton as she processed the question. Did she still love Mark?

"Do I . . . still love . . . Mark?" She paused, then said, "Absolutely not."

His brow furrowed. "Are you sure?"

"Dalton, I did love him once, and I wanted to make our marriage work, but I fell out of love with him long ago."

"Then why were you crying?"

Paige looked down at her hands in her lap and sighed. She was embarrassed to tell him. She cleared her throat and twiddled her thumbs for a moment while she searched for the right words. Finally she said, "Seeing him with her reminds me of my struggles. You know, it just opens up old wounds. I guess I haven't worked through all the anger I feel toward him for what he did to me and Jared."

Dalton nodded and continued listening, letting her say what was in her heart.

"But it's also because . . ." this was the hardest part to admit, "I know it's stupid, but I feel protective of Jared. I don't want to share him with his father. It's like I want to punish Mark for leaving us by not letting him see his son. But I can't prevent them from seeing each other, because I know Jared needs to have a relationship with his father. Jared needs that, and I know Mark loves his son. After he left, it was hard for him to come back to important events in Jared's life— like when he got his Eagle Scout award and all of his basketball games. But now that they live so close together, it scares me," she admitted, feeling another knot of emotion clog her throat, which she promptly tried to swallow away.

Dalton brushed a strand of hair off her cheek and left his hand cupping the side of her face for a moment. "What scares you, Paige?"

"What if he wants to be with his father more than with me? I couldn't take having Jared reject me too. Especially when Mark sets such a horrible example for him. What if Jared wants to be like his father? I couldn't handle that, Dalton, I just . . . couldn't . . ."

She couldn't go on. After all they'd been through, and as wonderfully as Jared had turned out, Mark just couldn't mess it up now. He just couldn't. But she was terrified that was what her ex-husband was going to do.

Dalton pulled her into his arms and held her, rocking her and stroking her back. He didn't talk, he just held her, letting her cry. She stayed in his arms as her tears dried, cherishing the strength she received from Dalton's hug, the soothing effect of his touch.

"I'm sorry," she whispered. "I think I need some serious therapy."

Dalton chuckled. "I think you've done pretty good with all you've been through. Your feelings are understandable, Paige."

She pulled back so she could look into his eyes. "You think?"

"There's nothing wrong with feeling the way you do. If I were in your shoes, I'd feel the same way."

"Really?"

Dalton nodded and winked at her, "You're an awesome woman, Paige. Jared loves you. No one can ever take your place."

A sudden flood of warmth and a speeding of her heartbeat proved Paige's feelings for Dalton went much deeper than mere attraction. He was kind and gentle, understanding and giving. And his words of encouragement and support meant more to her than he would ever know. She didn't know where their friendship would take them, but for now, she was just grateful to have him there for her as a friend. No one but Lou had ever filled that role in her life, especially a man.

"Thank you for being here for me," she said.

"Anytime," he replied.

She gazed at his face—his understanding eyes, the kindness of his smile, the charm of his dimples, the scar on his forehead. She'd never noticed that scar before. It was just below his hairline on the left side of his head.

She reached up and ran her finger along the shiny length of the scar. "What happened here? That's quite a scar."

Dalton blinked, the look on his face changing to one of pain.

Paige mentally scolded herself for apparently broaching a sensitive subject. "I'm sorry, I didn't mean to—"

"No, it's okay. It happened in the war."

"Weren't you supposed to wear a helmet?"

"I was. That helmet saved my life," he said.

He was just about to continue when there came a pounding at the door. Then the door opened. It was Jared. "Hey, you guys, we're all going swimming. Are you coming?"

Paige looked at Dalton. "You want to go swimming?"

"I don't swim," Dalton answered abruptly. "You go ahead, though."

Wondering why he didn't swim but sensing this wasn't the time to press for an explanation, Paige told Jared they'd be out in a minute.

"By the way, Mom," Jared said before leaving, "Lou wants you to sing something with her. Something by some group called the Carpenters. I think she said the song was 'Close to Him,' or 'Close to Me'—"

"'Close to You,'" Dalton and Paige said together.

"Okay, whatever," Jared said. "Just hurry up. You're missing all the fun."

Silence filled the room after Jared closed the door. Their heart-to-heart talk was over for now, but Paige felt a closeness with Dalton for having shared thoughts and feelings she hadn't even shared before with Lou.

"Guess we better get back to the party," Paige said.

Dalton helped her to her feet, and they walked together toward the door. He stopped her before she opened it.

"For what it's worth," he said, "your divorce was Mark's loss."

Paige smiled. "I doubt he thinks so, but thanks."

* * *

After a quick dip in the pool, Paige decided that the night air was just too cool, so she dried herself off, then helped Lou clear away some of the food and dishes to make way for the karaoke numbers. She scolded Lou for volunteering her to perform, but her protests fell on deaf ears. Lou reminded her of the times they'd sung together in high school and maintained that they were still as good now as they were then. Paige highly doubted it, but didn't want to be both the guest of honor and the party pooper.

By the time the patio was cleared and chairs were pulled around the karaoke machine, the kids were tired of swimming and ready to start the singing. Paige had glanced at Mark and Brindy occasionally through the evening and noticed that they'd barely spoken to each other and that Brindy looked bored out of her mind. Mark, on the other hand, had an amazing gift of gab and could strike up a conversation with about anyone he met. He had no trouble mingling and enjoying himself. He made his rounds, greeting and meeting all the people there, and occasionally Paige heard his loud laugh over everyone else's. Paige knew that Mark thrived on attention, something that annoyed Paige now as much as it had when they were married. No matter what the event was, he managed to turn the focus toward him. Paige knew that was another reason, however juvenile, that she didn't want him there. This was her night, not his!

Paige noticed that Brindy seldom spoke to anyone. Of course, she didn't think that Brindy's distance was all her own fault. It was possible that she felt out of place and unwelcome at the party. After all, she was Paige's ex-husband's wife. And no matter how nice of a person Brindy was, her outfit presented a questionable image of her.

"Okay, folks," Bryant said once he got the microphones working. "Let's really get this party started. Our first number stars Paige's son," then he added as a quick afterthought, "and Mark's son, Jared, and his roommate, Nate, plus a couple of 'dudes' from our ward, Landon and Trevor." The crowd cheered, and Bryant continued, "They're going to sing a song the Beach Boys made popular a few years ago, 'California Girls.'"

The four boys had actually pulled together a few moves to go with the song, and once they all got together on the words, they sounded pretty good. The audience clapped along with the song and gave them a standing ovation when they finished.

The next performer was the elder's quorum president, a man who worked with computers and struck Paige as being rather quiet and reserved. "Wait until you get a load of this," Lou warned her just as the music started. Paige watched as Brother Jeffries transformed himself into "The King," complete with curled lip, hip swivels, and a Nashville accent. Paige nearly died laughing, not necessarily because he was funny, but because he was *so* good and *so* unlike himself. Brother Jeffries' wife, Lara, clapped the very loudest after he finished his song.

Paige glanced over and noticed the look of boredom on Skyler's face and wondered how she could include her in the fun. She thought for a moment, then came up with an idea. Leaning over to Lou, she whispered the idea into her ear. Lou agreed it was perfect.

The decision was made just in time, since Bryant announced Lou and Paige as the next number. Paige then reached for Skyler's hand and asked her to join them. Skyler protested but after some coaxing from Jared and Dalton, she finally went up in front with Paige and Lou.

"If I have to do this, so do you," Paige told her.

"I don't know how to sing," Skyler said.

"Mouth the words then," Paige said.

Lou told Bryant what song they were doing, and as he located the CD, Paige looked out over the audience and caught Dalton looking at her. He winked, she rolled her eyes, and they both laughed.

Then Lou whispered another suggestion in her ear. Paige looked at her as though she had completely lost her mind. But Lou, being Lou, managed to talk her into it. Hesitantly, Paige agreed.

Lou went to the microphone and invited Brindy to come up front with them. Paige thought the girl was going to fall off her chair with shock, but Lou persisted, and the crowd clapped and cheered until Brindy had no choice.

When she joined them in front, she gave Paige a worried look.

"Think of it this way," Paige told her, "you probably won't see many of these people ever again."

"I can't believe I let myself get talked into this," Brindy said.

"Come on," Lou told her. "It will be fun."

Lou huddled all four girls together, and they made a quick plan. Luckily they were all familiar with the song.

"You girls ready?" Bryant asked.

They broke their huddle and took their places in front of the microphone, striking a pose they'd discussed.

"Hit it," Lou said to her husband.

The song started and, following Lou's lead, they started stepping side to side with a little Motown flare. Together they sang, in between mistakes and giggles, "We are family, I got all my sisters with me . . ." The catchy beat soon had everyone clapping, and even though they had never rehearsed together, they managed to perform a respectable rendition of the song. By the time they were finished, even Skyler and Brindy seemed to be having a good time. When the song ended, the four girls wrapped their arms around each other's waists and took a bow.

Skyler and Paige quickly took seats on either side of Dalton just as Bryant took his place at the microphone. It was his turn to sing, and Paige knew they were in for a treat. The man had an incredible voice. The music started, and everyone recognized what it was—the Stevie Wonder song, "I Just Called to Say I Love You."

Dalton leaned over and gave Skyler a kiss on the cheek and told her how wonderful she'd been. He then slipped his arm across Paige's shoulders and gave her a squeeze. "Not too bad," he said. "Where'd you learn to sing and dance like that?"

"Lou and I used to sing a little when we were in high school. We did that song for an assembly once. It's been a long time since we've sung together."

"Well, you've still got it," he said.

They stopped talking so they could hear Bryant sing. He handled the microphone like a pro, crooning the words to the song with his smooth, rich voice. Every time he sang the chorus, he looked at Lou. Paige decided this was undeniably one of the most romantic moments she'd ever witnessed between a husband and wife. When the song ended, he gave Lou a kiss, and she wiped at her eyes and buried her head in his shoulder.

Bryant asked the audience if anyone else wanted to perform, and Skyler did her darndest to convince her dad to get up in front and sing, but she just couldn't persuade him to do it. Paige laughed at how flushed with embarrassment his cheeks were.

Paige half expected Mark to get up since he wasn't one to miss a chance for the spotlight, but to her amazement, he didn't even show an interest.

The hour had gotten late, and it was soon time to end the party. The men pitched in and folded and stacked chairs and tables while the women cleared away leftovers and picked up any trash around the pool or yard.

Paige was twist-tying a plastic garbage bag when she felt a tap on her shoulder. She turned and found Brindy standing behind her. "Hi, Brindy." She couldn't imagine what the girl was going to say, but she expected a tongue-lashing for them making her get up and perform.

"I just wanted to thank you," Brindy said.

"Thank me?"

"I appreciated you making me feel welcome. I didn't want to come tonight at all, but I'm glad we did. I had a lot of fun."

Paige smiled. "I'm glad you did. Thanks for coming."

"I'm sure we'll see each other from time to time," Brindy said.

"Probably." Paige felt like the girl was making an effort to bridge the Grand Canyon–sized gap between them. While they would probably never be friends, if they were going to be in each other's lives from now on, it would be nice if they could be civil toward each other instead of feeling awkward around each other.

"Well, I better go. Mark's waiting for me." Brindy turned to leave.

"Wait!" Paige cried, and Brindy turned. "Sometime I need to get a recipe from you," Paige hurried to say before her confidence could fail her. "Jared says you made a killer dessert when he came to visit once."

Brindy thought for a moment. "Oh, yes, the chocolate fudge cake. Sure, I can get that to you."

"Thanks."

"Why don't you give me your phone number and I'll give you a call?"

Brindy wrote Paige's number on the back of a deposit slip in her checkbook. "Guess I'll talk to you soon then." She gave Paige a warm smile, pausing a moment to peer into Paige's eyes. Paige expected her to say something, but Brindy's eyes shifted to look over Paige's shoulder. "I better go," she said, then left to join Mark, who was talking to Bryant and Lou.

"What was that all about?" Dalton asked Paige as he took the bag of trash from her to carry to the garbage.

"I just asked her for a recipe," Paige said, "but I felt like she wanted to talk to me about something. I don't know what it could be. She just seemed . . ." Paige shrugged, ". . . bothered about something, maybe."

"Wonder what it could be," Dalton remarked, tossing the bag into the garbage can.

"Probably just my imagination," Paige said.

The backyard was empty except for the stereo and karaoke machine, which were playing some of Bryant's favorite oldies. The guests had either gone home or were inside the house.

"Oh wow," Dalton said as the next tune began. "I love this song."

Paige listened for a minute and bobbed her head to the beat. "This brings back memories of high school," she said.

"Hey," Dalton said with a twinkle in his eye, "wanna dance?"

Paige laughed. "Sure," she said, unable to refuse such an offer.

Dalton slipped one arm around her waist and pulled her close. Together they swayed to the music, the only light around them coming from a half dozen burning Tiki lamps. Softly in her ear, Dalton sang with the chorus, "Ain't no mountain high enough, ain't no valley low enough, ain't no river wide enough, to keep me from gettin' to you."

Chills tickled Paige's neck as he sang and held her close. She shut her eyes, drifting along on the magical spell that seemed to capture them in a timeless moment. She'd thought the walls she'd built around herself had been strong and sturdy, but there, in Dalton's arms, she felt those walls crumbling, her defenses weakening. How was she supposed to protect herself from getting hurt by a man when he was as charming as Dalton was?

As the last notes of the song faded, Dalton held her close and dipped her back, holding her in a dramatic Fred Astaire and Ginger Rogers pose. Paige laughed, feeling giddy at his playful spontaneity.

She turned her head as he pulled her upright and was surprised to see Mark standing near the gate, watching them. Dalton noticed him too and pulled Paige protectively close to his side.

"I, uh, forgot the car keys," Mark said, walking to the table where they'd eaten dinner and retrieving a set of keys. He held them up for Dalton and Paige to see. "Good night, then."

Dalton and Paige didn't reply, just watched him leave.

"How long do you think he was watching us?" Paige asked.

"Long enough to decide he didn't like it."

"What do you mean?"

"Didn't you see the look on his face? He clearly didn't like seeing you in the arms of another man."

"That's ridiculous," Paige said. "He couldn't care less about whose arms I'm in."

"Maybe so, but the man didn't look very happy at all to see us together. In fact, he looked a little green, if you ask me."

Paige scoffed at his comment, but she had noticed an odd expression on Mark's face. Still, she knew jealousy was the last thing Mark would feel for her.

CHAPTER TWENTY-FOUR

To Paige's surprise, Jared actually spent the next afternoon with her instead of Nate. Of course, it was only because Nate's girlfriend was up from San Diego visiting, but Paige didn't care what the reason was. She was just glad she finally had some private time with her son.

They went shopping, frivolously spending more than usual. She needed some updated clothes for her wardrobe, and Jared found plenty he wanted at Niketown, but settled for a Nike baseball cap and basketball shorts for practice.

It was over lunch that he managed to completely throw Paige into a panic.

"Hey, Mom, I've been thinking about what I'm going to do next summer." He gave his hamburger an extra squirt of ketchup and replaced the bun on top.

"What do you mean?" Paige's forkful of salad stopped in midair. Suddenly she'd lost her appetite.

"Well, I was going to try and leave on my mission sometime at the end of May or the first of June, but it wouldn't be a big deal if I waited until the end of August, would it?"

"Ah . . . well," Paige chose her words carefully. "Is there any special reason you want to wait?" Her mind flitted to several possibilities of why he "couldn't" leave the end of May, all of which were not good.

"Kind of," he said. "Nate's going to Hawaii this summer to work at a pineapple plantation his father owns. The pay is out of this world, and his dad has a condo right on the beach."

"Condo?" Paige repeated. "Hawaii?"

"Mom, it's the chance of a lifetime, and it only means waiting three months. Three months isn't that big of a deal."

Paige felt her wiring start to crackle. Her worst fears were coming true. Sure, Jared was saying he'd only put off his mission three months, but would it really be only three? After the summer, would the coach talk him into playing one more season? And if he did great that season, would it just be "too hard" to leave when he was doing so well?

She had a bad feeling about this, but she didn't want to overreact in front of Jared. He would only get defensive and angry, and then he'd quit talking to her and end up doing what he wanted to do anyway. She had to handle this delicately and prayerfully.

"Besides," he went on with his sales pitch, "all that money I make would help pay for my mission."

Paige had to control herself from laughing outright. Did he really think she was stupid enough to believe that his motives for this were purely unselfish? He knew very well that they had plenty of money saved for his mission. For years Paige had put a little bit away each month, and Jared had helped build his savings with money from his jobs through summers and high school.

"I know you've always wanted to go to Hawaii," she acknowledged, reminding herself to breathe. For as long as she could remember, Jared had wanted to go to Hawaii. He seemed to possess some type of affinity for the place. He knew all the history about it and was fascinated by the Hawaiian culture.

"Finally, this is my chance to visit it for three whole months. It's like the ultimate dream come true," he said.

Or the ultimate temptation, Paige thought. The adversary certainly knew where to hit her son. Dangling carrots like these would be hard to resist.

"Why don't we talk more about it a little later?" she said, trying to buy some serious praying and thinking time. Plus she wanted to talk to Bryant and Lou and get their input. More than anyone, she wanted to talk to Dalton. Maybe he could give her some ideas on how to handle this.

* * *

"I have an idea," Dalton said over the phone later that night, "why don't we switch kids for a while? You get along better with Skyler than I do—and she listens to you—and I think I could talk some sense into Jared."

Paige laughed. "So you agree that he shouldn't put off going on his mission? Even if it is just three months?"

"Absolutely not," Dalton responded without pause. "The longer he waits, the easier it will be to put it off again and again until he ends up not going altogether. I agree with you completely."

"You don't know how good that sounds to me. I've been wondering if I was overreacting or being an overprotective mother."

"Paige, your instincts tell you he shouldn't wait. I believe in those motherly instincts."

"You sound pretty confident about that."

"I am. Even though it used to frustrate me sometimes, my mother was very close to the Spirit, and when she felt something, we learned to pay heed. She sure ruined a lot of fun for me in high school though."

Laughing again, Paige ventured, "Like not feeling good about you going to a party, or hanging out with a particular group of friends, but not really being able to explain why she didn't feel good about it?"

"Exactly!"

"I'm sure I drove Jared nuts, but I was the same way. If I felt uncomfortable about something, I wouldn't let him go. We spent many nights not talking to each other because he was so mad at me."

"Jared is a great kid. He'll do the right thing," Dalton told her. "Don't lose faith in him."

"I'm trying not to. I'll tell you what, though, I'm sure glad I moved here. I'd be going nuts in Salt Lake if I were there right now." She couldn't imagine being so far away from her son and was very grateful that the opportunity to move to California had presented itself.

"I'm glad you moved here too," Dalton said.

A knock came at the cottage door, and Paige glanced over to see Lou through the window.

"Lou's here. I guess I better say good night."

"Okay, but don't worry yourself over this, Paige. I have a lot of confidence in your son."

She thanked him and hung up the phone, cherishing his friendship. No matter what happened between them, she would always be grateful that Heavenly Father had brought Dalton into her life.

"Hey, Lou," Paige said as she opened the door. "I'm still not used to being so close to you. Instead of having to pick up the phone, we can just pop in and see each other."

"I didn't mean to interrupt. Who were you . . ."

Paige smiled.

"Ahh, it was Dalton."

"I didn't say that."

"You didn't have to. I could tell by the look on your face." Lou plopped down on the leather chair.

"What look?"

"The look of love," Lou said, propping her feet up on the ottoman.

Paige cast a sidelong glance at her friend. "So," Paige opted to change the subject rather than justify Lou's comment with a reply, "what brings you by?"

"Oh," Lou sat up a little straighter, "I wondered if you'd be okay at the store alone for a while Monday morning."

"Alone?"

"Just for an hour or so. I have a doctor's appointment, which won't take long."

"With your plastic surgeon?"

Lou nodded.

"Oh," Paige said, not wanting to add to Lou's concerns. "Sure, I'll be fine. It's not too busy in the morning."

"There aren't any appointments scheduled until afternoon either."

"Okay, no problem," Paige replied. "Anything else I can do to help?"

"Nope, just love having you here. How are you feeling about Jared?"

Paige had discussed her son's summer plans with Lou and Bryant earlier. They also agreed with Paige, and Bryant assured her that he would make sure the head coach wouldn't pressure Jared to play another year. The coach wasn't LDS, but he'd had several players who were, and he was very supportive of missions. In fact, the experiences he'd had with returned missionaries gave him the opinion that missions made players even better.

"I'm worried, but I'm trying to be positive and not overreact. I'll tell you what, though, I'd like to throttle Nate."

"Nate doesn't understand," Lou reminded her.

"I know. And Jared's a big boy. He needs to make his own decisions. I just want them to be right ones."

"Did you talk to Dalton about it?"

"Yeah. He agrees that Jared shouldn't put off his mission. He offered to switch children for a while."

Lou laughed. "Are you sure that would be a fair trade? Skyler seems like she'd be a handful."

"She is. But there's something about her I'm able to connect with."

"That's good. I bet Dalton's grateful to have you in his daughter's life."

"He says he is," Paige said wistfully.

"What else does he say?" Lou asked, her question born out of nosiness but also out of love, reason enough for Paige to feel comfortable opening up to her friend.

"Dalton is such a fine man," Paige said. "He's kind and warm, he's got a rock-solid testimony of the gospel, and the way he lives his life totally reflects that."

"He's darn handsome, too!" Lou added.

"I was getting to that," Paige told her. "He's very handsome and so charming. I find myself thinking like a schoolgirl, acting like I'm a teenager again."

"That's wonderful."

"It's ridiculous," Paige countered. "My heart gets ahead of me sometimes, and I have to remind myself to slow down."

"Why?"

"Because," Paige paused for a moment to allow her emotions to settle, "I can't trust my heart. I've learned that the hard way. No matter how I feel about Dalton, I can't let those feelings cloud my good judgment. I have to act responsibly. I'm an adult, and I am not going to make any more mistakes when it comes to matters of the heart. I've learned that there's much more to relationships, especially marriage, than love."

Lou thought for a moment, then nodded. "Okay, I can agree with that. Go on."

"I loved Mark with all my heart, but all the love in the world wouldn't make him devoted to me and Jared. I think having things in common, such as beliefs, goals, views of family, marriage, and life, matters as much as love."

Lou nodded again.

"So even though I may have feelings for Dalton, my head's going to take a lot longer to be convinced. Besides," she added, glancing down at her hands, "it doesn't really matter how I feel because I don't know what Dalton would think if he knew everything . . . about me. I mean, why in the world would he want damaged goods when he can have anyone of his choice?"

"What do you mean 'everything about me'? Just because you're divorced?"

"No," Paige answered. "Although that adds plenty of baggage to the situation."

"Then what do you mean?" Lou was clearly baffled.

"I mean my cancer surgery. Compared to other women, especially the ones Dalton dates, I'm half a woman."

Lou sat up in astonishment. "You're kidding, right?"

Now it was Paige's turn to be baffled. "About what?"

"You honestly think Dalton is that shallow?"

"To not want a woman with a big scar on her chest when he can have a one with a perfect body? I don't think that makes him shallow—just normal."

"That's ridiculous!"

"That's the way it is, Lou. I'm just facing facts, you know . . . reality. Mark left me because of my scar and everything that led up to it. If my own husband couldn't love me, why would anyone else?"

Lou shut her eyes for a moment, then opened them and looked directly at Paige. "You listen to me, Paige. Mark was a selfish jerk. He wasn't committed to your marriage from the beginning. Your cancer and your surgery just gave him a reason to leave—they weren't the cause of it. A good man would have stood by you. He would have loved you and taken care of you. A man like Bryant. A man like Dalton."

Paige kept her eyes down. Bryant was that way. And probably Dalton too. But how could she ever know for sure? "It's dumb to even have this discussion," Paige said. "We're assuming Dalton even wants to have a relationship with me beyond friendship. He's given me no reason to assume that."

"He hasn't?" Lou challenged. "You think he sings love songs in other women's ears? You think he kisses all his lady friends?"

Paige shrugged. "I don't know. I seriously don't. I just know that I have to take things very, very slowly, and I have to stay clearheaded. I can't get caught up in silly romantic notions or let my expectations become unrealistic. It's for my own protection and happiness, and I guess Jared's too."

"Well, I think you're wrong about Dalton. He's a wonderful, incredible man. And if you think for a second that God didn't have a hand in bringing you two together, you're wrong. I know He did. You and Dalton's lives have been linked together twice now—once when you were sixteen, and now thirty years later. It isn't by mere chance or coincidence."

Paige shrugged again and shook her head. "I don't know, Lou. Like I said, my head's going to take a lot more time to convince than that."

"Don't listen to your head," Lou counseled.

"I have to. When my heart and my head agree, then I'll know it's right. And right now they don't."

Lou got up from the chair. "Well, I hope the day soon arrives that they do. I think Dalton is perfect for you, and you are perfect for him. And, by the way, maybe you should take a look in the mirror more often. You are an attractive, beautiful woman. Any man would feel privileged to be with you. But what's even more important is that not only are you beautiful outside, but you are beautiful inside, Paige. You've got a heart of pure gold."

"Thanks," Paige said, amazed at her friend's ability to say just what she needed to hear when she needed to hear it. Still, she felt ill-equipped when she thought about the competition for Dalton. "The problem is, people don't always look at what's inside. I mean, I feel like I'm D.I. Barbie—you know, the one whose head was pulled off and won't stay on and who's lost an arm. No little girl would want a doll like that when she can have a new one right out of the box."

"Will you stop with the analogies already," Lou pleaded. "You know, the worst thing Mark did to you was make you feel like you weren't good enough. You're an amazing woman, Paige. I just wish you could see yourself the way others see you, the way Heavenly Father sees you."

Paige swallowed, feeling tears well up in her eyes. "I appreciate what you're saying, Lou. And I don't want you to worry about me. I'm happier now than I've been in years, and more than anything, I'm just grateful to be alive so I can be here with Jared and with you, Bry, and the kids. That's what's really most important."

Lou nodded and reached out to hug Paige.

As Paige hugged her friend, she realized that she truly did feel that way. Surviving breast cancer had helped her appreciate life and loved ones. Sometimes the things of the world distracted her for a time, but when she really stopped to think about it, she always came back to the gratitude she had for the important things in life—the gospel and her loved ones.

Still, as she watched Lou walk back to her house, Paige thought about their conversation and about Dalton. She couldn't imagine ever telling him about her surgery. She couldn't handle the rejection that she was sure would come with it.

* * *

The week flew by, and Paige found herself settling into a comfortable routine. Between working at Lou's store and taking on some freelance design work as a result of the basketball program she'd done, Paige stayed plenty busy. She was glad when the weekend rolled around not only because it meant getting a break, but because Dalton had invited her over to his house for a barbecue Saturday evening.

"I don't know which shirt to wear," Paige fretted as she pulled blouse after blouse out of her closet and tossed them onto the bed, where Lou was reclined on a mound of pillows.

"I still think that eggplant-colored sweater is my favorite," Lou offered, leaning forward to dig the sweater from the bottom of the pile.

"But I've had that for years," Paige said, noticing the lateness of the hour. It was time to leave, and she still wasn't dressed.

"Trust me, Paige, no matter what you wear, you'll look great. But this sweater says classy and comfy, and it looks great with the highlights in your hair."

Lou and Paige had gone to the hairdresser together and gotten more color than Paige was used to. Instead of her normal pale blonde and golden highlights, she had a few streaks of caramel and deep red woven in. The rich contrast of colors gave her hair great texture and movement and added warmth to her complexion, which was a few shades darker from her time spent reading by the pool after work.

"It's always been my favorite," Paige said.

"Then go with it. You don't want to have to sit and worry all night. Wear something you know works for you."

"You're right," Paige said, holding the sweater up to her chest and taking one last look in the mirror. "You're absolutely right."

"Of course," Lou said, raising her hands in a "so what's new?" gesture.

Paige pulled on the sweater and finger-combed her hair into place. Adding a few spritzes of her favorite perfume, she gave her appearance one last look, then stopped and held her stomach.

"What?" Lou asked in alarm.

"I'm nervous," Paige said. "I don't think I'm going to be able to eat a thing. Why am I so nervous?"

"That will all go away as soon as you get to his house," Lou said. "You're probably just excited about being with Dalton. And maybe a little nervous that he might kiss you."

"Lou!"

"Well, he might. Why wouldn't he?"

"I don't know. It's not like that between us. We just talk, you know."

"Well, just in case, take your toothbrush with you in your purse so you can brush your teeth after dinner."

Paige looked at her.

"What? You don't want onion breath all night or something. Just do it. I promise you'll thank me later."

"I don't need to pack a toothbrush," Paige said.

"Why not?"

"Because I already have a spare in my purse," Paige confessed. "You know, for after lunch when I'm at work and stuff."

Lou gave her a big smile. "Then you're all set."

"I hope I can find my way over there."

"You'll be fine." Lou walked from the bedroom with her and followed her through the cottage to get her keys and purse. "I feel like you're my little sister, off on your first date."

"I know," Paige said. "That's how I feel too."

"We'll be up late, so if the light's still on, drop by when you get home tonight. I want to hear about everything."

"I will," Paige told her, putting her hand on her nervous stomach again.

"C'mere," Lou said, giving her friend a big hug. "Everything's going to be great. And for once," she told Paige, "let your heart lead the way. Maybe your head will get the message this time."

Paige chuckled. "You don't know how thick my skull is, do you?"

"Come on, I'll walk out with you."

Lou and Paige followed the flower-lined path through the trees to the driveway. Lou reached to open the gate, then stopped, holding tightly to the wooden post.

"Lou, are you okay?" Paige asked with alarm.

Taking a deep breath, then blowing it out slowly, Lou nodded. "Sorry, I got dizzy for just a minute. I get light-headed sometimes. I think it's a precursor to becoming an airhead," she attempted to joke.

Paige laughed but felt a twinge of worry prick her heart. Lou seemed to push herself too much. She wished her friend would take it easy, give her body a chance to heal, and adjust to the changes from the surgery. But that wasn't Lou's way. Still, Paige often worried that Lou was overdoing it.

"Hey, I'm fine," Lou assured her. "I'll go lie down and rest. It's nothing."

Paige gave her an encouraging smile and a hug. "You just take it easy, will ya?"

"I promise. Now go have fun and stop in when you get home. I want to hear about everything."

Paige added her promise and was off.

* * *

Tender rib-eye steaks grilled to perfection, baked potatoes, a wonderful salad, and plenty of conversation filled the table that night. Soft music played in the background, accompanied by the sounds of the ocean and a gentle breeze. They ate on the terrace and watched as a heavy sun sank slowly into the endless sea. Dalton was a marvelous chef and a wonderful host. Skyler was gone for the evening, so the house was all theirs.

"This is heaven," Paige told Dalton. "I don't know when I've been so relaxed or felt so peaceful."

"It's nice when you can take a vacation from your worries, no matter how short."

"How about you?" she asked. "Do you ever get a vacation from your worries?"

"Sometimes between the hours of four and six in the morning, when I am finally asleep and I know Sky is asleep, I can relax and know everything is okay for a short time."

"How's Skyler doing? Has she spent a lot of time at the dance studio this week?"

"She has. It's been nice. She's the type of kid who needs to have a lot going on in her day. She's much more productive when she has to budget her time, rather than when she has a lot of free time on her hands."

"Jared's that way too. He could spend the whole day playing video games or sleeping if he didn't have to go to school or basketball."

They visited for a while longer until the sky grew dark and the breeze carried a chill. Paige was grateful she'd worn her maroon sweater, but even with it on, she folded her arms and rubbed them to keep warm.

"Why don't we go inside," Dalton said, "before your lips turn blue."

"I'm sorry," she laughed. "It got cold all of the sudden."

"The evening breeze off the water can get chilly. Let's go in. I'll turn on the gas log, and we can have some dessert."

"I'm stuffed," Paige protested.

"It's cheesecake," he replied.

She didn't waste any time following him into the house.

Together they loaded the dishwasher and put away the leftovers. Once the kitchen was clean, Dalton pulled a tantalizing New York–style cheesecake out of the refrigerator.

"Make my piece small," she requested, wishing she had enough willpower to resist the dessert altogether.

With a low fire glowing in the fireplace, Dalton and Paige sat on the couch, enjoying every delectable bite of cheesecake. Paige tried but she just couldn't finish hers. She'd eaten too much already. "Thanks for the wonderful meal," she told him. "You really know your way around the kitchen and the grill."

Dalton laughed. "Funny you should say so. We usually have take-out every night."

"That's what I do," Paige said. "It's too much work to cook just for one person." She glanced at the clock, wondering how it had gotten so late.

Dalton also noticed the time. "Sky should be home any minute. She wanted to see you. Can you stay awhile longer?"

Paige complied, reasoning that since church wasn't until eleven o'clock the next morning, there was no reason she couldn't wait until Sky got home.

Swapping stories about their childhoods, Paige and Dalton told about their families and the memories they had of growing up. Paige's heart went out to Dalton as he told her of the fun he and his brother had when they were young—building tree houses together, racing dirt bikes, and collecting baseball cards. He missed his brother terribly, and Paige wished that Jared would have had a brother or a sister to grow up with. Maybe that was why he'd bonded so quickly with Nate. Maybe he needed to fill that void in his life.

Paige rested her head against the back of the couch as she listened to Dalton tell about Christmases at his grandparents' house in Salt Lake City and going to see the lights on Temple Square. "I'm taking Skyler there this Christmas," he said. "She's never been there, and I want to show her how beautiful it is at that time of year. She wants to go snow skiing, too, but I'm not sure about that yet."

"Sounds fun," Paige said, feeling fatigue set in.

"Hey," Dalton said, his voice soft. "You're not going to fall asleep on me, are you?" He reached out and stroked her cheek. She smiled and leaned her face into the palm of his hand. "I'm not that boring, am I?"

"No, of course not. You're actually the most fascinating man I know." She hoped her comment didn't sound like more than it was. She was merely stating the truth.

"Wow," he said, leaning closer. "That's quite a nice thing to say. Especially when I think you're a pretty amazing lady."

Paige felt color rise to her cheeks, not only because he'd paid her such a kind compliment, but also because their faces were only inches apart. Lou had been right! He was going to kiss her, and she hadn't even brushed her teeth!

Even though she was blushing, she couldn't help smiling. Dalton had a way of making her feel good inside. The gap between them closed even more, and Paige was waiting for the brush of his lips against hers when the shrill ring of the telephone broke them apart with a start.

They both laughed.

"Excuse me," he said. "I better get that. It might be Sky." He looked at the clock, which read ten-thirty. "It'd better be Sky. She's half an hour late."

Paige tried to calm her heart as he answered the phone.

"She was supposed to be with you," Dalton told the caller. "She knows she's not allowed to go to that club again." He listened for a moment. "Are you sure?"

Paige braced herself for the news, which she guessed wasn't good.

"I'd appreciate that, Abigail. You can call me on my cell phone. You've got the number, right?"

He mumbled a quick good-bye, then hung up the phone.

Paige closed her eyes and uttered a prayer for Skyler and for Dalton. This was going to be a long night for both of them.

CHAPTER TWENTY-FIVE

Paige paced back and forth from the kitchen to the living room window and back again. She had stayed at Dalton's to wait while he went out looking for Skyler. The girl had told her dad she was going to a movie with Abigail, but Abigail had phoned Dalton and told him that Skyler went with some other kids to Remix, the club where Skyler had gotten into so much trouble before.

Dalton called Paige at every stop he made. Of course, the first place he went was Remix, but didn't find any trace of Skyler there. No one had seen her or knew where she was.

Paige was getting sick with worry. Where in the world could that girl be? And why didn't she at least telephone and let her father know she was okay? She sat for a moment on the couch and rubbed her throbbing temples. She could only imagine who Skyler was with and what she was doing.

Just then, the telephone rang, sending a shock of adrenaline through her. Lunging for the phone, she answered it on the second ring.

"Is this Skyler?" a woman's voice asked.

"No, Skyler isn't home," Paige answered.

"Oh, I see. Is Dalton there?"

"He's not here either," Paige replied, getting the feeling that it was Darlene on the other end.

"He's not?" the caller said with disappointment that quickly turned to confusion. "Could you tell me where he is?"

"He had to run out for a while," Paige said, not wanting to give the woman any more details than she had to. "May I take a message?"

"I'll just call him on his cell phone, but just in case I miss him, could you tell him Cassandra called?"

"Cassandra?"

"We dated before I moved to San Diego. I'm sure he still knows my number."

"I'll let him know," Paige said with forced formality. She didn't mind helping out to find Skyler, but she wasn't excited about being Dalton's answering service.

Paige hung up the phone and conjured up a picture of Cassandra in her mind. The woman was likely in her late thirties or early forties, with polished white teeth, a suntan, and thick, gorgeous hair.

Trying to shake off her annoyance, she focused her mind back on her worries. What in the world was Skyler doing?

Noticing Dalton's photo album on the far end of the coffee table, Paige picked up the book and thumbed through the pages. Most of the pictures she'd already seen the first time she met Dalton. Now she had a chance to study the pictures, to see the man he was thirty years earlier. The photographs fascinated her, and through the eyes of the camera lens she got a taste of what Vietnam was like, what he'd seen while he was there.

She gazed at the pictures of him in the hospital after his release from the Hanoi prison. His shrunken frame and gaunt, hollow expression struck a painful chord inside her chest. No wonder the man didn't sleep. After all he'd lived through, after all he'd seen, it was a wonder he could function at all, let alone be the influential and incredible man he was.

He had a smattering of bandages on his face and arms. One leg was bandaged, and his left arm was in a splint, plus he was hooked up to several monitors and machines. She wondered what had happened to his arm and leg and made a mental note to ask him later. He looked terrible, nothing like the good-looking young soldier he'd started out as or the handsome man he'd become. In fact, the person in the bed barely resembled Dalton.

She closed the book and rested her head in her hands. Dalton didn't deserve any more heartache. He'd had his share and more. Anger at Skyler flared up inside of her. Didn't the girl understand all her father had endured? All the death and horror of war and prison, then the suffering and pain of his wife's tragic death. Right now

Dalton needed his daughter to get her life together and make right choices, living her life as an example for others.

The handle on the back door rattled, and Paige got to her feet, hoping that Dalton was home and hopefully not alone.

To her surprise, Skyler stepped through the back door.

"You're home!" Paige ran to her and gave her a giant hug, then let go and grabbed her by the shoulders. "Where have you been?"

Skyler's original expression of defiance suddenly melted in front of Paige's eyes. Color drained from the girl's face, and a frightened look crossed her glazed eyes.

"Are you going to be sick?" Paige asked, the odor of alcohol on Skyler's breath suddenly assaulting her nostrils. Skyler nodded and clamped her hand over her mouth as she raced for the bathroom.

Paige stood outside in the hallway, feeling her own stomach lurch at the sound of Skyler vomiting. Her first thought was to call Dalton and tell him Skyler was home. She ran to the phone and dialed his number. After several rings, he answered.

"Paige," he said, his voice full of anticipation.

"She's home," Paige blurted out, wanting to relieve his worry as quickly as possible.

"Is she okay?"

Paige didn't know how to answer that question. After some hesitation, she said, "I think so. She's in the bathroom. We haven't had a chance to talk yet."

"I'll be home in about fifteen minutes. Can you stay a little longer?"

"As long as you need me."

"Thanks, Paige," Dalton said, audible relief softening his voice. "I think my hair is turning grayer by the minute."

With a sigh, Paige hung up the phone. His hair might just go completely white when he got home and found out the true condition of his daughter.

Hurrying to the bathroom, Paige went to see if Skyler needed any help. She knew it wasn't her place to lecture, but it would be difficult to not say anything to the girl. Skyler was making some big mistakes, and Paige didn't feel she could stand around and just let her ruin her life.

"Sky?" Paige said when she saw the girl slumped over the toilet.

She tried to rouse her, but Skyler's arms were limp, her whole body like one big blob of Jell-O. She had passed out cold.

"Boy would I hate to be in your shoes," Paige said to the girl as she hooked her hands under Skyler's armpits and slid her along the floor to her bedroom. With considerable effort, she managed to get Skyler onto her bed, and then removed her shoes and covered her with a blanket.

"Why are you doing this?" she asked the sleeping girl. For a moment, she gazed at the peaceful expression on Skyler's face, then knelt down and stroked Skyler's cheek. Tears welled up in her eyes. "If you only knew how hard this was for your father." Paige sniffed and wiped at her wet cheeks. "You're breaking his heart."

Paige sat on the floor and rested her head against the bed.

Heavenly Father, if there's anything I can do to get through to this girl, please let me know what it is. I care about what happens to her and I want to help her.

In the distance, the wail of a siren broke the silence of the night. Gratitude filled Paige's heart to have Skyler home, safe in her bed. But her tears fell anyway. She'd shed many tears over her own son, as well as for the young women in her ward. Watching a teenager with such promise make such grave mistakes made her heart ache. If they only understood how much they were loved by their Father in Heaven, as well as their own parents and others. If they understood how important it was for them to be strong.

Borrowing a corner of Skyler's blanket, Paige wiped her tears and expelled a long, slow breath, shaking her head with despair.

She jumped when she felt a hand on her shoulder.

Turning quickly, she saw Skyler was awake.

"Paige," Skyler whispered. "You're crying?"

Tears filled Paige's eyes again.

"Why?"

Licking her lips and blinking furiously to try and stop the tears, Paige finally said, "I'm worried about you. I'm worried about your father too."

"My dad?"

"He loves you so much, and he's so worried about you."

Skyler shut her eyes, a pained expression on her face. "I know."

"Why are you doing this, Skyler? Why?"

"I don't know," Skyler said, blinking tears from her own eyes. "I don't know, Paige. I just feel so lost inside. And angry. And confused."

"About what?"

"About everything. Who I am, where I fit in, why my mother killed herself. I miss her, but I'm so mad at her. Why did she do it? Why didn't she love me enough to try harder, Paige?"

Paige's heart ached for the young girl. "I know she loved you, Skyler. You were her whole world."

"How can you say that?" Skyler's voice grew angry. "If she loved me, she wouldn't have done that. She would have wanted to stay around and be with me. She would have wanted to watch me dance and help me when I had problems. But she didn't care. All she cared about was herself."

"That's not true, Skyler," Dalton's voice came from the doorway.

Paige and Skyler turned to see him, his face etched with worry lines, his eyes red and tired.

Skyler turned away.

Dalton walked into the room and sat down on the edge of Skyler's bed.

"You were the greatest blessing in your mother's life. She thought God had completely turned His back on her because He'd taken everything from her—her parents, her brothers, her country, her husband and child. She wanted to have another child for years. She struggled constantly with the memories that haunted her from the war. She saw things . . ." Dalton had to stop. He swallowed and pulled in a quick breath. "Things that no person should ever have to see. Horrible things that hurt her so deeply she never recovered. Things that would drive anyone to madness."

Skyler looked at her father.

"She loved you with all her heart. Don't . . ." he stopped again, his bottom lip trembling, his voice growing gravelly with emotion. "Don't judge her too harshly, Sky. She did the best she could. She experienced sorrow that many will never know. She was a very special woman, and I loved her very much. I miss her too."

A stream of tears cascaded down Skyler's cheeks. "Oh, Dad. I'm sorry." She reached toward her father, who scooped her into a giant hug and held her close, rocking her gently.

Suddenly, Skyler broke away and dashed for the bathroom.

Wiping his cheeks on his shirtsleeve, Dalton composed himself and pulled his shoulders back with a cleansing sigh.

Paige felt like an intruder, an outsider who was eavesdropping on a very personal family moment, but when she made a move to leave, Dalton reached for her hand and pulled her toward him.

She sat on the bed next to him and they embraced.

"Thank you," he whispered.

Paige nodded but stayed silent, appreciating the feelings that were being communicated by their hearts.

In her heart she felt that Skyler had finally turned the corner. The communication barrier between her and her father had broken down. They had shared their deepest feelings and strengthened their bond of love. It was a moment of healing, drawing them closer together.

* * *

With her stomach empty and her body completely worn out, Skyler fell asleep for the night.

Dalton and Paige sat on the couch, physically and emotionally drained, hoping that the nightmare was over. Of course, Skyler was going to have a whopper of a headache in the morning. She also faced a serious talking-to by her father. But tomorrow would be a new day, full of promise. Paige wanted to believe with all her heart that it would be the first day of a new life for Skyler.

Paige had called Lou earlier to tell her she was going to be late. She knew Lou didn't expect a report of her comings and goings, but she didn't want Lou to worry about her.

"I feel like my body is velcroed to these cushions," she said to Dalton, lacking the energy to even lift her head.

"I'm sorry it's so late. I should drive you home. I don't want you to go home alone this time of night."

"I'll be fine—" A yawn crept up on her, and she couldn't stop it.

"I insist. I couldn't stand it if something happened to you."

She patted his hand. "Nothing's going to happen to me," she told him. "I just hope Skyler's okay."

"We've got a lot of talking to do, but I'm sure she'll be fine." He propped his feet up on the coffee table. "I knew she was still upset about her mother's death, but I had no idea she was dealing with all of that."

"She'll feel so much better once she gets it all off her chest," Paige said. "Talking about it is going to help her process her feelings better, and maybe that will help her move on."

"I've tried to get her to talk to me all along, but she just won't open up," Dalton said. "You must think we're pretty dysfunctional."

"I think you have a lot to deal with in your family, but I don't think any other family could do any better than you two are doing."

"I just wish she'd open up more. I don't know why she's like this."

"Part of it is just being a teenager," Paige said, "but I think she's a little bit like her father."

Dalton looked at her with one eyebrow raised in amusement. "Oh really?"

"Yes, really. You keep a lot in too."

"I do?"

"I think that's part of the reason you don't sleep well. You keep it all inside."

"I wouldn't know where to begin letting it out. I'm afraid one little hole in the dam might just cause a flood, you know?"

"Maybe," Paige said. "Or it might help take some of the load off your mind and the burden off your shoulders."

Dalton was silent, apparently thinking of what she'd said.

"Dalton, I'm sorry. I shouldn't have said anything."

He turned to look at her. "You know what I have nightmares about?"

She shook her head.

"It's not always the same thing. I mean, flashbacks, reliving stuff from the war, guilt over my wife's death, worries about Skyler, these are things that weigh on my mind. But the one that wakes me up and sometimes keeps me up is . . ."

Paige could tell that relating this was hard for him.

"You see, it was my last mission before I got captured. I took six men on a top-secret recon mission. We were close, these men and I. Like brothers. I would have given my life for any one of them. Instead . . ." he swallowed, then cleared his throat, ". . . they ended up giving their lives for me."

"Oh, Dalton." She wanted to hold him, help him, strengthen him.

"After the drop, we waited behind some trees to make sure it was safe to move to the mountains. In my gut I felt we should wait, but I ignored it. My men waited for my signal, so it was up to me, my decision alone." He shut his eyes and leaned his head back against the cushion. "If only I'd waited a little longer," he agonized. "One minute longer, maybe they'd all be alive today. I thought the Viet Cong soldier knew we were there. It almost seemed like I sensed it. If I'd only waited just a few more . . . seconds."

"Dalton, it wasn't your fault. You did the best—"

"It *was* all my fault. I made the call. I got them killed. And now, all I see are their mangled bodies, and their eyes, their lifeless eyes, staring at me. Haunting me." He barely got the words out when he covered his face with his hands. "I can't get the image of those eyes out of my head."

"I'm sorry," Paige said, reaching for him with caution. She wanted to let him know she was there for him, but she didn't want to intrude if he didn't want her to.

She touched his forearm, and he looked up, his eyes filled with tears. He moved toward her, and she gathered him into her arms, holding him and letting him release thirty years of guilt and pain.

* * *

"What in the world?" Paige woke up to a stream of sunshine on her face. One quick glance at her surroundings told her she was in Dalton's front room on his couch.

She sat up with a start. She couldn't remember falling asleep the night before, but she must have because she had a blanket over her.

I better call Lou, she thought. She didn't want her friend worrying about her, especially when church was about to start and she wasn't home to go with them.

She placed the call and found Lou to be her usual understanding self. Since sacrament meeting was the last meeting in the block, Paige had plenty of time to at least get back for that.

Folding the blanket, Paige thought about the events of the previous evening, recalling pieces of conversation.

Paige heard a door in the hallway open and looked up to see Skyler, looking like roadkill.

"Hi," Paige said.

Skyler squinted, then grabbed her head with both hands. It was obvious she was feeling the effects of the previous night's shenanigans. "Tylenol," she whispered.

Paige fought the urge to help the girl get some pain reliever. Skyler had made a poor choice and was suffering the consequences of her actions—a painful lesson to learn.

After taking the medicine, Skyler joined Paige in the living room, shielding her eyes from the bright sunlight. She sat on one end of the couch and groaned. "So stupid."

"What is?"

"Me," Skyler said. She pulled a face. "Ugh, what a yucky taste in my mouth."

Paige felt bad the girl was miserable, but she was also grateful that Skyler didn't feel well. Hopefully the natural consequences of her decision would deter her from doing it again.

"What was I thinking?"

"That's what I was going to ask you."

Squinting, Skyler looked at her but didn't speak. Neither did Paige. She had plenty to say but didn't feel like it was the right time to say it.

"Where's my dad?"

Paige shrugged. "I haven't seen him this morning. I woke up just before you did. Guess I fell asleep on your couch. Last I remember looking at the clock, it was almost three."

"I'm sorry."

Giving her a nod, Paige smoothed the blanket she'd folded. "Guess I'd better take off." She got to her feet. "Where does this go?"

"I'll put it away," Skyler said.

Slipping on her shoes, Paige then located her purse and dug out her keys. "I'll see you guys later."

She was walking to the door when Skyler said, "Wait!" Paige turned and saw the girl trying to push herself up from the couch. Skyler finally stood on wobbly legs and walked toward Paige. "Thanks for being here last night," she said. "I'm so mad at myself for what I did. It was so stupid."

"It really was," Paige told her.

"I didn't mean to hurt my dad. He's probably so disappointed." Skyler's bottom lip began to tremble. "And you are too." Her chin dropped, and a great big sob shook her shoulders.

Paige couldn't resist. "C'mere," she said, putting her arms around the girl.

She helped Skyler back to the couch and patted her back, smoothing tangles of hair from her eyes.

"I didn't even mean to drink," Skyler confided tearfully. "It was some kind of sparkling, fruity drink, and it tasted funny at first. My friends lied to me when I asked them if something was in it. They wanted to get me drunk because I always said I would never . . ." She broke down sobbing. "I would never drink . . . or take drugs," she finished.

"They don't sound like very good friends," Paige remarked.

Skyler shook her head.

"And you lied to your dad about going to a movie with Abigail."

"I thought we were going to a movie," Skyler said. "We all met at her house, then I found out they were all going to Remix, and I told her my dad said I couldn't go there anymore. That made Abigail mad because this boy she likes really wanted us to go."

"She called and asked for you about ten-thirty last night. She told your dad you went to Remix."

"She did that just to get me in trouble," Skyler cried. "She's mad at me because I don't hang out with her anymore because I'm always at my dance studio. She had big plans last night, and I messed them up."

"So where did you go?"

"Some of the kids didn't want to go to the club because they didn't have enough money to get in. So they were just going to some-body's house to watch DVDs. I thought that would be safer than going with Abigail, so I went with them."

"What happened?"

"The parents weren't home, and we made popcorn and stuff so we could watch a movie. We were having so much fun I guess I just didn't worry about what we were drinking. We kept drinking and laughing and . . ." Skyler shut her eyes. "I'm so stupid. I should have been stronger."

"How did you get home? You were in no condition to drive."

"One of the guys brought me home. I left my car at Abigail's."

"Was he drunk?"

"I don't know," Skyler answered.

The telephone rang once, then stopped. A moment later, Dalton came down the hallway looking for his daughter. He was surprised to see Skyler and Paige sitting on the couch. "Abigail's on the phone," he said.

Skyler looked at Paige, then said to her father, "I don't want to talk to her."

"She sounds pretty upset. I think something's wrong."

"Oh, all right." Skyler took the phone from him and said, "Hello?" As she listened, the color drained from her face leaving an expression of disbelief.

"No," Skyler said. "Are you sure?" She listened for a moment as fresh tears filled her eyes.

"Yes, he brought me home last night." She shut her eyes and whimpered softly as she listened. "Okay, I'll call you later."

She hung up the phone, then turned to Dalton and Paige.

"Joey, the guy who brought me home, was in a car accident last night. He's dead."

CHAPTER TWENTY-SIX

By Thursday of the next week, Paige found herself thinking her boring life back in Salt Lake City might not have been so bad after all. It was certainly the opposite of what her life had become since moving to California.

She hadn't talked to Dalton since she'd left the house Sunday. She worried about how he and Skyler were doing, but didn't feel it was her place to call and find out. They knew how to reach her. So she waited and wondered.

Jared was doing great with school and with basketball. As the beginning of the season approached, the coach clamped down on the boys and gave them strict curfews and restrictions. Paige loved every rule that came with being on the team. Even Nate had to toe the line or risk being kicked off the team. Paige didn't forget to thank her Father in Heaven for small miracles. And she was even more grateful that the Hawaii pineapple-picking summer idea hadn't come up again. Hopefully it would disappear as quickly as it had come up.

It was a rare moment that Paige had time to watch her big-screen television, but that evening she felt like turning it on and just relaxing, giving her brain a much-needed break.

Flipping through the channels until she found a documentary on Katharine Hepburn, Paige sat back with a bowl of teriyaki chicken and rice from a Chinese drive-through and a tall glass of raspberry ice Crystal Light. Heaven. Pure heaven. No worries, no thinking, just relaxing.

She didn't even get to the first commercial before the phone rang. Hesitation to answer it filled her. "I can't handle one more crisis," she said to the television. But curiosity got the best of her, and she leaned over and grabbed the cordless phone, checking the caller ID.

Mark St. Claire.

Why would Mark be calling her?

She put the phone back down. The machine could take a message.

After four rings, the machine clicked on, played her quick message, and beeped.

"Hi, Paige, this is Brindy."

Paige looked at the machine in surprise. Brindy was calling her? She couldn't stand it—she had to answer.

"Brindy, this is Paige."

"Oh, Paige, hi." Brindy sounded surprised. "I was hoping you were home. I need to talk to you."

"What about?" Paige reached for the remote and muted the TV.

"Well," Brindy started, then there was silence. Paige thought she heard sniffing. Was Brindy crying?

"I, a," Brindy continued, her voice tremulous. "Mark's in the hospital . . ." Again, silence.

"What's wrong?" Paige asked, clicking the remote to turn off the television.

"He had . . ." Brindy paused. "He had a heart attack."

"Is he okay?" Paige knew there was a history of heart problems in Mark's family. His father had died of a heart attack in his early forties. But Mark seemed to take pretty good care of himself, and Paige had never thought he would have one.

"The doctors are keeping a close watch on him. He's doing well now. We just have to wait and pray."

"How are you?" Paige asked, imagining how hard this was on her, especially since she was expecting a baby. Brindy had to be wondering if her husband was going to live long enough to see his own child.

"I'm doing okay. It scared me so bad. We were at a restaurant, and I thought he was choking on a piece of chicken. A man at the table next to us knew CPR and determined Mark wasn't choking but having a heart attack. The paramedics came and took him to the hospital." Brindy's voice was so heavy with emotion that Paige could barely understand her words. "I thought it might be better for you to tell Jared instead of me."

Paige appreciated her thoughtfulness and agreed. After getting the hospital and room information, Paige told Brindy she'd tell Jared.

"Thanks for calling, Brindy," Paige said, then added, "Let me know if you need anything."

Brindy thanked her tearfully and hung up the phone.

* * *

It took some work to track down Jared. He was with a bunch of friends and couldn't hear his phone ringing. When Paige finally reached him, he was in a hot tub. In the background, Paige heard all kinds of talking and laughing. She pushed away images that surfaced in her mind, but she couldn't help but wonder what he and his friends were doing.

His jovial tone quickly grew somber with the news. "Is he okay, Mom? Is he gonna . . ."

"He's going to be fine," Paige assured him, knowing she couldn't guarantee anything, but she wanted to say something positive and encouraging. "Your father is young and healthy."

"Can I go see him?"

"Sure. Anytime you want."

"Will you go with me?"

Paige's heart grew warm at his request. "Of course I will, hon."

* * *

Early the next morning, Paige woke up to the ringing of the phone. "Oh no," she groaned. "Now what?"

She and Jared had gone to the hospital to see Mark the night before. He was asleep when they arrived, but Brindy was there and told them the doctors were encouraged by his stable condition.

Jared hadn't said much on the way home from the hospital, and Paige worried about him. He assured her he was okay and promised to call the next day.

Checking the caller ID, she saw Dalton's name and number displayed.

She quickly answered, hoping everything was okay.

"Sorry to call so early," he said. "I wanted to catch you before you left for work."

"How was the funeral yesterday?"

"It was hard. You wouldn't believe how many kids from school showed up. I really hope that they learned something, especially Skyler. She could have been in that car with Joey when he crashed. It happened while he was on his way home from our house."

"You're kidding! I heard sirens going off about that same time. I'll bet they were for him."

"Probably. The accident wasn't too far away."

Paige's heart went out to Joey's parents. What a horrible tragedy, all because he'd felt he needed to drink with his friends.

"Sky's pretty shook up," he said, "but I think something good might come out of it. I think it woke her up."

"That is good."

"She made an appointment to meet with the bishop on Sunday."

"I'm happy to hear that. She's a great kid, Dalton. She's going to be okay."

"So, how are you doing?" he asked.

Paige told him about Mark's heart attack. He expressed concern and asked if there was anything he could do.

She appreciated his offer, but there was really nothing anyone could do. "I guess all we can do is pray and hope he's okay," she said. "And if there's anything I can do to help you with Skyler, I hope you'll let me know."

"I'm glad to hear you say that, because that's why I called. I need to ask you a favor, but I understand if it's not going to work out."

"What is it?"

"Skyler's Young Women group is having a mother-daughter sleepover Friday night. Her Laurel advisor called to see if there was any way Skyler would consider coming."

"Oh dear," Paige said, knowing how difficult it would be for the girl without her mom there.

"Oh dear is right. I was wondering if you had anything going on Friday night."

"Me? You mean, to go with Skyler?"

"You're the only person she said she'd even consider going with."

Paige was flattered. She loved hanging out with the young women, and if she could help Skyler, she was willing to do anything. "I'd love to."

"You know you probably won't get any sleep," he said. "Our family is having a bad influence on you that way."

Paige laughed. It was true for last weekend and would likely be true this weekend. But she wasn't worried about it in the least. "That's okay. I have plenty of catch-up time."

"It would be nice if Sky could get some sleep. She has a precompetition performance Saturday evening."

"What's that?"

"It's kind of like a dress rehearsal, but they have a panel of experts to critique the girls and help them with things they need to work on. It's kind of a big deal, and Skyler will do much better if she's had some sleep. If I didn't think this Laurel activity were so important, I wouldn't let her go. But I do. I think she needs to be around the girls in our ward."

"I'll do what I can to get her to bed at a reasonable time," Paige promised.

"By the way, I have to tell you—after our talk the other night, I had the best night's sleep I've had in a long time."

"That's good news," Paige said. The man deserved a good night's sleep.

"I think you were right about something."

"Me?"

"Yeah, I think you were right when you said that part of the reason I can't sleep is because I'm not talking about the things that are keeping me awake."

"I said all that?"

"You did. I think you missed your calling in life. You should have been a psychiatrist."

Paige laughed. "I'd get too involved in my patients' problems," she said.

"Maybe, but you sure know how to make a difference."

"Glad I could help."

"It meant a lot to me to have you listen. I don't know what it is about you, Paige. I've never been able to talk to anyone about all of this before."

Paige was flattered, but didn't think she could truly take all the credit. "Maybe you just weren't ready to talk about it until now."

"Maybe, but you've really been wonderful."

"Don't think you haven't helped me out too," she said. "You've done your fair share of listening to me too."

"That's what friends are for, right?"

"Right," Paige said wistfully. "That's what friends are for."

* * *

"C'mon, Paige, you can do it," Skyler screamed. "Just a minute longer."

Paige's eyes crossed as she looked down at the spoon hanging from her nose. She always knew that the little pug tip of her nose was good for something. The other mother sitting next to her lost the spoon off her nose, and Paige was declared the winner.

The next thing the girls wanted to do was teach their mothers how to dance. Paige hated to disappoint Skyler, but she could no more do hip-hop moves than she could fly to the moon.

"Skyler," Sister Buchanan said, "why don't you get up in front and lead us?" Skyler stepped back shyly, but the girls in her class and others in the group coaxed her to do it. Taking a few hesitant steps, Skyler took her place in front of everyone and just stood, apparently not sure what to do.

"I don't know where to start," she said to Sister Buchanan.

"Why don't I just turn on some music, and you start dancing. We'll try and follow you."

"Wait," Sister Powell, a devout scrapbooker, said, "let me record this."

Skyler's face went red when she knew the camera was rolling, but Paige caught her eye and gave her an encouraging smile. She knew the girl had the ability, she just wasn't in her comfort zone.

The heavy beat of a dance song started, and Sister Buchanan said, "Okay, let's boogie." The younger girls laughed, and stiffly at first, Skyler started to move. The group followed, and Paige felt as uncoordinated as she had the day she and Jared had gone water-skiing with a family in the ward. She'd been a pretty good water-skier in her youth, but the trend had soon become wakeboards, and she found that she was the world's biggest geek when it came to getting up on a wakeboard. She'd finally managed to get up after a dozen attempts or more, but the minute she tried to cross the wake, she fell. She didn't walk straight for a week.

As the group mimicked Skyler's every move, Skyler began to forget about being self-conscious and began to concern herself with helping the others get the moves. "The more relaxed you are, the more natural it's going to feel," she said. "You have to be loose." The women and girls tried to loosen up, and while the girls managed to look like Skyler, the women managed to look like drunken gorillas.

Skyler stood back to watch the group and had to cover her smile with her hand. Paige saw her laughing and pointed at her. "Are you laughing at us?"

"No," Skyler said. "I'm just . . ." She couldn't hold it in. "I'm sorry."

Some of the women laughed good-naturedly and sat down, letting the girls dance. One or two of the mothers seemed to pick up the feel of the moves and didn't look half bad. Paige was not one of them.

Repeating the same sixteen-count combination of moves several times, the girls all got together and performed it with Skyler leading the way. Paige marveled at how easy the girl made it look—almost as though she was born dancing that way.

After the piece was over, the audience clapped, and Paige gave Skyler a giant hug. "You're so awesome," she said.

"Thanks." Skyler beamed at the compliment, especially when the other girls in her group told her the same thing and asked all about her dancing. Skyler then told them about her upcoming competition, and the decision was made that all the girls would attend the precompetition performance the next night to support her. Paige smiled at the encouragement from the other Laurels and realized that Dalton was right—this was the exact place Skyler needed to be.

"You know," Paige joked, "your dances are fine, but it's not like we didn't have a few dances in our day."

"Oh, yeah?" Skyler said, one of her eyebrows lifted. "Why don't you show us?"

Paige looked at Sister Buchanan. "You don't have any disco music, do you? Maybe a little 'Disco Inferno' or 'Le Freak'?"

The younger girls laughed at the names of the songs.

"I don't have either of those, but how about 'Stayin' Alive'?" Sister Buchanan asked..

Paige clapped her hands together. "Perfect." Being around the youth brought out the kid in her. She'd missed hanging out with the young women and was glad this group had been so accepting of her.

"Who's joining me?" Paige asked the other women. All of them were great sports and jumped to their feet. "You remember the hustle?" Paige asked them. Most of them didn't but were willing to fake it. Paige wasn't sure she remembered either, but she was confident it would come back to her. She'd been a huge fan of disco in college.

The famous introduction of the song started, and the younger girls sat down and clapped along while the women picked up the beat, ready to move when the singing started. Stumbling over their own feet at first, it took several tries before the ladies finally got the dance together, but before long they were moving and clapping in sync and having a great time. The dance wasn't anywhere near as complicated as the dances Sky was doing, but it was just as much fun, and in no time the girls were also on their feet, moving right along with their mothers. Every time the chorus came on, the group sang along.

After dancing, it was time for snacks and serious desserts. They had an ice cream bar with several choices of ice cream and dozens of toppings. Groaning after their midnight pig-out, the girls and their mothers settled down to watch the movie *The Princess Bride*.

Most of them didn't even make it halfway through. By two o'clock, everyone was sound asleep. Paige checked on Skyler one last time and relaxed peacefully in her sleeping bag. This was the kind of fun teens should be having.

* * *

"How's she doing?" Dalton asked as Paige joined him in the lobby of the auditorium where the precompetition performance was being held. Paige had gone back to the dressing room to check on Skyler.

"Does she usually get nervous before performances?" she asked, not telling him that Skyler nearly passed out in the dressing room.

"A little, but she's performed so much of her life it doesn't usually hinder her dancing. Why?"

"Oh, I just wondered," she said, not wanting to alarm him. There was no sense getting him overly worried. It wouldn't help Skyler if he was a basket case too.

"Look," Paige said, noticing the Laurels coming through the doors. "I'm going to say hi to the girls."

"Okay, I'll go find a seat up close," Dalton said, wringing his hands.

"She's going to be wonderful," Paige tried to console him. He looked like he was going to pass out too.

"I hope so. The girl who does the best at this performance usually goes on to win the real competition. She's up against some talented girls. She has to do her best."

"She will." Paige nodded in encouragement. "I'll see you in a minute."

The Laurels were excited to see Paige. After one overnighter, they'd all bonded like close friends. One of the girls already had pictures developed from the night before and showed them to everyone. Paige laughed at some of the silly shots of her and Skyler. She hadn't let her hair down and been so crazy since the last time she was with the Young Women.

Sister Buchanan greeted Paige with a hug. "How's Skyler doing?"

"Nervous, but she's very excited all of you are coming."

"Why don't we go in and get a seat, girls?" Sister Buchanan suggested. "I need to be up close so I can see."

Paige walked into the auditorium behind them and searched for Dalton. He'd saved a group of seats so the girls could sit close by. "Over there." Paige pointed.

The girls giggled and goofed around as they made their way to the seats. Paige noticed they were such sweet, wholesome girls. She hoped that Skyler would forge friendships with them and spend time with them instead of her old friends.

They were just about seated when a woman approached Dalton, a frantic look on her face.

It was Miss Mandy.

"Have you seen Skyler?" she asked Dalton.

He leapt to his feet. "What do you mean, have I seen her? Isn't she backstage?"

"No," Miss Mandy cried. "I've been looking everywhere for her. It's almost time to start, and she's disappeared."

Dalton looked at Paige with desperation. He couldn't go backstage, but there was no way he could sit by and do nothing.

"I'll help look for her backstage," Paige volunteered. "Why don't you check outside or in the parking lot? Maybe she had to go to the car for something."

Dalton shook his head with concern. "I hope you're right. I can't help but wonder if she's up to something, though."

"She'll turn up. I'm sure everything's fine," Paige tried to offer words of comfort but found herself also wondering if Skyler was up to something.

After checking the ladies' room, all the dressing rooms, and every nook and cranny of the stage, Paige and Miss Mandy both came up empty-handed.

The introductory music started, and the lights went out. "If she misses her turn, she's disqualified," Miss Mandy told Paige.

Where are you, Sky? Paige wondered. *Father in Heaven, help me find her. Please bless her that everything is okay.*

The stage lights came on, and a woman acting as emcee began introducing the first number. Paige felt pure panic course through her veins. Skyler had worked too hard to mess this up now. Paige wasn't going to let her miss this opportunity.

Stepping out of the way so a prop could be moved onto the stage, Paige walked around to the dressing rooms where she'd last seen Skyler and tried to think where the girl could be or what she could be doing.

The curtains opened, loud music started, and the first girl began to perform.

The knots in Paige's stomach tightened.

She noticed a broom closet next to the exit and wondered if Miss Mandy had already checked in there. Why Skyler would be in there was anybody's guess, but Paige didn't want to rule out any possibilities.

Reaching for the handle, she turned the knob. It was locked. Disappointment flooded her.

The performer on stage was now halfway into her number. Skyler was next.

"Darn it, Sky!" Paige said, banging her fist against the door.

A moment later, she felt the door push against her hand. Paige stepped back as it opened, and out stepped Skyler.

"Sky!" she screeched, grabbing the girl in a crushing hug, grateful that the music on stage was loud enough to drown out her outburst. "What were you doing in there? We've been looking everywhere for you!"

Skyler looked at her like she was crazy. "I went in there to pray," she said.

"You're on next!" Paige exclaimed.

"What?" Skyler put her hand to her chest. "You're kidding! How long was I in there?"

"Long enough to make us worry that something had happened to you. Are you ready to go on?"

"Yes . . . no . . ." Skyler took several breaths. "I'm so scared, Paige. What if I forget my number? What if I can't dance?"

Paige took Skyler by the shoulders and looked her square in the eye. "You have worked hard for this, Sky. You're going to be great. Just go out there and do the very best you can, and you *will* be a winner. That's all anyone asks you to do."

Skyler shut her eyes and nodded. With one more deep breath, she opened her eyes again. "Okay. You're right, I can do this."

Paige hugged her again. Then she remembered Dalton was outside looking for his daughter. "I have to go find your dad."

"What? Where is he?" Skyler panicked.

"He's looking for you."

"Go," Skyler said. "I'll be fine."

Paige gave her a thumbs-up for luck and ran off to find Dalton. She tore down the outside hallway to the lobby and burst through the front doors, nearly colliding with him. But he wasn't alone.

"I found her," Paige said, glancing quickly at the woman with him. It was Darlene. "She's fine. She's ready to go on."

"What a relief." Dalton hugged her. "Where was she?" Dalton ignored Darlene, who gave Paige a look of murder.

"In a broom closet, praying."

Dalton burst out laughing. "How about that."

They pushed through the doors and rushed back inside with Darlene trailing behind.

"What did she say?" he asked.

"She's nervous, but she's going to be great. I think the prayer helped."

They stopped at the auditorium doors and noticed the emcee introducing the three experts on the critique panel. Paige was grateful for the extra time it gave Skyler to get ready.

Not wanting to make the situation more uncomfortable than it already was, Paige let Dalton and Darlene get seated while she went around by the Laurels and sat next to Sister Buchanan. Dalton looked over at her with one eyebrow raised, but Paige didn't respond. She turned her attention forward, anticipating Skyler's performance. She'd worry about Darlene later.

CHAPTER TWENTY-SEVEN

"I can't believe it," Skyler said again, jumping up and down, hugging Miss Mandy. "The critique panel really said that?"

Miss Mandy glowed as she repeated her news. "That's right. They said that had this been a real competition, without question you would have won first place."

"What about Kelsie? Everyone thinks she's going to win," Sky asked.

"Not anymore," Miss Mandy replied. "I knew you would do well, Sky, but you danced better than I've ever seen you before. Every member of the panel agreed that you were better than Kelsie."

Skyler blinked several times as tears glistened in her eyes.

Darlene stepped forward and handed Skyler a bundle of flowers. "Congratulations, Skyler." She air-kissed the girl on the cheek. "You really were quite amazing out there. I'm so glad I got to finally see you dance. Thanks for inviting me."

Paige fought the smile that played on her lips. She knew very well that Skyler hadn't invited Darlene to the performance.

"They're beautiful," Skyler said, sniffing the flowers. "Thank you."

Darlene smiled proudly as if she got extra points for bringing flowers, then stood next to Dalton.

"I don't know what you did differently tonight," Miss Mandy remarked, "but you were amazing."

Skyler thanked her teacher, then said, "Tonight was the first time I was really scared to perform. But even though I was scared, I knew I would do my best. I think the fear of going out there and making a fool of myself made me concentrate and try harder."

With a nod of agreement, Miss Mandy gave her one last hug and handed her a manila envelope. "These are the sheets from the critique panel. They all have some very positive things to say, and there are some helpful comments about things you might consider working on. But overall," she smiled at Skyler, "they thought you were terrific. I was very proud of you tonight. I knew you could do it."

"Thanks," Skyler told her teacher.

"I think this calls for a celebration," Dalton said. "Why don't we all go out for pizza."

* * *

Somehow Paige wasn't surprised that Darlene didn't go with them for pizza. It obviously wasn't her type of gathering, especially after Paige, Sister Buchanan, and most of Skyler's Laurel class joined them. But it was all for the best. Dalton was so busy puffing out his chest and hugging Skyler every few minutes he wouldn't have had time to pay attention to Darlene. Still, Paige had watched out of the corner of her eye as they'd said good-bye in the parking lot. It was obvious there was still something between them.

After the celebration, Skyler and Paige had a few moments alone while Dalton paid the bill and went to get the car.

"So, how do you feel?" Paige asked.

Skyler beamed. "This is the most amazing day ever," she said. "I never thought I would be the best at anything, especially at dance. But you know what?"

Paige shook her head.

"I worked hard for this. Maybe I could have worked even harder, but I feel I did the best I could."

With a smile, Paige reached for Skyler's hand and gave it a squeeze. "You made a lot of people proud of you today."

"I know," Skyler said. "I doubted myself the entire time, but you and Dad and Miss Mandy never quit believing in me. And now that I know I can do this, I'm going to work like crazy getting ready for the competition next week."

"It's great to see you so focused on a goal. A lot of kids just live for today, you know? They don't look down the road to see where their choices are taking them."

"Yeah," Skyler scowled. "I've been such a dork."

"True," Paige said, getting a "gee thanks" look from Skyler.

"But you've also learned a lot, haven't you?" Paige hoped for a positive answer. She wasn't disappointed.

"When I think back on some of the dumb things I've done, I wish so badly that I could do them over or erase them," Skyler confessed. "But I know I can't. So I figure the best I can do is not make the same mistakes twice. And somehow," she said wistfully, "if I can make something out of my life, maybe it will help make sense out of Joey's death."

Paige nodded. "I think that's a good way to look at it."

Sky shrugged. "Thanks. I'm trying to do better."

"I can tell, Sky. So much of what you do reflects who you are inside."

"What do you mean?" Skyler cocked her head to the side, absorbing everything Paige had to say. Paige knew she had to make her words count.

"How do you feel when you're with your friends—like Abigail and those guys at the club?"

"I don't know . . ." Skyler thought for a moment. "I mean, they can get into trouble sometimes."

"Sometimes?"

"Okay, it seems like every time we get together something happens. But they are fun to hang around. They're crazy and cool, you know?"

"Do you ever feel pressure to do things you don't want to do?"

"Sometimes, but it's mostly that when I'm with them I just get caught up in what they're doing, and I want to go along with them."

"And how did you feel when we were with your Laurel group?"

Skyler laughed. "They're a blast. I didn't realize how much fun those girls could be."

"Did you worry that anything bad was going to happen or that you were going to get into trouble while you were with them?"

Skyler looked down and shook her head slowly. "No."

"So are you saying you can have just as much fun doing good things as you can doing bad things?"

Skyler looked up at her. "Yeah, I guess that's one way to put it."

"So, what's wrong?"

"I just never thought of it like that. Those girls know I've gotten into trouble and that I've had some problems, but they still accepted me and treated me like I was one of them. That was really cool."

"Do you think that some of the clothes you wear and the music you listen to is influenced by your friends?"

"Totally," Skyler said without hesitation. "You think I'd listen to some of that junk if my friends didn't listen to it?"

Paige smiled. She couldn't have thought of a more appropriate word to describe the music those kids listened to.

"I was wondering if some of your other friends were going to come and watch you tonight."

"Yeah," Skyler said with disappointment. "I told them to come. They think I'm wasting my time with dance because I can't have any fun when I'm going to classes all the time."

"What do you think?"

"I think they're wrong. Every minute I spent dancing was worth it when I was up there performing tonight. It was the best feeling ever. I've never done a split leap like I did tonight. I've never been so solid with my routine or felt so strong. Being up in front of an audience seemed to make me dance even better. I loved it."

"It was fun watching you. You looked like you loved it."

Skyler nodded.

Dalton pulled up to the curb in front of the pizza parlor.

"There's your dad," Paige said, grabbing her purse.

They stood up to leave, but Skyler grabbed Paige's arm and stopped her. Without warning, she gave Paige a hug. "Thanks, Paige," she said.

CHAPTER TWENTY-EIGHT

"Hey, girl," Lou said. "Where did you just go?"

Paige blinked a few times, then looked at Lou, her thoughts returning to the table in the deli where they were eating lunch. "Sorry," she said, picking up her turkey sandwich to take a bite.

"You've been a major space case lately. What is going on?"

"You want the short list or the long list?" Paige asked with her mouth full.

"We have to be back at the store in an hour. You decide."

Paige took a quick sip of her lemonade and wiped her mouth. "It's nothing you don't already know. I'm just trying to figure out how my life suddenly got so complicated. You know, when I was in Salt Lake, I actually had days at a time when I was so bored I didn't know what to do with myself. Now I've got so much going on I don't have time to think. I've become one of those women who put their mascara on at stoplights."

"Have I got you working too many hours?" Lou said, full of concern. "I could easily cover for you while you take some time off. This isn't really our busy season anyway."

"No, no, I'm fine. You need to take it easy," Paige insisted. Lou had thought she'd bounce back from her surgery, but the truth was, she was more tired and more sore than she'd expected. "Work is the only place I feel sane. It's everything and everyone else that's making me crazy."

"Like who?"

"For starters, Jared. He and Nate are definitely spending the summer in Hawaii, but now he tells me they plan on taking two weeks off to take Nate's dad's sailboat and sail to each of the islands."

"Does Nate know how to sail?"

"He claims he's spent his whole life on sailboats, but that doesn't mean a whole lot to me. If he sails like he drives, they're in big trouble."

Lou laughed.

"I feel like Nate's the little devil on Jared's left shoulder and I'm the angel on his right shoulder and we're both trying to tell him what to do. But he will only listen to Nate."

Lou nodded thoughtfully. "What else?"

"My house in Salt Lake hasn't sold yet, and I think I need to hire a new realtor, one who's more aggressive and works harder than the one I've got. Plus, Ross called the other day."

"What did he want?"

"Guess who up and left the company out of the blue?"

Lou shrugged.

"Lance. The guy who took over when I left."

"I bet that didn't make Ross happy."

"Ross is fit to be tied. He's begging me to come and help for a month or so until they get someone else trained. He offered an outrageous amount of money to do it, but I can't do that to you. Not with all you're going through."

"First of all," Lou said firmly, "I've told you a million times, I'm doing much better. I feel stronger each day. And I have a lot of help in the shop right now. If you need to go to Salt Lake for a while, do it. Maybe you won't need to be gone a month. Besides, you want to be back for Jared's games. They start the first week of November."

Paige appreciated Lou's support. Somehow knowing there was someone standing behind her, willing to help however she could, gave Paige an added measure of strength to make decisions and to face her challenges.

"What else?" Lou asked, nibbling on a barbecued potato chip. "Is Mark doing okay?"

"Jared stays in touch with him more than I do, but he says Mark is home now and doing great."

"That's good." Lou nodded. "So, what else?"

Paige wasn't quick to answer. This was a topic she wasn't sure she wanted to talk about because she was so confused about it.

When she didn't spill her guts right away, Lou took a stab at it. "It's Dalton, right?"

Paige couldn't deny it.

"Have you talked to him yet?"

"No." Paige pushed her plate aside. Talking about Dalton took her appetite away. "I think he's hooking back up with Darlene."

"Are you sure?"

Paige nodded. "I got a call Monday night from Skyler. She wanted to make sure I was coming to her competition on Saturday. I think she called mostly because she was upset. Dalton was with Darlene."

Lou pulled a face.

"It's hard for me, though. I mean, I need to encourage her to give Darlene a chance and to think of her father's happiness, but it's so hard, because . . ." Paige ran her finger along the outside of her lemonade glass, sending trickles of condensation down the side.

Lou waited patiently, her eyes full of sympathy.

Paige tried to gather her thoughts to make sense of the confusion inside, but her feelings swirled around like a whirlwind, not slowing long enough to understand.

"You love him, don't you?" Lou said.

"No. Yes. I don't know," Paige said as the whirlwind inside her upgraded itself to a tornado.

"C'mon, Paige. You can be honest with me. Maybe if you talk to me, it will help you sort out your feelings."

Paige knew she was right. It was just so hard to admit she was in love with a man who didn't return her feelings. She was embarrassed to think that she had actually hoped a man like Dalton would be interested in a woman like herself, a woman who wasn't physically complete and who dragged so much baggage around from her past she looked like an old plow horse.

From the determined look in Lou's eyes, Paige knew she wasn't leaving that table until she had laid all her feelings out on it.

"Okay. Yes, I have feelings for Dalton," she admitted. "I am in love with him. I think about him all the time. I'm happy when I'm with him and miserable when I'm not. I get nervous when I think about getting into another relationship, but then, when we're together, I forget that I'm nervous. But . . ."

Lou rolled her eyes.

". . . but, Dalton still loves Soon Lee very much and is having a hard time with his past. Not just his wife, but stuff from the war."

Lou opened her mouth to speak, but Paige held up her hand and stopped her.

"Also, he loved Darlene very much and was heartbroken when she called off their engagement. Darlene isn't hiding the fact that she wants Dalton back, and I think he still has strong feelings for her. But—" she said again quickly before Lou could interject any thoughts, "even if things don't work out with him and Darlene, there are hundreds of other beautiful women out there he could be with. Why would he want me when he could have them?"

Lou's forehead wrinkled. "And what's so wrong with you?"

"C'mon, Lou, don't make me say it."

"Say what? That you've had a mastectomy?"

"Yes."

"What's the big deal? Why can't you tell him?"

"Heavens, no!" Paige exclaimed.

"Why not?"

Paige looked down at the crumbs on the table in front of her.

"Are you afraid he won't want to see you anymore if he knows?" Lou guessed.

With a broad sweep of her hand, Paige cleared the crumbs away to the floor. Sheepishly, she nodded.

"You don't give him much credit, do you?"

Paige shrugged.

"I think the man has more inside of him than that, Paige."

"It doesn't matter. I wouldn't tell him unless our relationship got serious enough for that. But it's not, so I'm not telling him something he doesn't need to know."

"I have a feeling Dalton would surprise you with his reaction," Lou told her. "He's been through too much himself to let something like that stand in the way of his feelings for someone."

"Maybe, but I just don't think the time is right. In fact, there may never be a right time because I don't see a future for us. And the crazy thing is, I swore I would never let myself get in a position to get hurt again, and here I am, willingly stepping in front of a veritable firing squad. What kind of idiot am I?"

"You're in love," Lou replied.

* * *

That night, Paige actually sat down in front of the television with her Marie Callender's microwave chicken pot pie and watched the evening news. She finally couldn't take one more negative, depressing story, so she changed the channel and found a rerun of *The Dick Van Dyke Show*. Watching it brought back memories of her childhood, which, even though it wasn't full of happy memories, was still a time of innocence and simplicity.

The ring of the telephone startled her. By habit, she checked caller ID before she picked up. It read *McNamara, Dalton*.

She was tempted to let the answering machine pick up just to hear what he had to say, but she answered before the fourth ring.

"Paige, I'm glad I caught you home," Dalton said, implying that she was so busy she was usually gone.

"Hello, Dalton," she said with a tone of formality to her voice.

"I'm calling from the hospital."

Fear struck her heart.

"I brought Skyler to the emergency room."

I don't believe this! a silent voice screamed inside of her. What else in the world could go wrong? "What happened? Is she okay?"

"She fell in gym class while they were playing volleyball. The doctor thinks she broke her ankle. She's in a lot of pain, and even worse, she's falling apart because she probably won't get to compete this weekend."

"Dalton, no."

"I know, I can't believe this. Is there any way you could come down?"

Paige felt herself melt inside. He wanted her there.

"She's been asking for you."

Feeling as if a pair of hands tightened around her throat, she managed to choke out, "Sure, I'll come." He was only calling because Skyler asked him to. Still, if Skyler needed her, she wanted to go.

He gave her the address and directions and thanked her.

Paige hung up and sighed. How had everything gone so quickly from hot to cold? They had connected—she knew they had. But things had changed between them.

And she knew why.

* * *

The day after Skyler's injury, Paige went to visit her at home. The girl's ankle was fractured, and the doctors had told her she wouldn't be walking for several months, let alone dancing.

Skyler had been so upset at the hospital that the doctor had given her a sedative along with her painkiller. Paige didn't blame her. The fact that she couldn't compete after all her hard work and when she had a good chance of winning wasn't just annoying and discouraging. In Skyler's book, it was worst thing that could have happened. And no matter how much Paige and Dalton tried to reason with her, the girl refused to be comforted.

Dalton was worried about his daughter—for good reason. It had been an amazing feat to even convince her to participate in the dance competition, but now this. He was afraid it would push her over the edge, and Paige didn't blame him for being worried. She was too.

Dalton answered the door when Paige arrived at their house. She half expected Darlene to be there and was grateful the woman wasn't.

"Thanks for coming over," Dalton said.

"How's she doing?"

"Okay, I guess. She's been sleeping most of the day, not really awake enough to talk. She's taking this pretty hard."

"I wish there was more I could do," Paige said.

"Just being here helps," Dalton said. "Sky feels very close to you."

Paige nodded but didn't speak. She was mad at herself for caring so much about Dalton, but she couldn't alter her heart. They'd been so close. They'd been friends. She was going to miss that.

Pushing her feelings aside, Paige went to Skyler's room and looked at the girl sleeping peacefully. She didn't want to disturb her, so she sat quietly in a chair next to the bed and watched her.

A picture of Skyler's mother on the nightstand caught her eye. She picked it up and looked at the Vietnamese woman in the picture.

Soon Lee had been a beautiful woman. But even though she was smiling, there was a haunted look in her eyes, a look of ultimate sadness, of hardship and suffering few people knew. Paige wondered how different Skyler's and Dalton's lives would be had the woman still been alive.

Deciding to just let Skyler rest and maybe come back later, Paige got to her feet. Just then, Skyler stirred, her eyes flickering, then slowly opening. A smile crept onto her face when she saw Paige.

"Hi," she said, her voice groggy.

"Hey there," Paige answered, sitting back down and taking Skyler's hand in hers. "How're you doing?"

Skyler shut her eyes and took a deep breath. Paige wondered if she was in pain, but then Skyler's eyes opened again, and she gave Paige a big smile.

"I'm doing great."

Paige's reaction was one of sheer surprise. "You are?"

"Yes. My ankle is killing me, but I'm doing great."

"You mean, you're not upset about missing the competition anymore?"

"Well, it stinks that I worked so hard and don't get to compete, but hey," she shrugged, "those are the breaks, I guess." They looked at each other and burst out laughing at Skyler's unintentional pun.

"I don't get it," Paige said. "Yesterday you thought your life was over. Now this morning, you're okay?"

Skyler's eyes lit up, and she clasped Paige's hand with both of hers. "I had this amazing dream! But it didn't seem like a regular dream—it seemed more like I was being shown the future."

Paige couldn't help raising her eyebrows.

"No, listen," Skyler urged. "My mom came to me. She told me that this all happened for a reason. Going through this was the only way for me to learn and grow."

Amazed, Paige listened to Skyler's story.

"In my dream, I stood next to my mother. It was like I could feel her presence with me, Paige, it was so cool . . ." Her thoughts drifted for a moment, then she continued, "Somehow, together, we were able to watch me compete. But the music was different, the dance was different. I can still see the costume and the props. In fact, I want to write down the choreography and the song, because I know it was me next year at the competition."

"Wow, Skyler, that's pretty incredible."

"It was incredible. Totally incredible. I know I could have won the competition this year, and that's enough for me. I'm okay with waiting until next year. Maybe what happens in my future depends on me winning next year—like a scholarship or an opportunity to pursue dance somewhere. I don't know what it is. I just know that it's worth waiting for and working hard for."

"Have you told this to your father?"

"Not yet. It's weird because yesterday I was so disappointed. And I was really mad at . . ." she pointed to the ceiling, "you know, Heavenly Father. I couldn't believe He let this happen to me. But now I know it's all part of a wonderful plan. Something awesome is in store for me, Paige. You just wait and see."

Paige wasn't sure what to make out of Skyler's experience. She believed that people could be taught in their dreams because her patriarchal blessing told her so. But this was so profound, so utterly amazing, that it almost seemed unbelievable.

Then Paige looked at the pure joy in Skyler's eyes, the peace and hope in her expression, and she knew that something spiritual had happened to Skyler.

"Can I make a suggestion?" Paige said.

"Sure." Skyler was still grinning.

"Do you have a journal?"

"Yeah, it's around here somewhere. I think it's in the drawer in my nightstand."

Paige opened the drawer and dug through some papers, candy wrappers, and school pictures of Skyler's friends. At the bottom she found a hardbound journal. Pulling it out, she handed it to Skyler.

"You need to write down everything you remember about this dream, especially how you feel. A year is a long time, and there will be moments of discouragement for you. When you feel that way, you can always come back and read about your experience and it will give you the strength to keep going even when it gets hard."

Hugging the book to her chest, Skyler nodded in agreement. "Yes, I need to get all this down on paper. I'm so glad you thought of that."

Paige was astounded at the change in Skyler's attitude and entire countenance. She truly beamed. A light shone in her eyes, and a radiance surrounded her. Paige knew Skyler had been touched by the Spirit. No other influence could have such an immediate and profound effect on a person.

* * *

"So how do you like Nate's new car?" Jared asked as they drove the sleek BMW down the freeway.

Paige was still trying to figure out how she got talked into going to Mark and Brindy's house in the first place. She'd never been there before, and she never wanted to go. But Jared had insisted, and even Brindy had called and begged her to come over for dinner.

"Mom?"

Paige snapped out of her thoughts and answered, "It's nice. Sure has a lot of bells and whistles, doesn't it?"

Jared looked at his mother with total confusion. "What?"

"You know, all the extras—a DVD screen, global positioning thingamajig, seat warmers, drink holders, front and side air bags."

"It's fully loaded. He got a great deal because it's last year's model. And, Nate told me," Jared flashed a look of excitement her direction, "that when we get back from Hawaii, his dad will buy him next year's model when it comes out and I can have this car."

"*Have?*" Paige asked. No one *gave* a car like this to another person.

"Yeah, he's giving it to me for helping out in Hawaii."

"He's giving it to you," she repeated with skepticism. "Aside from the money you get paid while you're there?"

Jared nodded, almost giddy with the news.

"Plus you get to live in a condo free all summer?"

Jared nodded again.

"Why would Nate's dad do this? I mean, what has he got to gain from giving you all this free stuff, plus paying you all that money in Hawaii? It just doesn't make sense. People just don't do that. It's like he's trying to buy you to be Nate's friend."

Jared's eyes opened wide, and his mouth dropped open in shock. "I can't believe you said that," he shot at his mother.

Paige knew she was pushing the limit, but she couldn't let the subject rest. "I'm serious, Jared. People just don't do things like this. I'm not sure what to think about all of it."

"There's nothing to think about it," he replied with annoyance. "Nate's dad is really generous. He gives stuff to people all the time. There are probably tax write-offs or something. And he's not trying to buy my friendship for Nate. It's just because I'm Nate's best friend. In fact, he said I'm the best friend he's ever had."

"Oh, really," Paige said, wishing she could keep the sarcasm from her voice.

"Yes, really. He said I was the only friend who didn't like him just for his money."

So, ironically, he's willing to pay you to keep your friendship, she thought. Even Bryant had mentioned that he noticed how Nate didn't really fit in with the team, but the boys pretended to like him because he was rich and always paid when they went out to eat or went to movies and clubs. The guys on the team used him, and Paige didn't want to believe that Jared was using him too. But she knew how much her son liked expensive things.

Paige knew she needed to remain silent. She'd made her son mad enough.

"And what will you do with your new car when you leave on your mission?"

"Uh, that's something else I wanted to talk to you about. I'm not sure I'm going to go on a mission."

CHAPTER TWENTY-NINE

"I'm so glad you made it," Brindy gushed when she answered the door. "You're just in time."

She invited Jared and Paige into the house and offered them a seat and something cold to drink. A delicious aroma filled the air, but Paige couldn't appreciate it. She was still reeling from her son's shocking news.

"Mark is just finishing the steaks on the barbecue, then he'll be right in and we can eat. I hope you're hungry. I made enough to feed an army. I can't help it, though. Ever since I got pregnant, I eat constantly."

Paige couldn't imagine Brindy overeating. The woman was rail thin.

"What do you think about being a big brother?" she asked Jared.

"I'm excited," Jared told her. "I always wanted a little brother or sister."

He looked at his mother as though she'd let him down. She resisted the temptation to tell her son, right there in front of Brindy, that his father wouldn't allow her to have another child. She'd always wanted four or five children.

"How's Mark feeling?" Paige asked.

Brindy smiled broadly. "He's wonderful. I like this slower pace in our lives. He pushed himself much too hard, and we didn't have a lot of time together. In a way, I think this was a good thing."

Paige nodded. Staring death in the face had a way of changing people.

The conversation lagged, and Paige shifted uncomfortably in her seat. The last place she wanted to be right now was here with them.

And worse, Jared had surprised her with the devastating news about not going on a mission. Slowly but surely the adversary had pulled him away from the things he'd believed in, the goals he'd strived for. His entire life he'd planned on serving a mission, and suddenly his life course had changed from following the straight and narrow path to setting down the broad and winding road of materialism, glittering with the temptations of wealth.

"Jared," Brindy said, "why don't you go see if your father needs help?"

"Sure." Jared jumped to his feet and left the room.

Paige certainly wasn't in the mood for idle chitchat and wondered what in the world they were going to talk about. She felt the stinging threat of tears every time she blinked her eyes. She wondered why she was even here. It was understandable why they wanted Jared, but why in the world would they want to have *her* over for dinner?

"Thank you for coming tonight," Brindy said.

Paige stirred the ice in her glass with her straw. This was going to be a long evening. She was so preoccupied with Jared she didn't know how she was going to deal with her ex-husband and his wife.

"I wanted to talk to you alone for a moment," Brindy said to her with a lowered voice.

Uh-oh, Paige thought, *now what?*

"Ever since Mark's heart attack, I've taken a lot of time to think about things. Maybe being pregnant has something to do with it. But I've been doing a lot of soul-searching, and I just wanted to," she looked down at her hands, "tell you how sorry I am for what happened in the past. I am ashamed of myself, and I know that I can never expect you to forgive me, but I at least want to apologize to you."

Paige just looked at Brindy, not knowing what to say.

"I really admire you, Paige. You're such an independent woman. Beautiful, intelligent, accomplished. And such a good mother. I hope I can be as good of a mother as you are."

Paige thought wryly that, based on her relationship with her son at that very moment, she wasn't the best role model for parenting.

"I wanted to invite you to dinner for two reasons," Brindy continued. "First, so I could tell you that I hope we can find a way to all get along. With Jared being a part of both of our lives, it would be nice for him if we could all be on good terms."

Paige detected the note of sincerity in Brindy's voice and felt the hardness in her own heart melting. They'd all been through a lot together, but it was in the past; it was behind them. And what mattered most was what was happening here and now.

The fact was, Paige was glad she wasn't married to Mark anymore. They hadn't been good for each other. She was better off without him, and hopefully he and Brindy could make their marriage and family work. Jared was the one she worried about. The divorce had been hard on him, but Mark seemed to be a much better parent now than he was when they were married. And that's what really mattered. Maybe Paige didn't agree with Mark's lifestyle, but Jared loved his father, and Paige loved her son enough to want him to have a good relationship with Mark and with Brindy.

"I agree," Paige said. "Even though what happened in the past was very hard for me, it made me a stronger person and, I think, a better person. I'm happier now than I have been in years."

Brindy blinked several times. "Thank you," she said, laughing with embarrassment at her sudden onset of emotions. "Sorry, hormones."

Paige laughed, remembering well how easily she'd cried when she was pregnant.

"You said there were two reasons you invited us for dinner," Paige reminded her.

"I'll let Mark tell you about the second one," Brindy told her.

The sound of Mark's and Jared's voices in the kitchen brought their conversation to a halt, but Paige found herself glad that she and Brindy had shared a private moment with each other. With forgiveness came the capacity to understand, and with understanding came acceptance. She finally felt like she could let go of her bitterness.

* * *

Paige couldn't understand how a woman as thin as Brindy could be such a wonderful cook. Brindy told her that her father had worked as a chef at a casino in Reno, Nevada, then took over as head chef for a cruise line. As she got older, she got a job also working with the cruise line, and that's where she'd been discovered by a modeling agency. She did swimsuit modeling for a few years, then began designing her own line of swimwear.

Over dessert—a deep-dish apple crisp with homemade vanilla ice cream—Mark finally revealed the purpose of the dinner.

"Brindy and I have made some big decisions these last few days," he told them, "and we wanted both of you to be the first to know."

Jared and Paige glanced at each other, then listened with interest.

"We're putting our house up for sale tomorrow."

"Why?" Jared wanted to know.

"Well," Mark reached for Brindy's hand, "we're moving to Arizona."

"What? When?" Jared exclaimed.

"It definitely won't be until after your basketball season ends, son. I'm not about to miss any of your games."

"But why?" Jared demanded.

Paige knew why her son's reaction was so extreme. Finally he lived close enough so his father could actually come and watch him play, and now, his dad was leaving.

"Brindy and I have decided we want a new start. I can do most of my work out of our home so I can follow the doctor's orders and eliminate some of the stress in my life. It will also give me a chance to help with the baby so Brindy can have time to work on her new swimsuit line."

Paige saw a different side of Mark, a side that was actually, finally, putting his priorities in the right place.

"We feel good about this decision, son," Mark reassured Jared. "And I'll be able to fly here to a lot of your games when you get home from your mission."

Paige and Jared exchanged looks that didn't escape Mark's notice.

"What?" Mark said. "Is something going on?"

He looked at Paige, but she refused to be the one to tell Mark about Jared's change of plans regarding a mission. She didn't want to give him the satisfaction of knowing that he'd won. His negative influence on his son had worked.

He looked at Jared. "Son, what's going on?"

"I just told Mom tonight that I don't think I'm going to go on a mission."

Mark's eyebrows lifted in surprise. "Why not?"

Paige looked at Mark, wondering why he cared. He'd won. His plan had worked.

Jared told his dad about Nate's dad, Hawaii, and the BMW. He explained how well he was doing in basketball, and that even though the coach supported missions, he would be thrilled to have Jared stay with the team.

"I don't think a mission is right for me right now, that's all. I mean, look at all these awesome opportunities I have. I guess I just want to do this other stuff. I'll probably still go, but not right now."

Paige marveled at her son's thinking, his complete rationalization of what was going on in his life. Those things weren't opportunities—they were distractions, temptations. If he could only see them for what they really were.

"Well, son, that's surprising news." Mark looked at Paige. "When did you find out about this?"

"On the way over here tonight," Paige said, feeling her anger rise inside.

Mark nodded, studying his son's face. "You're a man now, and I think it's time you made your own decisions."

Jared flashed a look of victory at his mother.

"I know I didn't serve a mission, son, but I think you ought to think more about this decision before you make any commitments to Nate and his father."

"You do?" Jared asked with obvious disbelief. Paige knew he hadn't expected this reaction from his father. But she wondered if it was possible that Mark's heart attack had opened his eyes and helped him take a different look at life and loved ones.

Mark nodded. He didn't say more, but he'd said enough. Paige was grateful he hadn't given their son the permission he was seeking.

Paige looked at Mark with amazement and, for the first time, with appreciation. He'd finally assumed the role of parent just when she needed him to. The fact that they weren't married anymore had nothing to do with it. They were still Jared's parents, and they both wanted what was best for him.

* * *

"Mark, what are you doing here?" Paige slid her pen behind her ear and pushed herself away from the desk in her office. She was filling out a special order form for a customer.

"Do you have a minute?"

She paused, wondering what this was all about. "Yeah, sure. Sit down."

He took a seat across the desk from her and took a deep breath.

"So," she said, wanting to start the conversation so it could get over quicker.

"So," he said, then paused. "The reason I'm here, well . . ." He licked his lips and pursed them together, then spoke again. "I need to get something off my chest."

It was all Paige could do not to roll her eyes. She did not want to hear this.

"You see," he cleared his throat, "the day when I was in that restaurant and I felt this crushing pain in my chest, I knew immediately what was happening. Inside, I knew I was having a heart attack. And in that split second, my mind thought a million things all at once. It was amazing. I thought about my father dying of a heart attack and how I'm older than my father was when he died. Then I wondered if this was it for me. Was I going to die? Then I thought about Jared, how much I loved him and how much I've missed out on things in his life. I suddenly wanted another chance to be a better father. Then I thought about you."

"Me!" Paige exclaimed.

"Yes. I thought about how . . . how . . ." He cleared his throat again. "I, uh, thought about how horrible I treated you and how you didn't deserve it. And I vowed in that split second that if God let me live, if He gave me a second chance at life, I would make the changes I needed to make, and I would set things right with all the people I've hurt."

Paige raised her eyebrows with interest.

"Well, I guess out of all the people I hurt, you're the first person I should apologize to."

Paige was taken aback. She'd never, ever heard him once apologize to anyone for anything he'd ever done, especially to her.

"You didn't deserve what I did, and I want you to know I am sorry for how I treated you—and for leaving you when you needed me. I look back on it now, and I can't believe how selfish I was."

This was good. Paige had never thought the day would come that Mark would actually feel bad for what he'd done.

"I can never undo the damage I did, but I want you to know that I feel terrible for it and that I'm sorry I hurt you."

Paige blinked, wondering what to say. She'd held on to her anger for so long it was like a part of her character, like a scar that faded but never really disappeared. What happened after she accepted his apology? Those feelings had defined their relationship for so long she was unsure how it would change if they were . . . gone. Yet she found her heart softening.

"I plan on talking to Jared also," he said when she didn't speak. "I owe him an apology too. I feel responsible for his confusion about his decision to go on a mission."

"I appreciated what you said last night," Paige finally said.

"It's how I feel. I would like to see him go on a mission. He can go do all that other stuff when he gets home."

Paige nodded, processing Mark's apology. It probably wasn't easy for him to come talk to her like this. She recognized that and appreciated his effort.

Mark grasped the arms of the chair. "Well, I just wanted to tell you that."

It had been a long time since she'd seen Mark humble and sincere. In fact, she wasn't sure she'd ever seen him that way. His cocky, confident personality and overbearing manner were Mark's trademarks. She didn't know what to think about this new Mark.

"Anyway," he pushed himself to his feet, "thanks for taking a minute to let me come and talk to you."

Paige didn't know why, but she stopped him before he left the room. "Thanks, Mark."

He turned to look at her.

"I appreciate you stopping by."

The right side of his mouth lifted.

What she said next surprised even herself. "I'm glad you're okay."

A smile grew on his face. "Me too."

Long after he left, Paige reflected back on their short conversation. She'd been angry at him for years, and now, after a five-minute conversation, everything had changed. Sure, there was still the memory of her pain, but the anger was gone. It was over. Heaven had blessed her with the capacity to forgive. Mark had moved on and was showing signs of making big changes in his life, changes she was glad he was making. But more importantly, she now felt like she could finally let go and move on herself. The feeling was freeing and empowering and . . . wonderful.

* * *

With her suitcases stowed in the back of her car, Paige drove the familiar path to Dalton's house. She was on her way to the airport, but first she wanted to tell Dalton and Skyler good-bye. She was going back to Salt Lake for a week or so to help Ross and to get another realtor for her house. She was excited to go back and see old friends and familiar faces and places, but she was even more glad it wasn't going to be permanent. California felt like home now. It felt right. And that felt good.

Several times she'd tried to reach Dalton or Skyler on the phone to let them know she was coming, but their phone had been busy. She figured one of them was probably on the Internet or Skyler was on the phone with a friend. And, for some reason, Dalton wasn't answering his cell phone either. She'd just have to surprise them.

She turned the corner onto Dalton's street and pulled up alongside the house. The day was warm and sunny. Overhead a gull called, and another one in the distance answered. She loved the sounds of the ocean and the noise of the beach. She thought about all the winter clothes in her suitcase and chuckled at the drastic differences in climate and how quickly she'd become accustomed to the California weather. Already she was spoiled.

Paige walked the length of pavement to the gate of Dalton's house and froze, quickly shrinking back into the shadows of a tree. Standing only twenty feet away in the courtyard of his home were Dalton and Darlene. They were kissing.

Hot, angry tears filled Paige's eyes. If she'd had any doubts about their relationship, she didn't anymore. What she saw before her was proof enough. Quickly, before anyone saw her, Paige backed away until she was a safe distance to turn and run to her car.

It hurt. It hurt like crazy. She and Dalton had no understanding between them. Sure, they'd spilled out their hearts to each other, they'd even shared kisses, but that didn't mean they belonged to each other.

Why don't I ever learn? she asked herself. She was a horrible judge of men. She blamed it on her parents but knew it was her fault. A grown woman should know better than to fall for the first man she met.

But her self-scolding didn't help. She cried all the way to the airport.

* * *

"So guess who called?" Lou said to Paige on the phone the day after Paige arrived in Salt Lake City. She had rented a car and was staying in a hotel, since her house had no furniture or power. There was also six inches of snow on the ground, and it was freezing cold.

"Who?" Paige stretched out on the hotel bed and kicked off her shoes. She'd spent the whole day at the office trying to make heads or tails out of the mess Lance had left.

"Dalton."

Paige's heart leaped, but she ignored it. Her heart wasn't reliable. In fact, it had gotten her into more trouble than she cared to remember. Nope, she decided, from now on she listened only to her head.

"What did he want?"

"He was looking for you."

"What did you tell him?"

"That you went to Salt Lake City."

"Why did you tell him I was here?"

"Because that's where you are," Lou said.

"Why does he care anyway? What did he want?"

"He needed to talk to you. I told him you'd gone to help out at your old job and do some stuff with your house."

"That's all?"

"Yep, that's all."

"Did you ask about Skyler?"

"I did, and she's doing great. She's on crutches and can't put any weight on her foot. Still, she's excited to be out of bed."

"That's good," Paige said.

"So, what are you going to do about all of this?"

"All of what?"

"The situation with Dalton."

"The only thing I'm going to do is forget about him."

"Forget about Dalton?"

"Who?" Paige said snidely.

"Funny," Lou said. "You think it's going to be that easy? You can just turn off your feelings like that?"

"No, I didn't say it would be easy. But I can do it. Lou, I have to do it."

Lou gave a snort of disapproval.

"Listen, Lou. I saw those two together, smooching away. What else can I make of it? He was totally in love with her. They were going to be married until she called it off. Well, she's calling it back on, and they are obviously picking up where they left off. I'm out of the picture, if, in fact, I ever was in the picture."

"Are you sure they were kissing? Maybe he was trying to get something out of her eye."

"With his lips?"

"Yeah, I guess not. But you guys are so good for each other! Things were going so well! I was convinced you two meeting up after thirty years was all by heavenly design."

Paige didn't have any answers. She'd thought herself that there was a special reason they crossed paths and hit it off like they did. Even Dalton had thought so.

"Maybe whatever the purpose was for us to meet has been fulfilled. Maybe this is something I'll look back on in a year . . . or ten, and see the purpose behind it," Paige offered.

"Baloney! It's all that self-obsessed Darlene's fault. She's not right for Dalton. She's not good enough for him or Skyler. They need you in their life, not a mannequin like her."

Paige snickered. "Mannequin—I like that. I'll have to tell Skyler next time I talk to her—if I ever get to talk to her again."

"You will. It's not over, Paige."

Paige didn't listen because for her, it was.

* * *

"Are you okay?"

"Lou, I'm fine."

It was early Sunday morning, and the ringing of the phone woke Paige from a wonderfully deep sleep.

"I just feel bad you're there all alone. Are you going to your old ward for church? Maybe someone will invite you over for dinner or something."

"I was going to go but I've decided I'm not in the mood."

"To go to church?"

"No, to see all my old friends from the ward. I'm not up to putting on a happy face and pretending everything is hunky-dory."

"So, what are you going to do?"

"Probably go down to Temple Square. Thanks to you, it's early enough that I can catch the Mormon Tabernacle Choir broadcast. I'll just hang out down there for a while."

"I wish I were there with you. I hate thinking of you all alone."

"Lou, I'm fine. Really I am."

"Okay, well, call me later if you get lonely or bored."

"I will."

* * *

The day was sunny, and the snow on the roads had turned to black slush. Paige drove along State Street, the main artery of Salt Lake City, and turned onto South Temple, where she was lucky enough to find an empty spot at a parking lot adjacent to the temple.

Temple Square was swarming with tourists, and even though she was surrounded by people, she felt very alone. The Tabernacle Choir broadcast had been uplifting and inspiring. Afterward, she wandered through the visitors' center, studying artwork, absorbing the reverent atmosphere, hoping that it would penetrate her soul and bring peace. But turmoil continued to rumble inside of her.

She strolled the grounds as the day grew warmer. Couples, hand in hand, meandered the walkways, some with rosy-cheeked children laughing and chattering as their parents gazed up at the spires of the temple.

Spying a bench in the sunshine away from the crowds, Paige sat down and drank in the beauty of the day. Leaning her head back, she basked in the warmth of the sun's rays.

Lately she'd felt as though she had a constant prayer in her heart. Even now, she communicated with Heavenly Father in her thoughts, asking for His help with Jared and for a blessing of strength for herself. He alone knew what she was feeling inside. Heavenly Father was the only one she could be completely truthful with.

She knew God loved her. And she'd learned not to confuse her feelings about God's love and life's challenges. It was easy to question His presence when things were bad and just as easy to neglect Him when things were good. But she'd come to realize over the course of her life that Heavenly Father was there through it all. The closeness of their relationship was up to her.

Hearing a shuffle of feet nearby, she sensed that someone had sat down on the other end of the bench. She kept her eyes closed for several moments more, not wanting her private moment to end. But the moment was gone. She lifted her head and looked at the Tabernacle ahead. Clusters of tour groups, guided by young sister missionaries, filed in and out of the building. She thought of Jared as a missionary and felt a rush of excitement and anticipation. He was hardworking, responsible, and kindhearted. She thought of the people's lives he would touch and knew that he would love missionary work. He just had to stay strong until he could go.

The person next to her cleared his throat, pulling Paige from her thoughts. She clutched the strap of her purse, deciding she was ready to go back to her hotel and get some lunch. As she stood to leave, she turned and let out a startled cry.

"Dalton!"

His blue eyes sparkled as he smiled from the other end of the bench. "Surprise."

"What . . . how . . ." she sputtered.

"What am I doing here? How did I find you?"

She nodded dumbly and sank back onto the bench.

"It wasn't easy," he said. "I called Lou and bribed her to tell me which hotel you were staying in and where you might be this morning."

"Bribed?" Paige repeated in disbelief.

"It didn't take much, actually. She wanted me to bring her some fudge from a place called Lucretia's Sweets."

Paige laughed out loud. She knew the place well. The place had been around since they were young girls. Chocolate was Lou's downfall.

"She likes their rocky road," Paige said, still in a daze.

"That's what she requested. She said you two used to go there every Saturday afternoon when you were young."

"We did. I'm surprised we have any teeth left after all the candy and fudge we ate." Then a realization struck her. The last time Paige had seen Dalton was when he was in Darlene's arms.

Her cheerfulness faded quickly. "So," she sat up tall, holding her chin high as she spoke, "why are you here?"

"I came to find you. You left without saying good-bye."

She stared at him for several seconds.

"Actually, I did drop by, but you were busy."

"You came by the house?"

She nodded.

"What do you mean I was busy?"

He acted so innocent she could have sworn he didn't have a clue as to what she was talking about. Figuring she had nothing to lose, she told him what had happened.

"You and Darlene were lip-locked when I saw you, okay?" She looked him straight in the eye when she spoke.

His smile faded, and his shoulders slumped. "You saw that?"

"Yes, Dalton. I did. So you might as well go back home." She meant to sound strong and confident, but her words sounded as sad as she felt in her heart.

"It's not what you think, Paige."

"It doesn't matter what I think. I know what I saw." She pulled her shoulders back in an effort to strengthen herself. "I've enjoyed getting to know you and Sky, and I hope we can always be friends." She stood, feeling her stoic front crumbling. She needed to get out of there fast. "Good-bye, Dalton."

"Paige, we need to talk. Please, won't you let me explain?"

"You don't owe me an explanation. There was no agreement between us." She wanted to cry and stamp her feet and have a full-blown tantrum.

"Paige." He stood and reached for her hand, but she pulled it away. "Listen to me. I was telling Darlene good-bye. Forever."

She stared at him. What did that mean?

"She was trying to convince me that there was still something between us by kissing me."

Paige rolled her eyes.

"It's true, Paige. She thought it would reignite the feelings we had for each other. But it didn't."

Paige shook her head. "I have to go." She turned on her heel.

"Paige, please," he begged. "All it did was make me realize how much I love you."

She stopped. Slowly, she turned to face him. With her voice barely a whisper, she spoke. "What did you just say?"

"I said . . . I love you."

Tears flooded her eyes. She shut them tightly and bit on her bottom lip to keep it from trembling. She felt Dalton's arms wrap around her and pull her close. Unable to hold it in any longer, she dropped her head onto his shoulder and began to sob.

"Shhh," he said, stroking the back of her head. "It's okay. Don't cry."

He helped her back to the bench, where they sat together. He rocked her and soothed her with soft kisses on her forehead.

Paige fought to control her emotions. Using his handkerchief, she dried her cheeks and dabbed at her eyes. "I'm sorry," she said.

"Hey." He lifted her chin with his finger and looked lovingly into her face. "You don't need to apologize. I can't imagine what you thought when you saw us." Then he added, "Actually, I can. I would have thought the same thing. How awful for you. I'm sorry."

"I didn't want to care that you were with her," Paige said.

"But you did?"

She nodded, blinking to stop the tears from starting up again.

"Why did you care, Paige?" he asked, stroking her cheek.

"I didn't mean for it to happen, but I've fallen . . ." She swallowed. "I've fallen in love with you too." She looked away.

"All right!" Dalton said with excitement as he grabbed her and hugged her so tightly she gasped for air.

"Sorry," he said, releasing his squeeze and looking into her eyes. "This is wonderful. You're wonderful."

Paige's eyes filled with tears again.

"What?" he said. "Paige, why aren't you happy? This is cause for a celebration."

"Dalton, you can't love me."

His forehead crinkled. With a laugh, he said, "Too late! I already do."

"You don't want someone like me."

"Are you kidding? Paige," he took both of her hands in his, "listen to me. I haven't known such joy was possible until I met you. You are the only person I've ever been able to share my soul with. You are my best friend, Paige. You are the person I want to be with always. You are the person I want to grow old with."

"Grow old with? Dalton . . . what exactly are you saying?"

"Paige, I'm saying I want to marry you. I love you. I can't live without you."

She liked that last part. That meant this was serious love. But there was something they needed to discuss, something he needed to know about her.

Looking around, she noticed that many of the tour groups had gone inside the visitors' centers. There were still a few people moseying around the grounds, but for the most part, they could speak in private.

"There's something about me you don't know."

He lifted one eyebrow with interest and waited.

She couldn't look at him while she spoke. Staring down at her hands, she said, "When I was diagnosed with breast cancer, I had to have some surgery. And . . . I don't have . . ." She clasped and unclasped her hands. "They removed . . ."

"You can tell me, Paige."

She finally looked at him with tear-filled eyes. "Dalton, I don't have a left breast."

"Paige, sweetheart, that doesn't matter to me. I love you for who you are, inside and out."

"But I have this huge, awful scar. I'm a freak."

Dalton's face had a gentle smile on it, but he quickly explained, "No, don't take me wrong. It's not your scar I'm smiling about, it's just that, well, I think there's something that might make you feel a little better." He reached down and pulled up his pant leg. He exposed his right leg, but Paige didn't see anything. She shrugged and peered closer. Dalton knocked on his shin with his knuckles. It made a dull, thumping sound.

Her mouth dropped open.

"It's not real. I have a prosthesis from my knee down."

"You do?" She reached out, then pulled back her hand.

"You can touch it."

She pushed lightly on the flesh-colored rubbery surface of the prosthesis. "That's why you favor the other leg sometimes."

He nodded.

Paige started to chuckle. "I can't believe I was so nervous to tell you about me when all along . . ."

"I had the same situation," he finished for her.

They laughed together as the news brought them even closer together, strengthening the bond between them.

"Did it happen during the war?" Paige asked.

"Right before I got captured. If I would have been taken to an American hospital, they would have been able to save my leg, but the Viet Cong didn't care until gangrene set in and the smell got so bad they finally took off my leg."

Paige winced. "Was it awful?"

"It was pretty bad. I finally passed out from the pain." He looked at her with twinkling eyes. "Does this change how you feel about me?"

"No," she said. "I think it makes me love you even more."

He smiled and reached for her again, hugged her tightly, then sat back. "We're certainly not complete when we're alone, but you know what? Together, we are whole."

She nodded.

"Thirty years ago God made our paths cross, and now here we are, with our paths joining together into one path we will travel together."

Paige smiled. It was true. Dalton filled the gaps in her life and the empty space in her heart. They needed each other.

"Do you have any plans for the rest of the day?" he asked.

"No, nothing, why?" She held tightly to his hand, never wanting to let go.

"Good, because while I'm in town I have to go see Hobart. I've already called him, and he's expecting me for lunch. Would you come with me?"

"Are you sure it's okay to bring someone with you?"

"I told him I might have a date if everything went well."

She snuggled into his chest, resting her forehead under his chin. "I guess it went well?"

"Better than I even hoped it would." He tightened his hug. "Better than I'd dreamed it would."

"What do you think Skyler's going to say about all of this?"

"She's going to probably reinjure herself jumping up and down with joy."

Paige laughed. "No seriously, though, I want her to be okay with this."

"You don't know how many times she told me to grab you while I could. She has never liked any of the women I've dated, especially Darlene. When I told her I was flying to Salt Lake to go after you, she had my suitcase packed before I hung up with the airline."

"I want her to like me. I think we've been able to connect."

"She thinks so too. Now it's my turn to ask—how do you think Jared's going to react?"

"He's going to be thrilled. He's worried about me being alone. That's why he wanted me to move by Lou—so I'd have somebody else in my life other than him."

"Lou!" Dalton said. "We have to call Lou."

"No, let's surprise her when we get back. We'll take her more than fudge."

Dalton smiled at her. "Then we better make this official." He got down on one knee in front of her. "I love you, Paige. Will you marry me?"

Paige giggled as he placed a kiss on her hand.

"I love you. Yes, Dalton, I will marry you. And thank you for coming after me."

"I'd go to the ends of the earth for you, sweetheart."

CHAPTER THIRTY

"This is it," Dalton said as he pulled up in front of a small, red-brick rambler with bikes and toys littering the driveway. Before getting out, they stole one more kiss. Paige's heart soared as she watched Dalton climb out of the car and come around to her door. A welcome calm filled her soul because, finally, she felt peace in her heart. This was right. She felt no fear about moving ahead. The future was full of promise, and with Dalton at her side, she looked forward to every moment ahead.

Hand in hand, they walked up to the door. The sound of children's voices and the pounding of footsteps seemed to drown out the doorbell, but the knob rattled and soon a little girl, maybe four or five years old, with wild red hair and a pixie nose answered the door.

"Hi, there," Dalton said. "Is your daddy home?"

"He's in the potty."

Dalton and Paige both laughed. "Is your mommy home?"

"No, she's at a meeting."

Just then, a gray, striped cat escaped through the door. "Misty," the little girl yelled, "you get back here." She pushed between them and ran after the cat.

Wondering what to do next, they looked at each other and shrugged. "What do you think?" Dalton asked her.

"I guess we just wait here until—"

"Lieutenant Mac, you're here!" Hobart's voiced boomed from the other side of the room. "Come in, come in." Hobart shuffled them inside and was closing the door when the little girl burst inside carrying the giant cat with both arms.

"Misty get out again?" he asked his daughter.

The little girl nodded. "I'm taking her to my room. She needs a time-out."

"Good idea," Hobart said.

The little girl stomped from the room, and Hobart found a chair near Dalton and Paige, who were seated on the couch.

From another room, the television blasted.

"Benji," Hobart shouted, "turn that thing down."

"Okay, Dad," a voice replied.

"Crazy kids. You'd think they were deaf." Hobart smiled and welcomed them again. "Janie is so excited to meet you. There's also someone else here who has waited a long time to see you."

"Really?" Dalton said. "Who?"

Just then, a back door creaked open and slammed shut.

"Janie, is that you?"

"Yes, Bart," a female voice came. "Did you remember to turn down the oven?"

"Sure did, honey. Come in here. There's someone I want you to meet."

Janie was the opposite of her husband. She was petite and had beautiful curly red hair. She looked like a porcelain doll. As soon as she came in the room, she shook Dalton's hand. "My husband has talked about you for many years," she said. "It's wonderful to finally meet you."

"Sit down, Janie," Hobart said. "I was just getting ready to give Lieutenant Mac the you-know-what."

"Oh, okay," Janie settled back into a chair.

Hobart went to the hall closet and brought out a box. "Here's something I'll bet you never thought you'd see again." He handed the box to Dalton, who looked at Paige first, then back to the box. She couldn't imagine what it could be.

Dalton opened the flaps and looked inside. His face literally went white. "I don't believe it," he whispered. "How did you—"

Hobart started to answer but stopped when Dalton reached into the box.

Out of curiosity, Paige leaned forward and watched as slowly he withdrew an army helmet with a fist-sized hole blown clear through one side. He turned it over and checked inside, then put his hand through the hole. No one spoke, and no one moved. It was an emotional moment for Dalton. He cleared his throat several times and shook his head as if he still couldn't believe what he was seeing. Paige remembered hearing about his injury. Judging by the size of the hole in the helmet, Dalton was lucky to be alive.

"This helmet saved my life," he said quietly. "How did you get it?"

"I didn't get it. Someone else did," Hobart told him.

"Who? None of my men . . ." He looked down at his helmet with a pinched expression. "Nobody survived."

"That's not true, sir," a voice from the hallway said.

Dalton swung around to see who was speaking.

A thin man with a long, straggly ponytail inched forward in a wheelchair, looking directly at Dalton.

The silence was powerful as emotions played on the man's face.

Dalton squinted as he studied the man. Then he stood and approached him, stopping several feet away. Their gazes locked, and they both remained silent. Then suddenly, as if in total shock and disbelief, the realization of who this man was dawned on Dalton with such force his knees buckled.

Hobart jumped to Dalton's aid. "Hold on there, Lieutenant," he said, grabbing Dalton's trunk and holding him with a sturdy grip. Dalton squeezed his eyes shut and opened them several times. It was obvious he couldn't believe who he was seeing. Hobart gently released his grip, allowing Dalton to stand on his own.

"Beckett? Beckett, is it really you?" Dalton's eyes filled with tears and spilled onto his cheeks, rolling down his face. He didn't even bother wiping them away.

The man sat up straight in his chair. "Yes, sir," Beckett said, giving Dalton a salute with his left arm because, Paige realized, his right arm was missing.

Dalton's head dropped forward, and his shoulders shook as great sobs overtook him. Thirty years of anguish and guilt came forth in a rushing flood of tears.

Janie handed her husband a box of tissues. Dalton took several and wiped his eyes and blew his nose. "I'm sorry," he said. "But all these years I thought . . ." He wiped at his nose again. "It's like having someone come back from the dead. How?" he begged to know. "I thought you were dead."

"So did the Viet Cong," Beckett told him. "I thought we were both going to make it, sir. They almost left us behind, and I thought we were safe. Then they came back and took you, and that was the last I saw of you." He wiped at his own eyes. "I kept your helmet, sir. I wanted something to remember you by."

Dalton shook his head. "That day has haunted me all these years." He knelt down by his friend and gave him a hug. "I can't believe you survived."

"And I didn't know you had survived until Bart saw you in October. I'd heard you died in prison, sir."

"I wanted to," Dalton said. "I deserved to. All those men died because of me."

Beckett's forehead wrinkled. "No, sir."

"Yes," Dalton countered. "It was all my fault. I gave the orders. If I would have waited, maybe they wouldn't have seen us."

"I know you did the right thing, sir. They did see us."

"How do you know?" Dalton implored.

"The North Vietnamese soldier saw me. Our eyes made contact."

"You're sure?"

"Yes, sir," Beckett assured him. "You made the right call."

Dalton heaved a sigh.

Paige knew he'd released a burden he'd carried for over half of his lifetime. He would always mourn the loss of his men, but the knowledge that an attack was inevitable and not brought about by his bad judgment would finally lift the load of guilt and pain from his heart. Bad luck, not bad judgment, had cost those men their lives.

"Thank you," he whispered to Beckett. "Thank you for surviving."

* * *

When emotions had settled and the shock had worn off, Beckett was able to tell Dalton how he'd managed to stay alive.

"I knew when they took you away, Lieutenant, that I had a small window of opportunity to get out of there. My arm was useless, and I could barely move my legs, but I managed to drag myself through the brush until I came to the main road. I'd heard helicopters in the distance and hoped they were ours. I barely made it to the landing zone before I passed out. Luckily one of our soldiers was securing the area and found me in the bushes. I would have died had he not found me in time."

"I made it to the same landing strip the next morning, but you'd already pulled out. That's where I got captured," Dalton told them. He explained about his trip to the prison and the conditions, giving details that made Paige shudder.

"Do you ever think of going back?" Hobart asked them.

Beckett answered first. "No. I left enough of myself there the first time I went."

"I do," Dalton said. "All the time. I think it's the only way I'm ever going to close that chapter of my life. Maybe I feel more of a pull because of my deceased wife, Soon Lee. She was South Vietnamese. I'd like to meet her family. I'd like my daughter to have a chance to meet her mother's family."

"Then you should do it," Hobart said. "After all these years, you deserve to have peace in your life."

"I'd just settle for a good night's sleep," Dalton said. His expression grew somber. Paige reached for his hand to offer an encouraging squeeze. Dalton had been through a lot that day, an overwhelming roller coaster ride of emotions.

"How can I thank you?" he said to Hobart and Beckett. "What you've done today . . ." The muscles of his jaw clenched as he paused for a moment. "This has been such a wonderful gift. Thank you."

The bond of brotherhood the men had shared in a time of war still remained and provided peace to Dalton's tormented soul. And for that, Paige was grateful beyond words. Even though Dalton would never accept the praise, in her eyes and the eyes of his men he was a leader and a man to be admired. He was a hero.

* * *

"So, where do we go from here?" Paige asked as they drove along the foothills of Salt Lake. Dalton pulled the rental car over to the curb and parked, giving them a view of the Salt Lake Valley.

"The first thing we need to do is call Skyler and Jared. You're sure we shouldn't call Lou?"

Paige chuckled as she thought about the excited reaction ahead. "Yes, we should call her. She'll feel bad we didn't call her the minute you proposed."

"The next thing we do is find you a ring. I want to make this official," he said, taking her left hand and kissing her ring finger.

"This has been quite a day, hasn't it?"

"It's been like a lifetime of Christmases all on one day." He kept her hand clasped in his. "I'm so glad you were with me."

"I want to share everything and every day with you," Paige told him.

"I wish I could promise you it was going to be easy, but I know we'll have challenges."

"I can handle the challenges as long as we're together."

"That's how I feel too," he said, pulling her toward him. "How long are you planning on staying in Salt Lake?" he continued, leaning closer.

"I was going to stay until next weekend, but I'm ready to go back home. I think I can wrap things up at work tomorrow. Then I just need to find another realtor, someone who will get my house sold."

"Tell you what, I'll take care of the realtor, you take care of things at work."

Paige smiled. "That would be great. You'd do that for me?"

Dalton leaned closer and gave her a kiss. "Sweetie, I would do absolutely anything for you. Your wish is my command. I want to make all your dreams come true."

Tears stung her eyes. Never had any man said something like that to her.

"You already have," she said, knowing that being with Dalton was the place where all her dreams really would come true.

"I love you, Dalton."

"I love you, Paige."

EPILOGUE

Paige wiped at a tear in her eye as she read the last paragraph of Jared's letter.

> *Tell Dalton and Skyler hi from me. Thanks again for the box of sugar cookies. My companion ate so many I finally hid the box from him. You're the best mom in the whole world. The gospel is true! Missionary work is great. More next week!*
> —*Elder Jared St. Claire.*

Paige folded the letter and thought about Jared's wonderful news. He'd been in Suva, Fiji, barely a month, and already he and his companion were baptizing a couple with one small child.

She still remembered the day he'd opened his call and found out he was going on a French-speaking mission to Fiji. Of course, at first Nate thought he could go over with Jared and hang out while Jared did missionary work. Jared had to explain how the whole mission thing worked and let Nate know he wouldn't get to see him for two years. The news didn't make Nate happy, but after Jared explained things to him, he seemed to understand.

"Everything okay?" Dalton asked as he brought the last of the groceries in from the car. Paige had just returned from the market, but when she saw Jared's letter had arrived, she had stopped everything she was doing to read it.

"They have a baptism on Sunday. Isn't that great?"

Dalton nodded. "Sure is." He dumped the armload of bags onto the kitchen counter. "I wish I could have gone on a mission. I envy Jared for what he's doing."

"You can still go on a mission, you know," Paige said.

"That's right." Dalton sauntered over to her and pulled her into a hug. "And the best part is, you'd be my companion."

"Twenty-four-seven," she reminded him. "You don't think you'd get sick of spending every waking moment with me?"

"Are you kidding? That's the best part."

Their kiss lingered for a moment, and Paige realized her love for Dalton grew with each passing day. Marriage to him was pure bliss.

"By the way," Dalton said, planting tiny kisses on her forehead, "I left the birthday cake in the car. I didn't know where you wanted to hide it."

"Mmmm." Paige had her eyes shut, enjoying his kisses. "I'll go get it in a minute." It was Skyler's seventeenth birthday, and they were throwing a surprise party for her.

"Is she home?" Paige asked.

"She got home just before you. I wanted to give one of her birthday presents to her before the party tonight."

"What is it?" Paige asked.

"It's a surprise for you too. You'll have to wait until she opens it."

"What is it? A trip to Fiji?" she asked eagerly.

"Hardly. I'll go get her."

Paige put the groceries away while Dalton went to get Skyler. She was still elated about Jared's good news. He truly loved missionary work and the people of Fiji.

"What's up?" Skyler said when she entered the kitchen. She spied a package of Oreo cookies on the counter and grabbed them, ripping open the end. "Thanks for getting these. They're my favorite." Pouring herself a glass of milk, Skyler sat on a bar stool at the counter and said, "So what did you want, Dad?"

From one of the cupboards Dalton produced a long, thin gift box tied with a silver bow.

Skyler shook it close to her ear. "Doesn't sound like keys to a new car."

Paige laughed. Skyler was working her dad over for a new car. Her Honda had close to 200,000 miles on it and more rust spots than paint.

"Just open it," Dalton said. "I told you, straight A's your senior year and we'll talk about a car for graduation."

"I already have a scholarship, Dad. I don't need straight A's to get into college."

Skyler had been offered a full dance scholarship to the University of Utah in Salt Lake City. Paige and Dalton had joked that now that she was moving, they also needed to move to Utah to be with her. Paige loved Skyler as much as she would a daughter of her own. She was almost willing to put up with the snowy winters to be close to the girl. But Dalton refused to move. The cold weather bothered his leg too much. He promised his daughter that they would fly to Salt Lake as often as they could to visit her.

Paige sighed with content. Life was good. No . . . life was great! Skyler and her father were getting along better than ever, and the marriage adjustment had been easier than anyone had dared hope for. Sure, there were tense moments at times, and Paige never felt completely comfortable disciplining Skyler. She usually left it up to Dalton, but Skyler had become so focused on dance and her future that she didn't have time to get in trouble like she used to.

Then there was Jared, who was flourishing on his mission. He'd had a great basketball season, playing more than most freshmen. While it wasn't quite as much as he would have liked, it was enough for the coach to assure him they wanted him back as soon as he got home.

Lou's story was still ongoing, which was another reason Paige was glad she'd moved to California. The doctors discovered that Lou's cancer had metastasized. They'd found a cancerous tumor in her colon, and she was now recovering from surgery. Paige hated to think what the future held for her friend, but Lou had taken on the philosophy to live one day at a time and not worry about the future. All she had was now. Paige spent several hours each morning at her house, doing whatever she could to lighten Lou's burden. She was determined to help her friend fight this battle. If anyone could beat cancer, Lou could.

Skyler finally pulled the ribbon off the box and lifted the lid. Inside was a white envelope. She looked at her father. "What is this?"

"Open it," he told her.

She lifted the flap of the envelope and pulled out something that looked like airline tickets. Her eyebrows arched with surprise, then, when she checked the detailed information on the tickets, she actually screamed out loud. "Dad! I don't believe it. I absolutely don't believe it."

"What?" Paige asked, wondering what was on the tickets.

"Paige," she squealed, "we're all going to Vietnam."

"We are?" Paige couldn't hide the shock on her face.

Dalton smiled. "We've talked about going long enough. It's time to actually do it. And I can't think of a better time than the summer after you graduate from high school."

"I don't know if I can wait that long," Skyler groaned. "It's forever away."

"It will be here before you know it," Dalton said. "This year is going to fly by."

Skyler jumped up from her seat and gave her father a hug.

Paige shook her head in amazement. It had been Dalton's dream to go to Vietnam, and it had become Skyler's too. It was a place that was a part of all of their lives; a place that was filled with stories from their personal histories and hopefully, answers to their pasts.

"Did you notice there were four tickets?" Dalton pointed out.

"Four?" Skyler looked inside the ticket jacket. A giant smile grew on her face. "There sure are."

"The other two—"

"Are for you and Jared," Dalton told her.

Paige felt a bubble of excitement swell up inside of her. "We're waiting until after Jared gets home?"

Dalton nodded. "It wouldn't be right to leave him out of it. I wanted our whole family to be together." Paige loved Dalton more at that moment than the day they'd been sealed together in the temple.

Yes, she thought, that did make it perfect.

"Thanks, Dad." Skyler gave her father a hug, then turned to Paige. "I'm so glad you're coming too. It wouldn't be the same without you and Jared."

Paige grew warm inside. For the first time in her life, she felt complete. Whole. A flood of gratitude filled her, enriched by the love surrounding her.

"Hey," Dalton said, touching her gently on the cheek. "You okay?"

Paige nodded and smiled. "I'm better than okay," she told him.

Dalton returned her smile and pulled her into a hug.

Yes, she thought, better than okay.